UNDER THE MAGIC MOUNTAIN

by

PAT SILVER-LASKY

Under the Magic Mountain ©2018 by Pat Silver-Lasky

All rights reserved. Except for the use in a review, the reproduction or utilization of this work in any form or by an electronic, mechanical, or other means, now not known or hereafter invented, including xerography, photocopying and recording or use or sale on the internet or in any information storage and retrieval system is forbidden without the written permission of the author.

Cover painting and drawings by Pat Silver-Lasky
Front cover design by Alexander Niles
Back cover design by Peter Betts
OuroborusBooks.Biz
California USA

OTHER BOOKS by Pat Silver-Lasky
2017 HOLLYWOOD ROYALTY A FAMILY IN FILMS Hardback ISBN: 978-1-62933-185-0, Paperback ISBN:9781629331843 BearManor Media|
2015 A STAR CALLED WORMWOOD: ISBN: 978-1-78510-586-9, OuroborusBooks.Biz
2013 THE OFFER: ISBN: 9781492759669, OuroborusBooks.Biz
2012 SCAMS SCHEMES SCUMBAGS: (with Peter Betts) ISBN: 9781478282037, OuroborusBooks.Biz
2010 RIDE THE TIGER: ISBN: 0-9544194-3-X, OuroborusBooks.Biz
2005 SCREENWRITING FOR THE 21ST CENTURY: ISBN:0-7134-8833-6, (B.T. Batsford, UK)
2006 (Republished by Ritchie Books, UK)|

With Jesse -Lasky Jr.
1978: LOVE SCENE, ISBN: 0-690-01412-9, T.Y. Crowell, USA Angus & Robertson UK
1977 MEN OF MYSTERY ISBN: 0-491-02460-6, W.H. Allen/Star U.K.
1977 DARK DIMENSIONS: ISBN::#0-89696-001-3, Everest House USA
1980 LOVE SCENE ISBN 0-207-95824-6 (paperback), Sphere Books UK
1981 THE OFFER: 0-385-15767-3, Doubleday, USA
1982 THE OFFER:0-425-05549-3, Berkley-Jove USA (paperback)

This work of fiction is dedicated to the memory of
Jesse L. Lasky Jr.,
who knew the lay of the land.

If some readers find a reflection of themselves in certain
characters, it is purely by chance.
But some things are truer than others,
and that is the way of fiction.
And some things live only
in the world of imagination,
and that is the way of
truth.

CHAPTERS

1. Santa Rita
2. The Smuggler
3. The Chair Affair
5. The Man Who Came To Puerto Banus
6. La Tormenta
7. Pushing Up Daisy
8. Party Time
9. The Man Who Was Sly
10. Come Buy Barata
11. The Man In The Dream
12. The Unknown Gentleman
13. Watering the Trees
14. The Salamander
15. Manilva
16. Then Who Am I?
17. The Road
18. The Walking Man
19. Percy
20. The Fortune Teller's Prediction
21. The Orchard
22. A Castle In Spain
23. I Have The Key
24. One Man's Medicine
25. The Fiesta
26. Spanish Days & Spanish Nights

1: SANTA RITA

She was looking back over her shoulder at Santa Rita, seeing it diminishing from the taxi heading towards Malaga airport. 'Santa Rita pray for me...' she sighed under her breath.

'What?' Jeff asked, turning his attention from the fastener on his decomposing briefcase.

'Santa Rita,' Jean repeated. 'Pray for me.'

Mm,' he said. 'For us both then, please.'

That Santa Rita was the patron saint of the deaf was important to the original owner of the house he'd named after her. It was more important to a pair of writers like Jefferson Thwaite and his wife and collaborator, Jean Varry because Santa Rita is also patron saint of the impossible. The Impossible, as both Jeff and Jean well knew, was for writers always a close companion. And anyone, saint or otherwise, who could accomplish it on their behalf was to be honoured, and indeed worshipped, Not to mention prayed to occasionally.

Santa Rita was the rack-going-to-ruin that the Thwaites had purchased in the hills of Andalucia from a hard-of-hearing British comic named Dykes who, it was reported (and Jeff never doubted it once inside) had sketched its design on the inside of an empty cigarette packet over a plate of fried calamaré one drunken lunch at Puerto José Banus, facing the Mediterranean Sea. The house was constructed according to his gastronomically-charged specifications by a Scottish architect, who wisely dropped dead before the comic could sue him. Jeff pointed out that the back hallway looked as though Cyril Dykes had accidentally dropped a calamaré on the cigarette packet floor plan, and there was nothing comical about that when you got up to go to the bathroom in the middle of the night. Cyril's architect, fortified no doubt by the inspiration of his national beverage, produced on a hill top above a Spanish valley and looking down the opposite vista towards that blue expanse, the

Mediterranean—a sprawling rustic concoction of sinking floors, porous roof tiles, and waterless plumbing.

But the over-shoulder sight from the Thwaites' moving taxi had indeed changed since that day so long ago when they first clapped eyes on it. For then, Casa, or more grandly, Finca Santa Rita, as the Thwaites had renamed it for its farmhouse charms, had evoked a sensation of distrust rather than love at first sight.

Not without reason. It was then under siege by a French woman and a pair of Alsatian hounds more savage than Transylvanian wolves. All three were awaiting the return of her jailed husband, Olivier Deguere, who had been sentenced to six years by the Spanish Courts. The French couple—or at least the male member, had been caught in the enterprise of smuggling, via sea-going visits to the nearby North African coast. What specific Tangier commodity he brought back was still in question among the American and British colony. Those more kindly disposed said cigarettes; a few hinted at other mind-altering possibilities. There was even the suspicion of human cargo. Certainly, Deguere's appearance fulfilled the role of modern-day pirate—who would if need be, produce a long-barrelled shotgun to maintain his position at Santa Rita as squatter-in-residence.

For squatters is precisely what the Degueres were when Jeff and Jean first stayed in the house next door, that balmy Spanish winter while they were working on a film script. They were renting it from an English school teacher named Belnapp who only used his house in the summers or on school holidays and had furnished it like a boarding school dorm. Not unreasonable, since he often brought a bevy of schoolboys down on their 'hols' for musical practice and sun. Belnapp taught maths and music, which are thought to go together. When the Thwaites were finally in residence in Santa Rita, they would occasionally see a pride of twelve year old boys marching up the dirt road from the tiny village carrying musical instruments. Later, as the cool of evening descended on the hill, they would hear the slightly discordant sounds of *Eina Kleina Nacht Musik* by Mozart wafting across from Belnapp's dorm.

Jean and Jeff had lived together for one year before they got married. Six years now since that happy day. They'd become instantly enamored at a Writers' Guild meeting in Hollywood, and when they found themselves serving on the same committee they began having a drink together afterwards, which gradually turned into dinner. And then the evenings got longer until they ended up having breakfast together. She was twenty eight with a modest list of TV and minor film co-credits. Jeff was thirty-five then, not totally decrepit and could still play a fair game of tennis. Before they met, he'd written a few blockbusters, but then his ex got alimony, the house, the Mercedes, the furniture and his boyhood collection of Indian Head pennies. He consoled himself that he'd outgrown them anyway. The pennies. He rather missed the Merc.

Together, Jeff and Jean had successfully written a few episodes for various TV series and managed to be assigned three films: *The Passionate Pirate, The Return of the Ninja-Yeti,* and *Haunted Surfboards*—sex, violence, and the supernatural—all dogs that Jean and Jeff had barked with when hungry, which now had come back to bite them. That is to say, nobody was offering them a job, until a quasi-producer named Mat Windsor came into their world. Enough time had passed since that fateful episode for them to get on with their lives—and perhaps the one good thing that Mat had done was to introduce them to Spain.

⌘

'But how did the French couple get there in the first place?' Jeff had asked Jean that first winter, studying Santa Rita from Belnapp's roof terrace, and trying not to be seen by the Alsatians who had finally stopped barking.

Jean was a collector of information that frequently turned out to be useful even though she often gave Jeff more than he asked for or needed when filling him in. 'It seems the two of them used to run a restaurant further down the coast near Estepona called "El Marinero". After all, Olivier Deguere was a mariner of sorts. His troubles started when he stretched his fishing trips into more lucrative waters, Jeff.'

'Hmm. That part Elliot Gray told me,' he acknowledged, settling his long frame back into a hammock, his swimming trunks revealing where the red line began at the top of his thigh. 'But how did they come to have squatters' rights in our comic friend's house in the first place?' He was referring to Dykes, whose cigarette packet design had grown into Santa Rita at least twenty years earlier.

'Easy,' Jean explained. 'Cyril had an Irish friend whose wife's Welsh cousin kind of set himself up as a local property manager for the British colony here on the Spanish coast. Named Davies. You remember him.'

'Davies...?' Jeff's eyebrows arched in a sun-bronzed brow beneath his straw-coloured thatch of hair.

'Jeff, really.' She shook her head. 'You met him at the Gray's cocktail party before the last.'

'Oh, you mean Davie Davies. That guy with the hat who never took it off?'

'Australian hat. That's the one.' Her eyes sparkled with the same cornflower blue enthusiasm they had at twenty eight, when Jeff first met her. That enthusiastic dedication always tugged at his heart and made him willing to listen to her most outlandish suggestions which somehow became less outlandish when he actually got involved. So once again, Jeff was listening.

'Davie speaks perfect Spanish, which is something his English clients haven't bothered to learn.'

'Even if he didn't, who'd know the difference?'

'The Spaniards, Jeff!' she exclaimed. 'Davie pays all his clients' gas bills and impuestos—that's their taxes—and the like,' Jean continued coming over to rub some coconut sunscreen on him. They had both heard plenty about Davie—beloved of lonely single ladies, equipped with a smile that flashed out faster than a pole dancer's bum and God knew what else. She dropped a pool of sunscreen on Jeff's belly and started spreading it.

'But I thought he was Australian,' Jeff said thinking of the hat, 'and if you keep doing that, I'm liable to get all worked up.' He grabbed her, pulling her into a kiss.

'Umm,' she said getting up and back to business. 'Davie likes to give an Australian impression. But Cynthia Gray explained about him. You see he's Welsh and...'

'Wind down, Jean,' he said sitting up. 'Right now I want to hear about Davie and the French couple, not his identity crisis.' Jean had a way of trailing off a subject leaving Jeff trailing after. She was looking over the railing again, at the house in question.

'Well, Davie met the Degueres in Alice's Book Bar in San Pedro.'

'I thought they were from Estepona,' Jeff said testily.

'Whatever. Anyway, one drink led to another bar as it has a way of doing in these parts, and the Degueres told him they needed a place to live just until their house got built. So Davie arranged to rent Santa Rita to them for ten quid a month.'

'Ten pounds? That's about fifteen dollars. *Jesus Perro*!' He said it with a Spanish accent that came out Haysus Perro!

'Please don't swear, Jeff. Particularly not in broken Spanish.' She went back to her mat to bake the other side, buttering herself with coconut sunscreen. Her slender legs were browning to a golden tan with a freckling shadow that went with the sandy blonde hair. 'Anyway, maybe that was more money in those days.'

'Everything was more money,' he growled. 'And you won't let me say Jesus Maryland anymore, so I've got to say something.'

'Jeff, how can you say Jesus dog? Besides being irreligious, Haysus Perro doesn't make any sense.' Jean's eyes were closed. 'Now about Davie... It seems Cyril didn't like Santa Rita standing empty because of burglars. They'll steal the roof tiles and have even been known to take a whole house down, cement blocks and all.'

'What for?'

'To build another house, of course.'

'So he rented it to the French couple, Jean. What I don't understand is why Cyril can't get them out.'

She sat up, opening her eyes to take him in. 'Jeff, we've lived in London long enough to know the rights of squatters there. Well, 'Squatters Espanole' have an even stronger law on their side. All a squatter has to do is prove he has no other place of residence in the world and you can't get rid of him for life or forever which ever is the longer-Jeff-you're-getting-too-burned.' Jean had a disconcerting way of putting two thoughts into one sentence.

'You just buttered me and I smell like a fruit salad,' he growled.

'Not enough.'

'What about the house the French couple were building?' Jeff asked not unreasonably, grabbing back the coconut sunscreen.

'The minute the Degueres were settled into Santa Rita, they downed tools on the building and sold the plot of land, so then they had no other place of residence, get it?' Jean loved to turn a statement into a question, which Jeff never seemed to mind, because it opened the conversation for more thorough discussion. Their life together—working and living—was a constant dialogue.

The facts as Jean explained them, were simple. Even though Olivier Deguere had been found guilty of transporting cargo without the formality of informing the Customs and Excise and was now absent from the premises since he was languishing in the Spanish clink, his position was unassailable. Madam Deguere continued to share the casa with the hounds and certain visiting gentlemen she claimed to be members of her family. What's more, the Spanish authorities, occasionally brushed by pangs of compassion, permitted Olivier to come home for the odd weekend after his first two years of imprisonment.

⌘

That was all the Thwaites were able to glean about the mysterious casa Santa Rita on that first winter in Belnapp's Spanish dormitory which they had rented at the suggestion of Elliot Gray, a producer of British films who'd hired them to write a screenplay based on a book he'd bought from a Frenchman. He'd offered them the opportunity to work alongside him in Spain as a sort of working holiday. Gray was struggling to survive in a dwindling industry, and had taken early semi-retirement. Stout bellied, balding and heart-warmingly jovial, he and his wife Cynthia had a house on that hill on the other side of Clive Belnapp's. On the far side of the Grays were the Ridgeways, an older couple who lived there all year round, therefore part of the cocktail party circuit. A famous actress lived up the Ronda Road. An award-winning Romanian director kept a house at the Marbella Club. The Costa Del Sol was covered in stardust and Cynthia lived for cocktail parties, which was odd since nobody ever saw her drink alcohol. But she did like to talk, and had a big line in cutting remarks. The Thwaites had been thrilled with their first three weeks on the hill and couldn't wait to have a chance to visit again. And again...

Now the point of all this was that the presence of the squatters had somewhat devalued the sales potential of Dykes's property. And the following year, while Elliot Gray was still trying to raise the finance to film their screenplay, Cynthia Gray telephoned the Thwaites in London to ask, 'Darlings, how would you like to buy a holiday house of your own in Spain?'

She said 'buy' not rent and without asking the price, Jeff was quick to say they couldn't afford it. But when she told them, 'Cyril has decided to rid himself of Santa Rita, sitting tenants and all—and the price has dropped into range of even a writer's purse, my dears', it was a sort of challenge.

Jean, always one to pick up a gauntlet, pursed her lips indignantly. 'Doesn't she think we have any money, or what?'

'Well, we don't with what Elliot is paying us,' Jeff said practically. 'Not for castles in Spain.'

'This is hardly a castle, Jeff. Only a casa.'

'We can't afford it, Jean. Besides, we've never been past the front gate. We haven't a clue what it contains except the Alsatians.'

'I'm absolutely certain the dogs don't get included,' she said, her mind filling with visions of ownership. They had never owned anything together. They'd rented a tiny condo in Brentwood during more lucrative California assignments. They were renting their London flat where they'd written a few TV scripts for the BBC and were hopeful for an assignment from HBO. It was not that Jean could envision ownership just anywhere in Spain. No! Not just anywhere! It had to be specifically on that hill.

There was something about that particular Spanish hill—something soul soothing, peace inducing, heart warming, story inspiring. They had both felt it from the first moment. Something that brought on an emotion much akin to love. And it wasn't the view of the sea because you could get that in a lot of places. It was the mountain, La Concha. The mountain that loomed above the tiny village of El Salto del Agua like a painted backdrop in a hot blue sky. From Belnapp's roof terrace they had first peered north across the hundred feet of barren hillside towards the quaint, freshly painted white stucco houses, tile roofed, all jumbled together with barely a thought of passage for animal or human. The donkeys and goats, the villagers—mostly women in black-on-black with sunburnt faces—the noisy chickens pecking, the freshly scrubbed children shouting; it was all so colorful, so different, so inspiring to an American writer's imagination.

'What a place to put words on paper,' Jean sighed one drunken lunch on the Gray's terrace after too much Sangrias celebrating the fact that an English/Spanish magazine had accepted a story by Thwaite and Varry. Hardly a financial coup, but a small literary triumph, Costa-wise, nonetheless. 'We could write a collection of Spanish stories down here when we finish Elliot's screenplay.'

'Couldn't agree more,' jocund Elliot Gray said with a self-satisfied smile as he refilled glasses. Elliot often wrote travel articles for the same magazine and Cynthia did an occasional gossip column. It was Elliot who told them an ancient local legend about the mountain. Although La Concha meant 'the shell', it was called by many The Magic Mountain: La Montaña Mágica, because it was said to give off mystical vibrations and good health to anyone living close to it. Certainly both Elliot and Cynthia Gray looked healthy, although she was given to acid remarks.

Jean had ventured to say, 'If any of these houses are ever for sale, do let us know.'

Party talk.

And now Cynthia had called from Spain to London to ask if they wanted to buy a house on that hill! A place of their own on that magical hill in the Spanish sun.

'But we have never been inside that house!' Jeff pointed out. 'Have never even peered too closely into the garden because of all that barking and slavering.' And more crucially, although Jeff agreed that the hill was story-inspiring, they didn't even know when, if ever, they would be able to take possession and set up computers, should they be foolish enough to buy it.

And so naturally they did buy it, sight unseen. What they didn't then dream was that they were buying far more than a crumbling unpainted, run-to-the-ground haunted manse on a rubbish-strewn stretch of useless hillside. The Thwaites were buying an experience of compounded disasters, trials and delights, tribulations and exultations, misadventures, thrills and sorrows—and a love affair with a tiny corner of Andalucian Spain. How they finally came to live in Santa Rita was a convoluted tale.

⌘

2: THE SMUGGLER

It was true, the Thwaites couldn't afford Santa Rita. Not all at once anyway, or maybe ever, even though the total price came to about ten thousand pounds or sixteen thousand dollars. No one could say it was a lot of money for a house. Any house anywhere. And buying a house from the owner who had agreed to be paid in instalments because they couldn't take possession since it had a sitting tenant... Well, it had definite advantages to these buyers because they were not talking mortgages, were they? Jean was quick to point out.

'But we are talking that we have only seen it from Belknapp's roof terrace and we have no idea what's inside—or even what is on the other side of the house.'

He had a valid point. However to a couple of American writers who had visions of keeping a rented flat in London and a retreat in Spain, it meant one thing: They needed to sell another film. Or a television script. Or get an option on a not-yet-written book—which was getting harder these days. Most of their salary on Elliot's project was deferred, and since they'd decided to write Spanish short stories, getting an option from a publisher seemed unlikely.

'Publishers are never keen on books of short stories unless you're a Stephen King or a Pandora Moon, and then they'll publish your laundry list,' Jeff reminded Jean.

'Yes, but these stories are crying out to be written,' Jean said. "And you should always write what is in your heart. That's what you told me.'

That seemed to settle that, and anyway, time was on their side. Apart from the price being 'ridiculously less' than even Jean had imagined, Cyril Dykes was willing to wheel them a deal.

'Only because there are no other buyers queuing up to make him an offer for a house they can't move into and nobody's ever will, because of a sitting tenant!' Jeff pointed out, a touch disgruntled.

'Don't bite the hand that may be feeding us,' Jean warned. 'A deal is a deal.'

'Except when it isn't kept,' Jeff advised, thinking of the many film script assignments he'd been promised through the years which somehow never came off. Or when they did come off, the Thwaites never seemed to get fully paid. A bit up front and somehow they'd never see the rest, agents or no. Jeff was thinking specifically of their experiences with Mat Windsor. But since he had promised Jean never to mention that particular name, he changed the subject.

Mat Windsor and the film business in particular were what had driven the Thwaites to move to England and take up writing books and the occasional television script when the Brits wanted it to sell to America and thought that a pair of 'mid-Atlantic' writers might have the dollar touch. They had been modestly successful, which is to say they were still solvent and could still afford a decent meal and a fairly decent bottle of wine in their local London wine bar. Solvency and a good agent were all they asked out of a frenetic life. Their beloved American agent, Theo Offer, had died two years before and they had acquired an astute Brit. named Andrew Horton whom they had grown quite fond of, and whose judgment they trusted when he was sober—which they had to admit, was becoming less frequent.

If Jeff and Jean hadn't been writers, they would never have ended up owning Santa Rita in the first place, although it was a perfect spot for writers to live and work with just the right amount of distractions to keep them from working too hard. And in the second place, had they been successful business people, it would have been too 'rustico' and they wouldn't have wanted it. Reality versus fantasy.

Before they'd actually bought the house, there was one panic moment when Jeff finally seemed to have made some headway with Jean's sense of priorities. 'Do you want us to buy a pig in a poke, Jean? And then having finally gained entrance and you having been put off by the bad vibes—even with that fantastic view you mentioned, do you still want us to go through with this purchase? That is, knowing we will never be allowed to live in it as long as the Degueres are in possession which may be forever?'

'I wish you wouldn't talk in convoluted sentences, Jeff.'

But Jean knew that as arguments went, Jeff's went a long way. Because even if it were true that the Spanish would deport Olivier Deguere upon his release, his wife could legally stay on. And on. And on...

For example, what if he deserted her? Or what if he knew about her gentleman callers who all looked like stevedores? Or what if Deguere had committed some other crime while a guest of His Majesty's Iberian House of Correction? What if he remained in jail for more years than the Thwaites could care to count? Having creative minds, the 'what ifs' were lining up end to end and it was not a pretty earful. But more to the point, had they not been writers, Olivier Deguere would never have gone back to Paris in the third place.

At that point they had never laid eyes on the man. But several months later when the Thwaites were once again occupying Belnapp's dorm, the smuggler was allowed out on a weekend's compassionate leave. Compassion for his hormones, being a Frenchman and all. One morning Jean, peeking across a bank of purple Morning Glories covering Clive Belnapp's roof tiles and spotted Monsieur Deguere lying on a chaise in his garden burnishing his jailhouse pallor. She brushed an unruly curl out of her left eye and stared.

'He's home, Jeff!' she almost screamed. Then lowering her voice: 'That's him...!'

'Who?' Jeff asked, trying to look like a man dozing in his hammock and not be drawn into any speculative discussions.

'Olivier Deguere, of course.' Even at this distance she could see that the man was strongly built, stocky, muscular, with the look of one who could take care of himself in extremely bad company.

'Maybe it's one of the gentleman callers,' Jeff mumbled, knowing it wasn't.

'Too pale.' She headed for the stairs. 'Let's go over right now before he gets away—and talk to him.'

'Do you think that would be wise, Jean?' Jeff asked, feigning talking in his sleep.

'Wise? Now you want wise?' she stage-whisper-screeched. 'Do you want that house or not?'

'Do I have to answer that?'

'Really, Jeff, sometimes I despair of you altogether. Come on.' She dragged him up from where he was trying to soak up one of the things Spain was noted for.

'Wait, Jean. This requires some thought.' He followed her down the floral tiled steps past the wall of hibiscus and bougainvillea and into the house where she picked up an unopened bottle of whisky on the kitchen counter and handed it to him.

"You want a drink now?" he asked, surprised.

"Present," she said.

'Okay, come on,' he sighed with some resolution. 'I'm not going to chicken out now.'

⌘

The savage Alsatians barked their unwelcome at the gate. Olivier Deguere stirred himself. Seeing the Thwaites looking perfectly harmless in their bathing suits and holding a bottle of whisky, he rose, silenced the hounds and came to the gate.

Jeff broke out his best French: 'We're the Thwaites. Staying next door. The people interested in buying this house from Cyril Dykes.'

Deguere glowered at the name. 'For years he has been trying to get me out,' he said in French in a voice an octave lower than basso profundo.

'Bon jour. We just came to say hello,' added Jean a tad too brightly, in English.

'Bon jour,' frowned Olivier Deguere, who clearly understood English.

Jean smiled her most winning smile and crinkled irresistible blues at him. 'We're writers. Working on a book next door.'

There was a perceptible flicker of change in Deguere's expression. 'Writers...?' he asked in English. 'You write books?'

'Yes. Also television. Films. Short stories. Long ones, too,' Jean put in.

'Almost anything they pay us for, these days,' Jeff added, not unaware of the sudden scrutiny.

'Wait until I chain up the dogs,' Deguere said with growing interest and eying the whisky. He barked a command. The animals barked back but followed him into the house. They could hear him talking to Madam, and after a few moments both Degueres came out onto the terrace with a tray of glasses and some potato chips. Olivier returned to the gate and admitted them.

Once seated around the terrace table, drinks in hand and chips half chewed, Olivier returned to the subject. 'Writers? And professional?' he continued in English. 'I should very much like to know—how does one get a book published?'

Jeff wondered if this was purely a rhetorical question. But there was nothing rhetorical about the man and the eyes said it had a purpose. 'Through a publisher, Monsieur Deguere. That is, you submit it to a publisher - and they either take it or reject it.'

'Anyone can do that? Submit a book?' Deguere asked.

Jeff could see that Deguere was out of his depth, being more familiar with the intricacies of smuggling. 'It helps, of course, if you have an agent to represent you and submit your book for you to the right publisher.'

'You have one of these? An agent?'

''Several,' Jeff said. 'In different countries. May I ask what your interest is?'

Deguere cleared his throat as though about to reveal the location of Long John Silver's treasure trove. His voice came out in a horse whisper. 'I am writing a book.'

Of course! What else does a law breaker locked in a jail cell for several years do? He writes a book, Jeff thought. And as if to answer the unspoken question, Deguere informed him, 'I shall tell the whole truth about smuggling on the Spanish Coast.'

'But the other smugglers...' Jean began. Jeff gave her a look. 'You'd be writing it in French?' she added hastily.

'Mais naturellement, mes amis,' he assured them, as though to say he would in no way be competing with them.

Jeff said thoughtfully. 'Then you'll need a French agent, Mr Deguere. In Paris. When you get there.'

'Call me Olivier...' Deguere said. Suddenly his normally intimidating expression warmed with a friendly smile. It gave him the leer of Jean Gabin playing the Cheshire Cat. 'You perhaps could provide me with the name of such a French agent?'

'When are you getting out of... Out, Olivier?'

'In three months.'

Three months!!! That was sooner than they had expected. They would have to raise a lot of money quickly to close their deal with Dykes.

'Of course, you would definitely need to be in Paris,' Jeff said. 'You'd want to live there full time—to follow up your new career as an author.'

'Yes, but of course I intend to go back to Paris.'

'And of course... Madam would go with you?' Jean asked ingeniously.

Madam Deguere glared at her husband as though he might escape to the delights of Paris, leaving her hound-bound.

'Naturellement. I take Giselle with me.'

'And the dogs?'

'Mais certainment les chiens!'

'Then, Olivier, I think we can arrange for you to meet a top agent in Paris,' Jeff told his new friend, extending a hand to be shaken. Deguere got the message and they drank to his fledgling career.

⌘

Lying in Belnapp's Spanish cherubim bed that night, Jean mused over the curious turn of events. 'You know, Jeff - I really feel sorry for Olivier Deguere. I once smuggled a carton of ciggies. When I still smoked, that is. Anyone can be a smuggler. But not everyone can be a writer.'

'Exactly,' he said a bit smugly.

'We'll get the house, but... well, he's in for such a disappointment, I'm afraid.'

Jeff nodded. 'We told him we'd try to help. And we will.' He drew her into his arms and kissed her deeply. They made love wondering if they would one night be doing it in a bed in Santa Rita.

The impossible was getting closer. And knowing the Degueres were about to depart permanently, Jeff arranged for Olivier to contact the French literary agent who had represented them on their last moderately successful book, and the Thwaites arranged to make their final payment to Cyril Dykes before he discovered that Deguere was leaving—and they would actually became the proud owners of their own finca in Spain.

⌘

But that day in London at Cyril Dykes' business manager's office when they went to finalize the purchase, Cyril had raised the price of the house by several thousand pounds and Jeff almost backed out of the deal.

'No dice. Sorry, Cyril. The deal's off!' Jeff had told him angrily wondering what Cyril would have done if he'd known his squatter was un-squatting. 'I thought we'd agreed the price. A deal is a deal.'

'Not when, for example, it's not on paper,' Cyril told Jeff with avaricious charm. 'Our agreement was only over the phone. And you know what Sam Goldwyn said—a handshake isn't worth the paper it's printed on. Besides, you don't think I'm going to sell you Santa Rita and all that land for the price we were talking about last year? Prices in Spain have gone up, my friend.'

Something Cyril had just said made Jean sit up with a start. 'All that land, Cyril. . . ?' She paused, one eye on Jeff, secretly toe tapping his calf on the other side of Cyril's desk. 'As a matter of fact, you've never actually shown us a map of the property, have you? I mean, it's one thing to put a down payment on a house we'd never entered—which we appear to have done—but to not even know its boundaries does seem a bit over the top, Cyril. We may be crazy, but we're not stupid.'

'What...?' Cyril asked, pretending deafness, which in his case he didn't have to pretend. But Jean saw he was wearing his hearing aids and heard perfectly well what she was saying.

'Boundaries,' she repeated flatly.

Cyril shrugged, rubbed his ample nose, and wiggled a finger at his business manager. Tom opened a drawer and pulled out a huge roll of stiff white paper which he proceeded to spread out across the entire desk. The Thwaites stared at the map, trying to make sense of it.

'That's the hill,' Tom said. 'There's the Belnapp house—and the Gray's place next to it. And down here... Here is the one belonging to the Ridgeways.' He looked up. 'The rest of the hill is Cyril's. And the house and garden, of course.'

Jean and Jeff gazed in awe at the map. The vast hill ran all along the village and down the other side. All the way down to the irrigation canal, and skirted the fenced in gardens of the three other houses. All this was land that they had no idea was included in the purchase. They thought—always had thought—they were buying a house with a fenced in garden, just like the other three houses on the hill.

Jeff's eyes widened perceptibly, and Jean quickly intercepted what she knew he was thinking and dreaded he might say.

'Well, of course, Cyril...' She tried to keep her tone casual. 'You didn't think we'd pay you all that money without that land, did you?' She felt her voice cracking. 'How big is it, actually? All together. With all that... I mean...all that. . .' Her voice trailed off.

'About ten thousand square metres, give or take,' Tom said. He was a small grey man with a business-like air and looked capable of handling the vast sums Cyril made from his films, stage, and television appearances.

'Just what I thought it would be—give or take,' Jeff said, getting the message as Jean toe-bruised him for the second time. 'Well then, if you insist on this increase in price, you shall have it. But this time, Cyril, we want it in writing. With no telephone handshakes and no further increases. Understood?'

'A written deal's a deal,' Cyril said, and stuck out his hand. Jeff shook it gingerly. Cyril's lanky fingers were clammy.

⌘

The Thwaites needed time to investigate the possibilities of raising enough hard cash, not just for the house, but to keep them afloat for a year while they worked on the book. But when they mentioned the Dykes's house deal to their long-limbed London accountant William Pratt, he sat back puffing a cigarette cloud their way, squinting pale-eyed incredulity through it. 'A house in Spain? And one you've never been inside? You're both crazy but then I knew that from the beginning darlings so all I can advise you to do is be careful which I know you won't be so why do I bother?' It was said all on one breath.

'You and Edward will be our first house guests in Santa Rita,' Jeff assured him.

'Hmm. A bit of sun.' Bill Pratt smiled longingly.

The way Jean figured it, if they paid the immediate down payment Dykes demanded in London and then went down to Spain to try to gain entrance past the dogs—"for an inspection only"—and found it not to their liking—'the most we would lose would be our option money, Jeff. Right?'

'Or our lives,' Jeff replied, thinking of all those canine teeth.

But Jeff had also got hooked on the magic mountain and wasn't really objecting with any vigour, so he agreed to make another rental visit to Belnapp's dorm. This time, they would take the boat from Portsmouth to Santander and drive down through the length of Spain doing some research on the trip for their proposed short story book. And this time they invited house guests to meet them at Belnapp's dorm: their lawyer and his wife who had also been a lawyer—Angela and John Vane. Angela had inherited and managed a large estate and stately home in the English countryside and knew a lot about property. She could detect dry rot a room away, and understood the subtleties of sinking floors.

'Marvellous idea,' Angela said. 'We'll say I'm your sister and could we please just come in for a tiny look-see because while you are buying it from Cyril Dykes and will become their new landlord, naturally you have no intention of putting them out.'

'Me, pose as your sister?' Jean queried with some reason. 'Do you really think Madam Deguere would believe that? I mean, our accents, to say nothing of our looks.' Angela close to fifty, sounded and looked a bit like the Queen as played by Helen Mirren. At thirty five, Jean's American vowels had only softened slightly. Her fluff of sandy hair was as unruly as Angela's dark locks were neatly coiffed.

'We'll say: same father, different mothers, eh? Anyway, Jean, Madam Deguere is French, so she won't hear the difference. Don't worry. Just let me do the talking.' Angela, who spoke perfect French and Spanish knew Jean's French was painful.

The plan sounded great, and looking at Santa Rita from Belnapp's roof terrace the Vanes were quite impressed. 'It certainly sprawls across that hilltop,' John mused. 'Five bedrooms, you say?' He leaned his portly frame against the railing for a better look. Like many Englishmen of a certain age, he was not used to the sun. His pate was thinly covered with baby-fine hair and his fair complexion was already enlivened by a hostile glow. His arms, unused to exposure, were exhibiting an angry division below a short-sleeved San Tropez shirt—and he'd only just arrived.

'Five bedrooms,' Jeff agreed. 'And one of them will make a perfect writing room' he said, still not actually been inside. Although he was still playing it cool, Jean could sense the growing enthusiasm on her husband's part at the prospect of actually calling Santa Rita his own.

'Tomorrow morning then,' Angela said. 'We beard the Madam in her den.'

'I'll go into town with Jeff and check out the legal aspects with this manager chap, what's-his-name?' John suggested.

'Davies. Davie Davies,' Jeff told him. 'We met him at Elliot Gray's. He handles all the foreigners here.

So in the morning, as the sun sailed on its daily hover above the sea, Jeff set off with John Vane for San Pedro and the two women walked across the field to the neighboring gate. Her tight dark curls wrapped in a bright yellow scarf, Angela strode out ready to do battle. Jean had chosen a pale blue cotton dress for the occasion to make her, she thought, look reliable. She found it difficult to keep up with the older woman.

There was no bell to ring. The gate was chained and padlocked. But even if it had not been, they couldn't come very close. The Alsatians were already leaping about, teeth bared and barking the whole village below to attention. They tried to shout above the dogs for Madam Deguere. After a few moments, they saw a curtain pulled back and Madam peer out from a window. Recognising Jean, the front door was opened and the small figure in a flowered house dress stepped out, shouting at the Spanish Guardians of France to stop their yapping. They obeyed, teeth awaiting further instructions. At their mistress's approach Angela's quickly made the situation known.

Madam Deguere, who had the sturdy look of a French countrywoman, wore no makeup and her hair was short and mannish; yet there was something quintessentially chic about her that only a French woman—even a non-Parisian one—displays. She was somewhere in her forties, and Jean was stuck by the deep sadness in her face now that her husband was back in the clink. She hesitated for a minute, but when Angela repeated for the third time that they had no intention of putting her out, she told them with a thick provincial accent, 'Wait until I lock up the dogs and then I shall come back and let you in.' With that, she led the animals into the house to lock them in a bedroom.

⌘

The tranquillity of the once sleepy fishing village of San Pedro de Alcantara had been invaded by a traffic jam of double-parked cars with licence plates of many countries. Jeff led John through a little square whose freshly white-washed walls were covered in small clay pots of trailing red geraniums. They turned down a back street meant for a gentle stroll lined with flowering pink acacias, hibiscus bushes thick with bright salmon and yellow blooms and beds of pink roses. Past a stand of orange trees they arrived at a flight of bright blue-tiled steps up to a door marked: "Davies Property Management, S.A."

A plump but pretty secretary somewhere in her late thirties, was looking busy behind the desk. She introduced herself as Marge, was definitely British, told them to wait, saying 'Davie's with a client.' Wrapped in a sarong-splash of brightly cotton flowers beneath which her bust was spilling over a matching one-piece bathing suit, it was clear where Marge intended to spend her lunchtime siesta. No formality in San Pedro de Alcantara.

Marge poured them a coffee and from Davies's inner office they eavesdropped on a discussion of how the gardener was to water the pots on the terrace which he always neglected while Mrs. X was away. He must feed the cats daily, and start the car every few days. Agreement reached, a rather elderly lady with tanned, leathery skin emerged. She was dressed in too tight white jeans, a frilly pink shirt and covered in gold jewelry which looked genuine enough to Jeff. Davie kissed her on the lips which sent her in a flutter. 'Give a cheque to Marge, dear,' he said.

As the old woman stepped up to Marge's desk, Davie ushered Jeff and John inside. Marge's instructions drifted back, 'That'll be four hundred thousand pesetas, Mrs Froland. That will take care of the month.'

''Did she say four hundred thousand?' Jeff breathed as they entered Davie's office.

'Spain doesn't come cheap, it seems,' John whispered back.

'Sit down, sit down. Streuth, it's hot!' Davie said, bringing out the brandy bottle and some glasses. At forty eight, Davie Davies had a weathered look and thick brindle-colored hair that hung down his neck and tufted out over his forehead and ears in calculated casualness. It was true his image was more Aussie than Welshman and he played up the old Crocodile Dundee image for all it was worth under a curious 'Outback' hat with a shovel brim and a folded top that looked like wings. Davie travelled lightly through life. Blue jeans, a variety of denim shirts, and a red bandana around his neck that was almost a trademark. Jeff suspected that except for possibly clean socks and jockey shorts, that was the extent of Davie's worldly possessions. None of which stopped him from being attractive to women of all ages. 'Where's that beautiful Sheila of yours?' Davie asked of Jeff, a grin widening across his face.

⌘

The sitting room was dark when Jean and Angela walked in from the bright sunlight. Jean paused. An immediate sense of doom engulfed her. The very air felt fetid, thick and cold—as though she'd walked into a haunted house. Madame Deguere kept a wall of heavy dark green curtains drawn on the far side of the room, hiding the rear view. The curtains sagged gloomily, looking like they may not have been washed in the twenty years since the house was built. The sofa, covered in fake black leather, had known the careless claws of cat and damaging dentures of dog.

Momentary panic gripped Jean. She was unable to step further into the room. Until this moment she had considered herself a sensible, level-headed person. How had she been so crazy as to put down a deposit on a house she and Jeff had never more than stepped in the door? And Jeff had been crazy enough to listen to her! 'Jesus Perro,' she said under her breath.

No one heard her because Angela was pointing to the bank of closed curtains on the opposite wall and asking, 'Is that a back terrace out there?'

Madam Deguere drew open one of the curtains letting the sunlight flood in and unlocked french doors to what was definitely another terrace. When they stepped out they found themselves hanging in mid air, floating in a vista of sky and treetops. Jean's breath caught in her throat. They were looking down past an irrigation canal at the bottom of the hill into a long valley ringed by a fringe of mountains that was truly breathtaking. Vast open green fields were centered in the distance by one lone ancient crumbled farmhouse backing into a length of stone wall that must have dated to Roman times. Dotted here and there were massive aggregations of time-worn eucalyptus trees, their pink-tipped sabre-like froth of leaves dancing an elegant Saraband on the warmly seductive breeze sweeping up from the valley floor. The Thwaites had not been able to see any of this from Belnapp's roof terrace because the tree tops and Santa Rita itself hid the view. Angela stirred Jean out of her daze. 'Shall we look at the rest of the house, sister mine?'

⌘

They'd ordered a giant platter of grilled prawns at a chiringuito on the beach and compared notes as they ate. John was peeling Angela's prawns because she hated the shelling but loved the results. They were into their second bottle of Viña Sol before all the news was out and Jean had come to a conclusion.

'I know I said the house was ominous inside, Angela, but really, I think I was picking up the poor woman's vibrations. After all, her husband has been in the clink for almost three years and her only companions are those Baskerville clones, who I must say, are even more vicious the closer you get.' She turned to Jeff. 'One got out after Madam Deguere locked them up and would have devoured Angela, but after running that estate of hers, she could outstare even the Werewolf of London.'

'Thank you, I think,' Angela said and popped another peeled prawn into her mouth. 'Personally, I prefer those dogs from the distance of Belnapp's roof. But wait until you see the view, Jeff...'

He raised an eyebrow. 'View? Of the sea?'

Jean shook her head. 'The other side, Jeff! Of the valley. It's... it's—well... beyond description.'

'And you a writer?' John smiled. 'Well, Jean, Jeff and I have some good news for you. How long did you say the pirate had been in the pokey?'

'Two and a half years.'

'Your friend Davie Davies can certainly knock back the brandy. But he seemed inclined to be friendly. He told us that according to Spanish law, a person serving a six year term for piratical pursuits can get off in three for good behaviour.'

Jean nodded. 'Okay, so, he'll be out. How does that help us?' she asked, eating a fried calamaré that tasted like a rubber band in batter—and rubber bands were something she often chewed while writing. Jeff was grinning from ear to ear. She knew that look. 'Okay. What have I missed?'

'Really, John, you are being quite tiresome,' Angela put in. 'Tell us, for God's sake, before I drink myself into oblivion.'

He handed her another peeled prawn. 'It's a Spanish solution. The government will deport him the minute he's out.'

'What?' Jean squealed. ''Whatever for?"

'Because they always deport foreigners after they've served their sentence. They can't deport the wife, but chances are she'll go with him, wouldn't you think?'

Jean took a large gulp of wine and almost choked. 'I do think! Oh, Jeff, you knew all through lunch and you didn't say!'

'That's why certain things are called surprises.' He reached across the table and kissed her on the tip of her nose.

'But I don't understand—why would Davie give you that information and not give it to Cyril? I thought he was still employed by Cyril.'

'He is,' Jeff told her. 'But Cyril hates his guts because of this whole mess, and besides if the house becomes ours, Davie's got himself new, friendly clients who will occasionally invite him for drinks. The only thing Cyril would pour him is strychnine.'

'We want Davie to work for us?' she asked.

'You want to pay your own impuestos? In Spanish?' Jeff asked back.

⌘

'So what are you two writing here in Spain that you can't perfectly well write in London?' John wanted to know that night as they sat around a log fire drinking Carlos Trés in Belnapp's sitting room; a room composed of four metal-framed dorm beds draped in bright Moroccan covers in the hopes of making them look less like dorm beds. The hope had not been realised and Jean was always bumping her shins on the metal corners, annoyingly hidden by the covers.

'Short stories at the moment. A book of them. All inspired by our growing knowledge of Spain—in one way or another. We've just finished one about a bed.'

'Not one of these dreadful ones I'm sitting on?' John asked.

'More like the one in your room.' Angela and John were sharing Belnapp's own bedroom and they had been admiring the bed earlier. Not the mattress, but the ornately carved wooden Spanish headboard and footboard with cherubim and flowers, stridently painted in pink and green and silver paint here and there.

This particular short story had grown out of a dream Jean had about that bed, lying in it looking at the footboard—and somehow it had got all mixed up with a director they had met in Madrid on an earlier expedition. When she put it all together and told the idea to Jeff, it evolved into a story about a film director from Prague who had a problem. They called it *The Man in the Spanish Bed.*

'Want to read it?' Jeff asked John. 'Wouldn't mind an opinion.'

'Mind if I fall asleep half way through?' John grunted.

'Really, Johnny, you can be downright rude,' Angela snapped. 'I'd adore to read it, Jean, dear. I've always wondered how you writers make up stories. And this one's actually about the bed we're sleeping in?'

'Actually might be the wrong word, Angela,' Jean replied. 'I suppose like all fiction, it's when 'what if?' meets a truth and mixes it with imagination.'

The story, printed on a sheaf of paper from their computer, with a few pen corrections, and later that night lying in the Spanish bed, Angela read it by the thin light of the be lamp.

⌘

3: THE MAN IN THE SPANISH BED

Stefan stared at the crack in the ceiling. He'd been in New York—what? Six months— and it was still a forbidding place. Would he ever get used to it? He reached over to the bedside table and fingered his pipe. Slowly, carefully, so as not to waste a shred, he filled it with his special tobacco.

No. This morning, he would not get out of bed.

Downstairs, he could hear Antoni puttering about in his worn felt slippers. Making breakfast, of course. Well, Stefan had no intention of eating it, that was certain! He puffed, and his mind clouded with thoughts of his wife and child in Prague. So far away now. So longed for.

It had been after the preview of their film that it became essential to vacate his homeland with Antoni. Vacate? Get out fast. With the assistance of those friends who preferred him a cipher on a map to a number in a cell. Blessed friends… Without them… well, conjecture was stupid. All in the past. CUT. FADE

OUT. FINIS. Goodbye Anna goodbye Revekka goodbye... Was it his fault he had been unable to get them out, too? No.

Yes, maybe.

No, of course not his fault! All the letter's he sent - all those letters. How could he know if they had ever been received? He set the pipe in the ashtray with a sigh. Six months. Who in New York would want to hire a Czechoslovakian director? What could he have to say about life in America? To Stefan, a film was a statement and he had nothing left to say about anything. Perhaps he should have stayed in Spain.

Oh, yes, here in New York the ex-patriots still hung around, to string his pearls of wisdom into strands of propaganda. Czechs, yes, but what sort of Czechs? Would he have bothered to know them in Czechoslovakia? Let Antoni deal with them. What was he doing here without Anna beautiful Anna?

When he thought about her, he wondered, did he desire her still? How could he, when desire was an emotion he no longer felt? Or any emotion , if it came to that. Stefan felt nothing nothing nothing empty as a sack of air. He sucked smoke, head lightening under the grass cloud. The reverie was broken by Antoni's footsteps mounting the stairs.

'Eggs. Ham. This I made for you, Stefan. Fried. So...! You will eat now, for you must eat.' He set the tray down on the bedside table and waited silently.

'I am not hungry.'

Antoni disapproved of the hashish. Okay, then why did he not at least criticise? Then, maybe, there would have been something for Stefan to strike back at, instead of this endless swimming in this eternal void. 'No food today. Not today.' Stefan pulled the covers up over his chin, leaving his mouth free to puff.

Antoni watched, his smile enigmatic. They had been students together in the film school, Antoni two years younger. When the chance came for Stefan to make his first professional film, he needed someone to bounce ideas against. Someone to listen to his thoughts. Oh, yes. Because in those days, he still had thoughts. Ideas. And with the gentle devotion of a younger brother, Antoni had worked with Stefan making films for five years. Films that never escaped beyond the borders of their own country, except perhaps for some unimportant Film Festival like Cork, or San Sebastian.

The last film - the one they wrote together - changed all that forever. It skyrocketed them to fame.

If this bed in this room, was fame.

But they had 'made a statement' - their 'cry for freedom', heavily masked in satire. The Party got the joke but missed the humor.

Antoni had no wife. For Stefan, the loss of Anna was a visceral emptiness that could not be filled by all the drugs in New York City so generously supplied by his adoring Magi, along with sweaters, food, money, slightly worn winter coats, and Polish vodka that floated a straw of grass from lost fields of memory. And that girl who had brought herself and the caviar! What did they think he and Antoni were, these New York Czechs?

And what, after all, were they? What kind of people had he and Antoni become? People who take everything offered.

In Czechoslovakia had it been better? Stefan, Anna, and little Revekka all shared one room. Anna had a career. She was an actress, and so they could expect some special considerations. There had been the promise of an apartment. For two years they had listened to the promises and waited and manoeuvred within the sensitive area of string pulling. A government official Anna had met had promised to help. He had come to the theatre to see her about it many times. He would speak to the Commissioner of Housing, a distant cousin. There was a certain building where rooms might be found. A hot flush swelled in Stefan's temples when he thought of that official. Had Anna slept with him in order to solicit his help with the apartment? No. If she had, certainly they would have been given it. But then, maybe that bastard had his way with her and didn't come through. Had no intention of coming through! Just like those slimy government officials. And would Anna have told him if such a thing had happened? No, of course not. She would have kept it to herself.

Another scar on memory.

Stefan looked up. Antoni was still standing over him, watching him with the same patient smile.

'Why do you wait? I told you - I am not hungry.'

'Four days you have been in bed, Stefan. Maybe you should get up.'

'So, I have been. So? I am ill. So! As you can see.'

'Four days this time, yes. But you have also already spent almost all of the last four months in the bed, no?'

'So? I like this bed. And I will also spend the next six months, if that is my decision.' A puff of smoke spiralled towards the crack in the ceiling.

'There is a man who wishes to discuss a film, Stefan.' The eyes probed him though slits in a sallow skin under strands of drab yellow hair. 'I think you should see him.'

'You know what happened in Madrid! I am a sick man.'

Madrid. Everybody knew what happened there. Their escape from Czechoslovakia had been played up in all the papers. They had been wined, dined, heralded as 'courageous voices of protest against an oppressive regime.' Yes, they would stay in Madrid, yes, accept the one thousand American dollars each week to write a screenplay which, if the producer liked it, Stefan would also direct. It would be their first venture into the International scene.

Yes, Madrid. In that hot Spanish garden of the gigantic villa with the burnt grass and the limp red geraniums and Antoni at the typewriter waiting for Stefan to speak. For Antoni to give birth to an idea. But his pauses were not ever pregnant. It seemed that outside his native Warsaw, the great Stefan Kulefskaw was not fecund. Alienated by all that sunshine; by the flies buzzing, and his palms sweating; by struggling to learn English when all about him were lisping Castilian. But the Spanish garden offered peace and tranquillity if only he could just sit there. Sit and do nothing.

Yet Antoni patiently had sat at his typewriter in the garden, with the same smile as he was wearing now, the same smile as when they shared that crowded room in Warsaw with four other writers. Always, he wore the same smile. What could Antoni be thinking about when Stefan was thinking about Anna? Anna was all he could think about. Not story ideas, not screenplays for one thousand American dollars a week.

Every day, the American producer would appear in the Spanish garden to ask how were they progressing? And every day when Stefan said nothing, Antoni would tell him it was going 'fine, fine, but nothing yet ready to read.'

It was in that Madrid villa that Stefan had found the bed. Found himself in the bed, for it was in his bedroom. An old Spanish hand-carved wooden bed with cherubs and flowers entwined at head and foot facing the sleeper; only Stefan wasn't asleep. It was painted the color of dusty faded bricks, decorated with oxidized silver and gold, and rosy pink cheek cherubs, each with the chubby face of Revekka.

That was when Stefan first noticed that he was beginning to tremble. First, just the hands. Then Antoni noticed it. Then the producer noticed and Antoni took Stefan to the doctor. He should never have gone; that was the mistake. After that, there was no hope of continuing to sit in the garden and drink the blood red Rioja - continuing to collect the thousand dollars a week for not writing a screenplay this crazy American was paying them.

Two weeks - was it three? they kept him in that hospital. Every day, Antoni came to see him because the hospital in Spain expected the family to care for the patient and Stefan had no family so Antoni sat by the bed, not speaking unless Stefan spoke first. Then one day when Stefan was out of the hospital and lying in the Spanish bed, Antoni told him about the Poles in New York who would pay the air fare for both of them.

Stefan nodded and agreed to go, but insisted, 'I must take this bed.' He was looking at the face of the cherub and seeing Revekka.

'But you cannot take a bed to New York,' Antoni had objected.

'Then you go alone,' Stefan told him flatly. 'Tell the New York Czechs that I do not come.'

Finally, they settled on half the bed. The headboard was too large, and after all, if you were in the bed, Antoni argued with some reason, all you could see was the footboard anyway. So they took the footboard, unscrewing the legs, and put it through with extra baggage. The New York Czechs would pay.

Now, after six months in New York, Antoni was hovering over the foot of the bed speaking but Stefan had not been listening.

'...I said - you should see a doctor.'

'I saw a doctor in Madrid. Is that not enough for you? Doctors are thieves! Scoundrels...' Stefan set his pipe back into the ashtray.

'You must see this time a psychiatrist, Stefan.' It took courage to say it, and Antoni looked more sallow than ever.

'It is you who need the psychiatrist, Antoni. You go! I will stay here in bed until you get well.'

Antoni did not look too disappointed. He picked up the untouched tray and started down the stairs. About an hour later, he appeared again. 'I am going out, Stefan. In maybe two hours, I come back.'

'Where do you go for so long?' Stefan demanded petulantly.

'To the psychiatrist,' replied Antoni and headed back down the stairs.

Stefan stared at the ceiling and thought about Antoni. Yes, it was Antoni who needed his head shrunk, all right. That was obvious. Any normal person would crawl into bed and shut out this city which had no 'script continuity'. Christ! The world had exploded and Antoni padded about making eggs and ham. Yes, he was the one who was sick in the head.

A long time later the key turned in the latch below. Antoni. Moving about the living room as though no one was upstairs. As though Stefan didn't exist. The horrible thought struck him: maybe he didn't.

'Antoni...! what is happening down there? You have brought a woman, is that it?' he shouted, reassured by the sound of his own voice.

'Tea...' came the reply.

That proved how mad his poor friend had become. Tea - at a time like this.

Soft footsteps ascended the staircase. Antoni had put on his slippers. He handed a steaming cup to Stefan, who downed it in a gulp. Suddenly he felt hunger. 'Bread!' he cried. "Give me bread."

Antoni headed back down the stairs two at a time and returned with two thick slices of dark brown bread, apricot jam, and butter. Stefan wolfed it down. Antoni brought the teapot and refilled the cup.

'What happened at the psychiatrist?'

'I told him I was Stefan Kulefskaw.'

Stefan stared at him. 'You told him you were me?'

Antoni nodded. 'It is you who are ill, Stefan. And so if you will not go yourself, I must go in your place.'

'But how can you tell him you are me? What do I say to him?'

'I tell him what I think you are thinking. I tell him about your life. He listens.'

'What does he say - after he listens?'

'"Come back tomorrow," is what he said. He is a great admirer of yours and he says he will charge you only half his normal.'

Stefan slid up. 'But at even half his normal, how can we pay?'

'The Polish Countess,' Antoni replied. 'It is all arranged.'

'You have told her you are going?'

'Of course not, Stefan. I have told her you are going. For me, she would not pay.'

It made sense. Who would pay for Antoni? Stefan nodded, satisfied and turned his face to the wall and slept.

The following day when Antoni returned from the psychiatrist, he brought pills. 'Two of these. Take,' he said. 'The correct - for your condition.'

'And what have you told him is my condition?'

'I have said that I lie in bed all day. How I cannot get up. That is, you cannot - but then he asks how did I get to his office? And I say you get up only to come and see him. For I do go there, do I not? Which is maybe bad, because then perhaps he thinks I am more well than you are.' He handed Stefan a glass of water with the pills. 'Swallow.'

Stefan downed two little yellow tablets. 'How long before these make you well?'

'They will not make me well, Stefan. They will make you well, for it is you who are ill. He said I must take four of them a day. That is, you must.'

The following afternoon Stefan waited with great anticipation for Antoni's return. It seemed to give his day a focal point.

He sat up in bed. 'What did the psychiatrist say? How am I today?'

'His wife too, is a great fan of your films. She is dying to meet me. That is, you. I have told him that I am feeling better.' Antoni regarded his friend anxiously. 'You are better, aren't you, Stefan?'

Stefan pulled the covers back over his eyes. But he did feel better. Slightly. 'What does he ask? You must tell me of every moment. I want to hear it all, this amazing cure. Leave out nothing! How long were you in his office?'

'It was forty five minutes, exactly.'

'So...!' Stefan looked at his watch. 'Begin.'

Antoni recounted how he had put his head back on the couch and told the doctor about Stefan's life on the farm, and how he had come to Warsaw - and the film school. And the films. And Anna and the child. And how, after the great triumph of their film 'The Engine Driver's Circus', they had escaped together through an Underground group of friends.

Then, about Madrid. And the restaurant that Stefan liked in the basement that served the roast suckling pig which Hemingway had eaten there many times. And the hospital where Antoni had come to sit by his bed. 'For I had to explain about me as though you were me, since I am you, because after all there are two of us are there not?'

Stefan could not fault the reasoning. He grunted, glanced at his watch. 'But why do you stop? You have been talking for only half an hour. What have you left out? What are you not telling me? There is still fifteen minutes, unaccounted!' demanded Stefan angrily, sitting up on one elbow.

'Sometimes I say nothing, Stefan. And sometimes the nurse comes in to speak to the doctor. Or the telephone rings and it is a patient who is going to kill himself right now if the doctor does not tell him immediately that he must live. That is what happened to the other fifteen minutes.'

Stefan nodded, satisfied, and stuck his feet out of the Spanish bed. 'I am going out,' he announced.

He dressed himself in a black wool jumper raveled at one sleeve and pulled on his old black corduroy trousers. He did not take time to comb his hair or beard. 'Come, Antoni. We walk. We go to a bar. We drink vodka.'

Weeks passed. Antoni continued his visits to the doctor, reporting back every detail of Stefan's treatment. The director began to feel better. Each day, he took the four pills and the hovering cloud began to lift. Now he went to bed for only one day out of seven - and who wouldn't do that? But his mind was still like an empty screen. Yet Stefan knew he must be better because Antoni had begun to smile. And Antoni had even gone to dinner at the doctor's house.

Then one day Antoni said, 'Now that you are better, I must tell them the truth. It is not fair to you that he thinks I am you.'

'But I am not yet completely well,' Stefan objected. 'It must wait a little longer.'

However, Antoni had made up his mind. The next day Stefan waited anxiously for his friend's return. Yes, he was well now. Cured. If he did not think about Anna and Revekka with the bluer-than-blue eyes and blonde ringlets he could poke a finger into and pull if he wanted to make her laugh. Or was it cry??? He'd forgotten which.

'I've invited the doctor and his wife to dinner,' Antoni announced.

'What?' Stefan felt a pang of anxiety. 'Here? But why?'

'Because I think the doctor does not believe me. And therefore, he thinks that I am sicker than you are.'

'But it is you who made up the story!'

Antoni nodded. 'So. Now I must let him see you so he will know I am not crazy. And then his wife, she is such a fan of yours! And it is not fair she thinks it is me. Three times she has seen the film. It is playing now, in an Art House cinema here.

'Maybe we should go to see it,' Stefan mused.

But they did not go, and the night arrived for the doctor's visit. Antoni cooked a special dish, Beef Goulash. It simmered on the stove for several hours and the aroma drifted up to the bedroom. Stefan went back to bed to forget it.

Then he heard the doorbell and voices. Antoni's, soft, gentle, barely a whisper. Stefan could not recall ever hearing Antoni raise his voice. His friend was equipped to withstand the jolts of the world. Somewhere deep in his psyche was a cushion––a shock absorber that took the rattle out of happenings, the reverberation out of events. But then, Antoni didn't have Anna to think about. All he had was Stefan.

He slipped into the black jumper and trousers and paused before the mirror. What would the doctor and his wife see? A Czech film director, who dared to make a 'quick cut' out of his homeland and who would never dare to make a 'flashback'. He studied his features: skin smooth, oily, unlined. Slavic eyes, slanted darkly. He combed his hair with his fingers, picked up his empty pipe, and started down the stairs.

They were seated on the green sofa. His step turned their heads. The doctor jumped up. Antoni made a gesture. 'This is - this is Stefan.'

The doctor came forward, hand extended. Americans always liked to shake hands. Maybe, after all, it was better than kissing on the cheeks. 'So you are Stefan Kulefskaw...! Well...!' the doctor said in wonder. 'Well...!'

Stefan merely shrugged.

'In all my professional experience I've never encountered such a situation.'

Stefan nodded thoughtfully.

The doctor's wife said, 'Your film. So stimulating. Such earthy verity.'

Why was everyone always an expert on films?

Antoni was passing drinks. Stefan turned and started back upstairs. He could hear Antoni telling them, 'He will be right back. He has only forgotten his tobacco.'

Stefan pulled off his jumper and trousers and crawled back into the Spanish bed. He could hear them waiting downstairs. Waiting for him to return.

He could feel the Spanish bed beginning to shake again. It shook all through him.

⌘

4: THE CHAIR AFFAIR

And so it came to pass that Jeff and Jean found themselves with an entire hilltop in Spain. There was no road, only a winding dirt path that turned to mud in the rain and the villager's doors and windows opened right onto their field, not an inch to spare. But it was all theirs.

Or so they thought. They hadn't reckoned on the villagers. That first day when they entered Santa Rita after the Degueres had departed, Jean had a strange expression on her face as she pulled down the curtains on the far wall and let in the view. It was a look of relief.

'All right, what is it?' Jeff asked.

'That feeling of depression I felt the first time I came in here - it's gone. Vanished. Like it never was!' She turned to him as the sunlight flooded in from the valley side. 'Don't you feel it, Jeff?'

Not being as sensitive to the unseen as she, he sniffed the air as though trying to locate a dead body. 'Nothing, Jean'.

'That's just it. Nothing! It's gone. They took it with them.'

'All the way back to Paris?'

'And their plates and cooking utensils and the like,' said Jean peering in the kitchen cupboards which were bare save for a lot of dust and rubbish. 'Hmm. I thought our new village maid, Maria was supposed to have it all clean and ready for us.'

'Maybe her concept of spick is not quite as span as ours,' he told her, opening the kitchen back door and stepping out onto the small porch, looking beyond the village towards the lone mountain La Concha. Suddenly that sense of 'did we make a vast mistake?' having left him in a flash, he was glad they were there.

She was looking at him with that shiny-eyed expression of a child at Christmas. 'Oh, Jeff, it's ours, all ours! Can you believe it?'

He came over, threw his arms around her and gave her a bear hug that swept her off her feet. 'You made it happen, Hon. Perseverance, your middle name.' He kissed her deeply. 'Now let's hope we don't both regret it.'

They spent the morning checking out the useables that could be salvaged and what to throw away. The old stove that nearly exploded when you lit a match half way across the room and the near-useless refrigerator in which even the ice cubes were decaying, had to be scrubbed, sterilised and kept just for the time being. Along with the rest of the furniture, including the canine-chewed sofas and cat-scratched chairs which Jean hastily draped with brightly colored bed covers she'd bought on sale for the purpose, avoiding the Moroccan tapestries that the schoolteacher, Belnapp used in his dormitory next door. She tossed on a few colorful cushions, had some thin white curtains made at the tapiceria, hung them at the back windows and said 'There!' with as much satisfaction as though she'd just done over the drawing room of the White House. They were going to 'make do' until better days.

'Writing short stories, will hardly bring us better days, Jean,' Jeff pointed out. 'Why don't we write an original screenplay? At least if we sold it, we'd make some money.'

'Because there is no film industry left in England, Jeff. Or have you forgotten?'

'We're still Americans. Have you forgotten that?'

'Yes, but then if we did write one for the American market and sold it, we'd have to go back to Hollywood and I thought we weren't ready for that yet.

That shut him up. Jeff had grown up in tinsel town, being the son of a film director. He knew the place perhaps better than anyone. And at the moment it was not where he wished to risk his sanity. He turned his attention back to making Santa Rita liveable. And against all reason, somehow the room had taken on an air of cosiness.

Among the bits of furniture they were 'making do' with, were a set of eight carved pine dining room chairs with brass studded leather seats. They came with the house as a kind of booby prize, but they appeared in fairly reasonable condition considering that the worms had held conventions in them. Jean, always one to look on the bright side, said she liked the wormwood effect. 'It gives them character,' she told him a few days later polishing one until it almost gleamed.

'Why don't you let Maria do that?' Jeff asked, waiting for her to return to the writing work in hand. He preferred his wife slaving over a hot computer to a kitchen sink any day.

'Why? Because Maria advised us to throw them all out, Jeff. Along with the table. They're not good enough for us, she says.'

'Well, I'm inclined to agree with her. Now let's get back to our story.'

But Jean wasn't finished with her rant. 'She has a son who doesn't know any better, and presumably lives in a house full of apple crates. He'll take the chairs off our hands, and not charge us a peseta for hauling them away.'

'She didn't suggest giving him the sofas too, did she? Which I'd gladly trade for a few sturdy apple crates.'

'No. She said we should give those to the rubbish man. I've called the Pest Control, Jeff.'

'They've got one here?'

She nodded. 'Davie Davies gave me the number. It's run by an ex-Londoner with an East End accent. Davie says his warfare against certain insect invaders is changing the ecology all down the coast.'

He had noticed the Welshman's continued interest in Jean at the last party at the neighbouring Ridgeways. Davie had rushed about refilling her drink every time the ice melted, which on a hot Spanish night was often. 'When did you speak to Davie?' he asked.

'This morning. When you were out playing tennis.'

'I see,' said Jeff.

'When did he phone?' Jeff asked.

'He was here.'

'Unannounced?'

'Jeff... Are you suggesting I can't handle the situation? He came by to give me the bills for the telephone which Cyril never mentioned he hadn't paid for two months. And for the bombonas.'

'What's a bombona?'

'Those big gas cylinder things. That's how we get hot water.'

'You mean that trickle that comes out of the pipe when I'm trying to shower and then scalds me when I turn it up?'

Jeff was still thinking about Davie Davies when the Pest Control man arrived. The Englishman was in his early forties, cheerful, muscular, with a bent nose which made him look like his removal to the Spanish coast had some reference to gangland. His name was Pete and he carried the chairs out in big ham hands four at a time to the back terrace where he sprayed them from an oversize canister. He came back into the house all smiles and assured them that 'all them pollilas is now gonners.' Jeff could imagine him doing away with a few larger type pollilas in his time. Jeff went out for a look and spotted several small brown insects crawling out of their holes like deep sea divers with the bends.

'Sure you want to keep them chairs?' Pete the Pest Control asked, accepting a glass of wine while Jean wrote him a cheque. 'I could take 'em off your 'ands, and I wouldn't charge you noffink for hauling 'em away.'

Jeff was about to take him up on the offer but Jean put in a hasty 'no'. Jeff looked through the french doors at the chairs lying on their sides, all wet and miserable and he somehow felt sorry for them. Considering their traumatic twenty years of service, and the Deguere dogs and cats, they were not without a certain bravura charm.

But despite their ordeal by canister and Jean's spit and polish, time had taken its toll on the chairs. One night at a small barbecue dinner on the Thwaite's front terrace, the weight of Elliot Gray's capacious rump brought him crashing to the floor, which he had a habit of holding at the best of times. On close inspection, one leg was ripped from its socket - the chair's, not Elliot's - and the wood seemed to be turning to sawdust.

Elliot Gray, a man who could fall down a coal mine and come up with a handful of diamonds, seemed unaffected. He rose to his full height, brushing off his trousers, and saying, 'I told Cyril not to buy those chairs.'

'When was that, dear?' Cynthia asked. Elliot was a man to whom time was only yesterday and twenty years but a snooze after lunch. 'Still,' she added, eying the carving at the backs, 'why don't I take them off your hands, Jean? An auction in aid of the Home for Cats I'm starting on the Coast. And they won't charge you a penny to have them hauled away.'

Jean declined.

In the cold light of day, the Thwaites assessed the damage. Seven of the chairs looked rump-worthy. But the three-legged chair wouldn't even hold a one-legged man. To find a source of reparation was no mean task in Spain. Shoes, yes. Handbags, certainly. And they can whip you up a leather suit in an afternoon. But an old, rickety chair that you were fast becoming attached to? Where would one take it? Tapicerias only covered them. Tiendas only sold them. Where then, was that 'little man' Jean was always seeking and somehow finding in London who could fix anything from a broken curtain rod to an electric socket?

Davie Davies had the right 'little man'. He asked Jeff when he'd be playing tennis again, eyes on Jean, and then told them how to find the carpenter. 'It's a piece of cake,' he said. 'You know 'The Abolingo', that big ceramica on the main carretera to Estepona that sells all the hand-painted Spanish plates?'

Jeff nodded. They'd bought one with a picture of Don Quixote on it.

'That's where you turn. You head up the dirt road past it, over three badenas.'

'Three what?' Jean asked.

'Sleeping policemen. Then you look for a smaller road almost immediately after, about twenty five or fifty metres. The second or third, I can't remember which. But you'll see a place with a big hedge.'

'I think I know that road,' Jeff said. 'But every house there has a big hedge.'

'Too right, Mate,' Davie said, affecting his Aussie way of speaking. 'That hedge is just like the others, but there's a goat inside the right one. You can't exactly see him because of the hedge, but he's there. It's the turn immediately after the first one behind it. Got it?'

'Sort of,' Jeff said.

'Does the house have a number or name?' Jean asked, being a stickler for landmarks.

'It's not exactly a house, Jean. That's how you'll tell when you get there. It's a sort of shed. Set way back from the others, the houses, I mean. That's where José works with his sons.'

'Is it a left or a right?'

'Hang a left and then right. Didn't I say?'

'That is, after the goat?'

Davie looked at Jeff blankly. 'I told you, you won't see the goat. It's behind a hedge.'

'Then how do we know it's there?'

Davie, who was used to dealing with demanding clients was nevertheless losing patience. 'Look, do you want me to help you, or don't you?' He had three cash customers in the outer waiting room being fed coffees by Marge.

'Help,' Jeff said agreeably.

'No worries then. So you turn right and left....'

'I thought you said left and then right?'

'That's right. Then you'll see the fence and the gate. Rustic. Be careful of the dogs. José has four guard dogs.'

'Are they dangerous?' Jeff asked, remembering the Deguere's savage monsters.

'I've never entered that far myself. But call out to him. José usually comes out to meet me. Or one of his sons, if they hear you. José's the greatest cabinet maker on the Coast. It's amazing what he can do with only three fingers on his right hand.'

'Three fingers?' Jeff asked, his confidence shaken slightly.

Davie nodded. 'From the electric saw he had before, but now refuses to use. Tell him Davie sent you,' he said leaning back dangerously in his chair and lighting one cigarette from the stub of the last one.

He rose to kiss Jean goodbye, for what Jeff thought, was a little too long.

So, dutifully they went home and tied the chair to the top of the roof rack of their small white antique Renault, tossing the leg inside. This procedure was complicated by Miguel's attempts to help. The gardener, who had come with the house, had somehow got it through his head that not being Spanish, his employers were mentally incompetent and one of his duties was to see that anything that took brains, like tying a chair onto a roof rack, he would assist with. The simpler things, like working their computer or actually cleaning the garden, he left to them.

Jeff at the wheel, they made their way as best they could to the road of hedges. And 'Jeff at the wheel' was complicated by the long legs of his six foot and-then-some frame. He always slid the seat so far back it was in danger of collapsing. They had thought about getting a larger car, but money had evaporated by the time it came to transportation.

'Stop the car, Jeff and listen,' Jean said suddenly.

He obeyed, not sure why. But Jean had been right. Behind one hedge they actually heard a bleating goat. A few wrong turns and finally they found themselves face to face with the unmarked entrance of a gate in the middle of a hedge that led to the shed that wasn't a house.

They parked in front. Jeff unpeeled himself from the driver's seat and peered past the gate. No sign of life in the courtyard except four sleeping dogs and a distant sound of the thudding beat of hammer and the whine of saw.

'I think you'd better stay in the car,' he said.

She stuck her head through the window. 'Shall I honk or let sleeping dogs lie?'

'Give them the full symphony right in the eardrum.'

The honking alerted the beasts, who rose from their afternoon siesta in full slaver. 'We've come this far, and actually found the place.' he said grimly. 'I'm not to be intimidated. I'm going in.'

Jeff opened the gate. Instantly he had a dog's mouth around his leg. But the teeth did not close; they were gently holding the trouser, but not quite intruding on flesh. Jeff moved his leg. The mouth moved with him but the teeth still did not close. Dragging along the large black and now-that-he-noticed-it, mangy beast, Jeff headed into the courtyard. The other three barked the way ahead, heralds to the Court. The smallest, a wiry mongrel with a falsetto yap, nipped the air baring its teeth in case there were any doubts in Jeff's mind of its sincerity.

'Nice pair of molars,' Jeff told him in a friendly tone. Then he shouted above the sawing and pounding, 'José! Señor José!'

Two hulking dull-eyed sons emerged, one armed with a saw, the other with a hammer. 'Señor Davie has sent me. I bring you a chair with a broken leg.' He said this in Spanish, well rehearsed. The taller boy nodded, shoulder-gesturing towards the back of the shed. Jeff entered, still dragging the dog. José was bent over a drawer like a surgeon. He looked up with the face of a saint, snapped his fingers, and the dog released Jeff's leg. A thinly wired man with a well seasoned face and grey streaks touching his stringy hair, he gestured Jeff forward with a three fingered greeting.

'I have a chair,' Jeff began, and explained the problem in mongrel Spanish.

José nodded, then followed Jeff outside to where Jean was waiting by the car, having unstrapped the chair from its rack. Gently, José took it down as though they had brought the greatest treasure from the Escorial. Jean handed him severed the leg. His remaining fingers lovingly caressed it. He sighed, nodded, then conceded the obvious, 'Yes, certainly it is broken.'

'Can you fix it?' Jean asked.

'Todo es posible,' he smiled. It was a phrase they were to get used to hearing from every Spaniard worth his salt. Everything is possible. In Spain, nobody admits to the impossible. 'But tomorrow,' he continued, 'it is the fiesta.'

Since almost every tomorrow in Spain is a fiesta, it was only to be expected.

'Then when could we hope that you can repair it?'

'Since in the morning I must be with my family, I cannot do your chair then,' he told them sadly.

'Naturally,' Jeff agreed, estimating the time before the next fiesta.

'...Therefore I must have it ready for you by six o'clock.'

They looked at each other. Jeff's nose twitched. '*This* six o'clock? Today?'

'Si. There is no other possibility, verdad. For I am certain that you must have the chair for your own fiesta. Is it not so?' José asked.

Jeff shook the three fingers and parted from the carpenter, near tears of exultation.

Jean drove. Jeff was too excited. 'At last in this world of fading craftsmen, incompetent service, endless delays, overcharging, and under-consideration, we have found the one - the only man of a dying breed, Jean! Isn't Spain wonderful?'

They drove home in a high state of elation feeling like a celebration. 'Let's have a drink to Davie, bless him,' Jeff said and got out the vodka.

'I thought we didn't drink in the afternoon,' she said holding out her glass, happy to share his joy if not his certitude. He took it, poured liberal vodkas over ice and topped it up with grapefruit juice, handing one back to Jean.

'Every rule has its exceptions, Jean and this is a momentous occasion. We drink a Salty Dog - a fitting drink - to Saint José, and to all the dogs in Spain.' Jeff downed his drink in a gulp, then grabbed her up swinging her in a circle and kissed her. 'I love Spain, I love the Spaniards, I love Santa Rita and this hill and the mountain and the village, and most of all I love you, Jean.'

'Sometimes, Jeff, I feel the whole world is no larger than you and me.' He kissed her again and drew her into the sitting room. 'Let's make love,' he said.

'Now?' she asked, feeling a bit light-headed and managing to set down her empty glass.

'We never do it enough in the afternoon.'

'That's because the goat man or somebody is always looking in the window.'

'Good,' he said, 'we'll have an audience. I've always wanted to work in a dirty movie.' He slipped his hand inside her shorts and felt the wet warmth of her. 'Jean! You're always ready. My kind of woman...' he breathed, covering her mouth with kisses. He was swelling against her, rock hard and she was too excited to wait a moment longer.

'I'd better be.' She undid the top button of her shorts and Jeff tugged them off, pulling her down to their new fake fur carpet by the fireplace.

'I want to be in control. To fuck you until you scream,' she told him and pushed him to the floor unzipping his shorts. She moved on top of him.

'Jean! You said fuck!' He pulled her down tightly. The joy of him soared through her.

'You have to, in a dirty movie,' she replied, moving slowly and driving him crazy. 'Let's see who can last the longest.'

It was Jeff who won the bet.

They were lying on the carpet, in a half dream state, so totally relaxed they had forgotten the time. Jean sat up. 'He said six o'clock, Jeff. Do you think he meant it?' she had not entirely bought Jeff's enthusiasm over José. Jeff glanced at his watch. It was ten minutes to.

'Time to find out,' he told her exuberantly, pulling on his shorts and getting to his feet.

Once more they set forth. Once more got lost - heard the goat - found the gate - roused the dogs - and once more, Jeff dragged the black mangy one by his pants leg to the entrance of José's shed.

The glum-eyed sons were expressionless as ever. José was working at the back of his shop on the same cabinet drawer. Jeff guessed he hadn't got to the chair. But he was wrong.

'Your chair, señor.'

'It's not ready.'

José smiled at Jeff and came forward holding the three fingered hand in a wave of affirmation. 'Oh, but it is, most certainly. It is here. Strong as the young bull. You may sit a man of many kilos upon it and he will rise again without damage to himself or to this brave chair. For it has withstood much surgery.'

A son brought the chair forward holding it up. Jeff could barely see the break. José turned it over for Jeff's inspection. Underneath, the carpenter had affixed a brace of heavy wood so cunningly that it didn't show. José stood it on the floor, shook it about.

'It's stronger than any of the others', Jeff assured him and complimented him on the fine workmanship.

'Si, it will see you through many fiestas,' José said. 'And I wish you a fine day.'

'How much do I owe you?' Jeff asked?

José picked up a scrap of paper, holding a pencil stub between his three fingers. He scrawled some figures, then added and erased, and finally after much calculation arrived at a sum. 'It is true, Señor, I have not taken much time with this work. But still, I will have to ask you two hundred pesetas, if you find that not disagreeable.'

Jeff gulped. 'Two hundred pesetas, José?'

'You think it is too much, Señor?'

'No. no,' Jeff said. 'It's estupendo, José. Absolutely, estupendo.' He reached in his pocket and pulled out a handful of coins, pouring them into José's hand. He added a few extra. 'That's for the dogs. So that they too, can have a fiesta.'

He came out carrying the chair, and Jean hopped out of the car all excited at seeing it in one piece. 'Oh, Jeff it's like when my little brother had his leg set after a skiing accident'.

'Jean, I feel guilty,' Jeff said. 'Do you know what he charged me? Two hundred pesetas.'

'Jeff - that's one pound, sterling. One dollar eighty cents, for goodness sake. Can we bring him the rest of the house?'

Together they tied the chair to the roof rack without the help of Miguel and drove back up the hill singing a light-headed duet of joy and exultation. As Jeff pulled into the driveway, Jean glanced out at their low slung garage teetering on the edge of Santa Rita.

'Let's put the car away, Jeff. We never do and it's getting so dusty.'

'Good idea. We should get into the habit,' he agreed and drove straight into the garage, forgetting that the chair was tied on top until they heard the crunch of splintering wood.

For weeks the chair stood in a heap in the corner of the garage shrouded with an old dust sheet so that maybe Miguel would not notice it and ask questions. Finally, one day, Jean said, 'We're taking it back.'

'Jean...I couldn't face him,' Jeff told her.

'We'll tell him a burglar broke in and we had to cosh him.'

'I don't think I could say that in Spanish.'

'But they did take it back and Jeff attempted no explanation. José looked at it sadly and finally said, 'It must have been un Diablo de la fiesta, Señor.'

⌘

They were drinking an afternoon coffee, watching a yacht slope into the harbor and reading the papers in one of the street cafés in Puerto Banus. Jean was scanning the Herald Tribune's list of best selling books around the world. A best seller in

France was Olivier Deguere's CONTREBANDIER. It was to be made into a film starring Gerard Départdieu who was to play the role of Deguere.

A tight-lipped Jean handed Jeff the paper. He read it and set it down. 'Maybe we should take up smuggling, Jean.' He stared across all the boats in the port and imagined the kind of boat Deguere would buy on his newfound wealth.

'I'm glad for him. He turned out to be a nice guy.' Jean said, trying not to feel jealous. Their short story book had been interrupted by two television assignments for a top British detective series. Which meant they were solvent and could keep paying Davie Davies' charges.

Jeff's gaze moved to a table near them. His eyes rested on a woman sitting alone drinking a Negroni. An English woman they had seen at several of the larger cocktail parties. 'That woman over there, Jean,' he said. 'Don't we know her?'

Jean followed his glance. The woman was staring at the boats with a dreamy look. She was attractive, smartly dressed, in her forties, maybe. But when she turned, there was something sad in her eyes. 'We saw her at one or two of Cynthia's parties,' Jean said. 'I didn't speak to her. Did you?'

Jeff shook his head. "She looks like she's waiting for someone.'

'Or perhaps remembering someone,' Jean said.

He nodded. 'Waiting and remembering. I wonder who it was?'

'Somebody that meant a lot to her,' she said. She paused, setting down her cup. 'He came off one of the boats. And something went wrong.'

He looked at her with that special look when an idea was beginning to grow. 'Somebody important,' Jeff said.

'Important, yes. But not just to her. . .' she stared at the woman sharing the seeds of a story that would keep the two of them talking far into the night and over several days that followed. And when it was finished, they would call the story, 'The Man Who Came to Puerto Banus'.

⌘

5: THE MAN WHO CAME TO PUERTO BANUS

The sad-eyed woman at the table watched without seeing the two masts and great sails that brought the big yacht edging around the breakwater. Ellen sat alone. So often now alone, since rounding her own breakwater—a forty-second birthday. Her friends, whenever she brought it up, were quite insistent that she needed no face lift. Her mirror took the other side of that argument.

She was sitting in the port at a front table in her favourite restaurant looking out at the cluster of boats moored against the quay side. Mostly large and luxuriant, diminishing in their ranks of rigging, row by row towards the northern end of the beautiful port. She did not really see them. Ellen's Negroni on the table before her put a period on her afternoon. One only; she would allow herself no more. And no vino today. Aging was bad enough, alcohol had never been known to enhance it. She was not prepared to let down her jowls with the crowd at The English Book Bar. Appearances must be maintained.

But for what...? Ellen counted her sins like beads slipping through her fingers, like the years of her living. Well cared-for hands. Less care always taken in the selection of companions. Bad choices. Wasted chances. And yet, she could still draw a passing glance of admiration. She lifted the Negroni to toast a memorial to lost loveliness. Had her sins been mortal? Beyond all redemption? Marriage to a rich man because—yes, be honest—mainly because he had been so very rich. Until the day he had dug deep into riches to purchase his freedom for the most banal of all reasons: a younger woman.

The next sin: vanity. The assumption that all the seducing men at parties would really care beyond one assignation. Next, self-delusion. That the young 'guru' she had met in California really wanted more from her than the cheque to build his Temple of Inner Illumination on the Spanish mountainside behind the little village of Estepona. He had called her his 'astral sister' and made gentle love in the 'Tantric' position. He had said he needed her middle-eye wisdom to build his Commune of Enlightenment high above a sea that still bore ghost-galleys of vanished empires. And finally, he had chanted the mystic words of union that bound their relationship by a 'marriage of light'. Not recognised in any court.

And then, after she had transferred funds from her Swiss bank account to anoint the earth for the Temple, he had simply vanished leaving her only a woven cowl of 'celestial magenta' and a cavity in her capital.

Well, she would not be taken again if it meant the emptiest king-sized bed in El Madroñal. She finished the Negroni and gazed at a boat gracefully nudged alongside a mooring directly opposite her outdoor table. Even among Arab luxury liners with their midget helicopters, this craft stood out with its length of teak deck and shimmering brass.

She ordered a café solo and waited to see which Saudi prince might come ashore. Who else in these times, could still manage such nautical splendour? Then she noticed the Panama flag and the curious gilded name on the stern: 'PAPA'S NEST'. That hardly sounded Arabic.

The youngish man who stepped lightly across the mahogany gang plank looked weathered, arrogant, with the kind of bone structure that seemed carved, rather than modelled from soft clay. He had a wide inquisitive blue glance, a designer stubble of beard on a determined jaw line.

And he was making for her! Ellen glanced quickly around to see if the smile was meant for somebody else. He came over and stopped in front of her, enormously confident.

'Sorry to butt in on you, lady...'

But of course, American. She waited, uncertain how to react.

'Whenever I put into a new port, I mean for the first time, I have a kind of thing about asking the first native I meet which is the best place to eat. Not a lot of chichi. I mean honest food, waiters who don't grab your wine bottle away before it's empty.'

'I'm hardly a native. In fact, it's not a word we English use about ourselves.'

'English? Of course. But you sure don't look like a tourist,' he said.

'Actually I do live here,' she acknowledged. 'Part of the year. Nine years, to be exact. A restaurant...? Well, this one is excellent. Run by a French woman. Not the largest selection, but they serve Gallo, which is what the French call St. Pierre.' She paused. 'The vino de casa is very drinkable. Of course, I haven't a clue what you're looking for...?' One carefully plucked eyebrow went up just slightly.

She said no, she wouldn't mind his joining her and she helped him to order in Spanish. The afternoon slipped towards evening. It was all rather crazy and disconnected. He told her he was a Hollywood film producer who made films in different parts of the world. He mentioned several movies which she thought she might vaguely have heard of. Ellen never liked going to films alone, and when she was taken out in London, it was always to a play, or ballet, if anything these days. He explained that he had sailed over from Monte Carlo to search out locations for his next film which was at this moment being scripted in Hollywood.

'They'll give me a first draft and I'll knock it to pieces with the director,' he said. 'Unless of course, I decide to direct it myself. It's kind of an episode in the life of Ernest Hemingway when he was having his love affair with Spain.'

'Read him, of course. But I don't know awfully much about him, I'm afraid.'

'I picked this place, because it's near Ronda. I mean, that's where Papa Hemingway set some scenes in *For Whom The Bell Tolls*. He told her.'

Yes, she recalled having read it years ago. And she smiled very intelligently when he mentioned that it was the subject of this next movie that had led him to christening his new boat, 'PAPA'S NEST'.

She had decided almost at once that the stranger could be forty years old - which would make him roughly two years younger than herself; but after a bottle of Marques de Riscal, the more he talked the less it mattered.

Over dinner (for he had finally insisted she must dine with him) he told her that his name was Gary Lebonovitch, and that he had taken the film course at USC or UCLA, or both—she wasn't sure which, having been concentrating more on his eyes than his words. He was from Santa Barbara and seemed to have inherited enough money to do what he pleased, which was making movies. He was here to 'nose around quietly, pick some locations, take a few stills. Maybe get some ideas. You know, get the feel of the place without a lot of jokers trying to sell me the Ronda Bridge. That's how I always start pre-production 'reccys'. Incognito. I slip into a place, duck the public relations gang, get my own impressions. Then I come back later for the full publicity schmeer. Face all the crap.'

She hardly heard. She was feeling that special glow of being looked at by an attractive man who was actually, yes actually holding her hand and talking about 'we' meaning her.

'Where exactly do I fit in?'

'Where do you fit in...?' he asked.

'Yes, Gary, where?' He was Gary now, and she, Ellie. He had some reason for not liking to call her Ellen. A sun-tanned hand spread her fingers over his palm.

'Across the river and under the trees, Ellie.'

'What does that mean?'

'One of Papa's titles. His novel that got the worst ride from the critics, and yet contained so much of him. The way he wanted to be. The title comes from something General Stonewall Jackson said when he was dying. At Shiloh, I think. 'Carry me across the river and under the trees.' Something like that. It was the kind of thing that was important to Ernie. His whole life was a love affair with death. And courage.'

'Are you like him?' Her eyes dissected his mood.

'Who ever knows what he's really like?' He waved for the bill, changing the subject abruptly. 'So I've got a week to spend in an unfamiliar country finding out what makes it tick. I'd love you to spend it with me. Besides, you speak good Spanish, Ellie.'

'Kitchen Andaluz, that's all.'

'And I get the idea you have some time on your hands.'

'Time. . . .?' Time killed at the Garden Club, time passed pleasantly enough at the Book Bar, or bridge at Lillian's. The lunches and the dinners, when the retired Englishman known as the 'Widow Walker' had been invited to escort her and they wanted to make up numbers at the table. Or the cocktail parties where being a single never mattered.

'Time? Yes,' she said. 'I suppose I do. It would depend.'

As the week slipped by, she showed him through her house in El Madroñal. He showed her around his boat. She was beginning to treasure their moments. His easy flow of words, his open-faced American confidences. When he drove up to Ronda, she went with him. They walked the back streets, discovered a small church that was like standing inside a jewel. Around the altar, a baroque proclamation of faith; a peasant's vision of paradise: Oh, God! If man could find such love from you, could not pain and death be taken from him?

'What are you thinking?' he asked softly, taking her hand.

'Just trying to preserve this moment.'

They lunched in the shadow of the bridge amid sun-burned tourists, and drove slowly back down the mountain along the wide road that roughened just above San Pedro de Alcantara. It was their seventh day spent almost totally together; and on the night of it, they made love on her huge terrace where a near floral jungle brought insect clamor and a slivered moon.

She was glad to learn that actually he looked younger than he was. Forty three. That made her only one year older. He told her he had gone through three divorces, which in Hollywood was not considered wildly excessive. Just expensive. He had lost his taste for young birds with hair streaming down to their skinny bottoms. He told her how, as a rich man's son he had been under a star of suspicion and so had to drive harder to build a career. She listened, and in the listening, found her greatest compliment. 'A woman I can talk to.'

Then one night she talked more carelessly than she might have intended. She lived on the income from twenty million pounds. Safe as Geneva, in a glass and steel bank. She had a flat in Grosvenor Square, an apartment on East 56th Street in New York and of course, the house in El Madroñal.

Laughingly, yes surely laughingly, and so very casually, he mentioned film investment. His last picture had made a cool fortune for his backers. Then when her eyes had become suddenly uneasy, he had added quickly that he himself had no need of private investment on this film. He had it all. Distribution guarantees. completion bonds. Terms that meant she told him nothing to her.

'What does? Mean anything, Ellie?' was his next question.

When she couldn't answer that, he made his proposal. Would she take a flyer with a sailor? Keep him company on the sail back to England where he would be preparing scripts and budgets? He would induct her into the mysterious 'Masonic rites' of what he called 'pre-production'.

Her heart leaped, but her brain warned. Not another 'temple of enlightenment', thank you very much. But still, she knew how she enjoyed just being with him. Not just the love-making, but the sharing of moments.

She would consider it.

Torn between temptation and caution, she called on Carl Stellerman, oldest member of the British colony of former film makers. He weighed it on the scales of his seventy-seven years, and pursed thin lips in disapproval. "Gary Lebonovitch? Of course I know Gary Lebonovitch. Of the young film producers, he is surely one of the top. But that he is here, is surely impossible!' He headed for his bookcase. 'Wait! I show you, Ellen.' From his film shelf, he reached down the current Film Year Book that kept him active in information, if not in reality.

Under the heading of 'Lebonovitch' were listed credits for twenty films, either as editor, writer, director, and/or producer. Two Academy Award nominations, and one Oscar. Impressive. The book noted that Lebonovitch's hobby was sailing. With an enfeebled hand, Carl returned it to the shelf.

'I myself am one of Lebonovitch's oldest friends. Who introduced him to Steven Spielberg when Gary couldn't even get himself a reservation at The Ivy? But Ellen, this man you met, it can't be him.' The veins stood out on Stellerman's forehead like knotted cords.

'But it does say in that book that his hobby is sailing. And I did meet him coming off his yacht.. He has blues eyes and a slight beard.'

'Sure, Lebonovitch has a yacht. And a beard. Eyes, I don't remember. But so does everybody. Shouldn't I know? 1 was on his yacht at the Cannes Film Festival four years ago. But if Lebonovitch were here in Marbella, wouldn't l be the first person he would call? l am telling you, Ellen, he would not set foot on this shore without contacting me or Henry Mathews, who once was in a co-production deal with him almost. What I am saying is, Ellen dear, this man you met has got to be an impostor. A fake.'

'But you say that without even seeing him?'

'You think he would let me see him? He knows if members of the International film world saw him, they would show him up as some cheap crook, using Lebonovitch's name.'

Ellen's heart began to sink. "But the yacht, Carl! That's real enough.'

'So maybe this person is the engineer. Maybe he's brought the boat here to meet Lebonovitch who comes later. Sure! That must be it. One of the crew. Those fellows, they will do anything to sound big. Maybe get some foolish woman to open her legs.' He eyed her sceptically. 'Or open up her purse, even.'

Her heart was drowning in a dark sea. A sea that had tears in it.

'You're a rich woman, Ellen, which a lot of people know about. Did he happen to mention, maybe money? An investment?'

'Well, he never came out and asked for it.'

'Listen, my little baby in the woods, these fellows know more about how to get into a woman's cheque book than a fisherman knows how to pull up a herring. But I would think after all you've already been through, you could smell—what is the polite word? An adventurer.'

'Don't be silly, Carl. I never really planned to go away with him. I was suspicious from the start. I've just been leading him on. . .' Her voice died with the spark of happiness, briefly known.

That evening she told him, 'I'm not a total fool you know, Gary—or whatever your real name is. From the first moment I saw you, I knew what you were after. Who put you on to me, I'd like to know? Did they tell you that the richest woman in Marbella always sits at that particular table alone? I just wanted to see how far you intended to go. You might even have tried to sell me the yacht, which, like your name, was not quite your own.'

His face was inscrutable. His smile a bit twisted. 'Okay, lady, you win. What about a goodbye kiss before I take the boat back to a used yacht lot?'

She averted her eyes so he would not see the pain behind pride. He turned her face gently around to meet his lips. He kissed her first on each cheek, then the eyes, then the mouth. They were standing near the same spot where they had met. He freed her then and his laugh was a little harsh. 'If ever you stop by Devil's Island, San Quentin, or Wormwood Scrubs, look me up. Jokers like me always get caught in the end.'

She was fighting tears. 'I. . .I'd prefer our next meeting to be 'across the river, and under the trees,' she said.

⌘

Two weeks later, 'The Marbella Times' noted a gossipy scoop: 'Max Seaton, former head of Paramount in Europe let drop that he ran into Gary Lebonovitch at The Marbella Club recently. The shy young movie tycoon seems to have made an incognito appearance on our coast. Naughty Gary, not letting us know! The word is, he was on a very hush-hush location hunt for his next epic about Ernest Hemingway's romance with Spain.'

Ellen put down the paper and took up her single Negroni of the afternoon.

⌘

6: LA TORMENTA

From the village side of the field beneath La Concha, the Magic Mountain, the goat lady was eying Jeff and Jean as they sat on their front terrace. They had been living on the hill for almost two months when they began referring to her as the goat lady. It was not that she in any way resembled a goat, but she kept one goat who seemed to be her constant companion. It followed her around like a dog and day by day she was gradually taking it further into their field to eat the wildflowers.

The front terrace was a lovely spot to sit on. The winds blew directly up from the sea to the east, on over the house and down into the valley or, if the wind was coming from the south west, it would skirt the ring of mountains, sweep across the floor of the valley up to the crest of their hill and on down past San Pedro de Alcantara, all the way to the Mediterranean.

The back terrace was too hot to venture onto in midday. It hung unprotected from the elements above the lower field. But in the cool of morning or towards sunset it offered a vista down the sweep of valley to the far mountains that encircled their new world, and they were engulfed by the heady scent of eucalyptus wafting up from the southern slope behind the property. The first week they took up residence they had set out a long table on the front terrace and began eating breakfasts, lunches, and even dinners there because the sea view was so seductive, the breezes so cooling, and the aging bamboo skeleton overhead afforded some shelter from the steady summer sun.

That thatch of bamboo was no more than a mass of canes tied together in layers,—*el techo*, their gardener, Miguel referred to it grandly as he strung up new grape vines so that the grapes would drop down between the canes of that rotting covering. It offered shade and also served as home to a large family of friendly lizards—and not so friendly insects who had little difficulty in finding their way past doors and windows into the house.

'We'll have to replace it, you know,' Jean said firmly one afternoon after lunch.

'Jean, that techo has probably been there since Cyril built the house, and Miguel assures me it's perfectly solid,' Jeff said strumming his guitar and adding with finality, 'It'll stand a little longer—at least until we can afford to replace it—*afford* being the operative word.'

She sighed, watching the goat lady's goat devouring pink wild flowers in a corner of the field.

'You must admit the thatch keeps our terrace ten degrees cooler than down in San Pedro, as you continue to point out to Cynthia Gray,' Jeff added, knowing that would get her goat.

'Only because she thinks her terrace is so special! Still', she sighed, 'we must get a real roof eventually This terrace would make a lovely outdoor room.'

He squinted a look at her and struck an 'F' minor seventh chord on his guitar that a musician friend had taught him 'This *is* an outdoor room! Look Ma, no walls!'

'I don't mean us to replace it this exact minute, Jeff. More like, the first financial opportunity.' She sighed, staring down at the silvery sea far below.

'Let's hope we have one,' Jeff mused realistically. 'Working on our book of Spanish short stories is not high on the list of financial bonanzas. Perhaps an interview with a murderer on why he did it. But we agreed we wanted to do this and we haven't got any current TV assignments, so what else can you suggest?'

'Take that up with Andrew Horton,' she said, referring to their British agent, who did try to get them work when not deep in the bottle. They had both come to realise that the cost of putting Santa Rita into reasonably liveable shape, what with the daily pueso puestos delivered by the gardener-cum-major domo Miguel-of-the-Outstretched-Palm was causing them to sell sundry disposable possessions in London, including a small collection of antique porcelain dishes, some old firearms Jeff had collected, a few First Editions, and a watch Jean's mother had given her, which Jeff knew she treasured. But the Spanish days were increasingly bewitching and they were both thoroughly bewitched.

Jean's glance drifted along the stretch of sea dazzling a diamond bracelet across the edge of the horizon. Her attention shifted around to the outline of their tiny village nestled against the foothills under the La Concha, Magic Mountain. 'You know what I want, Jeff? I want to feel a real part of this place; to feel integrated with our village. We must get to know the villagers.'

Cynthia Gray had advised against it. 'Personally, my dears,' she'd told them over dinner one night, 'I would stay as far away from them as possible. Just let Maria clean for you and her son Miguel do the garden. Pay them and say gracias occasionally but not too often so as not to boost their sense of being needed. What would you talk about, anyway? Now why don't you join the Amegos de la Musica, Jean dear? They're a fun group. All Brits, though they don't mind the occasional American like you—and they do give such smashing cocktail parties. You'll meet simply everybody, even if most of them are old bores. Of course alcoholism is a big problem here. But then most of the residents think an alcoholic is someone who drinks more than they do.'

The Thwaites weren't sure how to take all that, and anyway cocktail parties weren't why they'd come to Spain. And so they sat on their terrace under the rotting techo, kept improving their Spanish, and looked longingly towards the village, afraid to venture too far too quickly.

The first month or so they didn't see much of the villagers, aside from the goat lady. Jean never did notice whether her goat was male or female, being more interested in the herbivorous end of it demolishing the wild flowers that spread in such profusion over their private hilltop. Purple and golden stalks that made great dried flowers if allowed to hang upside down; red poppies that wilted the moment they were cut, and something pink and creeping that grew thick on the ground and looked like a wild Morning Glory, occasionally allowing a daisy to pop through.

It was not that Jean minded one goat chomping all he could masticate. In fact it was certainly picturesque, the goat lady in her black dress and black head scarf. The goat in its black and white fur coat. For that matter, all the women in the village past the age of forty seemed to wear black dresses and black head scarves.

'Do you think that all those women have somebody dead in their families? Jean asked Jeff one morning, watching the black bustle of activity to-ing and fro-ing at the bottom of their hill.

'Since they all seem to be related to Maria, I guess if anybody drops dead, the whole village goes into mourning,' he replied.

To gaze down from their front terrace at the jumble of red tile-roofed and flat-topped houses, always immaculately white in the hot white light, the village back-dropped like a stage set by the grandeur of La Montaña Mágica, The Magic Mountain made them think they had really fallen into heaven and that their hilltop was indeed a magical place.

Their village El Salto del Agua of forty houses, was only a few miles from the mountain. Jeff had heard from an American sculptor holed up in the art colony at Benahavis, another of the mountain villages—who was chiselling out a crystal owl hidden in a stone—that most of the rocks taken from the mountain's base were solid crystal. So there was possibly some validity in their belief if you believed in the magic of crystals. Yet people in the village still died as readily as anywhere else.

'Are you happy here, Jeff?' Jean asked one day. 'Is it what you thought it would be?'

He paused in his strumming to look at her, touched by their closeness and the openness of her expression. 'No. Not what I thought. Somehow it's quite different.' Jean was not a person he could lie to easily. It brought a tightness to his throat.

'Do you realise we nearly didn't buy this miserable house, Jeff?' Her smile crinkled contentment in the corners.

'I do indeed, my love. And we might have been better off. At least financially.' But he didn't mean it. He loved it as much as she did.

One afternoon the goat lady arrived on the hill with three goats. Then donkeys began to join the goats for dinner. But since they all stayed close to the village side and were yet to eat their way up the hill to the Thwaites' crumbling picket fence, they remained picturesque.

A week later the goat man appeared with an entire herd; black, brown, beige, white, and permutations in between. His goats wore loud, discordant bells. One morning, working in their study at the back of the house, trying to finish another story for 'Curious Tales of Spain', they heard the bells very close by and looked out to see the goat man staring back at them through their study window. He was standing in their garden. It was not a pleasant sight. He had one eye and enough wrinkles in his face to hold a two day rain. He didn't offer a smile, merely peered in to see what he could see. Not much. Two writers, writing.

'What do we do? Wave...?' Jean whispered.

'You were the one so keen on getting to know the villagers. Think of it this way, Jean. We are the foreigners, and probably take some getting used to.'

Her voice held the tone of ownership-meaning-assertion of rights. 'But he is the invader in our private, fenced-in garden with a herd of goats who are no longer just eating our wild flowers, Jeff! There go our roses...!'

It was true. Goats of every gender and hue were methodically devouring the roses and gorging themselves on the leaves of the newly planted peach tree. To say nothing of climbing the Magnolia tree! Only the week before it had produced its first three blossoms which were immediately invaded by ugly speckled black beetles. Jean had refused Miguel's demand to spray them, on the grounds of ecology and went out with a jam jar of disinfectant, picking the beetles off one by one with a tweezers and dropping them into the jar. Instant death by bottle. 'You know, hon, I've never seen a goat climb a tree until this very moment,' Jeff mused, looking out the window with some awe.

'Really, Jeff! Why didn't they do this when the Degueres were here?'

'The dogs. Remember?' He un-pleated his lanky frame from his typing chair. 'But I agree. This is not the way we would like them to behave.' He considered the possibilities, running a hand through his thick shock of sandy hair. 'Maybe in the beginning the villagers were playing it cool. Staying away long enough to assess the enemy.'

'This is no time to philosophise. This is a time for action. Do something, Jeff...!'

'What do you want me to do, Jean? This requires careful thought.' Jeff waved at the goat man and smiled.

'Oh...!' she said with exasperation. 'I wish you weren't always so diplomatic. I give up!' Jean hurried out into the garden and asked the goat man not to bring his goats into it. She used all the Spanish she could muster, and with some confusion, the Goat Man led his goats back over the fence. Jean could see Jeff at the window still waving and smiling. He refused to get involved with chastising the natives.

And gradually the villagers returned to their old ways—which clearly had included using the hill as their own property.

Each morning the Thwaites observed a steady stream of villagers tramping across the bottom of their back field along the edge of the irrigation canal—presumably a short cut to the main Ronda road.

'I wonder why Cyril and his business manager forgot to mention that?' Jean said.

'That's not all he forgot to mention!' Jeff was thinking of the plumbing.

Then one evening as they sat out on the back terrace with long, cool spritzers, prepared to enjoy the glories of an astonishingly red sunset and the nightly aerial ballet of swallows and tiny tree bats, they noticed a small group of village women and children on their hillside below, digging in the weeds directly under their terrace. Jean leaned over the railing mustering her simple Spanish. 'What do you look for? Have you lost something?'

'Las Caracolas,' came back a cheerfully toothless grin. It was the goat lady. Jean nodded as though she understood and ran into the house to their newly acquired Larose English-Spanish dictionary. Caracolas?

Snails. . .!

Snails. Of course. They were gathering the rare delicacies from the hillside—to eat.

'It's clear,' Jeff conceded as he poured another wine spritzer, 'that property lines mean nothing. These people have been using this hill forever and just because some dogless foreigners have bought the house—are actually living in it—is no reason for them to stop,' he said. 'Think of it this way. If we had bought just the house and fenced-in garden as we originally thought we were doing, you wouldn't have given a tinker's farthing to these people running amok on the hill. It is ownership that's done this to you, Jean. Where is the simple bohemian girl I married?'

'I was never bohemian, Jeff. And the word 'encroachment' comes to mind.' Her expression was grim.

'Jean...' He came over, held her by the arms and kissed her. 'We have to accept it—live with it or go.'

"But we *have* bought the hill, Jeff! It's ours.' A look of determination illuminated her face. 'And I propose to do something to keep it ours.'

Jeff had met that look before and knew it was pointless to resist. '*Jesus Perro,*' he breathed.

And then it really began. Every day as late afternoon approached, the children marched onto the flat field at the top of the hill just opposite their front terrace and began to play a loud and noisy game of football. Why hadn't the Thwaites observed the tell-tale furrows in the earth? Where were those powers of detection that had served them so well through so many TV detective scripts?

Just as Jeff was about to take his siesta, the yelling, the encouragements from the side-lines, and the shouted arguments began. Finally, Jeff was starting to show annoyance. Jean smiled to herself.

⌘

'Spanish girls all shout like stevedores,' Cynthia Gray told them, smoothing her black hair back into a neat bun, which made her look as Spanish as any villager. 'The boys are macho as hell, smoke cigarettes by the age of seven, and are screwing everything moving by the age of ten, if they wait that long.' Cynthia was sleek and had probably looked sophisticated from the age of eleven.

Jeff was inclined to agree with her that there was nothing in the world like the voice of a Spanish village child. It had the power, the volume—the cutting edge of a fog horn in the midst of a storm at sea and could be heard the other side of beyond.

'Village children pride themselves on being able to out-shout anybody who crosses them,' Elliot Gray added.

'After all, It may be their only defence,' Jean said softly.

'Whose side are you on?' Jeff asked, staring at his wife.

Their gardener was from the village. All his family were from the village. When the Thwaites moved in, Miguel had informed them that his mother, Maria would be their creada and keep the house clean. No such thing as an interview. It was clear they had no choice in the matter. The village Mafia had decided.

A buxom creature of indeterminate age, Maria bulked up the hill when she saw fit. Since her health was not of the best, they could not expect dependability, she made that clear. An apparition in eternal black, worn for at least three of the eight husbands who had fathered her thirteen children. Unlucky for some. These children had now produced some twenty eight grandchildren, making Maria a tribal matriarch for the duration of her days. But more than that, she was 'Godmother' to the village Mafia. The gossip—gleaned of course, from Cynthia Gray (who else?) was that once, long ago, Maria was the village whore and that many of the marriages had been consummated but never consecrated. Some of the children didn't know their fathers. No wise child in that family.

Now Maria's pale blue eyes were rheumy and her fair complexion, damp and diabetic from too many sweets. Her hair may possibly have once been red but now it was grey and knotted into a rubber band at the base of her neck. Her face was weathered and creased like one of those dried apple dolls that American Girl Scouts used to make. Her mouth proudly flaunted one crooked, lonely, browning tusk in front. And yet beneath it all, Jean could see that her features were small, even, and once there had been beauty in that face. Now, she had kidney trouble from too many chorizos in pork fat and was liverish from too much wine. But with all her physical complaints, Maria was more commercially orientated than the Bank of Spain.

On the days when she was too ill to work, her daughter, Mercedes and daughter-in law, Candela instantly replaced her as a team; underlining the point that it took two of them to equal one of her. To Jean's astonishment, she discovered that all the money she paid the younger women was promptly turned over to Maria. They didn't even get to keep ten percent. Jean would have preferred either of the two to work for her permanently, because they left everything clean and shiny. But that was out of the question.

Untrained and untrainable, Maria didn't take orders, she gave them. She scrubbed holes into the clothes, refusing to use any soaps but a Spanish one called Lejija which Jean soon learned was the most powerful household bleach, so strong it could remove the hide from a crocodile. Every cleaning day Maria swabbed the floors, sending all the dirt into packed mud in the corners of the rooms. She shook out the rugs, sending clouds of thick yellow dust into the room. Jean could barely see her to shout, Afuera - afuera, Maria! 'Out on the terrace in the fresh air, of which there is much.'

Maria had a passion for mops and could wear one out in two weeks. Making the bed so they couldn't climb in was another of her special talents. Jean was convinced she was an 'ant whisperer' and fed the ants, because after one of Maria's scrubbing forays, the insects appeared in marching columns across the kitchen counter: Little red ones, giant black ones. Ant powder could disperse them only until Maria's next visit.

And one day after she'd scrubbed the guest room for an impending visitor, a double column of red-winged ants marched out from somewhere in the baseboards and down along the back hall floor to the garden door and once outside, found the freedom to wing it.

Hers were the wicked ways of a lifetime; of the crusty hill peasants and as self-assured as the ancient cave dwellers of Spain. Nor could the Thwaites fire Maria because no one else in the village would dare work for them if they did. A fact confirmed by the Grays, who apparently had accepted domination by the village Mafia as being the least stressful alternative.

'She's just likely to put a curse on you, though personally I don't believe in superstition; it brings bad luck,' Cynthia said.

Then one day Jeff noticed one of the little boys, Paco had climbed over their fence (the same boy who always stuck out his tongue at them as they aimed their ancient Renault across the bumpy dirt road down to where it met the main Ronda Road below leading into San Pedro). Paco was in their garden cutting their pink roses and digging up the freshly planted lettuce seedlings.

'My vegetable garden!' Jean cried and hurried out, Jeff shouting after her: 'Easy does it, babe...'

She calmed herself and in her best Spanish, offered the little intruder a piece of cake, patiently pointing out that he was on private property. He was not supposed to come into the garden which was after all, separated from the fields by the old picket fence and gate (padlock now removed).

Not one for gates or warnings, the boy grabbed the cake, hopped back over the fence and ran off to a safe distance, where he turned back and once again gave fresh air to his tongue. A distinctive looking child with wicked black eyes, a pushed-in face and a sassy smile, for a villager he always appeared unusually dirty. The Spanish country people, money not being a given, still pride themselves on keeping their children clean and beautifully dressed, and parading them every night in the cool-of-evening paseo—a walk-about that goes on until midnight. So then why was Paco so dirty and ill mannered?

In her growing Spanish vocabulary, Jean casually inquired about his family from Maria and tried to spot which house he came from. It was a ramshackle affair with a bamboo lean-to on the flat roof, perpetually decorated with hanging laundry. At least somebody else in the family was clean.

Paco? Part gypsy, Maria assured Jean with disdain. His family had no right in the village. But to Maria's disgust, she admitted that a few of the village girls had married real gypsies, generally some handsome boy who got her *embarazada*, and he agreed to marriage if he could move in with her family. But Maria was careful to remind the Señora that neither she nor any of the real residents of El Salto had gypsy blood. How could she tell? Because they were all related to her.

The following day Jean found Paco, the gypsy anarchist digging up their flowers again. On the off chance that she might make friends with him, she tried to engage him in conversation. Were the roses for his mother?

He tossed them at her and scampered over the fence and down the hill just far enough to turn back for his usual tongue lash. The other children stopped their football game to watch. Jeff, who had come out in time to see this last encounter, thought the other children showed a certain manic glee at one of their group tonguing up to the estranjeros.

And after that, the children became a little more aggressive, sending the occasional ball as far as into the front garden and demanding that it be returned. Once, Jean refused. Told them they had no right to be playing football there at all. They should find another place to play. There was a nice field at the bottom of the hill where they would bother nobody. A group of them approached the fence with menacing looks just as Jeff came out of the house.

'Prudence is the better part of valor, Jean,' he said and threw back the ball.

'Being writers with a huge desire to get away from it all does not include getting into a situation where we are the focus of attention of the entire village, Jean,' he told her over dinner on the terrace, staring down at the white houses below. 'There are more of them than us. Try to remember that we are 'civilised'. This village is still 'third world' even though most of the rest of Spain is not. We must try to communicate. Make friends, not waves. The villagers will learn to understand our simple desires. After all, we aren't tourists; we are going to live here at least part of the year, so they have to accept us. Eventually. And we have to accept them! Think "live and let live" and all those similar concepts. Right?'

'You're so goddamn condescending, Jeff!'

'Me... Condescending? I'm just making sense.'

'Are you through with your lecture?' she scowled.

He scowled back. 'Got any better ideas?'

'No,' she admitted.

'Well let me know when you do. And I'm sure you will.'

She nodded. 'Cynthia told me that some of our villagers have never been down to San Pedro, and it's not even a mile away, Jeff.'

They went to bed that night on opposite sides of the large bed, not even touching a comforting toe—and with an unusual sense of doom. Santa Rita was a house that was hasty to pick up the vibrations of its occupants and even though it was a warm night, the room felt chilled.

⌘

In the morning they learned that one of the women in the village had died. From beneath the techo they watched the funeral procession; mourners shuffling on foot after a plain wooden casket hefted aloft by six sturdy men. They would march all the way down the hill and along the main road a mile and a half to the local graveyard.

Jeff and Jean brought flowers to the house. The dead woman's husband sat behind drawn curtains in the tiny dark room with his four daughters and the older members of his family pouring brandy and smoking cigarettes. Black tears in a blackened room. No one spoke. Occasionally, the girls sobbed for their mother. The father was understandably drunk. Jeff and Jean stayed long enough to sip an offered brandy but were not asked to sit down.

Over the next weeks, Jean made friends with the family's youngest daughter, who was eight. Pepé told her that she wanted to learn English. Jean promised to help her if she would help Jeff and her with their Spanish. Pepé came up to the house and ran a small finger along every object. Jean gave her cookies and milk. She was bright as could be, and soon could say 'fireplace, table, chair, kitchen, water, milk and cookies.' She hated orange juice. She loved Jeff. Particularly if he played his guitar for her. She could not believe that an estranjero could play a Spanish guitar.

The Thwaites had made their first friend. One small member of the village.

Maria scowled when she observed it. Having polished away the remaining paint from the face of a treasured carved wooden Philippine Madonna until it was blacker than the Madonna of Montserrat, she told Jean not to trust the child; that she was a thief; that her family was no good. That the father was a drunkard and had beaten the mother. Jean ignored the warning.

One child always stood at the edge of the football games and watched—a vast, tender smile on his wide, flat face. He did not shout or speak. His eyes were gentle, but hazed with dimness of mind. His hair was plastered in a black mat across his forehead. Pedro was the village idiot according to Cynthia, who told them there were a lot of mongoloid children in the area, perhaps because of constant inter-marriage and older mothers.

About sixteen, Pedro always came up the hill on the hand of a two year old boy. Jean couldn't be sure who was leading whom. The others seemed to accept that he was part of the action and must be included. Sometimes he would rescue a stray ball booted into their garden, but he never took part in the games. A respected referee, his decisions were never disputed because he never made any. Although he was generally ignored, nobody ever teased Pedro or made fun of him.

This seemed as close as the Thwaites could come to knowing their villagers. The Grays, the Ridgeways, and Clive Belnapp thought themselves well advised not to get involved. 'Maybe they know something we don't,' Jeff mused. But he too, wanted to be part of the local life and would go down to the pub in the village sometimes with Jean, sometimes alone and order a beer and speak in his growing broken Spanish to the men. They would smile, and Jeff felt he was gaining ground.

⌘

Despite sensitivity to heavy noise factors, writers learn to tune out distractions or they would all go crazy. Because the Thwaites usually wrote as a team, they had the uncommon faculty of concentrating or getting distracted in tandem. One particularly hot day several months later, they were working on a short story they thought their agent might be able to sell to the BBC for a radio monologue. They were lying on their bed at the front of the house. They often made corrections flat out, to relieve the tension on their backs from typing. The story was told in the voice of one woman, so Jean was reading it out loud—to see if it would work for radio.

Don't you think she sounds too much like Cynthia Gray?' Jeff asked. 'I mean, if she ever read it.'

'She *is* Cynthia-esque, but then do people ever know themselves the way others see them?' Jean said, going back to her reading. Jeff was vaguely aware of a noise without listening to it. It sounded like a train. He hadn't heard of a local train in all the months they'd been there. Hadn't seen any tracks. The sound didn't belong, so he put it out of his mind like something one imagines he's not hearing and was concentrating on Jean's reading.

But it grew louder, until he was conscious of the absurd thought that an express train was coming across the valley, mounting their hill and aiming directly at Santa Rita. Since that was clearly impossible, he closed his eyes and went back to listening to Jean.

But he couldn't concentrate because the train was fast approaching and he could not dismiss it a moment longer. He opened his eyes. 'Jean...?' She was reading at full speed. 'Stop,' he said. 'Listen...!'

She became aware of the sound for the first time. 'Jeff, what is it?'

It was suddenly close now, thundering into a vibrating, deafening roar until it seemed—it was—right on top of them! The whole house shuddered under a booming barrage. An implosion of shattering glass shivered from somewhere. Musket balls fired by unseen hands stormed walls and roof. From the front terrace there was a detonation of crashing timbers as the ghost train roared right through the house. Right through them!

From the back of the house came one last shuddering crash— —and then the train wheels churned away down the front hill towards the sea.

Jeff's voice sounded hollow. 'Did you feel anything?'

'Nothing...' she whispered.

They lay frozen to their bed until the sound faded and was finally gone. Jeff looked above his head. Happily, the beamed ceiling stood firm.

'What was it?' she asked.

'God only knows. It came from the valley. Let's go look!'

They opened the bedroom door and ran out into the twenty foot living room, separated by a double-sided fireplace in the middle of the room. They rushed to open the back terrace doors. Hailstones the size of golf balls covered the terrace floor a foot deep. The back wall of the house had turned into a porcupine. It took a few minutes to figure out that the quills were eucalyptus leaves driven like arrowheads by the force of the blast, into the cement face.

'The kitchen...!' Jean breathed, hurrying to open the door. It was jammed tight and took both of them to force it open. They found themselves knee deep in glass shards from the shattered wall of windows above the kitchen counter. Thousands of hailstones like a golfer's dream, angled four feet down to the floor.

They hurried to the back of the house. One bedroom on the valley side was the same, the bed, covered in glass and hailstones. In the other two bedrooms, the windows being smaller, had held. Their writers' room had only a narrow strip of windows high on the wall facing the valley side and seemed only lightly damaged.

"Let's go see if Elliot and Cynthia are all right," Jeff said. 'Whatever it was, when it left our house it must have gone by theirs.' Clive Belnapp wasn't in residence next door, but the Grays and Ridgeways always were.

They hurried to the front door, only to find it hopelessly jammed! They peered out through the rejas that barred the windows, at a jungle of debris. The bamboo techo Jean had wanted to pull down had pulled itself down, free of charge.

Rotted timbers and bamboo had collapsed in a broken tangle of grape vines, filling the terrace floor and sealing the front door shut.

Then they saw him. Slack-jawed, limp-limbed, coming up across the field to their house. The village idiot, Pedro, the two year old boy in hand, trudged towards Santa Rita with his usual shambling gait. His expression was grim and in his other hand he carried a crowbar. Behind him was Paco, a leering grin on his flat, gypsy face. They were followed by a menacing band of children some of them, no more than six—carrying sticks and crowbars. It looked like the entire 'under twelve' population of the village was about to attack. A worried Pepé hung back on the edge of the crowd, as though she was afraid of what might happen to her new foreign friends.

'Jeff...' Jean whispered in a terrified voice. 'Remember the film, 'La Strada'?

'Sort of,' Jeff said, picking up her worry.

'Remember that scene—that absolutely horrific scene—when the village women come to the house of the foreign lady who has died, and strip her room, her body—of everything she possessed? These little monsters have the advantage of numbers, Jeff. They've come to pick at the remains of the usurpers of their land. Oh, Jeff... We're lost....!'

'Hola...! You are all right?' called a gravel voice in Spanish. 'It was La Tormenta, Señor. You are lucky to be alive, Señora,' The goat man had mysteriously appeared from the other side of the hill and spotted them through the window. Where had he been? Saving his goats, no doubt. They had heard that there was a cave below them. A tornado! They had lived through a twister!—and now they were trapped in the house.

"Do not worry. We shall get you out," the goat man said in Spanish, giving orders to the children, and appraising the situation with his one good eye.

Jeff smiled and kissed Jean on the cheek. 'Oh ye of little faith....! He kissed her again. 'Although, I've gotta admit—they had me going there for a second.'

Under the goat man's direction the children set to work, hoisting, dragging, unthreading the debris of fallen beams and bamboo. They carried it all out to a pile in the open field where they'd played football, until they had cleared the doorway and the Thwaites were able to emerge.

One young lad having got his hands on one of Miguel's rusty saws, was enthusiastically cutting down the old grapevine and also a charming climbing vine which was never more to produce scarlet bougainvillea across the roof.Once released, the Thwaites helped to clear the terrace. On the field a huge stack arose like a pyre for Guy Fawkes night or the Fourth of July.

Darkness was falling fast when the Grays and the Ridgeways came into the field. The twister or tornado was the first in one hundred years. It had miraculously missed the neighbours' villas. It had missed the village. La Tormenta had passed them all by, except for Santa Rita. Later they were to discover that it had wound a circuitous rout. Santa Rita was one of the few houses on the coast to have been hit with the full force of La Tormenta and aside from windows, it was defiantly still standing, a tribute to Scottish cigarette packet architecture.

That night the goat man set fire to the great stack that had once been the techo, and everyone danced around it and cheered, and Jeff poured a glass of wine for the goat man, and the children moved around the flames like excited gnomes and had Fantas and cookies and Pepé said 'roof'.Curiously, the other adults of the village did not approach. Nor did Miguel, the gardener and caretaker of the four villas who should have been the first on the scene to help.

The next day the Thwaites talked to Davie Davies about getting a builder in to put up a new solid roof with arches in front and planter boxes.

Davie said they should plan on two weeks to do it. 'Personally I always figure two days for a one hour job, mate.' Then to their amazement they discovered that the insurance Davie had arranged for them would pay most of the costs. But he told them to up the insurance on the house, just in case there was a next time. 'If it burned down tomorrow, what would we get?' Jeff asked looking over the policy.

'Probably two years, mate,' Davie replied with a grin.

It seemed the cocktail circuit were dying to hear all about the tornado. They had met the Hendersons a few times at the

Grays, who invited them to their beautiful home for a buffet supper. The husband was more than a bit younger than his wife and almost movie star handsome. She was a wisp of a woman and known to be the one with the money and it was whispered, quite eccentric. The house was elegant and the gardens were unusually beautiful. Cynthia told them that the garden was Henderson's hobby. He had won a prize the year before for the best garden on the Costa del Sol. There was certainly something different about this couple and their life style and it gave Jean an idea for a story that might be 'one for the book'.

She told it to Jeff later when they crawled into bed. Jeff felt it should have a narrator; somebody like Cynthia Gray. She thought the husband should be called Brian. Jeff thought the wife should be called Daisy.

*

7: PUSHING UP DAISY

Those of us who knew Brian, knew that he'd married money the year before he and Daisy came to Marbella and moved into that rather too large house overlooking the Puente Romano. How shall I describe him? Slender. Fortyish. An eleganté. His prematurely white hair set off that perpetual tan and the lively grey eyes. Even at the Marbella Club, he could make a certain Prince look parvenu.

They had been living on the Costa del Sol for five years when it happened. I mean, everyone's coming here now, aren't they? Even Henry, whom you couldn't pry away from Gstaad and Sardinia, and all that St. Tropez crowd.

Daisy bought that house because it offered Brian the possibility of the perfect garden. Since there was no need for him ever to work again, she wanted her new husband to fulfil his horticultural dreams. Greenhouses and terrace boxes brimming with orchids, cyclamen, angel-wing and elatior begonias. Gardenias, too - although Brian knew the soil had far too much lime. (I once saw him - no, actually - watering them with agua sin gas!) Roses, fuchsias, Brian had them all blooming in profusion. His lawn was agrostis, or 'bent' grass, which was lushly beautiful, though I sometimes wonder if he didn't plant it just for the pun. Bent. I mean Brian - well, you'll see what I mean.

And Daisy? How do I describe her? Nice enough, taken all in all. But though 'mousey' or 'sparrow-like' were suitable descriptions of her physical presence, it would hardly give you a true picture of Daisy's character. Ever since I'd known her, which was since we were at school together at Le Rosey in Switzerland. She'd been a free spirit, notoriously strong willed. I mean, in the face of a father who wolfed down lashings of Sunday roast every day of the week, Daisy had turned vegetarian. Come to think of it, her father might actually have been the reason.

Daisy's blonde hair was cropped short. Brian's hung down over his favourite Moroccan silk jacket and curled at the tips. She wore no makeup. He, as we all knew, tinted his eyelashes and brows. Daisy thought it looked romantic, and it did, in a sort of theatrical way. It was certainly true that Daisy cared more for Brian's personal appearance than for her own and had often told him in front of me that one beauty in any family was enough.

Speaking of family, they seemed disinclined towards having children, but then I think Daisy would have made a terrible mother and anyway, her health always seemed a bit too frail to take on such a project. Most projects, really. That was why it seemed so…

But I'm getting ahead of my story.

While Daisy quite fancied Brian in the role of amateur gardener growing his rare and exotic blooms, (did I mention the lilies?) she made him grow a patch of kale which was a favourite food of hers. If she liked vegetation at all except for eating, she was personally devoted to the lowly wild flowers. Even after Brian's garden was flourishing, Daisy continued to wander about the open hillside beyond their wall to pick fists full of wild poppies and lupines. She was especially fond of dandelions that Brian took such great pains to ban from his perfectly manicured 'bent' lawn. Daisy would come home with bright yellow bouquets of her weeds to arrange in those little crystal bowls she kept by her bedside. You know, the ones she won at the Don Pepé bridge tournament two years ago?

Mind you, she fussed over them as carefully as Brian did with his favourite white Iris. Brian loved to arrange them in the Chinese porcelain vases Daisy had brought from her Yorkshire estate. The blooms looked for all the world like open handkerchiefs. Daisy said that when one wilted, it looked like Brian had blown his nose in it. Brian pointed out—and there I had to agree with him—that because of the fact that Daisy was arranging weeds, her floral arrangements lasted for only a few hours.

But Brian bore her eccentric little bouquets with patience. After all, the house and its bounties did flow from Daisy's silk purse, and he could put up with a few sow's ears for that. He was not one to berate a wife who (upon the early death of her father from high cholesterol) had provided him with an agreeable way of life, far more suitable to his temperament than her Yorkshire downs would ever have been, even with two thousand head of sheep at last count. He preferred counting his blessings, and also blessed Margaret Thatcher who long ago had allowed the free flow of Pounds sterling into pesetas. I mean, think of the poor French, my dear.

It wasn't until Angel Cherubito (actually that was his name...!) was hired to assist Brian's head gardener, that Brian first became critical of Daisy. Angel was seventeen, lithe and tawny, with a body that was to die for. His deltoids and his aps were Romanesque and when Brian saw Angel stripped to the waist with those bronzed triceps glistening as he dug out a new bed for roses, he must have decided that Angel was the most perfect creature he had ever seen. Angel would flash his employer an uncomplicated smile (mind you, the lad couldn't have had a very complicated one at the best of times, since he'd had practically no schooling) and anyone watching could see Brian virtually melt. To hear Brian pronounce his name with that Spanish clearing-of-the-throat: *Anqchel* - one could smell trouble brewing. It was not difficult to guess that Brian was becoming dissatisfied with life as it was, as it were. Although his life style was certainly a vast improvement from the days when he'd managed that flower shop in Sloane Street, London, and Daisy first came in to buy some blooms. Would you believe, I think she'd actually asked him for pansies?

But nothing is ever so good that it couldn't be better, and who is ever satisfied with things the way they are? And when one gets what one wants, is it ever what one wanted at all? Suddenly Brian had a vision: Himself and Angel without Daisy. The notion made him quite giddy, and increasingly irritable to his darling wife. At the Flambert's dinner party, he twiddled his fork all through the prawn cocktails, and when Daisy nattered on about wanting to plant Eucalyptus trees at the back of the garden, I thought he would plunge it into her. I mean, it wasn't too clever of her, was it? Even I know about Eucalyptus roots, and Stephanie, who has no green thumb at all, noticed how they'd grown right through her drain pipes, and she's usually too sloshed to notice anything.

Then one day Brian actually caught Daisy scattering wild daisy seeds in his Agrostis grass. And when she said there was nothing prettier on a green lawn than a flurry of white daisies, he thought he could almost kill her.

And then he thought he really could.

In fact, the more Brian thought about it, the more clear it became. Crystal clear, and utterly simple. In Marbella, rat poison is the easiest thing in the world to come by. No one ever talks about the rats, but my dear, they ate right through my electrical wiring two years ago, just before my après bridge paella supper, which we pretended was meant to be served by candlelight (which we'd rushed out and bought every one we could find.) Anyway, there is such an abundant selection of drugs sold right over the counter. Or you can buy absolutely anything in front of that market in Marbella, from that little man with the green kerchief and the black hat.

Mind you, you must understand that I only found out about the details of this story much later. But I'm filling in the pieces and I'm telling it as it happened, so I hope I haven't lost you.

Brian was determined to dispose of Daisy and have the house and garden and Angel all to himself, because in Brian's mind, Angel had become the essential part of his dream.

Naturally, the first thing he did was to get rid of the head gardener and promote Angel.

Then Brian remembered those homeopathic drops, Gataegus something-or-other, that Daisy got for her heart in that shop in Duke Street in London. I've seen her take them myself when I stayed with them two summers ago while my house was being redone in 'burnt adobe'. She always put the drops into her breakfast orange juice. You could tell they were bitter by the face she made, which I must say gave her an even more rodent-like appearance. Beauty was not Daisy's most salient feature, and I say that as a close friend.

Brian must have realised that a dollop of a certain weed killer he had stumbled upon, would scarcely be noticed if added to her juice, particularly if she'd been drinking brandy in her champagne the night before which Daisy tended to do. It always left her with a bad taste in the morning. But she used to tell everyone that it was very good for her 'arrhythmia'

There had been a time when Brian thought that the arrhythmia itself might kill her. But Daisy assured him that the doctor had assured her that such a heart condition, though uncomfortable, would not stop her from reaching a ripe old age. She might even outlive him, she laughed. Brian never did have a sense of humor.

When he finally did it, he could scarcely believe how simple the whole thing had been. He wondered why he had dithered about for so long. After the one glass of orange juice (not even freshly squeezed because he'd let the creada have the day off), Daisy gave Brian a startled look, mumbled something like, "Brian... my heart!" and slumped nose down, right into her yogurt and Burcher Muesli.

Brian swept her into his arms, carried her to her bedroom, and laid her out carefully on her bedspread—the one printed with white daisies. Actually, he wanted her as flat as possible before rigour mortis set in. Then he went out to the garden shed for a spade.

It was evening when he returned to Daisy's bedside and to his distress, he saw that her arms had splayed out from her sides although he had left them neatly crossed over her chest. Her feet had also spread slightly, at an unseemly angle. But Daisy was now as stiff as a board so Brian had to take her as she was. Well, almost. She did have one eye open, which he managed to close.

It made little difference to his plan. Brian had spent the entire afternoon with Angel carefully digging (well practically peeling back) that narrow strip of lawn between the two garden paths bordering the rose beds. They had rolled the grass back on itself so no seam or cut would show when it was replaced. Brian told Angel that he was going to try out a new fertiliser from England (which in a way, was not entirely untrue although Yorkshire would have been more accurate). He said that they had to dig it under the grass for maximum effect. Like all Spanish gardeners, Angel, knowing less than nothing himself, assumed all foreigners were more stupid than he. But Angel just nodded and did as he was told.

After Angel went home (for as it came out later, Brian hadn't made Angel privy to his plans, not being exactly sure what the young man's reactions might be), Brian dug a deep hole in the very center of the exposed soil. It had to be wider than originally planned, because of the way Daisy's arms and legs had spread-eagled. He waited until after dark to drag her through the double-terraced doors, then plopped her into the earth like a doggie bone.

It took several hours to re-lay the grass all by himself. Had anyone seen him, they wouldn't have paid him the least attention, being so used to his puttering about in his beloved garden. When the first red rays of sunrise slanted over the top of his pergola, Brian surveyed his handiwork with satisfaction. His 'bent' grass looked quite unbent and velvety as a putting green. When Angel arrived a few hours later, Brian explained he'd had to replace the turf by night so the sun would not touch the special preparation he'd dug into the soil. Then he waved a large empty sack that had English writing on it under Angel's nose, tossed it into the pile of leaves Angel had raked, and set a match to it.

Brian told Angel (and me and all of Daisy's other friends) that his wife had suddenly been called to England by the serious illness of her favourite aunt. He thought she might be away as long as several months.

The thing was, Daisy had made a luncheon date with me in Fuengirola for the next day to plan the 'Amigos de la Musica' presentation for the following month. I considered it really thoughtless and unlike Daisy not to let me know because I waited at that little Indonesian place for nearly an hour, and ended up stuffing myself with saté, which did nothing for my waistline.

I phoned Brian several times after that, and he really was quite rude. I was rude back. I think it must have been a few days later that Brian suggested to Angel that while his wife was away, the two of them take off for Morocco in search of rare plants. Angel, it seems, didn't appear too awfully surprised. In fact, he told Brian where they could purchase some very rare plants of the hemp genus. They set off on that Saturday in Brian's Bentley, to take the car ferry across from Algeciras to Tangier.

They were away for three months in all, which must have been extremely rewarding because they returned looking like a couple of squeezed out dishrags, but obviously in the first stages of a 'meaningful relationship'. He'd sent a message of his return in Spanish to Alma, the creada.

Brian's heavy carved Spanish door was opened to them by Alma with a worried look on her face. 'Two Señors, Señor - they wait for you in the garden.' Brian set down his bags. Alma's voice recorded a healthy respect for the law. 'They are of the policia!'

Brian stepped out through the double doors to face a large belly bulking towards him above a shiny leather belt. Black eyes probed from fleshy pockets. Words sprayed him like insecticide.

'Señor Whidindon? We did not expect that you would come back.'

'Why not, Inspector? This is my home,' Brian assured him.

The policeman nodded. 'Well then, welcome home. You are under arrest, Señor.'

Although it hardly showed under the tan, Brian paled. (He was a bit wan anyway, from all that prancing about in Marrakesh.) 'Surely there must be some mistake,' he insisted. 'I renewed my Residencia Permit four months ago. What could you possibly arrest me for?'

The black eyes swabbed the innocence from Brian's face, then moved to the velvet carpet of 'bent' grass.

'For planting the daisies, Señor.'

Brian followed his glance. And right there in the centre of the bright green stretch between the two garden paths bordering the rose beds, grew the whitely dappled image of a woman, arms and legs splayed out like a gingerbread doll. It was perfectly formed by wild daisies. I tell you, it was quite a sight when I stopped by the house that morning to see if Daisy had returned, and saw it. It was what made me call the police who were now digging it up.

But really, don't you think Brian should have been more careful? I mean, telling me that nonsense about Daisy going off to visit her aunt, when I of all people, knew that Daisy never had an aunt! Now if he'd said uncle....

8: PARTY TIME

Jeff and Jean hoped that the charming couple, the Hendersons who'd invited them to that buffet supper, wouldn't end up like the pair in their story. Hopefully, fiction was stranger than life. When they sent the story (another radio monologue) to their London agent, to their delight, BBC Radio 4 accepted both stories and asked for a few more to complete a series.

'We're in the money," Jean cried, hoping that Cynthia did not listen to BBC Radio. 'But let's not mention it to the Grays.'

'Don't worry,' Jeff said. 'If she hears it, she'll think it's about her friend Audrey Bennett.'

They were in the car driving down to San Pedro to settle their accounts with Davie Davies. Jeff discovered that Davie had a neat system for living rent free. It all had to do with his clients being security conscious—and well they might be. Davie looked after quite a few people who, like Jeff and Jean, spent only part of the year in Spain. But unlike the Thwaite's tumbling down Santa Rita, most of his clients had fairly posh villas where they kept a goodly amount of personal possessions. Robbery, armed or otherwise, being the sole source of income for certain members of the Spanish community (not to mention the London 'wide boys' who'd settled in Spain, out of the reach of extradition but not totally out of the reach of the odd bullet or two) the Spanish private security services did a roaring trade.

So did Davie, on a more personal level. Unoccupied foreigners' villas held a special thrill for Spanish thieves. Nothing was too small or insignificant to attract their attention. They'd filch anything movable from bedding to barbecues and as Jean had earlier noted, did include the bricks and metal-framed windows. A respectable number of these ladronés were lads under twenty. That is not to say that they weren't dangerous. Maybe money for drugs was at the root of much of it with the younger brigands, but people had been injured, raped, and killed.

Yet curiously, few young thieves ever seemed to get caught in Andalucia and Cynthia Gray said it was because the local police were afraid to arrest youthful burglars for fear of a vendetta from their families. In the days of Franco, the Guardia Civil officers always operated in a different town from their own for that very reason. But the new-found freedoms brought by democracy had left the Defenders of Law and Order closer to home and consequently, produced an inevitable increase in crime.

'You wins some, you lose some,' Davie was heard to comment smugly since nothing he owned was ever worth stealing except perhaps his hat. But that was where Davie's special services came in. He would 'house sit' for absent clients, charge them running expenses and then live there, rent free. Davie had a licence for a rifle, and a pet Alsatian named Skippy. Both went everywhere with him. He told Jean the Spaniards respected Alsatians more than guns. 'Respect' translated to 'were afraid of'. When a villa owner returned, it seemed there was always another house available for Davie to 'sit' and moving his possessions meant taking his rifle and Skippy, jeans, jockey shorts, T-shirts and red bandana.

On the occasion of a house-move, Davie would throw a party for a select few dozen friends-of-the-moment in the ever-changing foreign colony. Of course, he never included any potential villa owner-clients who might envision such a thing happening in and to their own house. Marge, who appeared to move with Davie into the endless string of addresses, could cook for forty as easily as four. Huge salads. Bowls of pasta, fruit pies from the overflow of somebody's garden, and the like. As Davie said, 'Come on over. There'll be 'more tucker than you could shake a stick at.' And the guests always brought a bottle or two.

Naturally the houses always had pools and large terraces, and the nights were always balmy. Somehow, Davie managed to get hold of a small band that normally played several nights a week at the Bongo Club in the Port. Los Hidalgos generally wore bright satin shirts in various colours, cummerbunds—a cross between flamenco and gigolo. Davie only threw parties when they were available, and Jeff was positive he didn't pay them. The band picked up plenty of private gigs from one of Davie's soireés.

What a lotus land in which to spin out one's nights. It was easy to see how people forgot about working and slipped into drinking too much and getting mixed up about whom they'd come with—before or after the party.

It was the second of Davie's 'do's that Jeff and Jean had gone to because generally they didn't accept too many invitations when they had a deadline on a script. But they'd been working hard on yet another detective thriller for television which had interrupted the short stories book, and they'd sent off the TV script that morning to the producer in London and celebrated with a fritos mixtos lunch at the beach with all the calamarés they could eat—so tonight was a guilt-free chance to linger with the lotus eaters and the locals. There were always a few English-speaking Spaniards: lawyers, shop owners who managed to eke out a living selling property or clothes or jewelry in the port. Or doctors who liked to practice their languages on the foreign colony. It was sometimes a good chance to pick up material for their short story book.

This 'house sit' was a fantastic villa with wide marble floors. Davie didn't draw the top international crowd who hovered in more rarefied circles and swooped down occasionally to land in the Marbella Club, but from time to time he came up with a few minor celebs. It was generally a 'mixed age' bag, and very often there were golfers down for a long weekend house-guesting with someone. A handful of older men flashing gold from everywhere including their teeth—on one arm a Rolex and on the other, a beautiful girl young enough to be a daughter, preferably somebody else's. Teenagers hung about avoiding parents and looking for the moment to cut out after the food. First, they had to find out who among them had wheels and possibly a stash.

'Now here's a Sheila with a neckline a man can approve of and look down on at the same time,' Davie said, introducing Jeff to a tall German actress named Susie wearing a low-to-no cut dress with see-through frontage. Jeff was not immune to the visual impact, though if Jean had worn it, he might have felt differently.

There were a few old standbys of the British community: The Grays and the Ridgeways had arrived early so they could eat everything in sight and be home in bed by midnight. Peter Ridgeway was reminiscing about his mountain climbing days to a very bored Audrey Bennett. She was now Lady Bennett because her late husband had been knighted for some industrial coup years before, and she let strangers assume she had inherited the title on her own. Actually she started her career selling men's underwear in London at Selfridge's Department Store which is where she met the future Sir Andrew over a pair of jockey Y fronts.

Cynthia Gray eyed Betty Ridgeway eying Peter Ridgeway across a platter of tapas and whispered to Jean, 'You can always tell when a woman understands her husband. She stops listening to him. Unfortunately, friends don't have the same opportunity.' She turned back to Jean. 'How are you and Jeff settling in?'

Jean told her that she was trying to think of a suitable present for Jeff for their anniversary. She wanted it to be a surprise.

Cynthia lifted an eyebrow. 'Well, Jean, your marriage is still early days. I find I always surprise Elliot on our anniversary by simply mentioning the date.'

The Widow Walker had arrived with an anorexic widow in tow who never stopped talking about her recent trip through China. Jean wasn't certain how much of it she had taken in because from the sound of it, she never seemed to have left her hotel. After dinner, which she didn't eat anyway, she and the Widow Walker danced a bit and left. 'Certainly not to go home together,' Cynthia observed.

Elliot patted his growing belly recently stuffed with lasagne and nodded agreement. 'But they do play golf together. She wins. I hear she came down to Spain to avoid taxes.'

'Not much difference between taxes and golf,' Cynthia replied a tad too quickly. 'You drive your heart out to make the green. And then you end up in the hole.'

Her remark made Jean wonder if Cynthia boned up before parties from a joke book and had it all set up with Elliot to feed her the prompts.

The younger crowd were still dancing out on the patio at one o'clock. Jeff and Jean had their fair share of Spanish champagne and were relaxing by the pool where the band was playing. Jeff was in deep argument about the Common Market with the blonde Susie, who Davie had whispered was on the brink of starring in a German film. She had a curious habit of blowing a curl off her forehead with a toss of her head that fascinated Jeff who waited for it to fall down again. The

European Union was a subject Jeff knew little about, but Susie knew less so the argument was going rather well.

'No dead beats! This is an action party. Let's have a lash, Jean.' It was Davie, who had come outside from his hosting at the bar. He grabbed her hand and pulled her into a gyration around the blue rectangle. The underwater lights reflected ribbons of white that undulated and snaked through darker shadows above turquoise tiles. Marge had floated magnolia blossoms on the surface and it looked so inviting that one of the golfers ripped off his clothes and jumped in. Others followed, clothes still on. Girls were jumping in, yelling, 'Take 'em off!' The party was waking up.

Jeff stood up to watch. Susie came over behind him and pushed him into the deep end. As he bobbed up for air, she jumped in and pulled at his water-logged shirt and white ducks until he took them off. Susie, a natural beauty with long silky legs, a perfect figure, and large grey cat's eyes, was laughing as she tossed his clothes out of reach on the flagstones. By now several men were swimming in the buff. Some of the younger women, too. Susie took off the rest of her clothes and tried to pull off Jeff's jockey shorts. The other swimmers dragged Jeff into a contest to see who could stay down the longest for an underwater kiss. He and Susie were shoved into the center, a crowd paddling around, shouting and laughing. On a signal they all dove under, the man with the Rolex keeping score while Jeff kissed Susie. Somebody took an underwater photo.

Susie came up gasping for air. 'That is most certainly a wet kiss. But it does not work like in the movies...'

'Fancy a dip, Jean?' Davie asked. At least it's clean fun.'

'No thanks. Jeff's making a fool of himself for both of us,' Jean laughed with just a tinge of jealousy.

Davie danced her away from the pool to the edge of the garden. 'Susie's a beautiful sheila. Do you mind him flirting?' he asked.

'He's just having fun. I trust Jeff completely.'

'You shouldn't. You should never trust a man. Not completely,' he said.

Are you speaking from personal experience, Davie?'

'Would it matter?'

She smiled. 'You are handling our business affairs here, so I expect you want us to trust you.'

'I meant man-woman kind of trust. A sheila and a bloke sort of thing.' He held her at arms' distance for a moment, trying his Crocodile Dundee smile on her, his voice gravely. 'I do admire you, Jean. Brains, talent—and the way you look. Subdued sex. Much stronger that the blatant variety. A man doesn't need to see everything to know it's there. A hint of mystery is so much more exciting. I marvel how Jeff can work with you. You must drive him crazy.'

She laughed. 'Don't be a twit, Davie. We spend days and nights together. We're used to each other.'

'God, I'd never get used to you!' he said. 'Does that mean you bonk all day—or that you never do it at all?'

'Aside from the fact that it's none of your business, we have sex like any normal couple. Okay, now let's change the subject. Does Marge trust you?' It was Davie who did the subject changing. 'Let's go walkabout, Jean. You haven't seen the garden by moonlight. This place is really quite a spread. Belongs to Lady Abersquith. I understand she has the money and he has the title.' He was indeed leading her down the garden path. They paused in an oasis of flower beds. He pulled her along with a sense of ownership down through a stately row of dwarf palms. 'This garden won the prize last year from the local Garden Club.'

The sea was a ripple in their ears and the music lingered on the breeze. He lifted her hand quickly to his lips tracing a kiss across her fingers. 'Jean—the ideal woman. I think I could fall in love with you and never stray.'

She withdrew her hand. 'If I wrote a line like that, I'd never get it past the publisher, Davie. Let's get something straight. I'm not bored with my marriage and I really don't get turned on by flirting.' She started back towards the terrace.

He caught up with her. 'Variety is the spice, Jean. Jeff's in the pool, kissing Miss Heidelberg.' He pulled her to him and pressed his lips on her mouth so suddenly she barely had time to protest.

Davie was forcefully lifted away from her into the air. 'You sly bastard! The minute my back is turned!' Jeff had suddenly appeared in dripping jocks.

Davie gave him a sheepish grin. 'Hey, Mate, don't get me wrong. You were kinda' busy yourself...' Jeff finished Davie's sentence with a left jab at his chin. He was as surprised as Jean to see the pseudo Aussie crumble.

With a groan Davie stood up. 'Look here, Mate, no need to get the wind up. That's my glass jaw you're working on.'

Jean turned on her husband angrily. 'What do you think you're doing? Saving my reputation?' She started away towards the beach. 'Men...! You're all such... such... twits!'

'Jean...!' Jeff called after her but she paid him no attention. He called again.

'Chill out, Jeff...And put some clothes on,' she called back and disappeared through the trees.

'Good idea,' Davie rubbed his jaw then stuck out his hand, thinking of losing a client. 'Let the sheila cool down, eh? Fancy a drink?' He threw an arm around Jeff's shoulder. 'No hard feelings. You carry quite a punch there, Mate.'

'Sorry, Davie,' Jeff said, feeling like an idiot.

'Think nothing of it, Sunshine. What's a party without a punch-up? Let's go blow the froth off a couple.' They walked up the path and the steam whistled out of the situation.

The beach was deserted. Jean kicked off her sandals, her toes digging into the warm soft sand. A full moon streaked a trail across the pulsing water gently lapping the shore. Silver foam frothed the edges of small waves that tongue-caressed the beach in a slow, tantalising tango of water and sand. She felt lightly touched by moon madness. It seemed to smile full and wide, an incandescent glowing beacon to light the paths of thieves in the night, nocturnal creatures of all kinds, Jean thought, but especially of lovers. The silver, silvery, slivery moon. The music was still drifting down from the villa where they were dancing. Dancing, flirting, drinking, laughing. Couples in love. Couples on holiday. Couples searching for something—two by two, and one by one.

She skipped down in little leaps to the hard, wet sand at the edge of the sea. To hell with Davie. And Jeff. Screw all men! She was nobody's possession to be dipped into when convenient. She had a sudden urge to dance and began to move to the music with wild abandon like a night nymph reeling and twirling in the moonlight, skipping into the water, splashing up a froth of spray as she turned, whirling back up onto the beach, gyrating, pirouetting, arms ascending in graceful arches above her head, cutting the air, reaching, bending, swaying, and spinning spinning spinning...

And then she stopped. He was standing there watching her. She hadn't seen him come down the beach. 'Jean...' he said quietly, his voice tight.

'Fuck off, Jeff.'

'...You look like the fairy queen Titania in "A Midsummer Night's Dream".' There was awe in his words. ' Why didn't you ever tell me you were such an amazing dancer?'

'It's not one of the things one does best behind a computer.' She scowled, and started away heading up the beach to where she'd left her sandals.

'Wait...Jean! Don't be ridiculous,' he called, following.

'Why not? You don't have the market cornered! Did I punch out Susie? Think about it, amigo.'

He came over and tried to take hold of her. She pulled away. 'Okay, Jean... I owe you an apology. A dozen of them. I was a shit.'

'A perfect shit?'

'Okay, perfect. But I want us back like it was before my foot got in my mouth.'

She held herself tight, unrelenting. 'I'd like to stay angry for a little bit longer.'

He stared at her, his heart aching. 'What is it between us, Jean? I was never good at chemistry.'

Her expression relaxed into a tiny smile. 'I think I'm failing to set up a "negative force field" against you.'

He stood there for a moment, feeling the electric charge in the space between them. And then he reached out and drew her close. Their kiss was deep, tender; deeper from the depths of knowing. He traced her mouth with his tongue, arousing emotions she knew were awakened by Jeff and no one else. It was his warmth, his skin, his passion she hungered for, and she wanted him now and he knew it. He drew her down onto the warm sand.

'What if someone comes?' she whispered, not really caring.

'If anybody comes, it had better be us!'

'Oh, Jeff,' she giggled. 'This is no time to make jokes.'

His mouth stopped further conversation. The moonlight etched their bodies in the warm sand and the softly lapping waves seemed to call to them, to beg them to give, to need each other forever. He rose above her, inflamed with desire. 'My beautiful, precious own Jean—I don't want to love you this much because I couldn't go on without you.' He moved, building the passionate rhythm which they knew belonged solely to them. Their rhythm, their tempo, no other two people in the world would ever experience it in exactly the same way. Their magic, their chemistry that made it so special to them. Their love...

⌘

'Marge and Davie aren't married, you know,' Jeff said at breakfast the next morning.

'Ho hum. So what else is new?' Jean asked.

'But did you know that Davie has a wife?'

That threw her. She sat back in her chair. 'Has—as opposed to had?'

Jeff nodded, biting off the end of a almond paste croissant. 'Most definitely 'has'. She was there. Last night.'

She stared at him.

'I found out—after you took off for the beach. She came over to me and introduced herself.'

But I thought he lived with Marge.'

'He does. When he isn't screwing anyone else of interest to him.' He gave her a sharp look.

'What about Mrs. Davie? Did I see her?'

'You were talking to her. At the sangria bowl. She was the one refilling it.'

That little tiny woman? She must be a size zero and she isn't five feet tall! And Davie's at least six foot three.'

'Two. I'm six foot three,' Jeff said, a hint of hostility coloring his tone.

'And Marge is... well, to put it kindly, not very small width-wise!' Jean said thinking that if the sarong-wrapped Marge ever did wear a dress it would have to be designed by Omar the Tent Maker.

'He has Catholic tastes, I'd say,' Jeff went on, reaching for more butter.

Jean slapped his hand away. 'Hmm,' she mused. 'I asked her—Mrs. Davie where she lived and she was quite evasive.'

He gave her a questioning look. 'What did she say?'

'Here and there.'

Jeff nodded. 'Davie's got her on the house sitting junket, too. Just so long as it's not the same house he's in. But apparently he supports her. And she's happy with the arrangement.'

'Maybe she knows something we don't. And after all, he does include her in his parties, so obviously they're still friends,' she said with some wonder.

He smiled and reached across to kiss her with a buttery lip. 'So are we, my love.' He pushed back his chair and rose. 'What say we drive down to that little community we passed in the hills above the port? Barrio de la something. It's all small cottages and little streets and there seem to be mostly low income Brits in the Senior league living there. The types that Davie Davis doesn't represent. I'd like to have a look around—in line with getting the lay of the land. Remember that guy we saw the other night at the Puerto Banus cinema?'

'The night it was raining?' she asked.

He nodded. 'It does rain in Spain. But mainly on the plain. I was talking to that guy while you were in the loo.'

'You're becoming so English, Jeff,' she said.

'I was thinking international.'

'You mean that guy you offered to give a lift home because he didn't have a car?' She was curious now. 'And he said he preferred to walk. A little guy, in his late sixties, maybe. So what about him?'

I think I've got a story,' he said 'A story about that man. I'll tell it to you while we drive. And you can change it all around, like always,' he added with a smile.

He did tell it and she did change it like always and they wrote this story together about the man who was Sly.

⌘

9: THE MAN WHO WAS SLY

The rains in Spain... It was certain they no longer stayed mainly on the plain, Sylvester thought as he walked the mile and a half back from the Puerto Banus Cinema. He never took the car unless it was absolutely necessary, or if Millie was coming along. He liked to do a spot of walking and the rain never bothered him. He'd been to see a Rambo film because they were running the series and his head was full of his namesake, Sylvester Stallone. Millie wouldn't come with him, she never would, to see Rambo. She hated violence and would never go to the cinema in Puerto Banus unless they had on a good love story.

He kept up an even, steady pace with broad steps, arms swinging easily at his sides. Walking was the most healthy thing a man could do. Not all this jig-jiggedy-jogging stuff. That was maybe all right for a younger man, but a nice brisk stride, that was what put the old heart to work, and kept it ticking over. Kept you feeling champion, walking. Retirement doesn't mean rotting or drinking yourself to death on cheap vino, what most of them down here didn't get through their heads.

He thought about the movie and how John Rambo had stuck an open bullet full of gunpowder into the gaping wound clean through his side. And then he'd rammed a flaming stick into it. Right inside him! 'You taught me how to ignore pain,' Rambo told his colonel. And with that wound and all, he'd dragged himself up the sheer face of the cliff. 'If you're captured, or this leaks, we'll deny your existence,' the Colonel told him. And all he replied was, 'I'm used to it.'

That was Rambo - a real fighting machine.

Sylvester stretched out his stride a bit, feeling the pull in his thigh muscles. A weedy, wiry man, his mouth pursed earnestly down at the corners which made the furrows crease more deeply at the sides before they curved up again to greet his fulsome nose. His chin was round and strong boned, giving it an aggressive jut, which he had no intention of hiding behind a beard. Besides, his skin was still fairly smooth for his sixty two years; even Millie had to admit that. Good skin like his mother's. His brows were thick and dark, although his hair had gone thatchy-patchy with grey. But he hadn't lost a bit of it, as he also troubled to point out to Millie when she was on at him about his health and fitness regime.

No, if he had to say so himself because nobody else would, Sylvester kept himself fit and what was wrong with that? In Spain, you could swim even in the dead of winter, and then a brisk walk back home. And no red meat any more. No doubt about it, you are what you eat. Not that he was total vegetarian. He ate fish, which you could get freshly caught in San Pedro de Alcantara. And he ate chicken sometimes, particularly the Spanish chickens which were free range and bright gold in colour and exceptionally delicious; the way a chicken ought to taste and maybe did when he was young. And plenty of root vegetables and greens and fresh fruit, organically grown. Honey, not sugar. No liquor. Here in Spain he could and did grow his own lettuces and tomatoes and garlic and onions and they had their own lemon tree out back.

Take for instance oranges, he thought, as he walked past a small grove. He could just make out the outline of trees and wondered what all this rain would do to the early blossom. Probably wash off some of the pesticides that went straight into their skins, and right all the way through the flesh. No sir, organically grown was best, thank you. And he had found a small mercado right in his barrio of La Campaña, that sold organic produce. He put up with Millie's complaints, 'We'll zoon be skint, Zylvester Plethers, what with the way you shop and the prices you pay, bain' it?' She had never lost her Somerset accent or vocabulary, which seemed to be thicker than ever.

He would remind her that it was he who 'always cooks the supper, so just mind your own business, Millie, an' eat wot's put in front of you and loyke it, my girl.' She'd grump at that, but didn't she just enjoy his cooking? And her food! A bit too much, he thought. Particularly the potatoes, though he never fried them any more. Boiled. Better for you.

Every day Sylvester worked out in the portable gym he had set up on the back patio, breathing deeply, the fresh air filling his lungs. He had the weights and a rowing machine. He was saving up for the pulleys. Millie refused to work out, although it would have done her a world of good, he had no doubt.

'Zomebody'd think oye was fat,' she complained. 'Why oye've never put on more'an a pound a year and that isn't much, for heaven's zake!'

But he reckoned that over the last thirty years it added up, bit by bit to sizeable hips and an over sizeable bosom. And if Millie kept it up for the next ten years, he'd have to wheel her into the dining room. But that was another matter. Millie liked her cheese and it was true, they produced a fine local Manchego in Spain. But he still had to admit to a hankering for Somerset Brie which you could not get, even in Gibraltar. Too much cholesterol, anyway. And Millie was always on at him about the patio, too. She wanted to build a barbecue and said his equipment was in the way.

He wondered really what they shared in common? Did she care a toss about anything he cared about? Even though she knew how much it meant to him, he couldn't get her to go to one Rambo movie, or any other of Stallone's films. Take 'Cobra', for instance. Now she would have liked that one. But she'd seen the first 'Rocky' and that was enough. She said Stallone wasn't her type. Had too many muscles. Who would credit it? Too many muscles? A regular fighting machine, that's what he was. Sometimes he thought she refused to go with him just to get his goat. All the ladies loved Stallone, didn't they? He wasn't just a man's man. Stallone was built like a Greek god. The girls at the Port Cinema whistled when he came on. So did some of the men.

One day when he got into a row with Millie about going to the films, she told him he was off his head, 'all the time going on about this Zylvester Ztallone...'

Off his head? Aye, that's what she thought of him! So he kept buttoned up about his hero in front of her for a while. No more rows. Least said, soonest mended.

But he got his own back on Millie right enough, without telling her until it was too late for her to stop him. He chuckled, wiping the rain from his nose as he headed up the road, remembering how angry she had been when he told her what he'd done the last time they were in Somerset to visit their daughter. How he'd got himself a lawyer in Frome and had his name legally changed by deed poll from Plethers to Stallone.

Now he could rightfully call himself Sylvester Stallone, and Millie had to be Mrs Stallone and not Mrs Plethers anymore, whether she liked it or not. It was all legal and binding and on their passports and he'd even changed their Spanish Residencia Permits.

He tried to recall how he had come to propose to Millie in the first place. He couldn't remember asking her to marry him or having the courage to ask anyone, at the age of seventeen. Maybe it was she who proposed to him? Yes, that must have been the way of it. He could recall having an eye for a little blonde girl, what was her name? Betty, who lived down in Frome. She used to come to the local rugby club games with her sisters to cheer his team on. He wanted to ask her out to a film, but somehow he never got up the courage. He tried to remember himself that young. What had he been like at seventeen? Not much at studies. Good at athletics, and really, now he came to think of it, no real ambition. He'd fallen into that job as a painter when a mate of his got ill and asked him to step in. 'What der I know about painting?' he'd protested. 'Not much to know, bain' it? Dip the brush in th' paint, wipe eht off a bit, and zlap eht onter the old wall, there's a good lad. Oy'll zplit with yer fifty fifty.'

How life traps you. . .

True, there wasn't that much to know, though over the years he'd learned a trick or two. Millie lived just down the street and next thing, her father had asked him to paint their parlor. A disgusting shade of pink her mother had chosen. He was too unconfident to say what he thought about the choice of color, nor was it his place and afterwards, when they didn't like it, they blamed him. But he told them the brush didn't make the paint. Then Millie stood up for him, and she walked him home. He thanked her, and she said she'd stand up for him just any time because he was so wonderful. She blushed and told him she was in love with him and kissed him on the cheek. 'I guess that makes uz betrothed, Zylvester,' she announced. And since he didn't know what else to reply, that seemed to settle it.

A lifetime spent in the wrong life. He hadn't wanted to get married, and he hadn't wanted to become a house painter for the rest of his days, even though he'd made a good living from it. What he had wanted was to be a chef in some great hotel. Maybe even travel the world. Switzerland, France, China. Now there was a country that knew about cooking. Sylvester had enrolled himself in a cooking course. But then his father had taken ill, and the painting job came along which gave him a chance to bring home a few bob. Seventeen, and the family depending on him. No different from other lads he knew, for that matter. And there was pride in being a breadwinner.

The next year he and Millie were married. Not that he was really complaining, even to himself. Millie had been as good a wife as she knew how. A good mother, no denying it. But not much in the understanding department. 'Off your head, Zylvester Plethers!' Millie exclaimed when she heard that he had changed his name. 'Whatever got into you, goin' and doin' a crazy thing loyke that?' And his daughter asked if she had to change her name, too but he said no, she was free to be Plethers until she got married, which was just in a few months anyway.

But the local British colony in La Campaña, when they heard about it, all started calling him 'Sly', just like his hero. And they smiled and cheered him when he came into the Las Muñecas Bar or the Mercado to shop.

'Say there, Sly, killed any Cong lately?' they'd say over a pint of beer. 'Show us your chest, Sly...' 'Do us your imitation, Sly...' And Sylvester would quote favourite lines for them in his deepest drawl. "In America there's a burglary every eleven seconds - a violent crime every fifteen seconds - a murder every twenty four minutes - and two hun'red 'n fifty rapes a day. . .' They'd all clap and ask what this or that was from and he'd tell them, 'That 'une's from 'Cobra'. And Stallone wrote that script hisself, din'ee?'

Sylvester took to wearing a headband, and chewing on a match stick, and in Spain he always wore T shirts with the sleeves rolled up to show off his biceps. And everyone said, for a man his age, he was in fantastic shape. Weedy, wiry, unwavering as a wall, he was. Hell, some men called themselves old at sixty two, but this Sly did not! His eyes were clear, his legs strong, and he didn't have a speck of fat on his belly.

Millie said the gang who hung around the Las Muñecas bar were laughing at him, but he knew they weren't. What was wrong with living up to an idol? Maybe they even secretly envied him just a little bit, because he had made something special of himself by trying to be like Stallone. There were few enough men of stature any more. And a world with no more heroes was no world at all.

Sylvester had been too young to fight In the last war, but he had heard enough stories from his father's friends. In those days men counted on each other, depended on each other for their very lives. It was a time when lads were true buddies, and you were not considered 'gay' if you put your arm around a pal's shoulder. It must have been like that in Nam.

Not like today, when you could get knifed in the back just walking down some streets right here in La Campaña or down at the Port or even in Marbella. Hadn't a young girl been attacked right in her own house? And they said they knew who he was who did it but they couldn't lay hands on him. Supposedly, an ex-gardener who'd been arrested for theft and rape some years back. The men were talking about it down at the bar. When he got out, this bandido got up to his queer tricks all over again. If he couldn't break into a house, he'd hook up the garden hose and shove it under the front door. Flood the place. And what with the drought and all, old Ben Crampet said he'd rather the bastard raped his wife than use up all his well water. But it was no joke because another girl had been raped in a lane going home alone at night only last month and the bastard was still running around loose.

A drought, was it? The rain was beginning to pelt down harder. Sylvester pulled his collar up. He never carried an umbrella. A sissified appendage for women and Londoners. But his cap was dripping down his nose and he was forced to pause beneath a tree to shake it off. He hoped there wouldn't be lightning. He never liked lightning and in March there was always a bit of it along this coast. The rains in Spain could be torrential. His trousers were damp enough to wring out now. He started on again, purposely making his steps more brisk.

Of course he didn't look anything like his movie idol, but that was hardly the point, was it? It was how he felt, not how he looked. And he felt like a tiger inside. Millie didn't appreciate the purity of the image Sylvester carried within him of the self he wanted to be. He only wished that he had thought of it a few years sooner. Changing his name seemed to have changed his entire outlook on life.

Over the last few years he had written to his hero out in Hollywood telling him that one day he hoped to put aside enough money to make a trip over there to the states and meet him in person. Just to shake his hand. Maybe he'd even be invited out on the movie set and watch the actor filming one of his pictures. Only nowadays Stallone shot so many of them on location in places like Thailand and Pakistan and Arizona. Well, maybe he'd even go on location with him! Then Millie would see. She would know that he was appreciated by Stallone himself.

He must have sent the actor hundreds of letters. Birthday cards, Christmas cards, three page letters of his personal opinions about each of the films. He'd seen each one at least four or five times. They had them all at the local English Club Videos shop. And he intended to see them again and again. But tonight it was great seeing Stallone on the big screen, even though the sound quality at the Port cinema was bloody awful and they had scratchy prints.

But he'd never got an answer to any of his letters. Then one day, he wrote to Stallone's studio and told them he had started a fan club for the actor, which wasn't exactly true, unless you could count his mates at the Las Muñecas bar in La Campaña, to whom he talked all the time about the movies. They liked Stallone's films, too, though they never saw them more than once, and Ben Crampet had never seen a Sylvester Stallone film even one time, although he could easily have got one out of the English Club Videos shop for four hundred pesetas, which was no more than two pounds. But that didn't stop old Ben from having an opinion about violence in the cinema. No, he nattered on about that plenty, over his third pint of beer. Lethal? Talk about violence, look what violence that stuff did to a man's belly. Ben went on about how Stallone was bad for youth, making them all like animals, and he bet that the San Pedro rapist who attacked that young Spanish girl probably went to see all of Stallone's movies with Spanish sub-titles and thought it made him God's gift.

Sylvester really got hot under his collar at that. He grabbed old Ben by the lapels and would have shoved his beer right down his throat, but he didn't believe in violence himself, and besides old Ben wasn't worth it. So he let him go with the admonition, 'Yer oughtn't ter drink that bloody stuff. It's got yer talking outer'a side of yer head.' But Ben never listened.

Sylvester didn't take more than an orangeade or agua con gas which he rather liked, at the Las Muñecas Bar. But he liked to stop by for a chat because apart from Ben Crampet, lots of the local British colony came in there. Not the toffs who sat in the Marbella Club and lived up the Ronda Road above San Pedro, but retired working men like himself who lived in the small houses or urbanisations behind Nueva Andalucia or in La Campaña.

When Sylvester was employed by Hammeth Builders and Decorators in Frome, he reckoned he'd painted most of the houses around that end of Somerset, and the interior of the town hall in Frome twice. Magnolia, matte finish, and gloss woodwork with white ceilings was the usual demand. Now all the young marrieds were into this 'dragging' and 'rag rolling'. Yuppy homes. Well, he could do that, too. But now he was officially retired, except as a favor for a new 'ex-Pat' friend who wanted a coat of white wash and didn't want to cope with trying to talk to a Spanish painter. Well, he liked to keep his hand in, so no complaints.

Sylvester picked up his pace just slightly against the wind which was driving the rain straight at him. It was a hot wind and he knew they were in for lightning. He squinted up at the sky. Thick as a pig's snout and no sign of clearing. The rain in Spain. . .Who was it said they were having a drought?

When he'd written that letter to the film studio about the fan club, he'd asked for an autographed photo of the star, and even enclosed a prepaid return envelope. To his surprise, because although he wouldn't admit it to Millie, he'd secretly given up hoping, one day a photograph arrived all the way to Spain. It was Stallone in costume—or lack of it—from his first Rambo film. He wore a headband and it was autographed 'To Sylvester, from Sylvester Stallone'. Sylvester was certain the autograph was genuine because he had saved the actor's signature from a fan magazine. He saved all clippings about the star. He compared the handwriting and it was exactly the same. Identical! The same little squiggle at the end. So he went into San Pedro on the bus and bought a silver plated frame for the picture and set it in pride of place on the table in the sitting room, where the sun wouldn't fade it.

Millie took it in stride, even admitting that the actor was a lot more pleasant to look at than the photograph of Uncle Henry after he'd had all his teeth out, which she'd felt obliged to exhibit since he'd left them that legacy twelve years ago. Six thousand Pounds, which, with interest and their annuity, helped them buy this retirement home.

Their daughter Henrietta (named after Uncle Henry), kidded him about the photograph, but he didn't mind. And when she brought her new husband to the house for a holiday, she snickered and told him it was a picture of dad's brother. In a way, that was true. His brother of the soul. Because that's the way Sylvester felt about the actor. He was certain that Sylvester Stallone must be just as heroic in real life as on the screen. Hell, you couldn't portray such characters without being somewhat that way yourself! Hadn't Stallone suffered partial paralysis in the face when he was young, and overcome it and so many other obstacles and built himself up physically, to become the great star and hero that he was? Yes, this surely was a man to admire. Who knew what the years would bring in the life of a man like that? One actor had already been President of the United States, hadn't he?

Sometimes he sat up at night on the patio after Millie had gone in to bed and talked to the picture of his hero. He would pour out all his thoughts and feelings no matter how small, just the way you might do to a real brother. And somehow it made him feel better, doing that. Not that he got any answers, but thinking things through out loud helped him to see them more clearly. He'd read this article where it said that to meditate was a good way to clear your thoughts and this was a kind of meditation, wasn't it? Maybe one day he'd take up that transcendental meditation, if he could find out where they taught it in Spain. Maybe in Estepona. There was a sort of foreign art colony there, he'd heard. Mostly Americans.

He was a grandfather now. Henrietta and Fred had a baby girl six months old. He, a grandfather! He'd talked to Stallone's picture about it, and finally agreed that it wasn't so bad, just as long as they didn't treat him like he was ready for the scrap yard.

'As a matter of topicality,' Millie said one night at about 1:00 a.m. in the morning when she came out on the patio and found him still sitting there, 'Just wot do yer think you're doing, Zylvester Plethers?"

'How many times must I tell yer, Millie, that my name is no longer Plethers. Nor indeed is yours, my girl. You are, and oye am named legally and binding, as it were, Stallone. And I'm just having a word with my friend here. Loyke I might if he was really 'ere beside me. That is exactly what oye am doin', bain' it?'

'Well, he's not 'ere, is he, Zylvester Plethers? Zo come ter bed for Lord's zake, before yer catch your death in the night air.'

'This is balmy Spanish air,' he cried. 'Millie, my girl, I am in perfect health, Never felt better, And if oye should care to sit up for a chat and a spot of tea, then that is exactly what oye shall do. And if yer put on another kilo, my girl, I shan't be able to get into that bed with you, anyways. But that's another matter.'

Millie was so furious at that remark that she nearly threw the Bristol blue bowl that her Uncle Henry had left her. 'Zoft in the upstairs, you be!' she barked at him, turning on her heel. But then he came and put his arm around her and gave her a kiss and a cuddle. He didn't want war. All he wanted was to be left alone. "I put in my time. My war's over." That's what Stallone had said in 'Rambo 3.

Finally Millie got fed up with trying to talk sense to him, and since she reckoned there was no real harm in it, she just let him be. And so he made it a nightly routine before bed to have a little chat with his namesake brother.

⌘

Sylvester pulled his cap lower over his forehead. The rain was coming down harder now and dripping inside the collar of his storm jacket. The verge was muddy and he was glad he was wearing his garden boots. But this being Spain, it wasn't cold, and the weather man had predicted that it would clear during the night. Not that the weather man was ever too right these days.

But what could you expect, with a hole in the ozone layer? All the good weather was leaking out, bain't it?

'And we are all bein' left with the greenhouse effect, loyke somebody 'ad turned on a zprinkler zystem over all the world,' he said aloud. He wiped water off the face of his watch. Nearly eleven o'clock. He sneezed. 'Hope oye'm not catchin' a cold,' he told himself. 'Not bloody loykly, with all the vitamin 'C' that oye take. But you never know. These new flu germs are real buggers, they are!' Why, he knew several of the men who drank in the Las Muñecas, whose whole families had been laid up with it.

'Wouldn't think you'd get it in a climate like this...' he said out loud. Ten minutes and he'd be home, make a nice cup of tea, and he'd sit down for a chat with Sly about tonight's 'Rambo' film. He had lots of things to say. Congratulations were in order, first. And then he'd write a letter in the morning. But tonight, he would clarify his thoughts before committing them to paper. Tell him how much he loved the stick fight at the opening and how good the dialogue was. Sly had written the script with some other bloke. What he said was never what mattered: 'We don't want to make it easy for them. We'd better split up.' It was the way Sly read the words in that rumbling, scratchy voice, made them so strong. Simple but strong. But he didn't like that horseback scene where those Afghans played polo using a dead goat for a ball, even though Stallone beat them at their own game. He'd tell him exactly what he thought about that sort of sadism, even if they were only Afghans. Maybe Americans could accept that type of thing, but the British were against cruelty to animals. Famous for it. Although, here in Spain... But they looked at bullfights differently, somehow.

The bus from San Pedro whizzed past him, splashing up mud, as if he weren't wet enough already. It would stop about 100 yards up ahead on the outskirts of La Campaña. Maybe he should have taken it tonight. Should have waited for it. Too late now. He was almost there. He sneezed again. Damn..! Up ahead, he could see the bus pull in. Could see a young woman getting off. There was a row of new houses down that road. Must be somebody who lived in one of them. Yes, she turned and headed in that direction.

101

Then he saw a man step out from the shelter of a thick acacia hedge. A man wearing something over his face. He must have been completely hidden from anyone getting off at the bus stop. The man turned and went down the road in the same direction as the girl. The sound of the rain would drown out his footsteps. No question! He was following her, by Jesus!

Sylvester picked up his pace, almost breaking into a trot. He could barely see through the rain, it was so blinding. But he had noticed that the girl wasn't carrying an umbrella. Always a good weapon for a woman against an attacker. He was trotting down the muddy verge now, slipping and sliding along until he came abreast of the bus stop. He looked down the road just in time to see the man grab the girl and drag her into the acacia bushes that skirted the road. Sylvester picked up his pace. Then he heard the girl's scream. He shouted at them and before he knew what he was doing, he was racing into the bushes after them.

Sylvester growled deep in his throat, just like John Rambo and found himself gripping the shoulders of a scrawny creature straddling the girl. He pulled the man off, and threw him down onto the ground. The man let out a cry and began to struggle, but Sylvester wouldn't let go. The girl broke free, rolling away, sobbing. Although he was younger, the attacker wasn't too heavily muscled and Sylvester managed to force him over onto his back and straddle him. A balaclava covered his face. Sylvester ripped it off to see that the would-be rapist was in his early forties, maybe, with a pinched face and a scar on one cheek and scraggly black hair.

'Don't try anything, dirt bag!' Sylvester snarled in his best imitation of his hero. Then he turned to the girl who was huddled in the grass. 'Where do yer live?' Shaken, she did not appear at first to hear him. 'I said, where do yer live, girl?'

'Down there. . . Over there.' She pointed towards a row of houses further on.

'Well get home, will yer? And telephone ther police. I'll hold this villain 'ere. Off with yer now! Hurry.'

The girl got to her feet rather unsteadily and stared at them for a moment as though in a trance. 'He.. . . he tried to. . . ' Then she bolted for the house. Sylvester pushed the man's shoulders flat into the mud. The man was snivelling now in Spanish and beginning to struggle. He hissed invective at Sylvester. The meaning was clear, if not the words.

'Don't even try, dirt bag.' Sylvester slapped him hard across the face. 'You're a disease. I'm the cure!' He said it just the way Stallone did in "Cobra".

Up the road he could see the door of a house open and lights come on inside. The girl pointed back towards Sylvester, then darted into the house. After a moment, a man emerged, pulling on a thin plastic Mac as he ran towards where Sylvester was holding the attacker pinned to the ground. The man was obviously the girl's father. 'Spanish police - on the way...' he said huskily as he came up.

The attacker began kicking and the girl's father grabbed his feet and sat on them. That was when Sylvester noticed the knife. It had fallen out of the man's hand into the mud. Sylvester scooped it up and handed it over to the girl's father. 'Dirty bastard,' he said. 'Look at that, will yer now?' The girl's father punched the attacker right in the balls. He let out a pitiful groan.

The policeman spoke English and asked Sylvester a lot of questions before driving him home. By now he was sneezing heavily. Millie couldn't believe it when the Spanish Policia brought him in soaking wet and covered with mud. At first she thought he'd committed some offence, and then she thought he'd been in an accident. But then they told her what he had done, and how her husband was a hero. They had been after this rapist for months. For the first time since Sylvester could remember, Millie was speechless. After they had gone, Sylvester made himself a cup of tea and added some medicinal whiskey and sat down by Stallone's photograph to tell him the whole story. Millie listened with gaping jaw.

The next morning Millie kept him in bed. His temperature had gone up to 102 degrees. And over his protests, she called in the doctor, an Argentine who lived nearby.

'All this fuss,' he said. 'Nothing wrong with me. I'm champion.'

The doctor smiled. 'You are that, all right, Señor, But you have the flu. You are to take these antibiotics, one every four hours. And stay quiet the rest of the day.'

But quiet wasn't in the cards for Sylvester. After the doctor left, Millie brought in 'El Sol', the English language version of the newspaper, and laid it on the bed. 'You've made the headlines, yer 'ave,' she said with something like awe.

Sylvester stared at it. 'SYLVESTER STALLONE CAPTURES SAN PEDRO RAPIST'.

'Looks like ye're famous, Zylvester.' There may even have been a touch of pride in her voice.

Sylvester sneezed and picked up the paper. He put on his glasses, although he didn't like anybody to see him wearing them. He read, 'Sylvester Plethers, who changed his name to Stallone, has featured in a real life drama as good as his namesake's.'

'And there are news reporters at the door, Zylvester,' Millie told him. 'One of them's from the *News of the World* all the way from London, he is. They wants ter talk to yer personally. What shall oye do about them?'

Sylvester slid his feet out of the bed, and put on his bathrobe. 'Ye're supposed to stay in bed,' she reminded him.

"Can't let them see me like this, can oye?' He looked into the mirror. He pulled a brush through his thick hair, flattening it down. Then he started into the sitting room.

Later that afternoon, he had a long chat with Stallone's photo which Millie had thoughtfully brought into the bedroom for him. 'Well, they interviewed me for the papers, just like you, Sly,' he said. 'Only oye'm not used to et, like you are. Guess oye'll have to send you the clippings. So you'll know more what oye'm like. Maybe then, you'll invite me out ter Hollywood and we can have a real long talk.'

He received a letter from the girl he had saved. She said she didn't know how she could ever thank him and if he hadn't been there at just that moment she might not even be alive to tell the tale. She sent him a five pound box of candy. But since Sylvester never ate sweets except for honey, he gave them to his gang at the Las Muñecas bar. Because if they stayed in the house, Millie would have eaten them all.

But the biggest news came a few days later when Sylvester was well on the mend. Millie looked up from the telephone, covering the mouthpiece and stared at her husband in wonder. 'It's the BBC, Zylvester! They're doing an in depth programme on Ex-Pats in Spain and they want ter do an interview with you! Something about a day en ther loyfe of a real hero…'

He thought a moment about this. What could he possibly say that would be impressive? 'I'll show them moy gym equipment, and work out for them a bit. Do folks good ter see how important et is ter keep fit. Never know when you'll have ter save some damsel in distress.'

⌘

10: COME BUY BARATA

On a loudspeaker designed to carry across the deep valley to the far distant hills, the arrival of the mobile department store making its way across the roadless hill, sends up a cloud of dust from the rutted track, and produces a thunderous rendition of Julio Iglesias as he was never meant to be heard. The music is always accompanied by a harsh Andaluz sales pitch, arousing the villagers to come *buy barata*! Everything on the cheap!

The van pauses at the village side of the hill and from their terrace, Jeff and Jean can watch wild scenes of jostling and shoving in hectic commerce—not unlike the first day of a Macy's Black Friday sale, Jean thinks. And a large van it is, choked to explosion with fabrics by the bolt, yarns, threads, skirts, sweaters, crocheted covers, and candy to keep the children quiet while the mothers buy. They can hear the eternal bang and chatter of the children and the rasping harsh-voiced mothers' warnings wafting up to them. Warning, but never forbidding; for all Spanish children are the true tyrants of their families.

Next comes the 'fish man' with a much smaller van. And after him, his lesser brother who has only a wooden box laden with sardines attached to his motor bike. Also on a motor bike comes the 'bread man'. And finally, the 'vegetable man' with his van-cargo of lemons, oranges, lettuces, and radishes as big as parsnips. All of which makes it possible for the villagers to avoid travelling with their donkeys less than a mile down to San Pedro and the sea. These Andaluz, from whose shores Columbus once launched his ball-breaking Atlantic crossings, are no rovers at heart. Some have never been as far as Marbella, only sixty minutes away by foot.

⌘

One morning Jeff was alerted by a strange sound lilting and trilling through the still morning air; a softly, fluted melody.

'Where are you, Jean?' he called. 'Jean! Where are you?' he called for a second time, pausing at the keys of his computer which he'd taken out to the front terrace to enjoy the air. 'Come out here quickly!'

She emerged, paused starry-eyed, at the sound of the flute and shushed him quickly, gesturing vehemently, as though listening to the pulse of nature itself. 'You hear it...?'

'Of course I hear it!' he barked. 'That's why I called you.'

'What do you think it is?'

'Pannish pipes.' He smiled. 'Pipes of Pan.'

Jeff then proceeded to tell her that the Romans had used this coast as a retirement base for worn-out warriors about two thousand years ago. It was they who brought flutes, as played by one of their gods, Pan. Jeff was always trailing off like that on some historical fact which, while fascinating, only vaguely seemed to relate to the issue at hand.

'Roman gods in El Salto?' she asked as the fluted melody lilted louder. 'Really, Jeff.'

'And there he is! The Roman god, my love,' Jeff said, pointing out a lithe, amber-skinned gypsy boy who now appeared fluting away on a pipe down by the village.

'But why?' She left him at his computer, running out of the garden gate and full tilt down across the edge of that dusty field of rubble laughingly called their land. Laughingly, because no one else in the village regarded it as anybody's but theirs for goats, donkeys, children of all shapes and sizes. And recently to their horror, monstrous motos! Motor bikes that tore sleep apart like a Manchurian ripping silk! How they and their neighbours, Clive Belnapp and the Grays and the Ridgeways cursed them! And how helpless they all were to curb their increasing numbers being ridden in repetitive circles over the open field by the macho young bucks of the village, who equated riding a moto with straddling a bull.

Finally Jean ran back up the hill to Jeff, calling, 'You'll never guess what he is, Jeff. A vision from an Attic world, advertising of all things, knife and scissors sharpening. He's a knife sharpener!'

Jean came up behind her husband gazing in total delight, her busy mind sorting through a huge collection of knives, scissors, and garden shears she'd instantly decided needed to be sharpened. Every edged-metal object that their gardener Miguel (whose dedication to lack of maintenance approached fanaticism) had condemned to rusty uselessness. She jogged urgently back to the garage, with a shout, 'Go stop him, Jeff. Don't let him get away 'til I get back!'

But she did not get back. When Jeff found her, the musical scissors sharpener had long gone.

Jean was inside the garage leaning against the wall, shears in hand, nursing a fury worthy of a lady Lear. And she was quick to tell him why. Miguel, bright with self-congratulation, had decided to do something about his normal sloth and had seized upon their new electric Black and Decker they'd lovingly brought down from London. He had carefully sharpened every garden implement—on the wrong side of the blade.

⌘

'Impossible,' Cynthia Gray said, hiding a chuckle behind her large flat hand when Jean told her. The Grays and the other two houses shared the inescapable cost and services of Miguel and knew only too well his devilish ways. While quick to extol the virtues of the primitive life, they took a certain perverse delight in letting the Thwaites discover the down side of villa ownership on this particular hill above this particular village for themselves.

'Impossible, Cynthia. . .? Not for our Major Domo of Disasters. For Miguel, Jean added gritting her teeth, *'Todos es posible!'*

Until Jeff had signed Miguel's employment contract, put before him by Davie Davies as a necessary community expense, no one had bothered to inform the Thwaites that they could never fire Miguel. Ever! Not unless they wished to pay him one month's salary and equal Social Security benefits for every year he had worked—not just for them, but for the four houses from the day they were built, over twenty years ago. He knew it and they knew it, and that was the end of it.

They decided that since he was their gardener for life, somehow they would have to teach him to do at least some things their way.

'That'll be the day,' Elliot Gray said with a smirk. A friendly smirk, but a smirk is a smirk.

Jean sat up late that night writing down the Spanish names for all the plants they wanted to put in the garden. They had space for a small vegetable patch by the kitchen door where the lemon tree had taken hold nicely. Jean wanted salvia, tomillo, cebolleta, pepino, ajo, perejil, and rábano, tomate, and lechuga. She had read that if you planted marigolds along the vegetable patch, it kept off bugs. So she asked the nursery man for caléndula. The list grew to include flowers for garden flower beds, and some unusual goodies for the new macetas on the terrace.

'Jean, before you embark on this time-consuming and fairly expensive project, don't you think you ought to reconsider—based on your lack of knowledge of the plant world?'

'Whatever do you mean, Jeff?' she cried indignantly.

'Well, you've got to admit if you are honest, that you don't know one plant from another, having always lived in a flat or an apartment in a large city since you were an adult, and as far as I have seen, you've never been able to raise an African Violet successfully in a pot on a window ledge, without it dropping dead.'

'I can learn!' she insisted querulously. 'That's the opportunity Santa Rita is affording us. Learning about nature.'

'Mmm,' he nodded, knowing it was impossible to dissuade Jean from anything once she had made up her mind. So they took Miguel with them down to the nursery hoping he would absorb some of the planting instructions by osmosis if nothing else. They brought back all the things on Jean's list and she planted them with the aid of Miguel, who was very insistent, although illogical, about where things should go.

A few months later, Jean took Jeff out to inspect the planting. To her surprise, in the middle of the lettuce patch, mixed in with the herbs was a small dark green, bushy plant with shiny, stiff oval leaves. 'Mmm,' she said, 'Is this the laurel, do you suppose?'

'What's a laurel?' Jeff asked, knowing far less than Jean about plants and gardening and unlike Jean, not inclined to learn.

'You know. A bay leaf, Jeff. Great for cooking stews!'

'When was the last time you ever cooked a stew, Jean?' he asked, thinking one might taste good right now.

'Well I might, if I had bay leaf growing in the garden.'

Later, when she faced their gardener with the question, he was quick to reply. 'Si, Señora. This is something of which I do not know the name in English,' said Miguel, who had planted it in the lettuce patch without telling her.

'What is it called in Spanish, Miguel? I'll look it up in the dictionary,' she told him. It turned out he did not know the name in Spanish either.

Jean nurtured the plant, seeing that it got enough water when Miguel wasn't looking, and admiring its pointed, dark green leaves. True, it doesn't look very tall, and the leaves were almost black but then maybe bay leaves don't look the same in Spain, she thought.

Then one day, months later when the leaves looked big enough, Jean decided she would make a stew. With the meat patiently waiting in the kitchen, she went on a forage of the vegetable garden, now lush with verdure. Jeff trailed after her with a basket to put the produce in. A bit of marjoram. A snip of thyme. Sage? No. But bay leaf, yes. The plant looked like it could just afford to lose three leaves to the stew pot without total annihilation. She cut. Sniffed. Try as hard as she could and with the best will in the world and an imagination to match, she couldn't make it smell like a bay leaf. 'I've only ever seen them when they are already dried,' she admitted. 'You know, in those little plastic packets. Maybe this is how they smell fresh off the bush.'

Jeff was reluctant to point out to her that dried packets were all she really knew about any spices or herbs. 'That must be it. The Spanish variety is different,' Jeff suggested helpfully.

'Maybe it tastes different when it's cooked,' she said, biting into it with not much reaction and taking the basket into the kitchen.

It went into the pot, and was duly cooked. But somehow, even accompanied by a good bottle of Rioja and a great Spanish bread, the stew left much to the imagination.

'It doesn't taste like bay leaf,' Jeff mused. But otherwise the stew was quite edible.

Then one day, Jean went out to inspect the bay leaf bush. She was surprised to find that the little buds on it had burst into flower. White, lovely. . . and all too familiar. They most definitely has a heady scent but it was not of bay leaf! Miguel had planted the glorious little gardenia bush she had forgotten about among the humble lettuces.

'A gardenia, Jeff! I did ask for one but then I forgot. You know the word is the same in Spanish. I wanted it for the terrace. To plant in a maseta. A pot. Oh dear!' she exclaimed. 'Gardenias do not like the hot sun. They want to be in the shade.' With great haste, Jean dug it up and moved it to a large pot. She put it on the terrace away from sun and wind.

It promptly lost its glossy green and turned a sickly yellow.

'What do you think went wrong?' she asked a few weeks later, staring at it sadly.

'I think it loved life among the lettuces,' Jeff told her.

Jeff and Jean were spending three to six months of each year in Spain now and when they could afford it, they would make a trip back to the States to visit her family in Youngstown, Ohio, where her dad had finally retired from a lifetime of teaching history to high school students. Her dad would tell her, 'Jannie nobody cares about the past anymore. I'm not even sure they care about the present and certainly not the future or they'd be taking better care of things right now.'

But he still cared, and he still revelled in his mock historical battles with lead soldiers on the fifteen foot table that had occupied the garage ever since Jean could remember.

Jeff had no family any more. His father, old Jeffo, had died several years earlier. Jeffo had been a film director in the days of the big Westerns. Jeff liked to say that his dad had driven cattle from Republic, through Fox, overland to MGM. 'Junior' got started in the business despite nepotism, and some people in those distant Hollywood days, who thought they knew his name really were confusing him with his old man. These days Jeff owed Hollywood no allegiance. He and Jean had turned to writing books, and television—and London and Spain at this moment in their lives, were where they wanted to be.

Sitting on the back terrace looking down into the deep valley, Jeff gazed out towards the fragment of ancient Roman wall. He turned to Jean. 'That's a perfect sight for a Roman camp, you know.' There was no denying, the Romans had truly been there. And the Moors and the Conquistadors and God knew who else? But when? And going where, Jeff wondered? And coming from where? Whose feet had trod that path?

Jeff could imagine Roman columns marching through the dusty valley, down from the distant ring of mountains perhaps on an ancient trail no longer visible, and trudging up their hillside, approaching their hilltop with the force of la tormenta––the tornado that had travelled right through them. A story began to develop in his mind.

A few days later, Jeff told Jean the idea and they wrote it together. It was set on their own hill, looking down into the long, timeless valley they could see from their back balcony, and it was about a man who Jeff imagined lived in this very house. A man who met someone from the distance of time, in a worrisome dream.

⌘

11: THE MAN IN THE DREAM

He had never quite recovered from the operation. Not perfectly. Not to be able to feel that final sense of recovery that was like turning a page of flesh so that there was no sign, no aftermath—no itch beneath the scars, no sense of wholeness and inner refurbishment, no dance-of-the-blood feeling. And no tranquillity. Yes, that was the worst; the loss of the body's tranquillity, as though bad neighbours had moved in and brought perpetual turmoil into his physical inner workings and stolen all sense of well-being until he thought—and he told her so—that he would never again be what he had been.

And so, after the accident when the university agreed to moving his sabbatical forward, John and Belina took what some friends kept referring to as 'the plunge'. They rented their house near Oxford, bolstering financial security—and above a tiny Spanish village, they come across this sprawling, rustic house for rent that the real estate people had referred to grandly as a 'Finca'. The location reminded John of a Pancho Villa movie. Like one of those Mexican haciendas on a hill above a valley through which rising dust might produce a gallop of banditos coming towards you.

After the sun had lowered sufficiently to soften the abrasive, brazen fury of the day's heat, they would sit on the rear terrace that hung above the spreading fields and find a certain comfort in the ballet of bats and swallows swooping through the eucalyptus trees. They would sit side by side and drink a Spanish brandy. During the day Belina would busy herself with nursing the garden back to health, which was a kind of extension of her caring for him. He, and the derelict garden would be made to bloom after the lacerations of neglect and the aftermath of some unknown violence.

At first John and Belina were quite reasonably happy there. Walks on the beach, reading, or bouts of backgammon. Her effort to improve college years of Spanish and his, to learn the guitar. The 'foreign colony' neighbours were distant and in any event, John and Belina were not social. Certainly not now. The children's voices drifted distantly like gulls disoriented in a storm and the villagers did not trespass the small orchard belonging to the Finca's owner. Then one day sitting on the back terrace, John told Belina about a particularly troubling dream he'd had. He pointed down into the floor of the valley.

'They were just over there! Coming from far over those hills down into the valley, right below this house.' He paused, as though seeing them. 'I heard their horses first, when I was lying down. And a creaky wagon. So I came out of the villa—out here on the terrace—and I saw...' He paused. '...*them.!*'

The way he said 'them' was loaded with a particular significance, she noted. There was a pause after it, in which she could almost watch John trying to recapture in his mind the exact images he wanted her to see through his eyes. Through his words.

'They were there! He pointed towards the far end of the valley. 'Out there—a group of them. Not in any sort of real formation! Just a tired straggle of horses, mules, and men. And at the back—behind them, Belina—behind them was this wagon with solid wooden wheels and things hanging from it. Things I couldn't really see. Couldn't quite make out. Water, or wine skins, I think. And sacks of feed. Yes, oats I suppose, for the horses.'

He paused again staring out. 'And some of the men had on bits of armour like the one riding in front. Certainly the leader—the man in charge. I thought so at the time because he was wearing a sort of Morion helmet with a high comb.'

She looked at him with mild puzzlement.

'You know, I showed you those Morions in the museum that day.' She nodded in remembrance of the ancient iron helmet John had so admired. 'And his was rusty, like his armour. That was the thing about them all; they looked as though they'd been on the road a long time. Dusty. Their leather was parched and cracked. The armour—those who had any—was scarred and brownish. Nothing shiny. Even the leader's plume, the plume on his helmet was a scraggly, moth-eaten sort of thing.'

He turned to her with feverish excitement. 'I could see them so plainly, Belina! I mean, little details stood out. The rapiers, the harquebuses', the powder flasks, the kegs, the baggage slung across the mules.' He paused. 'And the monk. The Padre! He was the one who noticed me.' John looked at her with slight apprehension.

'Did he—say anything?' she asked, trying to focus on where his story was going, feeling she must.

'No. None of them spoke to me,' he said. 'But I could hear them talking to each other, plain as my own voice now. And they were coming this way, just down there!' His finger intruded on the present scene describing a gentle half-circle of movement down the long, summer-parched valley where only an ancient ruined wall, surely Roman, and the scorched, tiled roof of a farmhouse, perhaps only a few hundred years old, could be seen.

'Well, we all dream, John,' she said matter-of-factly, trying to sound as though it really didn't matter. Didn't make any difference. 'And you did write those articles on antique weapons recently, so that must have been what stuck in your mind.' She sighed. 'Not much of a contribution, I'm afraid. But what else can anyone aside from a psychiatrist say about anyone else's dreams? And who knows if the psychiatrists are right, for goodness sake?'

But Belina knew that the silences of the nights were punctured by his unstable breathing that gave his sleep a tentative anxiety from these dreams. *Dreams.* Not nightmares, exactly. No, not nightmares; just a troubling turbulence of unfinished pictures. Images, each leading fear like a leashed dog that would not be lost or abandoned. He would relate them to her in the morning with such concern.

He expelled breath as though he had been holding something back. 'The part that's crazy is, Belina. . .You see, it's the second time I've had that same dream!'

'Same? You mean the same group coming down this valley?' She looked at him closely.

He nodded, turning his eyes away. 'And this second time, they'd come some miles nearer. Closer. Closer to me!' He gulped breath. 'In the first dream they were only distant moving shapes in puffs of dust. Pink and yellow, with lance tips glinting sparks in the sun and a rag of a pennant.'

'Well then,' she suggested practically, trying not to sound flippant, 'If you dream them again tonight, try to have a word with them. I certainly would.'

He looked away and didn't tell her that it was exactly what he was planning to do. That he knew clearly and surely he would see them again through the eyes of sleep. Knew that they were not done with him. That they would come nearer—and their grizzled beards, unshaven cheeks, and shaggy strings of hair would be so close—so real that he would smell olives, and garlic, and sour wine.

⌘

He had not been wrong; they were there again in his dream. Not quite as close as he had hoped, but closer, more defined. They had stopped for the night. Some had rigged up tents or lean-tos. Knowing it was a dream (and he was consciously aware of that), he went to the garage and got out the hired Volkswagon. He found himself driving right down the hill straight towards the men. He stopped the car and got out when he saw the Padre mumbling his beads and taking small drinks of water from a clay receptacle.

'Hello, Father.' Being a dream he was not aware whether he was speaking English or Spanish, only that they were communicating easily.

The monk wore a robe with a cowl that would once have been black but had faded in suns and rains and rough washings against the stones of mountain village streams. The bulbous, scraggly face turned a pair of electric eyes towards John before he spoke. His words came soft and deep in his throat. 'Hello, my son.'

'Padre. . .may I ask a question?'

The man's eyes, soul-windows with a gaze that could see past the present into time-future, or read sins that darkened the minds of men and could offer the solace of confession. Eyes, the palest blue of skies wherein the pupils hunted like hawks to find something always unnoticed by ordinary gazes. Eyes that had watched the light go out in the eyes of the fallen on many battle grounds.

'What is it you wish to know?' asked the monk.

Under The Magic Mountain

And now John was aware that the monk's Spanish was clearer than the local Andaluz. It finished words with consonants, rather than letting them slur away into harshness.

'Who are you—all of you? Why are you here in this valley?'

'We?' The monk appeared faintly shocked by John's question. 'We are the company of Captain Francisco de Cordoba. We are making our way to Cadiz.'

'Why, Father?'

'Why. . ? Would there be any other reason to go to that devil's port, I ask you, but to take ship?'

'Take ship for where?'

The monk squinted a glance at John, veiling his thoughts. 'These voyages, we are not in the custom of discussing. Too much talk in the villages. It can bring out the thieves and harlots who follow soldiers like flies at the summer's end.'

'But I must know where you are going, Father!'

The man's face turned away like the closing of a door. 'We may speak of this another time. I am weary, and the strap of my sandal is in need of repair. Farewell, my son.'

⌘

'And those were his exact words as you remember them? Exactly?' Belina was at last showing some genuine interest.

John had felt until now—until this moment—that she didn't take his dreams seriously, with her remarks about a psychiatrist and all. And to him, every night was making the occurrence more real. More crucial. 'I don't know what exact means. I've told you the general meaning of what he said, Belina. I don't know if they were even there—or if I was! The landscape of dreams is not precise.'

'And yet you saw so many details. . ?'

'Details, yes, of course. You see them in surrealist images, don't you, but the whole thing has no reality. Like ghosts or telepathy, it doesn't add up, as your father used to say. And I'd say, "What does?" and he'd get peevish as hell. And I wouldn't blame him, really. Nobody likes to be told that what they *know* is not real, and what they *see* is not there.'

117

Belina looked at him over the beans she was stringing. Cooking was her reality And gardening. And love-making. All factual. All adding up. Yet, she too, could sense at times more than the mere presence of what was visible.

That night having tucked away a bottle of their favourite Valdepeñes and making love, John slid into sleep like a fall into a bed of feathers. She lay awake for a while watching him in the sharp light of a full moon, wondering if he were dreaming about them again. Wondering if she could see them, these men, in the flickering and fluttering of his eyelids. He had passed into the deep, dark haystack of the night, clothing him in uncertainty and she could not join him there.

⌘

John dreamed he was asleep and then got up and walked out onto the back terrace. They were there as he knew they would be, breaking camp this time. Tent poles that were spears held ropes which now set free the billow of canvas, to fall or collapse and be folded up for the further journey.

The leader mounted into a high saddle, thrusting his feet into triangular iron stirrups. It was the dark before dawn and most of the camp still drowsed under tents and lean-tos or in the shelter of that same ancient wall. Now, whenever 'now' was, there was no farmhouse to mar its antiquity.

And then inexplicably, John found himself down there among them. The Padre was dozing by the wall, awaiting the awakening sound of the morning drum. He opened his eyes at John's nearing step. There was, John thought, just the faintest touch of fear in them. 'It's you...' the Padre whispered, as to an unwelcome visitor.

'You said another time, Father. For my question.'

'Do not ask it, my son.'

'But I have to know where you are bound for. You must tell me!'

The pause lasted so long that John thought the grizzled face would never move to answer. Then sadly—strangely sad, like one crossing some unwelcome horizon—the Padre said, 'New Spain. We go, if you must be answered, to New Spain.'

⌘

'New Spain? Do you think he meant America?' Belina asked when John told her.

'Yes, it had to be. Mexico, that's where they went, actually. Where they landed. My history's somewhat sketchy on that period.'

'So what you dreamed up was a party of Conquistadors?'

'Could be. But there's something more to it, Belina. There has to be something more. Some reason why I. . . Why *I* should dream this!

John had that deeply troubled look again. Certainly, no question, he was becoming obsessive about this whole dream thing. But the doctor had warned her to expect the unexpected from him, so she let him continue without interrupting.

'I think there's something dark ahead for them, wherever they're going. I've had an image of their graves without seeing them exactly. Mounds of earth in a kind of jungle. Rotting bones, and shreds of flesh gnawed by insects. Their bones—housing serpents in their rib cages where the Indios who ambush them will leave them in the jungle.'

'That's in your dream, too?'

'Not exactly *in* the dream, Belina. It's more of an after-feeling of seeing into their future. What lies ahead for them. A sort of sixth sense of. . .of knowing. Telling me I must warn them! Stop them somehow. I don't really know yet, haven't seen anything about that part. Only this feeling that now I know I never want to dream them up again.'

'You probably won't,' she said in her most reassuring tone. But she did not reassure herself. And John knew better.

⌘

This time he was not in the house. Not on the terrace. And they were not in the valley! He found himself on a wharf with ships moored to it. Seamen were crawling up the rope ladders, fixing rigging, climbing to the crow's nest. Preparing their ship to sail.

He saw the leader supervising the swinging aboard of the horses. He saw some of the Men at Arms, the Hidalgos—gentlemen adventurers, their armour newly burnished after the long journey. He saw the soldiers staggering; many so drunk they had to be half-helped, half-dragged across the gangplank.

Then he saw the Padre, his back to the ship, watching the wharf with an anxious eye. An eye he knew at once was watching for him! But when he approached, the Padre tried to escape him. He ran down the wharf, John chasing after him. John called out to him. 'Padre! I've come to tell you. . ! You must not go on this voyage. Do not sail with this ship. Padre!'

The Padre paused for a moment to listen, then again turned from him and ran. The old man hid behind some thick-bellied casks, and John found himself moving towards him in slow motion. His feet became stuck to the planks of the wharf, heavy as lead.

Then he could not lift them at all. Could not move to reach the monk. He struggled to be free, tried to shout, but suddenly he had no voice. But now he was close enough to hear the Padre mumbling a secret prayer. 'Oh, Lord Jesus, do not let him come again into my dreams! Do not let him walk into my sleep and ask questions, this stranger from I know not where. Perhaps he comes from Hell as the Devil's servant. Or from around some further bend in time! But in the name of the Blessed Virgin, let me sleep quietly without this lay-Inquisitor invading my dreams night after night!'

⌘

12: THE UNKNOWN GENTLEMAN

Jeff and Jean were beginning to feel at home in Santa Rita just when their London 'short let' tenant was leaving and they had to head back to London to see to their affairs.

It was not until three months later that they returned to Spain, again taking their car via ship from Portsmouth to Santander. They drove the little Renault down the length of Spain stopping first in Madrid visiting the great museum, then spent two days in Toledo, the ancient city perched high on a hill above a winding river and a poppy-etched plain. A Greek painter had once lived there, Domenico Theotocopuli, known to history as El Greco. They brought back a small print of his portrait of a 16th century gentleman, a man with a long, elegant, Spanish face and sad, powerful eyes. Fascinated by the face, they hung it in their bedroom.

'I wonder who he was?' Jean asked as they lay in their bed, staring dreamily at the picture of the unknown gentleman from Toledo in the black velvet doublet with the high white ruff framing his face. His eyes were sad and haunting.

'Who do you think he was, Jean?'

'Tell you in the morning,' she said and when she woke up, she knew who he was, and it all began in 1585 in Toledo, Spain.

⌘⌘⌘

His knees ached. His mind was empty. All afternoon, he had been praying in the Church of San Juan de Los Reyes. Praying for solace for his troubled heart. Praying that tranquillity might visit his wife's disposition. That his son might find more fruitful occupation than dicing and drinking. That his wilful daughter might reconsider and accept the marriage he had arranged for her with the great-nephew of Count Orgaz.

Maria del Mar was no beauty, certainly. He wondered if the rich dowry he would provide her would compensate for the squint in her left eye. What more could she ask of a father than a rich marriage? And yet she was a defiant, ungrateful girl! True,

Don Miguel was a score of years older than she, but he bore the arms of one of the noblest families in the province. And was he not, like his famous forebear, a man known for great piety?

The Caballero rose from his knees a little stiffly, and walked out into the roughly cobbled street. It lead him down towards the bridge of San Martin. Beyond the crenelated city wall the open fields spread themselves in golden slashes on the green carpet of the plain. As far as the eye could stretch and further, fields of red poppies and purple wild flowers exploded in fiery bursts. From out of this plain sprang one harsh, abrasive crag of mountain jutting an accusation into the empty blueness of sky. Upon this swelling stone and earth, the fortress city of Toledo had been built. A thrust of river severed the flat openness from the all-seeing city; a city as cold and austere as the Caballero's own empty life.

A life which at this moment seemed devoid of meaning and purpose. If only he could look back upon one worthy deed, one virtue, one action, one accomplishment meriting remembrance, even from the grave, because the Caballero suspected that the only true immortality lay in the memories of others.

The Caballero walked on past the Church of San Tomé. The foreign painter, would be working inside at this very moment, perched upon a scaffold. He must look in on his way home, to see how the mural was advancing. The mural of Don Miguel's renowned forebear, Count Orgaz. The Greek had chosen to depict Orgaz being borne aloft on the wings of saints and angels; but what could any artist know of eternity?

In the Caballero's opinion, this artist knew little enough about his craft, much less eternity. Certainly he knew nothing of perspective. His colors were dark, brooding, his expressions, sad and strained. And his figures were elongated out of any reality and looked as though they had all been stretched upon the rack! But the Caballero's daughter's suitor, Don Miguel, who knew even less about art, was pleased enough with the mural. Art must be modern, he said. One must stay abreast of the times. Indisputably, through this Greek's painting being permanently affixed inside the church wall, Don Miguel's illustrious ancestor's name would live on in memory. And hence of course, his own name.

The painting would provide a crumb of conversation when he and Don Miguel dined together, later that evening. Better than harping on the emptiness of existence. To live out the rest of one's days awaiting only death. And what to follow? Total oblivion? For who could truly know what might come after? Together they would drink a bottle of fine Madeira and ponder those questions that troubled the souls of thinking men. Don Miguel fancied himself a philosopher. He would offer the usual council: more prayer. Solace through faith. Platitudes that the Caballero was exhausted from hearing.

And when faith seemed to fail, one could delve into the more arcane mysteries: visions and prophecies. So the Caballero crossed the street, out of the sharp rays of the late afternoon sun and into the sombre shadows of a lane so narrow that he was forced to flatten himself against a wall to avoid being bumped by a passing cartload of oranges. Purposefully he made his way to a thick wooden door where the blue paint was blistering, and the heavy iron nails were rusting. This was the house of the alchemist, with his medicines, potions, and herbs; and if the Inquisition was not too close by, it was also the house of prophecies. The Caballero climbed the stairs and knocked. He would be expected.

Even on the hot day, the old man wore a heavy velvet cloak with mysterious symbols embroidered on it in thick gold thread. The cloak was perhaps even older than the man. His room was tidy, with bunches of herbs strung up on hooks along the walls. They gave off a pungent smell with just a hint of some acrid potions. There was a wooden bench, two chairs, a tall wooden tripod holding a heavy brass bowl of water. Sometimes the alchemist used this bowl to foretell the future. He also possessed a rare deck of French cards for divination. He called them 'The Tarot' and handled them with great reverence.

The alchemist knew the Caballero to be a man of substance; one who would pay handsomely for a comforting prophecy, and who could be counted on not to discuss the cards with the wrong friends. He asked his visitor to sit across from him at a small table inset with marbles of various hues in a strange design worked like a star overlaid upon a star. Then he asked his visitor to divide the Tarot deck into four parts. The alchemist took up each pile in turn, searching though it until he found the King of Swords. This, he laid face up. Carefully, he laid out the other cards from that pile in a design on the table.

Facing the King of Swords came The Moon, The Sun, La Papess, The King of Pentacles. The alchemist's eyes narrowed, then lifted to study the aristocrat's face across from him.

The Caballero wore a rich black velvet doublet, a stiff white ruff at the throat that seemed to hold his head aloof from the minor trivialities of life. A long, distinguished face with powerful, sad, grey eyes, an aquiline nose, prominent ears, a greying beard, neatly shaped to an angular point. Close-cropped hair, frosting at the temples, brushed slightly forward to hide a receding hairline. It was the face of one who has suffered in the spirit. A face that must be told something of great import.

The Alchemist always took care to keep his predictions sufficiently ambiguous. No one could say that he was entirely wrong and often enough he was right. And who could ever say that his herbal medicines did not do some good, even when the patient died? That was the art of the matter. Make the customer feel he had received his money's worth no matter what the outcome. Not too difficult, if one kept one's ear to the gossip in the taverna. In his trade, it paid to have sharp ears and a good memory. Now what was it his servant had reported? What was it that the Caballero's wife had told the dressmaker...? Oh, yes, and his cook had repeated to the baker's son.

'You are going to have your portrait painted,' the alchemist said, eying the cards.

'Ah! But that is absolutely correct!' the Caballero cried in amazement. 'By the foreign artist, the Greek, though he is not very good in my opinion. But then he is fashionable right now, and he is not expensive. But how ever could you know? For I have told no one.'

A bony finger pointed, nails stained with the dyes of many concoctions. 'It is there - in the Tarot, Señor. A portrait.'

'But do not, please, think I am a vain man. For myself alone, I would not trouble. Portraits are the mirrors of pride. It is at the insistence of my good wife, you understand. Here, in Toledo, it seems that all the husbands of her friends. . .' His voice trailed off.

The alchemist swept the cards together and allowed the Caballero to cut them once more. It was true certainly, the Caballero was not a vain man. The alchemist turned over another card, then looked up sharply. This time, in front of the King of Swords, lay some of the minor arcana. Then Death: The Reaper. After it—the Sun: Judgment. His words surprised himself, even as he spoke them.

'Your face will be known to many more than just your wife, Señor. Or even to your children. It will be known in all parts of the world...!'

The Caballero laughed deprecatingly. His children? Just hovering about him waiting for him to die. This time, the alchemist had gone too far. 'You need not invent fantasies, Señor Alchemist. I shall pay you your two réals, whatever you tell me.'

The fortune teller felt a twinge of excitement. Once in a while, he actually saw—actually knew! Could actually sense through the tips of his fingers—with a tingling sensation —and his head would feel light, as though he might faint. That was how he knew the truth was this time being revealed to him through his cards. A truth he did not always understand, but nevertheless knew had a meaning which he must tell. For after all, he was only the messenger.

'But what I say is truly here in the cards, Señor! Many years from now, even centuries, travelers will come to our city and they will admire your face. And any who see it, will not forget it.'

The Caballero waggled his head sadly. His portrait would not hang in the church. He had not discovered the new world like Queen Isabela's admiral, what was that name? Ah, yes, Cristobal Colon. And already, nobody could quite remember what that great man had actually looked like because his portrait had been painted only from memory, after his death.

And after his own death what would there be but bones and rotting flesh? What possibility was there that he, coming to the end of his days, could accomplish any one thing, anything worthy of being remembered? More likely, his grandchildren, if there were to be any with his daughter's reluctance to marry, would let the painting gather dust amidst the sherry casks in the cellar until the damp rotted the canvas away.

The alchemist threw back his cloak and turned another card. The World. Then, the twenty second card in his deck: Le Fol. The Fool!

Now, the feeling that he could see into, could know the future was so strong within him that even the Inquisition could not have silenced him!

'Even in four hundred years, Señor, they will make copies of this portrait of you which is to be painted. Copies that will be sold. Yes, sold, even on the streets of this town! Your face will look into strange rooms in many lands.'

'I - I shall be that famous?' The Caballero asked incredulously. The older man studied the cards once more with wonder, for he himself did not understand nor could make sense of his prediction.

"Not you,' he said. 'No, not you. The Greek! El Greco. For no one will ever remember your name.'

13: WATERING THE TREES

'What are we going to do about the hill, Jeff?'
'What do you want to do about it, Jean?
'Something. And soon,' she said firmly. 'We've got to fence in our land. It's the only way to stop them.'

'We can't do that, Jean.'

'Why not? It's ours, isn't it?'

'The villagers. It would be a declaration of war if we shut them out.'

'We can't have the goats eating our orchard.'

He stared at her. 'Jean, there isn't one tree out there on the entire hill.' She was wearing that jaw-clenching expression he associated with pig-headed determination. 'Jean... we don't - do not - have an orchard. Or any trees. Not one! Except in the garden, and that magnolia hasn't looked too healthy since the goats climbed it.'

'We will have trees, Jeff. When we plant them,' Jean's logic was irrefutable. 'And the villagers wouldn't have any respect for us if we were to plant an orchard and not fence it in. So you see why we've got to have a fence. For the orchard.'

'Quit saying orchard.'

She sat down beside him, taking hold of his hands, a dreamy look in her eyes. 'Jeff, you've always told me about your vision of the Chekhovian life. Seagulls. Cherry orchards. Tutors by the lake on a sweltering hot afternoon. Uncle Vanya spouting poetry on a garden bench. White Panama hats fanning neat, bearded faces. Well, this is our chance! We've got the fields.' She looked at him closely, not entirely with approval. And you've got the beard now.'

It was true that in the last year Jeff had grown a beard. It was a soft shade of sandy brown, and it somehow suited his lanky frame and angular face. 'Jean,' he said, 'you're making a dramatchka.'

'What's a dramatchka?'

'A Russian drama.'

'You made that up.'

'Okay, so I made it up, but this is Spain not Russia, and that's your fantasy not mine. If you think back, I never much liked Chekhov. And trees sound like work to me.' Jeff was still able to defend himself in the clinches, but not against Jean, whom he claimed, didn't clinch fair.

'Green Peace would love it,' she said vaguely.

'But would we? Be reasonable, Jean. All I see out there is an empty hill, a few goats and too many noisy children playing football. We haven't got any relatives here, and certainly not an Uncle Vanya. Seagulls we can get at the beach. Besides, what would we plant? I don't think cherry trees thrive in this climate. They'd never survive the hot breath of Africa.'

'I've been giving that some thought.'

'I'll bet you have,' he smiled, weakening slightly. 'What have you come up with?'

'Well,' she replied, settling in for a good think. 'It's got to be something that doesn't need bottom land. Something that likes a high wind, the occasional Tormenta, and a soil composed mainly of weeds and children's discarded sneakers.'

'Were you thinking of telephone poles?'

'Come on, Jeff. You can do better than that.' She smiled, but her face was determined. 'What about avocados?'

'Jean, I know for a fact that avocados need lots of water, fine soil, a knowledgeable gardener—which lets out Miguel— and a well organised sex life.'

'Us, or the trees?'

He reached over and kissed her. 'I'd say ours was intensely organised. Let's slip into the bedroom.'

'Flickering pheromones...!' she said.

'What...?'

'It's an expletive. If you can make them up, so can I.'

A smile curved his lips. 'Then you've given up saying fuck?'

She nodded. 'It doesn't really suit me. Okay, Jeff... so avocados are out. We might plant a few down at the bottom, though. And the odd fig and an orange or two.' Her face lit with sudden inspiration. 'Nuts...!'

'Really, Jean, don't give up. We were just in the middle of a good discussion.'

'No, Jeff. I mean what's your favourite food?'

'You mean peanuts? Don't they grow on vines low on the ground and come from Georgia?'

'Yes, and they're going to stay there. But what did you say Andalucia was like the first day we drove through the countryside?'

'Old California, in my father's day.'

'Okay. It still is. And what nuts do they grow in California, aside from the cases on Hollywood Boulevard, from which we have thankfully escaped?'

His smile broke into a sudden laugh. 'Flickering pheromones, Jean? You actually made that up?'

She got up, pulling him with her. 'Did you say the bedroom, Jeff?'

⌘

The visit from the Vivero was both rewarding and disappointing. Yes, he assured them, almendros were the very thing for Santa Rita.

And how many could they plant?

The Vivero was wearing tight American jeans and he cut quite a dashing figure as he marched out onto the field, pacing it with a measuring macho stride, his jacket slung over one shoulder like a cape as though the bull would appear at any moment. His black hair was pomaded back as slickly as any matador's. Jeff could spot villagers coming out of their houses to peer across, as though something momentous was about to happen. Any stranger on the foreigners' field was food for gossip in an otherwise indifferent day.

'Do you think they know he's a Vivero?' Jean whispered.

'He's probably a cousin and they always know everything,' Jeff growled.

When he returned from his pacing, the Nursery Man informed them in passable English that they could plant exactly five hundred and fifty almond trees on the hill.

'What will we do with them?' Jeff croaked, having imagined in his wildest fantasy, a figure closer to twenty.

'Market the nuts.' Jean's blithe retort sounded as though she had been in the produce business for years.

'Market?'

'Sell.'

'And what is more, Señor, at the bottom of the hill where the soil is rich and near to the irrigation canal, you can have the oranges, the lemons, the apricots, the figs, the apples, the peaches, and the pears.'

'Not the Chirimoyas?' Jean asked.

'What's a Chirimoya? ' Jeff wondered.

'A Custard Apple,' she said.

'What's a Custard Apple?'

'Really, Jeff! Those fruits with the fish scale design on the green outside and inside the center is white with big black seeds. You said they were absolutely delicious.'

'Did I? When?' he tried to remember.

'Si, Chirimoyas, Señora. But nothing can be planted until next January. All the trees, they must wait until exactly before the season with much rain.' The Vivero's words put a damper on Jean's enthusiasm for instant action. 'The field, Señora, it too, must be made ready. Ploughed and prepared. This will take much time.'

'Right,' Jean said cheerfully as they saw him to his car. 'Perfect timing.' His car bumped down the rutted hill track and at the bottom he paused to talk to several of the villagers. Now all the villagers would know about the coming of the orchard.

'Perhaps I'm missing something, Jean.' Jeff was secretly relieved that they would not have to do anything immediately. Procrastination had its virtues in his book. 'Why did you tell the Vivero—perfect timing?'

'As you were the first to point out, Jeff, fruit trees are expensive and we'll need to raise more money.'

'What about raising the almond trees? Did your father grow them in the garage—along with his toy soldiers?'

'Okay, so I don't know anything about orchards. This will give us ample time to bone up. We're both very good researchers, aren't we? You've always said you could learn anything with the right book. '

'Don't you think the Vivero knows?'

I'm sure he does. But we don't want to appear stupid, do we? So what's the difference if it's for something we're writing - or for our orchard? We can learn.'

'Of that, I am certain, my undauntable darling.' He wrapped an arm around her waist and took a deep breath of the air. Up there on that hill beneath the Magic Mountain it had a different scent. Somehow fresher, cleaner, sweeter than anywhere he could remember except as a boy in the California hills above Malibu on the back of a horse on a warm summer's day in the long ago time of his youth. And so they sat down and wrote to a friend in California for help.

In due course, books of instruction arrived from the Department of Agriculture. How to plant an almond orchard for the best possible yield. How the trees must be laid out on a grid thirty feet apart so a tractor can pass between them to plough the field. And then there would be the machines that shake down the nuts at harvest time, which must be able to move about easily.

'Do you think they have such machines in Spain?' Jeff queried.

'Fred told me that they have a Sindicado. You know, an agricultural syndicate. They do all sorts of things for the small farmer,' she said.

'We couldn't get any smaller and who's Fred?'

'You remember? The little guy with the loud Hawaiian shirt at Cynthia's last party.'

'What the hell does he know about almond trees in Honolulu?'

Whatever he knew or didn't, Jean was not to be deterred. Then, or ever. But the day of planting was postponed until the stars were propitious. Jeff was wondering if they would have to anoint the earth with a ritual blood sacrifice to the local gods.

Jean said unnecessary.

One resident of Santa Rita was paying tribute to the household gods. A cat they had named Munchkin had become their protector. Seated in the terrace window betwixt the wrought iron rejas and the newly installed screens (to keep out flies and lizards and Munchkin), pacing in this self-imposed cage, this curious cat thought of itself as a lion. It chased away intruders and brought offerings. The intruders happened to be friends and the offerings happened to be horrible, but cats have a different way of looking at the world.

'Did you know that Marmalade cats are all supposed to be male, Jeff?'

'Really?' he asked trying to get a clearer view of Munchkin's anatomical structure and failing. 'I don't think that's a male cat, Jean.'

'Mmm,' she agreed. 'Either his bits are well hidden or missing.'

Jeff decided that Munchkin was a Marmalade of no affixed sex, since the male cats of El Salto never went near it 'in season'. And unlike the motley campo cats, Munchkin had most definitely at some time in the past, been house broken.

In Spain, cats are easy to acquire. In fact you don't acquire them: they acquire you. The day the Thwaites moved in, they found themselves regularly hosting twelve campo cats who arrived in tandem for breakfast on the kitchen terrace. These four-legged scavengers were wild and dangerous, demanding regular payoffs 'with menaces'. They operated a sort of Protection Racket in return for keeping the field mice at bay. Sometimes Jean thought she would have preferred the field mice. Alive. She was not keen on finding a half eaten dead mouse on the doorstep as the Cat Mafia's side of the deal, or the little well-loved lizards, or the feathered friends who perched too low on a bush and got caught by a stealthy Catman leap.

'We really must all feed them, you know,' Cynthia Gray had instructed Jean the very first day they moved in. 'The villagers give them nothing and they will all get cat fever from starvation.'

'...The villagers?' Jeff asked, thinking cat fever might do a few of the villages some good, especially Miguel.

Cynthia just scowled at him. 'I feed twenty, so you must take whoever comes your way.' Jean suspected that Cynthia liked cats better than people, judging from a few catty remarks. She stopped Jeff from eating Cynthia's hors d'oeuvres because she was convinced that some, particularly the ones called paté, were actually made of cat food. When she couldn't force-feed the Thwaites, Cynthia accused them both of trying to slim and informed them she herself, when going on a slimming diet, ate only potatoes.

Jean found that besides feeding twelve cats, a few extras were beginning to mooch in, who still had a hollow place left in their bellies after breakfasting on Cynthia's hors d'oeuvres. The Untouchables, as Jeff tagged them, would bat each other with a heavy paw to the jowls when one was too greedy at the bowl. Jean was forced to put out several more bowls to lessen the mayhem. Maria disapproved of feeding them at all, but went along with the foreigners' strange customs as long as she was paid regularly and nobody criticised her work. Who would dare?

Munchkin refused to fraternize with any of the campo cats and ate his/her dinner on the front terrace from her own bowl. The pack in turn snubbed her at every opportunity. All except one black and white male Jeff named Tio Rodrego. He had unusually short, slightly bowed legs and pointed his toes out, which gave him a rolling gait. Tio Rodrego took a shine to Munchkin and trailed after her everywhere, only to be ignored. It was a case of unrequited love and unless Tio Rodrego was gay, it was the final answer to Munchkin's sex. Munchkin made it understood in no uncertain terms that she only liked humans, and followed Jeff and Jean whenever they came outside. They were soon able to pick her up, put her in a cat basket borrowed from Cynthia, and take her to the local Vet for cat-flu shots and finally confirm that she was female and had been spayed. She forgave them the painful indignity, and would hop into their laps and purr when stroked. Munchkin had adopted them.

When they took the car into town, Munchkin was waiting on the hill in joyful leaps, eager to escort the car back (in case they didn't remember which was their house) and somehow managing to stay out from under the wheels. When they'd return to Spain after months away, Munchkin would be there waiting with psychic clarity, as though they'd sent her a telepathy FAX about the precise moment of their arrival.

⌘

But there was a new upset. The villagers were beginning to dump their rubbish on the field. One day Jeff saw a village woman fling her bucket of basura as if to say, 'take that for being foreign.' Maria told them the basura was meant as a deliberate insult from the cross-bred gypsies at the bottom of the village. Jean thought it might have been the tongue-wielding boy's mother. Once again she began to think about fences.

'Think about money instead,' Jeff told her. 'Ten thousand square metres of field would cost a fortune to enclose. Even a fence made of the cheapest wire mesh—and we'd end up looking like Colditz.'

It was in mid-December that Jean could wait no longer. Her green thumb was itchy with ideas. She grabbed Jeff and pulled him out to the front terrace. 'We'll plant a fence, Jeff! Of cypress trees. Along the edge of the village road, and all the way along the bottom by the irrigation canal!'

'Plant it? Hmm. Maybe that would work,' he said. 'It would certainly look less like a prison compound with us being kept inside, instead of them being kept out. But what about all those villagers in the morning who walk to work down along the irrigation canal?'

'We'll leave enough room for them to walk behind it. And along the village, too.' Her face suddenly lit up. 'We'll make them a Good Will present of land! A polite way of saying: don't enter' past the trees.'

It made sense even to Jeff.

The trees were only three feet tall when they arrived. Hardly ready to keep anything out, even a midget. The Vivero planted them. He dug long trenches, put in some fertiliser, some water - and he assured them, the acipréses would grow quickly. One foot at least a year. Better yet, they would only need regular watering during the first six months.

Miguel assured them that the Vivero was wrong. Spanish trees did not need water. Ever. If you gave them water, they would only get used to it and then you'd have to give it to them all the time. Besides, anything to do with the field was not his regular work.

Jeff wasn't sure what Miguel's regular work was, because if it was taking care of the garden, the only chore Miguel seemed to enjoy was running the electric lawn mower which they shared, like Miguel, with the other three villas. The Spaniard, his short frame rounded by a beer and brandy belly, rode the machine across the lawn, back and forth, to and fro, cutting the grass so close that the garden looked like a shaven head. Miguel shook his, and told them that the grass needed more fertiliser. He held out his palm which contained another gouging Presupuesto.

Finally he agreed to water the cypress hedge for a large number of pesetas extra.

Then one day as they drove up the hill from San Pedro, Jean noticed that all the new cypress trees were dying. 'No water! she screeched at Jeff as though it were his fault. 'He's not watering them. Do something, Jeff!'

'I'll speak to Miguel,' he said.

Properly rebuked, Miguel went down and watered the trees along the bottom land facing the valley. Since that row skirted the irrigation canal, they were surviving despite his attentions and were not the trees in need of water. But no amount of bribery seemed sufficient to make Miguel water the trees along the side of the village.

'Well, it's obvious, isn't it?' Jean told Jeff the next day.

'Don't keep me in the dark,' her husband said, knowing that was the last thing she'd ever do.

'Miguel doesn't want to be seen working so close to the villagers. It would ruin his reputation for being lazy. We'll have to do it ourselves.'

'What?'

'Water the trees.'

'Us?' he asked.

'You don't want them to die, do you? Think of all the money we've invested.' She knew exactly how to hook him. 'Besides, it's the only way to teach him a lesson.'

'Monkey see, monkey do?'

If you like,' she said. 'Come on.'

So an hour later found the Thwaites walking down the hill to inspect the trees, Munchkin trailing after, or popping up from behind a cypress in a game of hide and seek. The Marmalade cat sharpened her claws on a few trunks, nearly doing the little trees in. Jeff and Jean hauled the great length of hose they had recently purchased, and began pumping water along the row skirting El Salto. Dripping it into the trenches, letting the water reach the roots. This entertainment gained an audience of the entire village. Everyone but Miguel who had completely disappeared. No monkey to see or do.

There was much whispering behind cupped hands on the village side. Jeering remarks were muttered. Children giggled. Cats arched their backs at Munchkin, who was loyally guarding their efforts at every step. Tio Rodrego, the black and white cat Lothario ambled along the village side of the trees, afraid to enter for fear of mortal combat with Munchkin who was hissing at all comers.

Finally, little Pepé stepped forward. 'Hola, Jean. What are you doing?' she asked.

'Watering the trees,' Jean told her. Watering the roots with liquid love, she thought.

Pepé nodded as though Jean had said she was trying to catch the wind in a net. Munchkin peered at the villagers and Tio Rodrego as though they were from outer space. The bandy-legged cat stared back at Munchkin, a traitor to her DNA.

A woman who lived in the house with the colorful laundry came closer. It was the gypsy boy's mother. 'Hola, Señora. dime qué pasa?'

'Riego de los árboles. Watering the trees,' Jean repeated, wondering if she should ask her not to dump her rubbish in their field. She thought better of it. The woman nodded and backed away, but remained to watch. Her son came behind his mother, clutching her skirts and stuck out his tongue.

The goat lady came out, friendlier than the rest, and ventured close enough to ask, 'What is it you are doing, Señora?'

'Riego de los árboles,' Jeff said this time, although by now it seemed patently obvious.

'Oh. Riego de los árboles,' the goat lady replied and nodded, staring in wonder.

'They are watering the trees…!' came the report, spreading down the road and into the houses. Heads stuck out of windows. 'The acipréses. Imagine… The estranjeros are watering them…!'

One young woman in a loose black dress, her bare legs in broken sandals, watched from the wall of her house and pulled her brightly flowered smock tightly around a swelling belly. Jean had noticed her many times lately, because she had a distant look in her eyes as though she wasn't quite all there. Jean had never seen her with a man and usually the husbands and wives walked up and down in the cool of evening's paseo. Sometimes this young woman stood against the wall in the morning, knitting shawls like the other women. But she always stood apart, as she did now. She watched but she did not speak. And curiously, nobody ever seemed to speak to her.

'The acipréses. They are watering them...!' The latest 'news reader' was Maria, who had come up to join the others with a look on her face that said, "I work for the estranjeros. I can dish you the dirt on how crazy they are." Her son, their gardener was still nowhere to be seen.

Jeff did not doubt that the village, which did not boast any trees at all (unless you counted one rubber tree in a pot on somebody's roof), considered trees a foolish foreign concept. Jeff struck an aggressive stance as if to say, 'Here is a man watering his trees. And he doesn't give a flickering pheromone what you think of that.'

An old man in a soft grey hat and dusty jacket that had seen better years, stepped forward, toothless, wise, and full of ancient wisdom of the earth. 'Pardon, Señor, but why is it that you water the acipréses?' he asked finally.

'Because they must drink, just like you. Because they are dying without water.'

The old man's weathered face shook sideways at the curious ways of estranjeros and he walked back to his house and climbed up to his roof for a better look.

The girl in the broken sandals and loose black dress moved forward, a spark of light coming into her sad, strange eyes. 'The trees want only the rain. The rains will come soon and save them,' she said.

Four hours later as the coolness of evening descended, with aching backs and tired arms and still assisted by the faithful Munchkin, Jeff and Jean put away the length of hose and returned to Santa Rita.

Miguel was the only villager who had mysteriously stayed out of sight during the entire Operation Cypresses.

Love was made that night in the total relaxation of utter exhaustion. The good ache in the tired body that can explode into the wonder of desire and completion. And in the night, the rains came and it rained for five days without stopping and the little trees were nearly washed away.

During the rainstorms Jeff and Jean stayed in the house and hardly came out except to slog though the mud down to the tienda to buy more cat food. It gave them plenty of time to write another short story. And as writers have a way of doing, they discovered it was about the girl in the black dress with the swelling belly and brightly flowered shawl—and the sad, vacant eyes.

The curious thing was they did not ever see her again and could not find out from Maria what had happened to her. But she had found her way into the story they called *The Salamander*. They named her Leacadia.

⌘

14: THE SALAMANDER

Nacho had come to the high mountain village with the other men working on the new road. Before these men came, few strangers ever travelled so far in the hills that side of Ronda because really, there was nowhere to go unless to one more sun-baked Spanish village on one more rocky hillside of poor earth and poorer people.

Leacadia had lived alone in the same white-washed house with the broken tiled roof and the rusting rejas since the day her mother had been carried out through the narrow doorway to the walled cemetery. They had placed the bare wooden coffin in a high crypt. Every week Leacadia took wildflowers to the graveyard and cried in front of her mother's crypt in the marble wall.

Now the house belonged to her alone and no one could take it away from her. She had no memory of her father. But the old women in the village remembered him as they remembered everything. They told her that he had never married her mother. It made no difference to Leacadia, in any case. She kept to herself, sold the eggs from her chickens, the milk from the two goats, and the shawls. The shawls her grandmother had taught her to knit while standing against the hot white wall where she always stood, near, but not too near the old women in black.

When the men came to build the new road, she filled a bag with oranges and wild figs and went along to where they were working, to sell them. Nacho bought two oranges and twelve figs. His eyes were flecked with green and there were streaks of gold in his hair like strands of fire. He had tied his shirt around his waist and the sweat glistened on his bare skin. When he handed her the money, she wondered suddenly how she must look. Sometimes she glanced into the mirror to see if her hair was combed or if her dress was clean but today she had forgotten. As she brushed the dust from the fig tree on her black skirt she smiled at him. The smile was returned.

Next day Leacadia cooked a large tortilla with eggs, potatoes, and onions, flipping it carefully onto the pan lid, then sliding it back into the pan, over and over like a wish. until it was golden brown. She brought it to Nacho and he gave her fifty pesetas. That day when he asked, she showed Nacho which house was hers. He said he would visit her.

And when the sun slashed crimson along La Montaña Mágica above the village and day melted into dusk, Nacho knocked on her door. The villagers did not take notice. It would have made no difference to Leacadia, in any case.

She fed him a plate of lentil soup by the sputtering oil lamp. He told her his village was far from here, down near the coast. She laughed to hear about it because it was a place she had never been. He had brought a bottle and they drank fresh Chiclana, the young mountain sherry of the South. The thick glass tumblers captured the flame of the lamp and it flickered and danced in his eyes. The flame leapt inside of her and she went with him to her narrow white bed. It was not the first time a man had removed her dress and lay down with her but before, Leacadia had never cared much one way or the other. No, it made no difference those other times.

Soon she felt a smile growing inside her and spent each afternoon after she finished working on the shawls in preparing a dish to please him and each night Nacho came to her bed and wrapped himself around her body like a flame.

And then one day Nacho told her that he was married and would be returning home when the road work was finished. Leacadia did not mind. Not then. Not until he left with the others. Then she could only remember the strength of his arms wrapped around her so tightly like a flame. Arms that held her as close as life.

Four months had passed since Nacho left. Leacadia noticed her reflection in the mirror and understood that she was going to have his baby. She was glad, even though like herself, it would have no father's name on the certificate of birth. She opened her grandmother's painted wooden chest and took out her mother's flowered smock. Large enough to hide her secret from the old women who sat all morning by the wall knitting until the sun became too hot and they went inside for their siestas. But they paid her no more attention than before, which was little enough and the months went by.

Leacadia was out by the edge of the forest alone gathering twigs for making the charcoal when she felt the baby coming.

She hurried back to her house and all by herself helped the child to enter the world as best she could.

As best she could. . .

The baby did not live long enough to cry out. Only Leacadia cried out. And in the night she buried the tiny girl under the wild fig tree behind her house. When the sun rose behind it, the branches seemed to shimmer and glow with a great fire and Leacadia was happy for the baby sleeping under that blazing tree.

That night the salamander came. He crept in through the open window and crawled into Leacadia's bed. The salamander wrapped himself around her body like an icy flame. His huge tail twisted around her waist, his narrow head nestled between her breasts. Leacadia was not frightened. The salamander's speckled green eyes looked into hers and there was no scorn or contempt in them. She was not frightened, although she could remember that as a child her grandmother warned of the salamander. Warned that these creatures were poisonous. She remembered the tale her grandmother told: that of all creatures, only the salamander could live in fire and only it had the power to quench the flames with its body because the salamander was cold, cold as ice.

Leacadia fell asleep with the salamander wrapped around her and she knew a deep peace. When she awoke she thought he would be gone like Nacho, and that her arms would be empty once more. But the salamander was still there. When she climbed out of the bed it would not unwind itself from around her body, so once again she put on her mother's flowered smock. When the salamander was hungry, she nursed it from the milk still heavy in her breasts. The milk her baby had no need of now. She knew that it meant to stay with her forever and she was content.

Then one night it twisted itself so tightly around her chest that she couldn't breathe. The salamander drew all the heat from her body until she was as cold as it was. And then it uncoiled itself, arched its body up, and disappeared forever.

In the days that followed, the young bride next door noticed that crazy Leacadia did not come to stand against the white wall of her house to knit the woollen shawls with the old women. Another neighbor said that she had not seen Leacadia muttering down the road towards evening, the way she normally did, when she brought her goats home. Maria said she had not come to her shop to buy bread. Poor Leacadia. Not all there in the head. Even though they had never paid her much attention, they could feel an emptiness in the village without her familiar figure passing by. And so finally the old women in black went to her house. They found the goats tethered in a pen in the back and the chickens pecking at the hard ground and they crowded in through her doorway to see if Leacadia was all right.

They found her on the bed cold as stone, her white body ringed by a dark bruise that looked as though something thick and heavy had been coiled around her.

The women shuddered and did not speak of it to their men.

⌘

15: MANILVA

When Jean got the news that her father's illness was cancer and it was terminal, they both knew she would have to fly back to the States alone. Jeff would have to finish their new television script assignment on his own or they'd never meet their deadline.

'Don't know exactly how long I'll be gone, Jeff.' Tears in her eyes, she'd booked a flight back to London for the following afternoon, and then a direct flight to Chicago and on to Youngstown, Ohio.

'Don't worry, he said. I was writing before I met you. Guess I can get the job finished. After all, it's an adaptation of a Raymond Chandler. How wrong can I go, working from the master?'

'Just don't get in the habit,' she nodded, her mind on her father and how she feared this might be the last time she would ever see him.

Jeff studied her expression. 'Tell you what. Let's take the day off. Go for a drive. There's a spring at Manilva that Davie told us about, remember? The Romans used it as a bath. This whole coast has been a holiday resort since Roman times.'

'Some things never change,' she said.

'And some things always do. What say we pack a picnic and go? Have a day alone together.'

She looked at him with wonder. 'Jeff - we're always alone together. We work together, remember?'

'That's different. I mean just a day with no work. Just you and me. We can talk together, you know, without it being about story problems.'

'Oh, Jeff - you always say the right thing.'

'That's not what you tell me on a script. How about picking up a chicken from that barbecue place? Some potato salad and a bottle of vino. How does that grab you?'

'It grabs me right here,' she said, hugging him.

They drove down the coast road past Estepona, following a map Davie had given them. Jeff spotted the turning just in time and headed up into the hills. These hills, still untouched by 'progress', were covered in thicket and oleander, and further up,

143

blanketed in squat green pines. As they drove on, craggy juttings of rock face gave the land a stark, abrasive clarity.

'The Romans must have trod across every inch of these hills to find this place,' Jeff said. 'Manilva was a health spa for their Legions to recuperate from their wars. They must have loved this coast.'

'They loved it anywhere where they could hack the peasants to pieces, Jeff. Plunder, rape, and pillage, that's what the Roman Legions loved.'

He laughed. 'I guess you're right about that. They had mines in Iberia, with maybe thirty thousand slaves digging for iron and silver.'

'At least it was only spear and sword wounds they were recovering from,' Jean said. 'And my father will be impressed when I tell him about your newly acquired sense of history.' Suddenly the brightness faded from her voice and she started to cry.

'Jean. . .' he said, 'you're going to have to be brave for your mother.'

She nodded, wiping her eyes. 'I will be, Jeff. When I'm there.'

The little Renault had reached the crest of a hill on the rutted road. Jeff was surprised to see a paved road springing out of nothing and leading down the other side where huge placards pointed the way to the Baths. 'Hmm! Davie said it was only a donkey trail and that the Spaniards didn't even put up a sign to show where the Roman Baths were.'

'Guess Davie hasn't been here for a while. Must be part of the Spanish 'improvements' to boost the tourist industry.'

'Which will mean a litter of tourist debris everywhere we go.' He parked the car and they got out. It had been about a forty five minute ride and they were glad to stretch their legs. 'Can't be much of a walk from here,' he said, taking the picnic hamper. Jean took the blanket.

Jeff gave Jean a hand down a steep incline and onto a footpath that led further down towards a narrow, nearly dried-up river bed. In the adjoining fields wild golden wheat moved gently with the breeze. The air was heady with the sweet scent of wild flowers and abuzz with bees.

'I'm not sure about the wild life,' Jean said, ducking a bombing bee.

'They don't sting if you don't annoy them.'

'What did you think I was going to do? Call them names?'

Closer to the river bed the path narrowed, bordered by pink oleander and golden hibiscus bushes in wild profusion. It finally disappeared altogether except for some wide, flat stepping stones just above the river bank. Water was bubbling down in swift descent over the stony bottom, but there wasn't much of it. Jean peered down. 'That's odd,' she said, staring at it. 'It looks milky.'

They rounded a stand of poplars to face the unexpected sight of a small brick bridge. The same long, narrow, delicately pink bricks Jean had seen in ancient walls in Rome. The bridge crossed the river at a spot no more than thirty feet from bank to bank and had been built in the shape of an almost perfect half circled arch with solid brick walls.

'Is it possible the ancient Romans built this exquisite thing here two thousand years ago in the back of nowhere?' exclaimed Jean.

'It wasn't nowhere to them then, and anyway, they were great architects. Too bad more of their buildings aren't still standing on this coast. I suppose their camps were clay and straw.'

They started down the narrowing path. Directly beneath the bridge and hanging under it some six feet above the waterline, there was a round brick dome. 'What on earth would that have been for...?' Jean asked.

'Your guess,' Jeff said, taking her hand as they started across the narrow foot bridge. From the opposite bank they could see underneath the dome. It formed a cupola over the river, but for what purpose?

'Possibly the water was deeper then, in which case the entire dome would have been submerged under water. A giant wine cooler, maybe. The water's so milky'

Jeff nodded and led the way down the path. 'It's a natural sulphur springs.'

Here, the water had been diverted by the Romans to form a swimming grotto about fifteen feet square. Two thousand years ago, and it was still covered by a roof of the same slender pink bricks. Although the pool had been lined with white tiles at some more recent date, ancient remnants of the original Roman painted tiles still clung to the enclosure walls. And scratched into them was the graffiti of the centuries; visitors who had made it up this hill in donkey days and had carved their initials. Jeff spotted one dated 1795. Another, 1634. The grotto was deserted now. The whiteness of the water seemed opaque, bubbling up in a frenzy of a strong current.

'The first Jacuzzi,' Jeff said. 'And what luck. We've got it all to ourselves. Jeff stripped off his ducks and T-shirt. 'When in a Roman bath, let's do as the Romans do, eh?'

She hesitated. 'Isn't it supposed to be medicinal? What happens if you're perfectly healthy and you go in there?'

≈'We'll find out.' He jumped in with wild abandon; Jean stripped and followed, splashing naked in the milky water. A faintly pungent vapour rose around them forming a mystical haze on the surface. Yet the scent was somehow not unpleasant. 'It's like a dip into hell,' Jeff said. 'More like a milk bath from a friendly but aromatic goat.' Their voices sounded hollow under the dome and the grotto seemed mysterious, the water was almost heavy enough to hold their weight. It was not too cold, and it tingled the skin softly soothing. Jeff clasped her from behind, drawing her back towards him so that she felt the sudden hard desire of him. He pressed her slim hips to him and

≈'We'll find out.' He jumped in with wild abandon; Jean stripped and followed, splashing naked in the milky water. A faintly pungent vapour rose around them forming a mystical haze on the surface. Yet the scent was somehow not unpleasant. 'It's like a dip into hell,' Jeff said. 'More like a milk bath from a friendly but aromatic goat.' Their voices sounded hollow under the dome and the grotto seemed mysterious, the water was almost heavy enough to hold their weight. It was not too cold, and it tingled the skin softly soothing. Jeff clasped her from behind, drawing her back towards him so that she felt the sudden hard desire of him. He pressed her slim hips to him and

Later, they lay on the bridge and dried in the sun. When they were dressed, they climbed up the hill to a field edged with tall grass and hedgerow. Words were their everyday tools. Now they delighted in being together in silence, sharing feelings. Jeff broke a path through the grass and carried the hamper to a spot where the grass was soft as a carpet. Jean spread out the blanket, and a small cloth from the hamper. He opened the wine, arranged the food and paper plates, forks and napkins. They dug into the picnic as though they hadn't eaten for a week.

'Why is it that the Spanish chickens taste so much better than the British or American ones?'

'They're not full of whatever it is they pump our poultry full of,' Jean said biting into a leg.

They lolled in the grass, satiated with food. The last crumb was scattered to the birds when Jeff pulled Jean to her feet. 'Come. A good walk is what we need to work off that lunch.' Jean took his hand and they climbed to the top of the slope where they could look across to the sea which seemed miles away from them now. The air was so clear they could see the entire outline of mountains across the water in Morocco and the peak of the Herculean Pillar.

One large fig tree dominated the field, and they made their way to it. Wild figs were purpling on its branches and the fruit flies had not yet discovered its bounty. Jeff reached one down and took a bite. 'Mmm, perfect,' he said, and plucked one for her.

She bit into the creamy white and pink interior, savouring the richly perfumed sweetness. 'Jeff. . .we're in Heaven,' she breathed.

'I think we owe it to this tree to make love under it,' he said thoughtfully. His eyes captured hers.

They had been wanting, and waiting had made the feeling more urgent. It was as though they had just met for the first time. She often felt that with Jeff and since they spent so much time together, it was hard to understand why. She knew he could make desire last. Like that time in the producer's office when they looked at each other and felt like doing it right on the man's desk. But they did not. And when they got back to the car, Jeff pulled into a side street and they made love then and there. And now, right now, she was aching to hold him as tight as she could between her thighs. Her hand reached the hardness she knew would be there, the throbbing part of him waiting to be part of her and she melted happily into his tight embrace.

'You looked like a nymph from a Roman painting in that phosphoresce mist. I could see you in another incarnation, your hair braided with golden chains and daisies, wearing only folds of white diaphanous silk over that body I love so much...' Words stopped as lips pressed gently, tasting the wonder of this passion as though it were the first time. His eagerness overwhelmed her. Their bodies, still half dressed, clung to each other as though all time had stopped in magical solitude and there was nothing else but them between the earth and sky, desire flooding them with love.

When they opened their eyes to a world other than each other, they saw a goat staring down at them, close enough to nibble at their clothes. They sat up to see that it was the 'bellwether' of a flock. They had not even heard its bell. Behind the goat, a herd was ambling up the hill towards them, the new born kids tagging in little leaps after their mothers. And behind them, a lagging shepherd boy foot-dragged his way after his charges, his dog sniffing at his heels.

Hastily they pulled their clothes on, and got to their feet. 'I'm sure sex is no mystery to that kid,' Jeff said.

'Oh, Jeff, a pun at a time like this?'

The goat put his front hooves up on the trunk of the fig tree and proceeded to chomp at the leaves on the lower branches, swallowing the few figs within his reach. Jeff and Jean looked at each other and burst into laughter, then made their way back down the hill past the goatherd, arm in arm.

Tonight would be their last together for how long? When they got back Jeff asked Jean to take their latest story with her. She could read it to her father. It might help him pass the time. And there was also a magazine editor in Chicago she could send it to. It never hurt to have the stories published even though they were going into a book. It was about a man on holiday in Spain who got a little confused about exactly who he was.

Under The Magic Mountain

⌘

16: THEN WHO AM I?

Michael Burkett's eyes opened slowly and focused on white. A man floating in blankness. For a moment, he didn't know exactly where he was. Then the whiteness took the form of a stucco ceiling. His glance dropped to an open window where tropical flowers, what were they called? Yes, Bougainvillea'. . .blushed a trail of salmon coloured bracts across the curved iron rejas covering the window. Now how on earth did he remember that word from childhood? Rejas. The iron window grilles.

His 'Brush Up on Your Spanish' lessons; that was it. It really had come back for him to remember a word like that. Here he was. He'd actually made it to Spain after all these years. He closed his eyes. His head felt thick, throbbing, and everything seemed a bit fuzzy. Must have had a hell of a lot more to drink than he thought on the plane. And of course, before he'd headed for the airport he'd knocked back a few with the lads from the bank. That was it.

Michael Burkett lay still for a moment trying to get his bearings. His eyes were drawn to the white lace curtains framing the floral display and a bright blue sky beyond. The bed too, was covered in heavy white cotton lace. Was he in the bridal suite? This hotel had certainly given him the special treatment. All due, no doubt to that dynamite red head in the travel agency, Sally. But a bachelor in a bridal suite? He'd have to kid her about that when he got back. 'Come on, Sally,' he'd say. 'Was that your idea of a joke on me?' Then maybe he'd invite her around to his flat for a bottle of vino and a takeaway.

Sally was a girl worth getting to know. She'd taken a lot of time over him, gone through all the Spanish brochures and come up with this special holiday. The brochure photos promised oceans of water skiing, shoals of shellfish, and galaxies of girls swanning about the bluest of pools—and the price was right. He was going to have a good time all on his own—although he didn't intend to be alone for long.

But what was niggling at the back of his brain? For one split second a twinge of anxiety shot through him and he sat bolt upright. His glance fell on a card on the bedside table. For the moment his vision seemed as fuzzy as his mind. The card read: 'El Sol Del Mar: Room Service Tariff'.

The curious thing was, he couldn't remember getting here from the airport. He dropped his feet over the edge of the bed, feeling just a bit stiff. Must have been that long delay at Gatwick. Five hours late for take off. And yet another controller's strike in France. When would they get it together for the traveller who, after all, paid all the bills? He knew he'd been meant to take a bus to Fuengirola from Malaga Airport, but he couldn't remember getting on it. And then there should have been a taxi. That must have been how he got so stiff, from all that sitting.

He got to his feet slowly and did a few stretches and bends. He sure needed this holiday more than he'd realised. His body felt thick in the middle and impossible as it seemed, his waist felt inches bigger today! Well, as someone once said, you have your fat days and your thin days and somewhere inside him was a fat man trying to get out. Have to do something about the fat man, he thought. Swimming was the answer. And cutting down on the booze.

But not until he got back to London. No, he wasn't that big a masochist. He intended to overindulge on the sensational Spanish wines that he'd been too young to appreciate when his parents moved to England. Spanish mother, English father. If it had been the other way around, maybe he'd have grown up in Spain.

Staring out through the lace curtains into the garden below and thinking about his waistline made him realise how hungry he was. He glanced at his watch. 10:30 a.m. Still not too late for brekkers if he hurried. Girls, several of them, were draped around the pool, and to his surprise, some of them were not wearing the tops to their bikinis. What sort of place had Sally booked him into? Not that he'd mind taking a longer look at the shimmering, sun-oiled bounty of one dishy brunette down there. Hastily he pulled on shorts and a T-shirt.

Michael headed down the stairs two at a time but his step did not have the usual bounce. That trip must have been more tiring than he thought. He hoped he wasn't coming down with something. The desk clerk nodded courteously. "Buenos Dias, Señor Alverez."

'Burkett. Mr Burkett,' he corrected. *'Donde esta el comodor?'*

The clerk regarded him with some puzzlement before pointing the way through tall double doors of carved pine.

He chose a table by the open french doors facing the pool. The brunette was still out there toasting on a lounger. And still alone. This could be his lucky holiday. He glanced around. Other guests were already tucking into their breakfasts and the smell of the Spanish coffee was like heaven.

Muy tipico, he thought looking around the dining room. Dark beams, white stucco walls sparsely decorated with thick white plates in colourful designs and rusted black iron implements that had seen better days in some farmer's hands. And dotted around the room, an explosion of bright fresh flowers jammed into hand-painted earthenware jardinières. *Si, muy tipico*. He could feel himself in love with Spain already.

And why not? It was in his blood. Tomorrow he intended to drive to Granada to look up his grandmother's house, the house where his mother had been born. His memory of his grandmother and that house was formed only by photos. Then he'd drive on to Seville to see a bull fight and watch some flamenco. As far as his money would stretch, that's how far he would go. He certainly didn't intend to spend this entire holiday lolling around any pool or beach. But it might be a good idea to pick up a traveling companion, preferably female - to share expenses. Good company and money saved.

Two tall blondes, Swedish or German? sat down at the table next to him. About nineteen or twenty, he decided. Just the right age. Perhaps if he chatted them up, the three of them could split the cost of a hired car. A Round Robin tour on the cheap. No sex, he was British. Half, anyway. He'd tell them that for a laugh. He sent a smile across to the one in the pink shirt. She averted her glance. Generally, he rated better than that. He tried the direct approach. 'Where are you girls from?'

'Holland,' said the one in pink, returning her eyes to the menu. Oh well. There was always the brunette. He'd think of a better opening line.

'Buenos Dias, Señor Alverez.' It was the waiter coming up to take his order. 'Mucho calor, hoy.'

Why was it every Spaniard had to say how hot it was today, when every day in Spain was hot! He glared at the man with some annoyance. 'Burkett's the name. Churros, cafe, y zumo de naranja, por favor.' His accent sounded so good to his own ears that he surprised even himself. Maybe that was why they were confusing him with this Alverez fellow.

The topless brunette was in the pool when he came outside. She rose up out of the water like a sea nymph clinging to the edge. Her black hair was slicked back revealing a high forehead above pale blue eyes and she was a burnished bronze sculpture. He caught his breath. She was really something. And she returned his smile, which was more than the two 'Goudas' inside had done.

'Great place, eh? Your first trip to Spain?'

She nodded. 'Been here one week already. Got three more days.'

'I'm down from London. You on your own?'

'With a girlfriend, actually. She's gone sick on me, though. A touch of the Don Quixote's Revenge, I'm afraid. I think she swallowed a windmill.'

He laughed, then plunged in. 'You unattached, then?'

She nodded 'The way I like it. And you?'

'Snap,' he said. 'The answer to a single maiden's prayer.' She actually smiled and he came over to dangle his feet in the water beside her, trying to keep his focus above her shoulder line.

By the time he got around to asking her to join him for dinner since her friend was ill, the Dutch girls had made an appearance at the far side of the pool. From time to time, they glared across at him disapprovingly as though he were some sort of dirty old man. He ignored them, devoting his full attention now to the brunette. He broached the idea of sharing a car, including her sick friend, of course. 'To do a bit of touring. Granada. Seville. Cordoba. Jerez, maybe. Test out the sherry. That's where it's from, you know.'

'I'll have to ask Emily,' she said. But her smile was almost a yes.

A small, stocky man was heading towards them from the hotel lobby. He was dressed inappropriately in a black business suit and tie and wore a determined smile. 'Who is he?' Michael whispered to Andrea; for by that time he'd found out the brunette's name.

'That's the Manager, Señor Lazarza. You must have met him last night. He shakes everybody's hand like he's milking a cow. My girl friend and I call him 'The Greater Greeter'.'

'Ah, Señor, Buenos Dias. It is a shame you had the trouble on the road last night. The garage will bring your car by noon today. They say it is not too serious. But it must have given you a nasty bump. One cannot be too careful on La Carretera de la Muerte.' He looked at Andrea, adding in English, 'the Highway of Death.' He turned back to the man. 'It is good to have you back again with us. So nice to see old friends return, eh?' Lazarza extended his hand for a thumping pump.

'Return?' Michael asked, with some annoyance. 'No, no, I've never been here before. You're confusing me with someone else. In fact, it's been happening all morning.'

'But how could I forget such a fine old customer of twenty years, Señor Alverez? For when you come with your wife from Seville, always we give you and Señora Alverez the same room. One hundred and twenty four. Our bridal suite, as you request, with the view of the pool.'

'But I'm traveling alone, as you can see.'

'Si, this is the first time you come alone. And maybe that is why you do not pay so much attention to the highway. Which we all must remember is muy peligroso.' He smiled cheerfully. 'Let me know if everything is to your liking, Señor.'

Andrea got up, walking to a table nearby where she sat down glaring across at him. He turned back to the Manager. 'Everyone seems to be mixing me up with this Alverez fellow,' Michael protested He was beginning to feel peculiar. 'My name is Michael Burkett. I'm from London, Patron. I assure you I have never been to Seville or to this hotel before. In fact, this is my first trip to Spain since I was a child.'

Señor Lazarza glanced past him to the lithe brunette. He had not been in the hotel business for twenty years without understanding such things. And since the end of Franco, morals were more relaxed every year. 'Of course, Señor, you have not been here. Certainly. And my regards to the Señora.'

Michael caught the salacious glint in the man's eye. 'What time is checkout? I may leave tomorrow,' he said threateningly.

'Twelve o'clock as always, Señor Alverez. But we have reserved your room for the usual ten days as you requested.' He looked at him closely. 'You look quite recovered today. Last night I feared we would need the doctor.' Lazarza bowed with slight archness and retreated into the building.

Michael glanced towards Andrea. 'This is a mistake, believe me. I didn't come by car. I flew.'

'Well, all I can say is you certainly speak perfect Spanish for a single male from London,' Andrea dove back into the pool. Which was when Michael realised that his whole conversation with Lazarza had been conducted in Spanish, and he hadn't even been aware of it. He really had to hand it to that language school. The instructor had told him that in a few days he'd be speaking like a native. But in a few hours…? Fantastic!

Andrea popped up again. 'And you can forget about dinner. I may not speak very much Spanish, but I know what the word Señora means. I draw the line at married men.'

He got up and came over to the edge of the pool. 'Look, I'm not married. I'm from London and this whole thing is simply a case of mistaken identity.' He headed back to the lobby. 'I'm going to find out what this is all about right now!'

'Your key, Señor Alverez.' The desk clerk handed it to him. He stared at the number. 124.

How stupid not to have thought of it before. 'Look here,' he said. 'I signed the register last night, didn't I?' He spun the leather book around and looked for the entry. But he found no Burkett. Then he saw the name beside the room number 124. A name in neat handwriting that looked very much like his own: José Alverez, Seville. Beads of perspiration made his forehead prickle. He felt a sudden disconnect with time and place and a hollowness in the belly.

'And Señor Alverez, there is a letter just came for you.' The clerk drew it from his box and placed it in front of him. It was stamped URGENTE and addressed: Sr. José Alverez, c/o El Sol Del Mar, Quarto 124, Fuengirola, Province de Malaga.

He ripped it open with trembling hands. It was in a woman's hand and written in Spanish:

My own dear Pepé,

Our quarrel has diminished my life. I cannot forgive myself. This is the last time I will ever tell you to go to our special place without me. I love you still and will be there as soon as I can get there. Keep the bed warm in our honeymoon room. Forgive me.

Your loving wife,

Constancia.

Michael's stomach churned. He turned and bolted up the stairs two at a time. His hand shook so much that he had difficulty turning the key in the lock. He relocked the door behind him and leaned back against it. He had to think. Think! What was happening to him?

Somebody must be setting him up. For something! But who - and why? It made no sense. He didn't earn enough at the bank to warrant any intricate plot, no matter how incomprehensible. Was he becoming paranoid or just going crackers?

No, no. It must be some sort of joke. Certainly, that made sense. A joke arranged by the blokes at the bank. Envious of his trip, maybe. Thought they'd have a laugh at his expense. They could have rigged it up with Sally at the Travel Agency. Several of the fellows used that office. His head felt light, sort of buzzing. His heart was pounding so loud he could hear the blood rushing in his ears. Then suddenly he was afraid.

But what on earth of? Well he didn't have to put up with it, did he, whatever it was? He'd pack his bags and get the hell out. He could feel himself trembling as he opened the wardrobe cupboard, and pulled out the suitcase.

He flipped it over on its side and stared at two gold initials stamped into the leather strap: J. A. The suitcase was new and brown, and he had never seen it before in his life.

⌘

José Alverez finished folding the last garment into the new brown suitcase Constancia had bought him for his birthday. She'd even gone to the trouble of having his initials emblazoned in gold on the leather strap. Perhaps a bit ostentatious, but beautiful, nonetheless. So was he to believe that she had stopped loving him? The evidence was against it.

José did not know whether to feel anger or despair. What had happened—was happening, was not of his doing. Of that, he felt certain. No, this was entirely Constancia's fault. Hers alone.

But then, who was it said that it took two to make a quarrel? Just like it took two to make love. This certainly was the worst quarrel of their marriage, just as he had thought only a few nights ago they'd shared the best night of their love. The boat that was rocking their world was foundering uncertainly and he felt adrift. Would it be able to re-float itself so that their lives could sail on together? José felt he was drowning.

He crossed to the window staring out past the rejas. Perhaps he had never offered Constancia enough of the worldly side of life. Their house in Seville could be best described as modest and was hardly in the nicest district. But certainly, it was pleasant enough. Their wants had always been simple, and happiness was not to be measured in spare bedrooms and fancy tiled kitchens, after all.

He glanced across his fence at Señora Martinez's laundry drying in the bright afternoon breeze, riveted by the size of her braggas. Señora Martinez was a big woman, certainly. Bigger every year, it seemed. Constancia was still beautiful, even in her forties. She was a small eater, and watched her figure carefully. He could remember Señora Martinez's slim shape when they first moved next door. He peered down at his own belly. Perhaps he had spread three or four inches. But it suited a married man. Everyone said so.

He sighed and went back to his packing. A burden Constancia would normally have overseen. 'Did you pack extra socks, Pepé?' she would call him her pet name. 'And Pepé, my sweet, you must take three pairs of swimming trunks. It is no good to sit around in a wet suit,' she would say, always caring for his wellbeing. This is what made it so hard for him to understand.

For twenty years he had lived in this house with Constancia. They had been so very happy until this senseless quarrel on the eve of their annual holiday. On the eve of their anniversary. Tomorrow, the 11th of April would be twenty years. He was sad that there were no children to resonate their happiness. But they had always been an ideal couple, everyone said so. Until this terrible fight, and how had it all started? He could hardly remember. What had it all been about anyway? Time they had a breather from each other, she had told him the night of the argument. Maybe he would learn to appreciate her more.

He paused in his packing, a terrible thought crossing his mind. One he had never imagined possible until this very moment. Maybe she had a lover! How could he be sure? Had he been living in a fool's paradise? He could not help but notice how the men from his office stopped to chat with Constancia when they met her with him.

A lover? Why not? Could he ever forget how Constancia had looked that day on his first visit to Seville? Her long black hair pulled neatly into a soft pony tail at the back. A crisp white blouse with a lace collar fitting tightly over swelling breasts. A smooth black skirt that curved over slender hips. Black stockings on perfect legs and a wide, shiny black belt that accented a waist two hands could almost span. And most important of all, large innocent dark eyes and a smile that lit up the room. He had fallen in love with her like in a fairy tale, at first sight. A coup de foudre! When he was still so confused in his mind about everything else in his life, he had never had one moment of doubt about that feeling. About Constancia, he was certain from that first moment.

José sank down on the edge of his bed, recalling those terrible days after the accident so many years ago. Over twenty years and still he could not remember anything before that crash. When he'd regained consciousness in the hospital, they told him he had been there for several months. Months! Even now, he could not imagine it. They told him how lucky he was, because the Englishman who had been sharing the taxi had died in the accident, trapped inside the burning car. José had been dragged free by the driver. He could thank that man for saving his life. Could, and did.

Apparently he'd been on a trip from Madrid to Fuengirola. He could not remember anything about Madrid. But that was not so strange since he could not remember anything at all, really.

They returned his papers and passport, what was left of them. His photo had been burned to a crisp just like that poor Englishman's.

When he came out of hospital José thought about what to do. The concussion had been touch and go, but the burns had been superficial and there wasn't much scarring. Only the upper lip, and if he grew a moustache, it would cover it. But for some reason he himself could not explain, he could not bring himself to return to Madrid. The hospital had written on his behalf to the company for whom he worked, and to the building where he rented a flat. The letters came back saying he had no family there. As far as he could tell, he had none anywhere. There was no one to come for him. And no one to return to.

He knew he had been right to make a clean break. To start a new life, a man with no memory and no ties to the past. That day in Fuengirola, his decision to go to Seville had led him to finding Constantia. She worked in an Insurance office. And since José seemed to speak excellent English, he was able to get a job with her firm. The funny thing was his Spanish seemed more than a bit rusty. But the doctor told him not to be too concerned. Loss of memory after an accident played funny tricks and was highly selective. Some people forgot how to count or to read. His language would return.

And it did, very soon.

Constancia and he went together for almost two years before she agreed to marry him. She hesitated, as though she was expecting someone to turn up from his past. Someone or something.

And now she was not speaking to him. He was going alone to the place they had until now, reserved for anniversaries. The El Sol Del Mar. Where they had spent their honeymoon.

'Go by yourself, José,' she had told him and she never called him José unless she was angry at him. It was always Pepé. 'I am going to Madrid on a shopping spree. I want some time to myself to think without you telling me what to do every minute.' And she had left that morning early to catch the plane. Was she traveling alone, he wondered? Was that what this was all about? He snapped the bag shut and picked it up, wondering if that tall, good looking Pedro from her department might be joining her in Madrid—to help her think.

José Alverez hefted his new brown initialled suitcase and headed out. Since Constancia had taken the morning plane, there was no reason for him not to take the car. It was about a six hour drive and he still had an early start. Not too much traffic until he hit Malaga, and then only thirty minutes more to Fuengirola. The worst highway in Spain, they called it. La Carretera de la Muerte. Yes, he would have to drive carefully. On the Costa del Sol they drove like maniacs, wine in their bellies, and sand in their brains.

⌘

Michael Burkett's eyes travelled from the water tap in the bathroom sink up to the mirror. The water glass dropped from his hand, splintering into shards on the tiled floor but he paid it no notice because from the mirror, a stranger stared out at him. A man's face reflected eye to eye. But not his face!

Not exactly...Yet something about it was.

Who was this impostor, posing as himself? This man who resembled him just slightly? This much older man, with a thick black moustache and a brindle stubble of beard. And greying hair... with hairline receding where Michael's certainly was not. And look at those crow's feet around the eyes! You couldn't acquire those in just twenty five years of living, could you?

Why hadn't he looked in the mirror when he woke up? He'd been in too much of a hurry to join the world. His hand crept to his face. One finger ran along the line of his moustache. Beneath it, he could feel the pressure on his upper lip of a deep scar. A scar he never had.

All he could do was stare in disbelief at this stranger in the mirror. It was as though someone had cast a spell over him. There were no answers—and a woman claiming to be his wife was about to descend on him. Some woman called Constancia.

He returned to the bedroom and opened the brown suitcase. In it was a Spanish passport. Where was his British one? He flipped it open to stare at this same older face something like him, but certainly not him.

And this woman on her way to join him; who could pounce on him at any minute claiming him to some life not his own! What could he do about her?

Only one thing. Get out. Fast. Get himself back on the plane to London. Everything would sort itself out there. The plane. Where the hell was his airline ticket? He rummaged through the suitcase and through the dresser drawers. Surely he must have a ticket!.

He sat down on the edge of the bed. No... not if he came from Seville. Then there would be no ticket for a plane. On the bureau were a set of keys and documents for a Spanish-made 1992 Renault. 1992...? Impossible. That would place him twenty years into the future. . !

His mind fought to concentrate. He must think! Think. . ! The car. Yes, start with that. Could this be the car the manager said was being repaired? And if so, then it was his!

He rummaged through the wallet. It contained strange Spanish money with 'Euros' written on it. He wasn't sure how far that would take him, but enough to get to London, surely. He rammed his possessions, if they were his, into the brown suitcase. He would get in that car and drive to the airport. He would think of something on the way.

As he approached the door he stepped on a newspaper that had been slipped under it. Michael Burkett picked it up. The date glared from the corner: 11, Avril, 1993. His body felt like ice.

It was true! Somehow, somewhere he had lost over twenty years. What now could there be for him in London? For him anywhere?

There was a knock on the door and a woman's voice called through it in Spanish: 'Pepé, are you there? I looked for you by the pool.'

He dropped the suitcase, frozen to the spot. What could he do? Where could he escape to? She knocked again. He had to do something.

'Pepé, open the door.'

His hand touched the knob, heart pounding. He opened it to see her standing there smiling at him. He could not remember ever seeing her before, yet there was something attractive, something reassuring, vaguely familiar about her. She threw her arms around him and kissed him and her lips felt warm and sensual.

'Pepé, my own true love,' She breathed, drawing him with her into the room and down onto the bed. She paused, uncertainly. 'What is it, my darling? You seem so...so different. Are you all right?' Not knowing what to say to her, he said nothing.

He did not instigate it, she did. He eased his conscience with that thought afterwards when he found himself making love to this strange woman. Making love instead of talking. It gave him time to think.

Afterwards they lay side by side in the white bed and he put his thoughts together. Should he tell her the truth? No, not yet. This was not the time. He would pretend that everything was as...as she knew it. He would step into this strange life of *now*, the life about which he knew absolutely nothing. Life with this older woman who was actually younger than he. But what other choice was there? He could less easily step back twenty years. He was like a blind man who has never seen, and then by the miracle of modern science is given the gift of sight. He had read that sometimes it was too much for such a person and he killed himself.

'Why are you so silent, my own darling Pepé? Have you not forgiven your little Constancia?' she said, kissing his neck. He returned the kiss but did not reply. Maybe his memory would come back.

But what if it didn't...?

⌘

17: THE ROAD

'So what do you think happened to the man, Pepé. Who was he?' Jeff asked Jean over coffee and toast the morning after their story had been accepted by a magazine and they couldn't now do a rewrite even if they wanted to.

'That's for the readers to decide, Jeff. They need to do a little of the work,' Jean smiled. 'Besides, my mind's moved on to other things.'

'Like what?' he asked, knowing he wasn't going to like the answer.

'Like what we need.'

'What would that be, Jean?'

'A road.'

He sighed. 'Jean, you left plenty of room on the village side of the hedge for the villagers to walk or even drive a car, if they had one, which they don't. And an entrance for us to come up the hill to the house,' Jeff said, getting up from the table and picking up his guitar. He always strummed it in times of stress, which was what Jean was laying on him at the moment.

He was in no mood for a discussion of property development, having decided that now he'd got this far with a comfortable bed to sleep in and a mended roof over his head, he could contentedly ignore the waterless pipes and exploding stove and iceless fridge and would willingly let the place crumble slowly around him. It was an attitude he knew would not get to first base with Jean, who had a different concept of comfort.

'It's true what you say, Jeff. But now that the rains have finally started, this hill is Mud City. Some days we can't even get down with our car—as you yourself pointed out only yesterday.' She glanced past the arches holding up the newly built terrace roof, towards the field, still soggy from yesterday's rain. Her glance stretched to the distant line of the sea, flickering silver sparks under the grey sky. 'And Munchkin came back from her last hunting expedition with a field mouse in her teeth, mud boots on her paws, and looking more like drowned rat than cat,' she added.

'Jean, if we built a road, Munchkin wouldn't walk on it. And even if she did, I don't think we should aid her in her hunting expeditions. Not that she needs our help. I haven't seen a live mouse since we moved in. Plenty of half chewed ones, yes. But no live mice.'

It wasn't much of a counter attack and Jeff had to admit to himself, Jean was right about the mud. If they tried to get down to the local tienda to stock up on bread and milk or something, they were plodding in the thick of it, all the way up to the ankles.

'Plus,' she went on, ignoring his remarks as he knew she would. 'we should have the road in before we plant the orchard so that the tractors can use it to come up the hill.'

Jean always had a way of using logic against any illogical defence. Seeing that this was only the beginning of the discussion, he set down his guitar, stood up, looking towards the village and the Magic Mountain looming over them all. 'Besides,' he said, 'even if we had the cash to put in our own private driveway, the tractor would still have to travel up the entire side of the village and there's no way you could ever get San Pedro to build a road to a village as tiny as El Salto. Besides, nobody in El Salto's got a car anyway.'

'Miguel's brother-in-law does,' she countered triumphantly.

'Well, Luciano keeps it in a bedroom and doesn't drive it in the rain. And even if the village did build a public road, we still couldn't afford a private one. Do you have any idea what such a road would cost? Nearly as much as this house.'

'Mmm,' she said tentatively and flashed a mischievous blue glance his way. 'I wasn't thinking of paying for it, exactly.'

This was the sort of response from her that drove him around the bend. But he kept his cool. 'What did you have in mind, Jean? Sticking up a bank and saying, "I'll have all the roads in your cash box and make it snappy"? He picked up his guitar again because it helped him to think better, even though Jean said it helped him to avoid thinking which may have been the same thing. 'Okay, what have I missed?'

'I'm going to write a letter to the Alcalde.' Jean's face was grim with determination as she hurried inside to her computer.

'Who's he?' he called after her.

'The mayor.'

'El Salto del Agua does not have a mayor, Jean!' he shouted after her, testily.

'San Pedro does,' she shot back, cheerfully.

He shook his head in wonder. One thing he never did was to underestimate Jean. Nor once she was wound up, did he try to deter her from uncurling in her own design.

Jean's father had died three months earlier, and she'd remained in the States to help her mother settle her affairs. It was the longest they'd ever been separated since they'd met and Jeff chose to spend the time in London, where he felt somehow safer. They'd come down to Spain together only a week before, and things had finally returned to normal. Jean's mother promised to pay them a visit in Santa Rita very soon to see this marvel of a house for herself. But the loss was still keen for Jean and she cried easily. She busied herself with the problems of the living and wrote her mother extra long letters, which somehow made it easier.

Jean wrote the letter to the Alcalde in English and read it to Jeff. He had to agree it was a great letter and an even greater games plan. But having once met the Alcalde some months ago, they both knew he didn't speak a word of English.

'That's where Davie Davies comes in. I'm taking it to him to translate.'

'Into Welsh of Aussie?' he asked.

'How about Spanish?' she smiled.

They made several visits up the blue-tiled stairs and past Marge in a new sarong, this one mainly purple. The lanky Welshman greeted them with his normal 'Gu'day, Mate,' in faded blue jeans and matching shirt with red bandana around his throat. They had never seen him otherwise. Jean was welcomed with kisses, Jeff with handshakes. They were presented with cups of coffee from Marge and brandies from Davie, laced with a few bills to be paid for things they'd never heard of before. It was beginning to be the way of life in Spain.

'The Mayor wouldn't give Jean's letter the time of day', Davie assured them. And they shouldn't expect an answer. 'But you might as well have a lash, Mate. The idea's clever. Ingenious, in fact. Who thought it up?'

Jeff quickly deferred to Jean's scheming mind. Davie smiled at her with a shade of speculation. 'Who knows, Jean? As the Spanish always say, Todo es possible.' He kissed her goodbye rather too fondly for Jeff's taste, told them the letter would cost them only five thousand pesetas for his translation, and invited them for yet another swimming party at the latest mansion he was 'house sitting', and himself to come 'blow the froth off a couple' at Santa Rita the next day. 'To bring the letter, and see how the place is coming along.'

Davie showed up the following afternoon during the siesta with the translated letter which Jean later mailed (after discovering that the post office was not where one buys stamps in Spain. Stamps, are purchased at the tobacconist.)

Jeff actually asked Davie about his wife and Davie said they had an understanding. He went his way, and as long as she went the way he told her, he paid her maintenance in their old apartamento overlooking the sea near Estepona. She was working in a shop there and he didn't see much of her. 'But we're still good mates,' he assured them. 'Hell, I invite her to all the shindigs me and Marge put on.' It seemed that he and Marge had an understanding, too, which appeared to allow Marge to take care of him and left Davie free to play the field. They finally got rid of the Welshman about eight o'clock after they'd 'blown the froth' off all the beer in the fridge and there wasn't a potato crisp in sight.

But Davie was right. The Thwaites didn't get an answer from the Alcalde. Not directly, that is. What they got was more of a visitation than a visit a few days later led by Miguel's brother-in-law, Luciano, the spokesman for the village, the villager with the only car in El Salto that he kept in his bedroom. He organised all the fiestas and chose the under-twelve Queen for the Day,

This visit of Luciano's was 'official'. He did not hazard to drive his car up the fifty metres to the house, but strode up the hill in that macho way all Spanish villagers have that says: 'I'm really a bull fighter. You're just catching me on an off day.' Luciano was followed by Miguel whose macho walk, hampered by his growing belly, was more of a waddle. Miguel's colouring was like his mother's, blue-eyed and sandy-haired. He had one red-headed daughter with a nose-dusting of freckles. Most of the villagers were dark haired, so the Tinedo family stood out as not typically Andalusian.

Behind Miguel and his brother-in-law Luciano came a few men from the village (population: ninety eight, counting dogs, goats, and cats). Holding his worn straw hat in hand and straining at his belt, Miguel introduced the Thwaites to the committee of villagers, with a slightly worried expression. The men's sunburnt, work-creased faces were long and sombre. Nobody smiled. At Jeff's invitation, they sat out on the terrace. Luciano on the end of the bench, said that they had come about the Señora's letter to the Alcalde. Jean offered them cold beer and potato crisps, the accepted refreshment for such occasions, and wondered how the villagers knew about the letter. They had told no one in the village, especially Miguel.

Luciano's expression was grave and determined. 'What exactly is it you have asked of the Alcalde, Señora?' He was small, wiry and good looking with a thatch of black hair and an angularly cocky expression.

Detecting a note of disapproval in Luciano's unwavering gaze, Jean felt an unreasonable sense of panic. 'I have asked the Alcalde for a concrete road for the village. Coming from the main Ronda road.'

'Why…?' came Luciano's shrewd-eyed query. The others, beer cans clutched tightly, stopped crunching crisps, breaths baited, redolent with garlic.

'I have asked for a concrete road because a gravel road would be washed away in a few rainy seasons.'

'And where will they build this miraculous road, Señora?' There is no room in the village for such a road.'

Suddenly Jean saw the drift. The villagers were afraid the estranjeros intended to tear down some of their houses which were built exactly on the line of the Thwaites' land, not a centimetre to spare. And Jean remembered something Davie had told them. The land that the village houses was built on had been 'appropriated' by peasant farmers at least a hundred years ago. The houses were 'hand built' and showed it in their rustic charm. No doubt only recently arrived villagers held a proper deed to their plots and nobody knew what the Spanish government would one day decide.

Jeff too, caught the drift and hastily answered Luciano's question. 'We have told him that the Señora and I would *give* land from our field for this road.'

The villagers just stared. Jean added quickly, 'Give the land *free*, for this road for all to use.'

Luciano's black eyes flashed as he turned to the other men, a smile growing on his face at confirmation of what he had already heard though the grapevine, but could not believe. Who gave away land? The bombshell was defused. His glance swivelled back to Jeff and Jean. 'To give land. . . for a road to the village, this is. . .why, that is. . .' He was at a loss for words. 'Estupendo. Fantastico! Maravilloso, Señora, ¡que bien! What you propose is a most generous gift to the people of El Salto.'

Not wishing to sound like a saint, Jean added hastily, 'You must understand, Luciano. We do this for ourselves, too. As the saying goes, God helps those who. . .' She did not pursue that tack.

Jeff cut in. 'We have also asked for a road to be built from this village road to our house, which will service Señor Belnapp, too. And a separate road to the Grays across our field.' Jeff and Jean had talked it over and decided they were sufficiently indebted to the Grays for having steered them into buying Santa Rita, to give them a road, too. 'We have sent the Alcalde a map of where the new roads should go and asked for it in concrete,' Jean added.

Luciano nodded to the others. 'Las sospechas eran fundadas..." Their suspicions were founded. "So far - if it is as you say and no more, then it is a just request, Señora. A request of you to the Alcalde. Therefore the men of the village will go with you.'

She exchanged a quick look with Jeff. 'Go with us where?'

'To the meeting with the Alcalde, of course.'

'We haven't heard about any meeting, Luciano,' Jeff said. 'In fact, we haven't heard from the Alcalde.'

'Si,' Miguel put in. 'The meeting, it is at five o'clock this very afternoon. After the siesta.'

Jeff looked at his watch. It was already three thirty. 'But why didn't anybody tell us?'

Luciano nodded. 'I am telling you now, Señor. So! It is all arranged. Creo que obraste bien.'

The 'El Salto Mafia' knew everything. In fact, they had set up the meeting. Wondering which one of them the Alcalde was related to, Jeff phoned Davie and asked him to meet them at the Mayor's office.

'You caught me in the dunny with a bit of the Hidalgo's Revenge, but no worries, Mate,' Davie said. 'I'll be there.'

⌘

The men pressed together thickly in the crowded office awaiting the Alcalde. The older ones doffed their hats to Jeff and Jean and gave Davie and them chairs when they came in. Every male in El Salto turned up—but no women. The village was yet to be swept by the liberating broom of the San Pedro feminists, a mere one hundred kilometres down the Ronda road. Yet the village men did not think it odd that Jean lived in what they considered a man's world After all, the estranjeros could not be expected to know how to behave properly.

The moment the Alcalde entered the room, the villagers all began to shout at once. Luciano shouting the loudest, was the one voice to be singled out. Jeff and Jean hadn't a clue what was being said, it was all too fast, forceful, fervid, and fired up. The Alcalde listened, nodded, but said nothing. Somebody banged a chair on the floor in anger, and then somebody else took a swing at the man who was shouting and then everybody seemed to be punching each other. Luciano was standing on the chair and waving his fists for silence but nobody was listening. Davie dragged Jean and Jeff out of the room.

They went around to The Book Bar. The Boozer, Davie called it. It was a small library, lined with book and just room enough for a small bar and about 10 of the foreign population.

'What was all that screaming and fighting about?' Jeff asked.

'Streuth, nobody in Spain gives away land, not even for a road, Mate. They wanted the Mayor to accept your offer,' Davie told them.

'So what did he say?'

'The Mayor? You didn't hear a word out o' that old pelican, now did you?'

Jeff shook his head.

'No.' Jean sadly added.

'That's Spain, for you. Nice try anyway,' Davie said. 'But you can forget it now. It'll never happen, Sunshine.'

And it certainly seemed that Davie was right. The mayor never did answer the letter or make any official comment on the meeting. And no more was heard about the road in the next month before Jeff and Jean had to return to London for a new television assignment.

⌘

Three months later when they came back, they had forgotten all about their request. Until their airport taxi from Malaga turned off the main Ronda road and headed up into El Salto. For some reason, the taxi was not riding across the middle of the hill and bumping over rocks. Jeff stuck his head out the window to discover they were riding on a newly gravelled village road, a road in the last throes of being completed. The taxi trailed along it, up the hill between the edge of the village and the row of cypresses, now about five feet tall. It followed exactly Jean's proposed map. The driver turned sharply left between the opening in the trees where Jean hoped one day to put a gate and headed up towards the house ON A NEW PRIVATE DRIVEWAY!!!

Jeff couldn't believe his eyes. 'Jean. . . your road! You've done it! We've actually got one all the way to 'Santa Rita! I can't believe it!'

She put on a calm face as though this miracle of a thoroughfare was the most believable occurrence in the world and doesn't it happen all the time? But she could hardly trust herself to speak, gulping back a frog in her throat and tears. 'Mmmn,' was all she could say.

The road builders were actually there at the top of the hill, working on the parking area as they drove up. At sight of them, Jean's excited squeals suddenly escaped. She tumbled out of the taxi as an eager Munchkin appearing out of nowhere, bouncing over her shoes, nearly tripping her. Jean tried to introduce herself to the road builders, all Spanish words fleeing from mind. Before Jeff could stop her, she was showing them in half sign language exactly how she wanted the parking area to extend to the entrance of their garage and to Belnapp's gate, and the road builders were smiling at her enthusiasm and nodding agreement.

Jeff came over and nudged her, whispering. 'Jesus perro, Jean! Don't press your luck.'

'Flickering pheromones, Jeff! Do you realise we could park twenty cars here?' she whispered back and picked up her suitcase, heading into the house, Munchkin after her.

'We haven't got twenty cars,' he called.

Her face lit up with that determination so familiar to him. 'I've got to write another letter quick, Jeff,' she said over her shoulder. 'I hope the computer's working.'

'Another letter? What about?' he yelled.

'The road. They haven't made it of concrete.'

Jean's second letter was duly sent to the Alcalde. This time there was no delegation, no meeting, and again no reply. They were assured by Davie, the translator, that it was a marvel that there was a road in gravel. 'Hey, you shouldn't complain if they made it out of eggshells. If you'd 'ave made me a bet, you'd 'ave won a lot of money off me, Jean. I didn't think you had a hope in hell with that road.'

'Want to bet I get it in concrete?' she asked with a wicked grin.

'Don't like to take money from a lady, Jean. But you're on.'

'Ten thousand pesetas, Davie. Put your money where your mouth is.'

And four months later, when they next returned from London, they found the concrete road nearly finished and the villagers already the proud owners of cars, cars, cars! Not a single mule in sight. Davie paid his debt and the Thwaites took him and Marge out to dinner.

Jean looked down towards the village from their terrace, seeing four cars parked on the new road.

'No more donkeys. Do you think I did the right thing?' she asked sadly, seeing how the face of El Salto was changing.

'Time is on the side of the future, my love,' Jeff said and strummed his guitar.

⌘

The plaintive notes of an accordion drifted across to Jeff and Jean through the fragrant summer evening from the village of El Salto del Agua, meaning 'The Jump of the Water', meaning waterfall. And indeed the village had one. It gushed down into a large pool at the bottom of the village. When Jeff and Jean had first arrived, it had been the ideal place for the villagers to throw their refuse as long as you didn't mind the smell. Later, after the road was built, they paved the bit of land fronting the pond and turned it into something akin to a plaza. Then some energetic village council converted the sump hole into a duck pond and encircled it with a high wire fence so nobody could throw their basura in it anymore.

One industrious villager immediately opened a restaurant and named it 'Y Todo La Pesca' which meant "And all that fish." 'Y. T. L. P.' was right across the plaza from the pond and Paco the owner, tended the ducks with loving care hoping to attract tourists from San Pedro.

It worked. Strangers began to drive up to see this local beauty spot and have lunch. Their cars clogged the square but Paco didn't care. He set out tables facing the ducks and saw to it that the loaves always provided enough crusts for a toss across the fence to a quacking beak. Paco's fish was always fresh and tasty and on a winter's day, inside the hollow cement room with its tile floor the juke box echoed with a deafening blare.

Soon another bar opened next to it called 'El Pescozon', which had nothing to do with fish and really meant 'A cuff around the scruff of the neck'. There was even talk of a kiosk in the square for candy and cigarettes. But more of that later.

The villagers were going into business. And it was all because of the road. Next, houses began to expand as much as they were able; these houses hand-built, room by room, as sufficient cement blocks were acquired for expansion. and if there was not enough land, bedrooms became partly garages to accommodate the sleeping cars. After all, Jeff noted, it was not long since their goats and even donkeys shared bed room in the house. Now, the donkeys had disappeared, and cars suddenly lined the curb of the new narrow pink and white tiled pavement all the way up to the entrance to the Thwaites' finca. The Traffic Control Department arrived and painted red 'no parking' lines which was a joke. The villagers parked anywhere. They even began driving into the Thwaites' private driveway and parking half way up to their house. Jean went down to the papeleria and bought a NO PARKING sign to put up. And one that said Camino Privado.

That was when a bus as big as a London double-decker appeared and began to make the four minute run every half hour to their village from San Pedro.

A bus? The villagers had always walked everywhere. Now they were driving in their shiny new (somebody else's old) cars or taking a bus! It was, far too large for the road and it chugged up the hill on the newly laid cement, generally bearing one lone passenger to the end of the line. . .which appeared to be the entrance to the Thwaites' finca. There it paused while the driver chatted up any women who happened to be hanging about without their husbands. If the Thwaites happened to drive up at that moment, they couldn't enter their driveway.

Then one day they saw that three growing cypress trees at the bus turnabout had been knocked down. Their green fence was nearing six feet tall now and filling out nicely. It didn't take Philip Marlowe to deduce that the bus had done in the trees. Several days later it happened again. All in all, they counted twelve trees mangled by the bus and they still hadn't managed to catch the bus driver at it.

Jean was near tears. 'Let's go down there, Jeff, and wait for him. If we have to wait all day. Face him with his crime.'

We can't just stand in the field, Jean. It won't look right to the villagers.'

'Who said stand? The trees need watering, don't they? We'll go down with Munchkin and water them.'

She talked Jeff into it against his better judgment. They dragged the hose down the hill and began watering. Always good for a laugh from the villagers. The goat lady saw Jean trying to tie up three trees knocked down by the bus. She hurried over to lend a hand, holding a tree upright to be tied, and offering advice on the correct knot to use, her face old as time, and her toothless grin a wonder of warmth and kindness. Jeff held the hose to feed a little water into the dry earth around it.

The old man with the cap, whose job it now was to sweep the street, came by. 'Tying up the trees?' he divined. "It is the bus.' Up chugged the bus. "The Assassin of the Twelve" stopped right next to the place where he had thrice decimated their cypresses. Jean waved at him, but her expression was stern. He waved back, a wide grin on his swarthy face. He had dark curly hair, wore his sleeves rolled up almost to the shoulder, and looked like a prize fighter. 'I see you are watering,' he called over. When Jeff nodded, the driver cut his motor. The bus slipped slightly, edging towards a section of trees still upright. 'Your trees are dry!,' he announced. 'They need water.'

That's why we are watering them,' Jean downed hose and came over to the open bus door, Jeff beside her, to speak to the only living Spaniard who thought that trees required water.

'You have killed our trees,' she said. 'With your bus. Water will not save them.' He shrugged, the picture of innocence.

'Your bus is too big to turn around here. Why don't you get a smaller bus?' Jeff asked.

It is not up to me. I drive what they tell me, Señor'.

'But you hardly ever have any passengers. A smaller bus would make more sense and take less petrol.'

It is too expensive, a smaller bus.' he said, then smiled amiably starting his bus again, with no trace of guilt as he brushed his bumper against the three trees still right side up. 'You should water your trees, Señor.'

On the back of his bus was painted a picture of Groucho Marx, with a hat made out of two loaves of bread and puffing a long cigar. There was a balloon for a quote, but nothing had ever been written in it. If there had been, he would probably be saying, "Watering the trees?"

'There's only one thing to do,' Jeff told her that night.

'Blow up the bus?' Jean cried.

'Give them more land.'

'Have you gone mad, Jeff?'

'I was mad enough to marry you, my love,' he said and kissed her. 'More land for a turnabout and plant the trees further back, so the bus won't knock them down. And then we'll put up that gate you've been saying you wanted.'

Her eyes brightened. 'The gate...?'

'I've been talking to Davie. He knows a guy who can get us a cut rate on wire fencing. If we put the gate and fence only on the village side and down along the irrigation canal, it shouldn't cost so much and maybe it'll keep down the traffic a bit.

This time Jeff and Jean paid a call on Luciano, the village 'maven'. They told him their proposal. The only thing they asked was to make an attractive bus stop with a tree and a pretty bench for the village.

They didn't have to wait long. Three days later, the road builders appeared and built the bus stop. It was a vast improvement and the vivero came up and replaced the victim trees. Jeff and Jean went down to the ferreteria to order the gate. Davie gave them instructions. 'You know where my office is? Well it's two streets above it but you can't enter because it's one way but if you go three streets beyond you can come to a turn and go left then right and then when you run out of road drive onto the field straight ahead of you. That's where he is. His name's Paco.'

'Another one?' Jeff asked. Despite Davie's instructions, they found it. They often wondered what Davie would do if he ever really got stranded in the Outback. He'd really learn the meaning of the word 'Walkabout'.

The ferretero drew them many designs. The gate had to be wide enough for the tractor. They picked an arced number with long spokes up each door. It was his least expensive design and still cost a lot more then they'd expected. Then they ordered the fence. It was so expensive they decided to erect it only on the village side of the field. They were running out of money.

'It's like pouring it straight down the drain. It just disappears, Jean. We've got to remember we're only a couple of writers and this is not the Alhambra.'

'I know Jeff, but it's all for a good cause and if we ever want to sell the place it'll be worth so much more.'

'Hmmm...', Jeff had heard that song before and he knew they'd never want to sell Santa Rita as long as they lived, they both loved it too much.

The next day their attention was temporarily distracted by a story screaming to be written and after all, the rains were falling and their feet were not muddy and Munchkin was walking on the paved road. The last time they'd driven south from the ferry boat at Santander, they had spotted a man hiking alone in the hills. When they stopped for lunch further down the road at a quaintly curious wayside inn, the walking man came in and sat down at a table across from them. Jean was fascinated by his pale grey eyes and the stillness of his deadly glance. He became the prime topic of discussion all the way back to Santa Rita, which took them about a week. By which time, they knew who the walking man was and what he was doing walking alone in northern Spain.

⌘

18: THE WALKING MAN

He'd taken the bus from Santander as far as Potes. Travelled with only one pair of jeans. In his rucksack he carried a spare tee shirt, two pairs of thick socks, extra hiking boots. He carried a light game rifle, too.

He'd been climbing steadily for about two hours before he paused for a drink, hefting his canteen to thin parched lips. Below him, in the velvet October light, the hillside was gently traced by stone-bound, terraced fields, speckled with sheep; like a field of roving golf balls on a putting green. Beneath his feet, wild crocus and heather hazed the rocky meadow with lavender. Higher up, round stone pustules festered in the face of the lava mountain. Wrinkles of snow creased the brow's ridge. The slopes were veined with dark cords of iron ore, like a dowager's legs. Already, waterfalls and river beds sucked new life from the snow. He could see all the way to where the road above wound in tight hairpin turns, snaking up to the top of the divide—up perhaps six thousand feet. And in the still air, he was suddenly certain he could hear the faint echo of Spanish music drifting up from somewhere below. Somewhere ahead.

The sun was high and moving west when he spotted the tiled roof far below. The low slung structure clung steadfastly to the side of the hill above the narrow zigzag of road leading down into the craggy river valley. No more than a donkey track that had been paved—and that, certainly too long ago.

Lazy smoke drifted from the thick chimney. The walking man always carried bread and cheese, a tin of paté sometimes, apples always, chocolate, and a small bottle of brandy. But whenever the opportunity arose, he liked to stop for a proper meal. A few hundred feet nearer and he saw the sign: 'SANTA TERESA DE LA LIEBANA. CAMAS - COMIDAS'. Beds and food. Two cars were parked on the verge. He made his way around a gravel walk to the entrance in the back, past tomato plants tied up to sticks and ringed by old rubber tires; a neat border of an enthusiastic vegetable garden. He recognized beans, onions, radishes, and lettuces. The blackberry bushes had lost the last of their fruit. Above them, apple trees were ripe for picking. He counted four goats, two dozen chickens. The menu would be fresh enough.

The woman's almond eyes looked back at him from a face bronzed by other suns. Her straight black hair hung down in a long braid, thickly plaited with strands of colored wool. She had strong, flat features, full, wide lips; her figure was solid and large breasted. She walked heavily with the resigned step of one used to hard work; but when she smiled, the walking man found beauty in her face.

There were only five tables in the room. She moved between them carrying trays of food to the hungry mountain climbers, hunters, and one old Basque in a black beret who sat alone in a corner. A local man, certainly, by his proprietorial manner. The walking man seated himself at an empty table.

The walls were rough-hewn slate; mountain stone gutted from the surrounding cliffs maybe fifty years ago or more. Thick oak slabs linteled the windows and the ceiling was darkly beamed. It was an atmosphere of rustic beauty. There wasn't any menu; she simply brought what she had cooked, the same for everyone. A thick, spicy soup of beans and ham, its seasonings not too subtle. Only white pepper on the table in this part of Spain. He ate slowly, glancing across at the Basque, who seemed to be staring at him.

After the soup came rabbit stew. When he'd finished that, she brought flan, then apples and cheese. By now everyone had left except for the old Basque, who sipped strong black coffee from a pressed glass cup and smoked a twisted black cigar. . . a calinquño. He smoked it, stuck upright into the bowl of a curved pipe. His sharp eyes had scarcely left the walking man's face throughout the meal.

The old man finally spoke in Spanish, thickly accented with Basque. 'Where is it that you go, Señor?'

'Walking,' the man replied.

The man leaned forward on his elbows, puffing at his calinquño. 'For some, these mountains offer danger. Strange fevers get in the blood and creep into the mind.' His eyes seemed to be trying to penetrate some mystery just beyond his grasp. 'Keep walking,' he said finally. 'For some, it is not healthy to stop too long in these mountains.' With that he rose, going over to the woman behind her counter. She rang up his bill on an old steel and brass till. He paid and shuffled out with a sidelong glance at the walking man.

She came over to the walking man's table. 'Your flan. You do not want it?' she asked in English with a warm smile that showed large, uneven teeth. He could see she had no objection to company.

'You run this place alone?' he asked, moving the flan closer in front of him.

She nodded, eyes sad. 'I am the cook, waitress, dishwasher, and cashier.'

'And the owner,' he said, spooning flan into his mouth as she stood beside him, gazing absently at his rifle. 'It's beautiful here,' he said finally.

She nodded. 'If you are a hunter, then you will find game.' She pointed to the wall behind him.

He turned to face a boar's head with menacing tusks. Past it, he noticed a collection of artefacts: A round, wooden carving of an Inca warrior, an oversized macheté, its sheath decorated with strands of colored wool. Gigantic wooden salad servers, their handles carved with Aztec Gods.

'My husband travelled from this place, far away. Far away to Guatemala. That is where he found me and he brought me here, to his home.'

'Where is he?' the man asked.

'Killed. Last year, while hunting that boar. There is always so much to do here. It was much easier, when he was alive. We worked together. He did all the cooking.' Again her eyes were sad.

'It must be lonely for you then. And hard.' In contrast to hers, the walking man's eyes were pale, almost colourless. They seemed to need the light of his surroundings to give them life. Pale blond hair glistened wanly in the thin slant of sunlight from the deep-set narrow windows. His lean features were soft, unlined.

The woman sensed an emptiness. A need. Perhaps, she thought, this man was as lonely as she? She stood for a moment silent, then asked finally, 'Where are you from?'

He shrugged. 'From everywhere. I never stay in one place long.'

'You are not English?'

'American...'

'This place is hard,' she sighed. 'In the snow time, I see no one. The road can be closed for months. The nearest neighbor is ten kilometres away. It is hard to find someone to come so far; someone to help out. Now, it is the roof that needs repair before the winter snows. A hard life...' She picked up his plate and moved behind the small counter fronting the kitchen.

'Maybe I could fix it. Your roof.' His words made her turn to look at him more closely.

Three hours later, the walking man came into her kitchen. 'It's done,' he told her, beginning to scrub his hands at the sink. She handed him a towel, noticing that his hands were fine, and well kept. Not the hands of a working man. Then she returned to her work, cutting up a large side of meat on a chopping board.

'What will you cook?' he asked.

'A stew of lamb. Sometimes there are six, maybe ten people in the evening.'

That's no way to cut meat,' he said quietly. 'You're cutting it with the grain. That way, it will be tough.'

'It is the meat here in Spain,' she complained. 'We do not get good meat.'

'Don't blame the meat. Blame the butcher. Everything depends on how it's cut. How it's hung. How it is aged. Any meat can be succulent, when you know what to do with it.' He took the butcher knife from her, and began to cut. His hands moved gracefully, deftly separating carcass from gristle and bone.

'Where did you learn to do that?' she asked.

'In a butcher shop,' he told her. 'In France. Then, for a time, I was a chef. In Morocco.' He smiled. 'I told you, I never stay in one place long.'

She looked at him wistfully. 'You could stay here. For a while. I could use help. There is much to do before the snow closes the pass.'

The walking man stopped walking for a while.

Soon, he had taken over management of the kitchen. Before the snows set in, several times he drove her van all the way to Portillo la Riena to buy the meat. A whole cow. A sheep. A pig. He showed her the proper way to hang it, how to cut and carve the steaks. At the side of the kitchen door near where the tomato plants grew, he built a barbecue for grills. One day he went hunting and shot a deer.

Whenever he returned, her eyes lit up in their almond pockets, lifting the sadness of her strong, flat face into a smile.

'What is it makes you so sad?' he asked one day.

'Because it has been such a long time since I visited Guatemala,' she told him. 'One day I should like to see it again.'

Winter came. No one travelled the road now. She closed the restaurant. Still, nothing was said about his leaving. He stayed on in a room down the hall from hers. No one else ever seemed to stay at the inn. Every night he could hear the key rasp in the old lock of her bedroom door. It wasn't until mid-January that he noticed that she had left it unlocked for two nights.

Snow muffled all sound outside when he entered her room. She was waiting, thick black hair sheaved out across the flowered pillow case; thick round body awaiting his touch.

By the end of February, the road was once again open. Travelers began drifting back. The hunters. The hikers. They found the man running the restaurant by himself. And the menu was excellent. Steaks and chops on the grill, as well as tasty stews.

One day, the old Basque returned. He sat in the same corner and ate slowly, eying the walking man as he had done before.

'Where is the Señora?' he asked. 'It is the first time in six years that I have not seen her.'

'She was lonely to visit Guatemala,' the man said. 'I am running the place for her until she returns.'

'The food is much improved,' a hunter told him. 'But this meat. I am not familiar with its delicate flavour, Señor. What is this we are eating?'

'A small animal I shot in the snow.' Strange to these mountains I think, but not without a certain beauty. But then, if I hadn't taken its life, it would have died sooner or later, so unprotected in this climate.'

The hungry hunter nodded, saying, 'A very excellent flavour, Señor. One I have never before encountered.'

The old Basque got up so suddenly that he left his pipe on the table, his meal half eaten.

⌘

19: PERCY

'Las Cucarachas - las cucarachas...!' So the old Mexican song begins. Add to that, spider, cricket, bee, termite, water bug, beetle, grasshopper, Praying Mantis (which Miguel quite wilfully insisted were poisonous), pismire (yes, that's its name), ladybug, dragonfly, wasp, mosquito, weevil, hexapod, and a variety of flies too numerous to name even if Jean knew the names. She was trying to figure out where they were all coming from and why they seemed to prefer the environs of Santa Rita to the more natural surroundings outside, like say, el campo.

But it really wasn't too difficult to figure out. Cracks in the tiled floors produced a steady and generous harvest of insect life. Ants in a variety of colors and sizes from small red to extremely large black, all made an aerobic jigsaw across the kitchen with tiny muscles strong enough to hoist the tiles. And in the garden, a prodigiously large beetle climbed out of the lettuce patch one evening as Jean was picking a fresh head for dinner. Her cries for help stopped Jeff in his tracks in case she was being attacked by a mad dog.

The mad bug had a row of amazing black and red curved stripes on its back, unknown in Cynthia Gray's 'Illustrated Insect Guide to Southern Spain', published by the Amigos del Jardin. At the risk of being thought ruthless and before Munchkin could devour it, Jeff preserved the curious creature in a bottle. He had jarred an already dead iridescent green scarab beetle he'd found on the doorstep the day they'd first crossed it and moved in. Remembering scarabs were highly prized by the ancient Egyptians, and remembering that writers need luck, he kept it on his desk for luck from Ra, the Supreme Solar God. But could he tell if it was working?

When Clive Belnapp arrived for his summer holiday that year with a fresh troop of 10 year old boy musicians, the insect corpses were passed around for all to observe. The youthful etymologists claimed never to have seen the like before and Clive Belnapp informed them that beetles are a group of insects that form the order Coleoptera, in the superorder Endopterygota, and having said a mouthful, added that he would look up the red and black beetle in an illustrated lexicon when he returned to school. Since he never found it, or perhaps forgot to look it up, it was to remain a mystery.

Because of the invasions in their sinking kitchen where the floor was slowly parting company from the walls, Jeff began calling it the Black Hole of Andalucia. One day Jean caught Maria sweeping the dirt into the gaps. But trying to stop Maria from doing anything was like stopping a Tormenta in full blast, and Maria was working her way to being more forceful. Jean could just about cope with the ants, but Las Cucarachas! This newest invasion of cockroaches, was the last straw. After all, this wasn't New York City, where people became so accustomed to sharing their quarters with those tiny creatures, though not exactly as pets.

Then as luck would have it, the Thwaites had a call from an old friend and ex-publisher of Jeff's who lived in New York. Could he and his wife come for a visit on their way to Seville? Considering that their new book of short stories was going to need a publisher and soon! the Thwaites were only too glad to invite them; but gave the civilized New Yorkers fair warning of the primitive state of the house.

'Then what can I bring you from civilisation?' was Douglas Entwhistle's next question.

Knowing that New Yorkers have given up their civil war against cockroaches and rapprochement has been reached between factions, and that wise apartment dwellers wishing to maintain the status quo, provide the creatures with their own accommodations known as 'Cockroach Motels' So what should Douglas bring? Obvious: Cockroach Motels. Unprocurable in Spain or London where it has not yet been admitted in polite society that cockroaches exist.

These tiny residences for 'order Coleoptera', come in the shape of quadruple-size match boxes with a *door* at each end and sticky scented *wallpaper* on the inside—the smell of which seduces a curious cockroach to enter. Once inside, the greedy buggers are stuck for the remainder of their short and gluttonous lives. A cockroach has never been known to escape unless across the backs of his unfortunate predecessors. The motels work much in the manner of old fashioned fly paper and eliminate the need for insecticide, which Jean forbade on green principles.

And just when the creatures were looming as large as the beetle-typewriter in William S. Burroughs book 'Naked Lunch', (which had to be published in France in 1959, because it was so shocking), and the creatures were approaching plague proportions, their friends arrived.

⌘

Maria, who always had a difficult time accepting foreign-made objects, was holding one of the boxes to the light for a better look, although she was standing on the kitchen porch in the full Spanish sun, pronounced : 'Well, these might work in Londres or the Estades Unidos, but that does not mean they will work in España, Señora.' Maria watched in disbelief as the motels were arranged in inviting corners of the kitchen which she'd reserved to store the sweepings.

One day she looked inside one of the boxes and was amazed to see it lined with black and shiny tenants. 'They must be Americano cucarachas,' Maria decided.

Jean had to admit to being bug-shy, but she couldn't hold a candle to Douglas's new wife, Sally. A third-time-around wife whom the Thwaites had never met before, Sally cut a glamorous if somewhat silicone impregnated figure with blonde Marilyn Monroe locks, long 'ex-human hair' eyelashes and those terrifying false nails with blunt ends that look like they could scar a man for life. Sally was a part-time actress. Douglas proudly boasted that she had been a Playboy Centrefold five years before and even Jeff was certain that she'd had a boob job because she was skinny as a Mashie Niblick with everything on top and when she sun-bathed on her back in only her bikini bottom on the back terrace, her boobs stood at full attention, utterly defying the laws of gravity.

Sally wore slinky black satin pyjamas and black marabou feathered mules on the terrace for breakfast and she was quite a dish. Miguel began watering the garden every morning paying particular attention to the planters in the terrace arches, and Elliot Gray took to walking his dog, Percy over the field on a leash about breakfast time, to catch a glimpse of Sally in her black satin outfit. Now this was unusual, because Percy had never known a leash in his life and he had only one eye; but even he, being after all male, had it focused on Sally. Jeff couldn't really blame them.

How Percy lost his eye was a saga in itself and worth a small digression. It wasn't only the insects that could sting and bite in El Salto. Snakes had been seen, a small black variety who hid under flower pots on the terrace and sprang out and ran away before they could be attacked. And one morning to her horror Jean had witnessed a long green and black snake as thick as a man's arm exiting the back hall through the open garden door. She couldn't believe her eyes and thought she must be hallucinating. By the time she'd gone to get Jeff to 'Do something...!' the reptile had disappeared completely. He was reported to have come down from the mountain for water, and Maria told a tale of one so big it stole a village child. Jeff didn't believe it, but Jean was inclined to.

Then there were the poison toads, reported to have a spitting range of at least ten feet. They'd need it, Jeff noted, since they moved so slowly they looked like they were standing still. The toads were large, ugly, brown creatures with warts all over their backs. Not the sort any princess would be likely to kiss even guaranteed to turn it into a Prince Charming. One night as the Thwaites were finishing their coffee on the front terrace with the newly arrived Entwhistles, they watched a huge daddy toad's slow and majestic progress as he mounted the six steps to the terrace. It took him a half hour to get to the top.

'Some humans take longer,' Douglas Entwhistle was heard to remark. The toad tucked himself behind a pot housing a majestic Mother-in-Law's Tongue. The Thwaites did not disturb his nocturnal rest but made a mental note to be careful in future when bending down to water the pots. Jean thought the toads even had a certain ugly charm if you didn't stand in their line of fire.

Which brings us to Percy. Unfortunately, one day Percy did. Stand in it.

Percy was just an ordinary short-haired black and white campo dog with long pointed ears that stood straight up at attention like great shells in which to hear the sea—with a pointed, shiny black nose and a roguish smile that seemed to tilt up at one side showing strong white and possibly dangerous teeth if he didn't like you; but he seemed to love everybody. A native breed of Spain that no doubt traces its history back to the Moorish invasion, Percy in particular had an expansive, endearing personality. Everyone loved his cocky approach to life. Percy met up with this particular toad on the hill one day and would not let it pass without the password. Toads do not know passwords and do not like to be asked too many questions. So with deadly accuracy, it spat in Percy's eye.

The moment Elliot Gray found Percy howling painfully in his garden, he could guess what had happened. Percy's eye already looked like a helium balloon and the Vet could do nothing to save it. It had to be removed before the poison spread to Percy's mischievous brain.

Elliot made a black patch for the missing eye which hooked over one ear and didn't fall off and Percy cut quite a dashing figure when he met up with the village dogs. It was clear that his exploits were known to his merry band of canine compañeros who greeted him on the corner of the field every night for choir practice. From that moment on, Percy was ringleader of the nightly howling forays. Jeff could spot him of an evening setting off from the Gray's garden via a brisk hop over the low wall, and heading down to the corner of El Salto. A few yip yaps as the pack assembled, and off they would go to yelp up the moon. By midnight they are ready in full 'Perro cante hondo' to bark the stars out of the sky and the Thwaites out of their dreams.

Since he'd lost his eye, Percy had begun playing matador to speeding cars. Perhaps like his human counterparts, he had to show off his 'macho-ness'. One day he was finally side-swiped and hobbled home. 'Thank God, they didn't kill him,' Elliot sighed, carrying him in his arms to his car for the cyclic trip to the Vet.

This time the Vet wanted to remove Percy's right front leg. But Elliot, who thought quite enough bits had been taken from Percy already, insisted on strapping the leg to a splint and somehow managed to save it, and without the vet's approval, it seemed to heal with aid of the splint. With his eye patch and bound leg, Percy looked a lot like Admiral Nelson.

⌘

One morning Jeff was awakened by yelps of another kind coming from the guest bathroom. It was Sally Entwhistle being attacked by a weird, black furry creature writhing on the floor! Jeff came rushing to the rescue armed with a broom, to find Sally grabbing for a towel. Not an unpleasant sight. He swatted the intruder with a mighty blow and it sailed up into the air. But it floated down in a strangely light manner.

It turned out to be only a feather escaped from Sally's black Marabou slippers. It was clear that the occupants of Santa Rita were getting jumpy.

Not without some reason. Jeff himself was the next victim a few days later. He was standing under the feeble drip of the overhead shower, protected from invaders only by Jean's shower cap. The shower was adjusted from the bathtub faucet which came up to his calves. As he bent to turn the tap with the hope of increasing the dribble from the pipe, something small but long and leggy emerged from the spout. He stared in horror at the descending entity, trying to count the legs. This time it was Jeff's turn to panic. In Jean's 'Aunt Jemima' cap, he shouted for her.

'It's probably another feather,' she called as she came running.

'This one has legs!' he yelled. 'Hundreds of them - and they're all wriggling!'

She was quick to the rescue with a jar and a cardboard. The special solution she reserved for the purpose of removing bugish intruders. She would put the jar over the creature, slide the cardboard underneath, turn it over, then 'bottle' it.. Hey presto! Then she would release the creature 'afuera'. Outside, into the nearest tree. This earthling turned out to be a gigantic centipede which made a leg-by-leg legato descent from the spout, landing by Jeff's toe. Jeff was out of the tub like a shot in less than a towel. Normally Jean opposed the execution of any and all living creatures, with of course, the possible exception of Miguel. But Jeff grabbed the jar and saw to it that the centipede met a watery end down the toilet. 'Let's hope he can swim,' Jean sighed and

Jeff got back under the shower still in Jean's cap. She dashed out of the bathroom and returned with her camera to record the executioner for posterity, draped only in a shower curtain and looking like a mad Roman senator. Douglas Entwhistle said it would make a nice book jacket photo.

What exactly did the Thwaites know about having house guests? They'd never had an abode large enough to house one, except for the odd visitor who got too drunk to leave their London flat and spent the night on the floor. Santa Rita house guests came loaded with gifts and left with what Jeff and Jean trusted would be happy enough memories of rustic environs, barbecue nights on the terrace with star powdered skies or in winter, sitting with a Carlos Trés before an open fire that evoked an atavistic sense of union against uncertain layers of encroaching darkness when the moon was on leave and even the orchestrated 'barkastrations' of Percy and his long-eared friends was mercifully, if inexplicably silent. There were producers or occasionally directors who came to Santa Rita work on projects fated or ill-fated, because not all series episodes or film projects found eventual destinations on small or large screens. Many projects remained in limbo: scripts that almost, but finally never saw the silver light of screen, or when made, the finished film ended up being an embarrassment to the writers—if not the backers.

Guests like Douglas and Sally, came for no reason but to escape the daily grind of life and share friendship and the Grays invited the Thwaites to bring the Entwhistles over for drinks. Cynthia wanted to talk to Douglas Entwhistle about publishing a book of articles she was writing about cats. Elliot wanted to talk to Sally about anything.

'It seems to me,' Douglas Entwhistle said that night at the Gray's party sipping a glass of Gran Viña Sol, 'that when a film is good, they praise the director, and if it's bad, they blame the writer. Can't get away with that with books, you know. That's definitely always the author's fault.'

'You've noticed that,' said Jeff, wryly as he watched Elliot Gray turning a leg of chicken over on the barbecue and wondered if Douglas was making reference to a short story Jeff had left on the fireplace mantle with the hope of it accidentally being picked up and read.

'But why do they blame the writer for a movie? Isn't that unfair? I either like the star or I don't, and I blame him if the picture's bad,' Sally said.

'Who's talking fair? This is the film business. All actors want to think of themselves as directors and all directors want to think of themselves as writers and all accountants as producers and all producers as gods,' Jeff complained.

Elliot, a producer who hadn't produced anything for too long, winced. 'Ahh, directors,' he said turning the subject away from producers. '*Auteurs*, the French call them. They are the gods. They all want to separate you poor hacks from any identification with the finished movie. And the critics are on their side. It's always 'Ridley Scott's picture or Steve Soderbergh's picture. Not taking into account the script.'

'Was your father like that?' Douglas asked, remembering that Jeff's father had been a famous Hollywood film director of Westerns.

'Old Jeffo hated script writers on general principles, but he was no auteur. He thought of himself as more of a craftsmen. A technician. To him all writers were hacks, even F. Scott Fitzgerald,' Jeff mused. 'Jeffo started in the days of the Silents and he believed words were not essential to a good film. "Cinema is visual," he used to tell me. "If yer gonna be a writer, Jeff, don't use words!" He belonged to the "Yup and Nope" school of script writing. "They went thata'way" sort of dialogue. It was a good film for him if the hero kissed his horse at the end and rode away into the sunset.'

'I think they're getting back to that,' Douglas said. 'Not the sunset bit, but all action and no words.'

'I like Leonardo DiCaprio,' Sally Entwhistle sighed.

'I'll see that you don't meet him,' Douglas grumbled, trying to suck in his protruding waistline.

Elliot Gray looked glum and basted the chicken which wafted a sizzle of delightful aroma to the early arrivals sitting around his terrace. The producer had failed to get a film project off the ground for the last four of the six years including the one he'd hired Jeff and Jean to write, and had settled into the party circuit as an alternative to work. But when his film friends appeared from time to time, he insisted on his place as doyen of the British producers, although nobody could quite remember his last film. 'We all know how hard it is these days, but we all keep trying,' Elliot sighed.

'Why?' wondered Jeff. 'Why do we try?' But nobody could answer that.

⌘

Earlier that day before the Gray's dinner party, Elliot had come over to see Jeff with the news that one-eyed, three legged Percy had been gone for several days. Vanished with no trace.

'I understand they kidnap dogs in Spain and hold them for ransom. Do you think he's been kidnapped?' Sally asked.

'I'd gladly pay a ransom, but I'm afraid there's not much chance of that. Even the most depraved thief wouldn't steal Percy,' Elliot said. 'Still, it's unlike Percy to stay away like this. He's been known to take off for the odd romantic caper, but generally returns in time for dinner. He's a dog who looks to his stomach. Although I'll admit when I'm not looking, Cynthia sometimes substitutes cat food.' Elliot sighed. 'She tolerates Percy, you see, but she really doesn't care much for dogs.'

'Perhaps that's why he took off and decided not to return,' Sally put in.

'Or maybe he lifted a good leg at a tree and fell over once too often,' Jean mused. 'Since his front leg has been splinted, Percy does have a tendency to topple.'

Elliot gave it some consideration. 'A possibility. I've tried to teach Percy to squat to no avail. I think it offends his canine pride. I'm only worried that maybe he has wandered down to the Ronda road and has been hit by a mad motorist. There are few of any other kind.'

It was true, the highways were strewn with the corpses of dogs and cats. Elliot turned to Jeff. 'I wondered if you'd care to go with me and have a look. Four eyes are better than two.'

So Jeff and Elliot rode up and down the highway in the hopes of not spotting a three good legged dog with an eye patch, surely the victim of his eternal assaults on moving vehicles. But they didn't spot his corpse, which after all, was a relief.

Under The Magic Mountain

Before the Gray's dinner party, Jean heard Jeff tapping away at his computer. She wondered what he was writing because the only thing he liked to write without her anymore was poetry, and that, usually by hand.

She found out that evening when the small gathering were sitting around watching Elliot at the barbecue. Jeff pulled a sheet of paper from his pocket and read out an ode to the missing mongrel. 'It's called Campo Perro,' he said, and read:

'Rag tag Perro with only one eye/Did a star come down and teach you to fly?/Your ears are great wings to cut any sky/Campo clown, where did you go…?/To a strange town with some circus show?/Comedy canine who loves to roll/And be scratched by a foot or empty a bowl/That the cats had begun?/You leave us poorer in love and in fun./Come back to your house on our lovely hill./Rag tag Perro, come eat your fill/Barking up skies in the rooster dawn/Carnival dog, have you once again gone/To war with some toad/Who stole half your sight in a thicket of woad?/We miss you tonight./Rogue and noble, you are both of these./Gypsy and rover wherever you please/Campo Casanova, in the hot Spanish sun/Wherever you end, /You've gallantly won/Each human a friend./Rag tag rover - wild as a gorge/Come home! you've won the Order of St. George/ For you've fought every dragon, And bitten all tires /Corridas with motos. Teeth snapping like pliers./Perro, the campo needs you to start /A fiesta of food-stealing/ Now you've taken my heart./Come home to our hilltop that misses you well,/To the fields and the rubbish in our throw-away hell./Come home to our evenings, You dance with the stars. /Your barking is music That chases all cars./The landscape is lonely to see you again, /Now we are lonely,/For you're part of Our Spain. . . '

As Jeff finished reading the poem, there were tears in Elliot's eyes. And then as though on queue, up through the garden meandered Percy on his three good legs, returning from his lost weekend. He pranced right over to Jeff as though he had heard the poem, and without falling over, expelled a critical pee on the leg of Jeff's chair.

Behind him, a small spotted mongrel trotted up. She was white with black spots, a sort of negative image of Percy - and her body was too big for her head, but Percy eyed her with love and affection. Elliot called her to him and she came over shyly, not certain of a friendly reception until he handed her a bit of chicken. Percy gave a yap, and Elliot said, 'Well that's it then. Percy's found a bride.'

'Thank goodness he's back,' Cynthia said, turning to Douglas. 'Now we can talk about cats.'

The little white and black dog moved in with Percy into the garage, and they named her Mabel and she and Percy were hardly ever apart except when he went out for a night with the boys.

The Gray's party was soon swarming with dinner guests who ate everything in sight, and all the males crowded around Sally. Davie was at the front of the queue. In her white dress with the waist length cleavage, Sally flirted with them all and gave nothing away. Doug seemed to take it in stride and must have been used to it.

Douglas Entwhistle having successfully published one of Jeff's novels a few years back was marginally interested when he heard they were working on a book—until he heard it was of short stories. Although he was secretly curious to read them, he didn't want to ask, for fear he might be required to make some sort of commitment while on holiday. As for Jeff, he wanted to show Douglas their short stories but he felt he might be imposing on the publisher's good will. So again accidentally on purpose, Jean left a few stories lying about where Doug might read them and could pretend he hadn't. Jeff saw Sally pick up one lying on the dining room table and take it into her room that night. But in the morning it was back on the table. It was called 'The Fortune Teller's Prediction' and they wondered if Douglas had looked at it.

That afternoon when Douglas was off playing tennis with Jeff, Sally said to Jean, 'You know that story you left on the table? Doug asked me to bring it into our room. He read it last night. I know he liked it. Where did you get the idea for such a story?'

Jean smiled. It was difficult to explain how a story grew in a writer's mind. Or how two writers worked together. 'Well,' she said, 'there are a lot of theatricals living down here now. Not just older ones ready to retire, but a lot of the younger actor crowd.

And they rent or buy apartments or time shares. And of course, there are the types who prey on them. Like the fortune tellers.'

'Oh, Jean!' Sally said with some disappointment. 'Don't you believe in fortune tellers?'

'Sometimes I do. That's why we wrote The Fortune Teller's Prediction.' Jean told her. 'Because sometimes, you know, a prediction really does come true.'

Sally smiled. 'Maybe you should leave a few more stories lying around.'

And Jean did.

⌘

20: THE FORTUNE TELLER'S PREDICTION

He didn't know why he'd let her talk him into buying the place. It wasn't even a time share. They certainly couldn't afford it, either of them, and the whole urbanisation could only be improved by blasting. But it did have a great view. Dan had to admit that he liked the idea of having a place in Spain and Sue had wanted it so very much that he had finally agreed.

There was that certain something in the Spanish air from the moment when one got off the plane, a heady scent, not exactly floral, maybe just the scent of the earth, it was somehow alive. It hit one's nostrils in a warm glow of a smell that gave Dan a sense of well-being, made him feel wonderful for no, or perhaps because of, an earthly reason.

Approaching his thirtieth year as an aging juvenile, Dan knew that if he didn't make it as an actor soon, he was never going to, unless he kept his credibility long enough to graduate to 'character man' roles. Having a place in the sun made him sound successful when he mentioned it to anyone but his agent, who knew better. And sounding successful was an important factor in job hunting for an actor.

They split the mortgage fifty-fifty. But for Dan, coming down to Spain to get over the stress of working in a dying British film Industry, and the further stress of a half dead agent, was like stepping out of the frying pan into the furious 'no funciones' of their only toilet. The place had been empty for some time and the real estate man assured them it was only tree roots in the pipes from not being used. Eucalyptus always did that. Nothing going down, the roots get in. But the trees were so beautiful and gave shade and made the air so clean and healthy. So Sue found someone to clean the drains and they began to mend the cracking walls and the place took on a charm of its own.

There had once been a fish pond in the grounds the size of a swimming pool, but it was clogged with weeds and stinking with foul odours, caused no doubt by drowned tree squirrels and campo cats who had accidentally fallen in. The other owners in the urbanisation, eleven in all, never seemed to be on their holidays at the same time as Dan and Sue, so they could never hold an 'owners' meeting' to do anything about communal improvements. The only person who lived there all year 'round seemed to be an aging English woman who called herself 'Madam Zena'.

But in such matters as repairs, Zena was of little use. She didn't seem to care much for fresh air either, and usually had her curtains drawn and windows closed. Her apartmento was hung with dark, mysterious carpets from Morocco and she was fairly dark and mysterious herself, from her jet black-dyed hair to the tips of her weird 'earth shoe' sandals fastened on swollen ankles and off-putting bright red toe nails with silver stars stuck on them. She took an immediate liking to Sue and Dan, and when she discovered he was an actor, told him she had been an actress 'when I was younger, dears.'

Carnival, more likely, Dan suspected.

Like it as much as he did, the expenses of maintaining this home-away-from-home were 'grossing him out', he complained to Sue. And as optimistic as she was, she had to admit that nothing came cheap. Where, oh where were the days of jugs of wine for two hundred pesetas he'd heard about but never so far encountered? Before his time. All those good things---before his time. Wasn't that always the way?

Yet Dan could not complain entirely about his life. He'd had three roles on BBCTV in the last year, and one of them was a four-parter, even though his part was small, it was a windfall in these lean times. He poured himself a goblet of chilled Valdepeñes, and sank back into one of the rattan chairs Sue had picked up from the Barata for the terrace. His glance lifted some distance across the road to what was left of a once grand country club built on a jut of hill looking down to the sea. The club was the reason why they had discovered this place for sale.

So close to Marbella and once so beautiful, how and why had the club failed? He could still recall the night he and Sue attended the grand opening of its short existence as The Marbella Movie Club. The Spanish owner was a well intentioned but highly impractical entrepreneur with great ideas and no follow through. And now the building had been almost levelled by vandals. Not a window left, writing on the walls of assorted Spanish vulgarities, half the roof gone and tiles stolen to add to some Spaniard's room extension.

At that club opening Sue had caused a sensation, joining in the Flamenco along with the Spanish dancers. The Olympic-sized swimming pool was filled with floating candles and flowers. A Flamenco band was playing and Sue wore some sort of flowery see-through thing with flesh colored tights underneath. Her figure looked smashing, if revealing. Sue belonged to the 'if you've got it flaunt it' generation and Dan never minded that. She had been trained and worked as a dancer until at twenty four, she found that teaching aerobics in Covent Garden provided a steadier income. Scatty as she could be at times, she was sensible about money and also independent. So far, it was she who refused to get married. Dan would have taken the plunge the year before. Sue had kept her own flat in Fulham until they'd decided to pool resources to buy this Spanish place. Otherwise, he doubted he'd ever have talked her into moving in with him in Chiswick where a few actors they knew had moved..

Sue was a happy-go-lucky, uncomplicated girl. As normal as the morning dew except for one thing. FORTUNE TELLING in all its glorious aspects: Numerology, Tarot, and Tea Leaves; you name it, she believed in it. Sue couldn't leave the Chiswick flat in the morning until she'd read both their horoscopes and decided if the auspices were all right for them to go out.

So if she hadn't met Madam Zena at the Marbella Movie Club party, they probably would never have found the Spanish place. This aging, ex-whatever-she-was with phony airs was the deciding straw for Sue. A militant non-believer, Dan couldn't give a toss about Tarot and had a horror of horoscopes. But he kept his opinions to himself, since it meant so much to Sue. Whenever they were in Spain, Sue would slip upstairs to Madam Zena's for a 'natter' when he was having his afternoon lie-down. Sometimes she'd drag him along, because as she pointed out, their lives were tied together now. It was her pesetas paying for the occult prophecies, so Dan could hardly object. Although in his private opinion, Madam Zena made a dishonest peseta or two to keep herself in brandies at the Book Bar by enticing mentally vulnerable women like Sue into her parlor.

On the whole, it was a harmless enough entertainment. Generally, the old con-girl spilled out mind-numbing nonsense like: "don't wear green over the weekend", or "when you get back to England, Dan should expect a call from a casting director whose initials were either B, L, S, or D", which gave her a fairly wide chance to be right since she undoubtedly still knew the names of some of the more elderly casting directors.

Actually, he had a call from Jan Saldido, which amounted to a job. But he deliberately didn't mention the source of the assignment to Sue.

Then came Madam Zena's prediction that if Dan wanted to be a star, he must change his name which she informed him added up to a numerological disaster in conjunction with the date of his birth. Most of the time he'd gone along with Sue's obsession, even if she'd wasted a lot of two thousand peseta notes being told that Dan should "avoid playing men's roles over forty five, my dear". More likely the casting directors would avoid *him*! It had taken him years to outgrow that children's series he'd done for two years running. But to change his name…! Even though his agent had once suggested it. Not that Dan Bloggs was the best name since Cary Grant changed his from Archibald Leach, and Dan might have changed it anyway, except that coming from Madam Zena, it really got up Dan's nose and resolve.

That afternoon he found Sue sitting on the terrace with a tall orange juice, working out lists of names for him. The discussion ended up in an argument and he slept that night in the hammock on the terrace and woke up in the morning full of mosquito bites. Sue smugly pointed out that Zena had warned him to avoid night air.

The following afternoon, just as Dan was dozing in the hammock, covered in calamine lotion, Madam Zena hoisted her bulk downstairs to give Sue her latest prediction. 'Free of charge, my dear, I must tell you immediately, it's so vital!'

'Come in, Madam Zena. My, I've never seen you so excited,' he could hear Sue saying.

'My dear, I have just had the most powerful—the most dreadful premonition. It came up in the cards, the numbers, *and* the tea leaves. Would you believe, all of them the same! And this definitely affects your Dan's career.'

Dan sat up in the hammock to hear better and in doing so, almost spilled out.

'Sue, there's a blond man in your life...?'

'You mean Dan?'

'Are there any other?'

'No. No, the only blond is Dan.'

'That confirms it then! It can only be Dan.'

'What can only be?' Sue's words came strained and Dan crossed the terrace to put his ear to the door.

Madam Zena's tone lowered with a conspiratorial air. 'He must above all, avoid ships! Do you hear? There will be a death. Death! I have seen it!'

'Avoid ships?' Sue seemed confused. 'Avoid. . .? But Madam Zena, we always fly when we come to Spain. We never take a ship.'

Dan bolted into the room, feeling his temples throb in anger. 'For Christ's sake, Zena, you know how susceptible Sue is! Why do you want to scare her with death threats? Can't you keep your predictions to yourself, you old. . . old!' He turned on his heel and stormed out.

Sue didn't forgive Dan for his outburst until the following week when they were on the plane back to Gatwick and London. And then, it was only because shipboard possibilities seemed so remote from their lives. Their relationship soon returned to the status quo, and life in the Chiswick flat went on smoothly for another three months, both of them avoiding touchy subjects like horoscopes or any mention of the Boat Show at Earls Court. Then Dan finished his play at the Almeida Theatre to good reviews and it was time to go down to Spain once again.

They arrived in the Spanish flat to hear Dan's cell phone ringing. It was a call from his agent. The actor was to hop right back on the next plane to London. Reggie had got him a lead! The part of a murderer in a BBC four hour mini series. They had wanted Robert Pattinson, but he wasn't available and the director was willing to take a chance on Dan after seeing him at the Almeida. Yes, it was definite! A great part opposite the rising star, Oona Smithers and the best money to date. A real thrust to his career and sure to lead to other things. The best thing about it was, it was all to be filmed aboard a cruise ship in the Greek Islands. So he'd even make a bit extra in travel per diems, if he was careful.

Sue had her arms around him in celebratory hugs when she pulled back, face suddenly drained of color. 'You can't take the part, Dan. You can't go,' she said firmly.

'What in the devil are you saying, Sue? You don't want me to play a murderer, is that it? You've never tried to interfere in my career choices before.'

She shook her head. 'It's Madam Zena's prediction, Dan. Don't you remember? "Avoid ships! There will be a death." Don't you see, you must turn it down!'

'Nonsense! ' he said angrily. 'That was all months ago. You can't possibly be serious about that woman's rubbish?'

But he could tell by her expression that she was. Dan could feel himself losing it. Temper control had never been his strong point and yes, he was blowing his top. 'God dammit! This is my greatest career move, Sue. A chance I've been waiting for all my life!' he shouted. 'I'm not turning it down for the ravings of some fucking half pissed soothsayer!'

'You're actually going to take it, no matter what I think? Is that it, Dan?'

'Watch my lips! Of course I'm taking it. To go to Greece, which I've never seen, get paid for it, and a great role to boot? Once and for all change my TV image from kid shows. By ship, dog sled, or helicopter, I'm going, for Chrissake, and no Madam Zena is going to stop me.'

Sue could see that Dan meant what he was saying. She couldn't talk him out of it. But she had to have one last attempt to save him. She would have tried tears but she was too angry to cry so she used the anger instead. 'Well Dan, if you take it, don't expect me to go back to London with you. I'm not going to sit around and wait while you, knowing what the fates have in store for you! While you just insist on walking into certain death!'

'Are you jealous? That's what it is. Jealousy, Sue. Me and Oona Smithers on a cruise ship alone together, with only an entire goddamn film crew.'

'I'll admit the idea doesn't thrill me, Dan. You and Oona. Everyone knows she's just broken up with her boyfriend and she's a man-hungry bitch. But I do trust you with women.'

'But not with common sense?' he flared.

The argument got so bad, that finally in a rage, Dan grabbed Sue's arm and dragged her upstairs to confront Madam Zena.

The old woman rose from her lunch; a bowl of soup and a bottle of wine. Dan tried to keep calm, but he could hear his voice rising out of control. He tried diaphragmatic breathing to calm down and insisted she retract her prediction. Madam Zena left her soup, downed her wine, and sat down at the Ouji board. The planchet spun around the half moon of alphabet and spelled out two words: FIRE - and - DEATH!!!

Her cheeks were streaked with running mascara and she had the dour expression of a groggy ghoul. She gave a slight hiccup from the hastily downed wine and turned to him with large, sad eyes. 'There will be a burning inferno in a ship's saloon,' she said. 'It is in your fates. I see death. I cannot change it. I can only warn you.'

This was too much for Dan. He exploded his full fury at the fortune teller, calling her everything from quack to charlatan. Zena, whose heart was weak, collapsed into her chair. Sue brought her a brandy and she revived slightly, her eyes focused far away.

Dan calmed down enough to apologise and turned to Sue. 'I'm going down and pack my bags.'

'You never unpacked,' she reminded him.

'Well, I'm going back to London,' he said. 'Are you coming with me?'

'You can do what you like. I'm staying here.' Her tone was final and she turned away from him. Madam Zena looked at him as though he were criminally insane.

Dan went down to the flat, poured himself a copious brandy and gulped. He waited, sure that Sue would come down, say she was sorry, and go back to London with him. But an hour later she was still upstairs with Zena. He dialled his cell phone and after the third try, got his agent on the line. 'Reggie? It's Dan,' he said.

'Dan, my old sunshine,' came the agent's throaty voice; the product of too many cigarettes and too many whiskies. Dan put his glass down as the agent rattled on. 'Hope you're thrilled, my old son. I've got you a great guarantee and the director loved you at the Almeida.'

'So you said. The point is, I'm not taking it, Reggie,' Dan replied in a hollow voice. 'I can't explain because you'd never understand. But I can't accept. Sorry. But I am available for anything else. Anything that doesn't involve a ship.'

'A ship? What is it? You get seasick or something?'

'Not exactly.'

'Well then, have you lost your marbles, Mate? This is a chance of a lifetime,' came the agent's querulous voice. 'I'll supply the Dramamine.'

'Sorry, Reggie. That's my decision.' Dan rang off. He turned to see Sue standing in the open doorway. She came over, tears in her eyes, and threw her arms around his neck.

Dan almost lost his agent over the job turn down. But Sue and he were on an even keel once again. As the days passed, they watched the newspapers, Sue, with dire expectations. But no nautical holocaust was reported in Greece or anywhere else. Somebody fell off a ship, but that hardly counted as a dire prediction for Dan.

And three months later, the cruise ship that the BBC had bought for their mini series returned to the port of Piraeus outside Athens with all parties intact and the actor who had replaced Dan, a few thousand pounds the richer and already offered another starring role. But Dan was quick to forgive Sue because by not going, he had been available to take a running lead on a cop series for LWT. The biggest break he'd ever had! Even his agent forgave him. It was cause for a real celebration.

So when the new series called 'a wrap' on the first ten episodes and Dan had three months off, they decided to fly to Paris, pick up a new French car, and drive down the rest of the way to Spain.

The trip had been glorious all the way, the scenery changing constantly from little French towns with incredible meals and Spanish fields of bright red poppies, to craggy hills, to lush vineyards. They were falling in love with their life and before heading back to their haven in Marbella, they decided to skirt Gibraltar and drive a few miles further on and see a bit of the Atlantic Coast side. Someone had told them about a place right on the ocean called Zahara de Las Atunes, where they'd heard the swimming was great and the seafood unequalled.

They arrived at sunset and found a small, inviting hotel perched like a shack right on the beach. It had its own restaurant facing the ocean. They checked into their room, made joyous love on one of the narrow twin beds before they even unpacked their bags, showered and changed, and went to dinner in the local restaurant, having worked up an appetite.

The sound of the surf rose with the changing tide, and the moonlight illuminated a silver stretch of sand. The restaurant, now quite full of people, reeked of atmosphere, from its straw roof and lanterns, to the sawdust floors, fishnets, oars, shiny varnished ex-swordfish and tuna corpses decorating the walls. They ordered flaming rum drinks and tapas and settled down to a vista of moonlit surf. When the waiter brought the menus Dan ordered two more flaming drinks.

Sue picked up the menu. 'Do they have those miniature lobsters? You know. Langustina?' she asked the waiter.

'Si, Señora,' the waiter replied.

'And those tiny white clams in tomato sauce,' she added.

'Almejas,' the waiter said, heading back to the bar for the drinks.

Her eyes rose to the top of the menu and her expression froze. Her face went pale. 'Dan! Oh, Dan,' she breathed.

'Sue?' Dan asked. 'Are you all right?'

'The name of this restaurant, Dan! Did you see? It's called El Buque!'

'So?' he asked, not comprehending.

'El Buque, Dan. It means The Ship!' Sue's belief system had slipped into high gear. 'This place! This must be the ship Madam Zena saw. The place she meant in her prediction. Dan - we've got to get out of here. Right this minute!'

Dan took her hand and tried to calm her. 'I do not believe I'm hearing this, Sue. I do not believe you are serious. We are not on a ship. This is not a ship! Just like Magritte's painting, "This is not a pipe". Anyway, since when is your Spanish so good that you know the correct translation for El Buque? It could mean anything,' he assured her. 'A fisherman. Or a barge. I'm certainly not going to have this weekend spoiled by that crank fortune teller's worn out prediction which is now over a year old!'

'Look around you, Dan!' she said. 'What do you see? Ship's bells. Fish nets. El Buque has got to mean The Ship!' Sue rose in a panic. 'I am leaving, no matter what you say!'

The waiter was making a swift approach to their table with their drinks. 'Wait, Sue!' Dan said, trying to hold her back. 'Let's ask the waiter what the name of this place is in English. Okay?' Dan tried to grab her hand, but her handbag swung out slamming straight into the drinks on the waiter's tray and sending up fiery blue bursts. Flaming rum splashed out against the fishnet-draped window and dripped to the sawdust floors. Swiftly the blaze leapt up all around them spreading out irrationally. In less than a minute the rustic wooden shack flared into an inferno. The sound of pop music mixed with the panicked screams of pushing, frantic diners. That was the last thing Dan remembered of the conflagration.

He woke up in a hospital with a lung full of smoke and bandages on his face and hands. He couldn't make out what the nurses were telling him. Finally a doctor who spoke English came into his room.

'What has happened to Sue?' he demanded. 'The woman I was with?' The doctor shook his head sadly. Dan tried to get out of bed, but he was too weak.

'Many were killed. You are lucky to be alive. I am afraid, Señor, that the lady was not so lucky. She was one of the fatal victims of the El Buque fire.'

Dan was numb. His mind could not take in what had happened. Long after the doctor left, he lay there staring out the window at the bright, shiny day, not able to believe she was gone. Later that day the nurse brought him an English language edition of El Sol. The headline read: TRAGEDY STRIKES THE SHIP'. Sue's name was listed among the victims.

Half demented with grief, Dan was released three days later, still in bandages. He arranged for Sue's remains to be cremated, and carried the box of ashes with him. It seemed to Dan like a lifetime, but it was just four short days after the fatal accident that he returned to their Spanish flat. He had no sooner deposited his suitcase, than he raced upstairs to Madam Zena's. When his pounding and shouting could get no results, he kicked his way into the fortune teller's apartment. But Madam Zena was not there. He couldn't understand it. She barely ever left her apartment. Making his way back down the stairs, he nearly knocked over Mrs Fanter who lived on the first floor when in residence. He grabbed her by the arms, giving her quite a start. When he realised he had frightened the old dear, he apologised.

'Oh, it's you Mr Bloggs. Back from London so soon?'

He nodded. 'Sorry, didn't mean to frighten you, Mrs Fanter. I'm looking for the woman upstairs. Madam Zena. Where is she?'

'You mean the Fortune Teller? Dotty as a fruit cake, she was, Mr Bloggs. And now she's drowned, could you believe it?' Mrs Fanter told him.

'Drowned? Was she...on a boat?' He felt the blood racing to his head 'Where? When did this happen?'

'Oh, Mr Bloggs, you're hurting me!' she cried and he realised he was gripping her arms again.

'When did Madam Zena die?' he asked letting go of her.

'Why it only happened just four nights ago. The dear old thing came running down the stairs and knocked on my door babbling about seeing a ship on fire. Something about you and that darling wife of yours. Then she just ran out into the grounds. Must've fell right in the fish pond. That's where she drowned, you see.'

'Drowned in the fish pond?' he asked, feeling quite faint.

Mrs. Fanter nodded. 'But the doctor says it could have been a heart attack made her fall in. None of us heard her, not that it would have done any good because she must have been dead before she fell in—or there would have been water in her lungs. You'll have to break it gently to your wife, won't you? She spent so much time with the old lady.'

Sue and I were never married,' he said numbly.

'I see,' she nodded. 'So much of that going around these days.

⌘

21: THE ORCHARD

'Any more predictions for today?' Jeff asked setting down the English newspaper in front of Jean with the horoscope on top.

'Oh, Jeff, don't be silly. You know I don't believe in that stuff. And right now I've got a lot on my mind.'

Everything was happening so fast. The rainy season had started, and one day the Vivero showed up to announce it was time to plant the much discussed orchard. And so the field was ploughed yet again by the huge tractor that the Vivero rented from the Sindicado. When it was done, all the wild flowers were gone and it looked so tidy Jeff couldn't believe it was the same football-weary hill they had looked out upon for so long. Not one old sneaker in sight.

They'd finally put up a low chain fence behind the cypresses where it couldn't be seen too clearly although Jeff thought it still looked a bit 'concentration camp'. The footballers got the message and had taken to playing on the field at the bottom of the village; a field that belonged to no one and where their shouts could echo out to sea without disturbing the siestas of the estranjeros. The new gate was now in place and really looked rather grand, Jean thought, with its curlicue wrought iron design.

In the clean-up, the Thwaites dug up an odd assortment of objects from the hillside. Miguel helped them carry the debris to be collected by the Basura man who drove his lorry up the new village road to the bottom of the field twice a week now to collect village garbage. An improvement over villagers throwing it on their hillside.

No Roman coins were uncovered. Their treasure trove consisted of some interesting small, turn of the century green beer bottles which Jean cleaned up and put on a kitchen shelf to become a focal point for discussion with visitors, and stopped them asking about the slipping floor tiles. Jeff was longing for a metal detector, certain there must be something of historic interest buried there somewhere.

The last television script had put enough money into the kitty to pay for trees, so Jeff finally sat down with the Vivero and showed him the illustrated planting instructions from the California Department of Agriculture. This was a new Vivero. The other one had disappeared without a trace. This one, like one third of all the men they'd met in Spain, was called Pepé. He looked at the pictures with the sort of unseeing eye they had first observed when they showed Miguel the Costa de Sol Garden Club's book of planting instructions for their garden.

Pepé replied in English, 'They may plant them that way in California, but the almond tree was invented in Spain, Señor. It is we who taught the Americans how to grow them many hundreds of years ago!'

'They have made a few improvements in agriculture since then,' Jeff suggested, not mentioning that the Arabs grew almonds before the Spaniards. But it would have made no difference, so they gave him the benefit of the doubt. The Vivero carefully ignored California's more modern concepts. He sent his men out to dig and prepare the holes, and the trees arrived tied in great bundles, all about three feet high. They looked no more than sticks when stood upright and sunk into each hole; five hundred and twenty five almendros. Nuts. And down by the irrigation canal, twenty soft fruit trees were to spread their fragile roots in the search for water. Jeff and Jean gazed across the field after the workmen left and walked up and down the hillside examining the trees carefully, as though they knew what they were looking for. 'We've planted our own private Garden of Eden,' Jean sighed.

'Next you'll be wanting chickens and a cows.'

'Not while we're travelling back and forth so often,' she replied, not ruling out the possibility as a retirement plan. The trees seemed terribly barren and they found it hard to imagine that one day there would be real leaves and nuts and fruit to pick.

But in four months the weeds had grown higher than the trees and Jean looked across the field with some worry. 'I think we should stop by the Vivero's and ask his advice.'

They found Pepé in the garden center. He looked at them as though they were both mad. 'You must have back the tractor again to clean the field. The trees, they must breathe, Señora. My responsibility this is not.'

It was Miguel who came to the rescue for a change. He knew the man from the Sindicado that the Vivero had hired. Of course Miguel knew him; he was a cousin. He would contact him and arrange for the tractor to come back.

And so on the appointed day, all morning Jean waited with Jeff on the terrace unable to concentrate at her computer. 'He said ten o'clock, Jeff. To have the trees ready.'

'How ready can they get?' Jeff wondered, remembering that in Spain, time meant nothing. And then around four o'clock in the afternoon the tractor chugged its way up the road and turned through their new gate, side-swiping and bending another curlicue into it. The Thwaites ran down to guide the driver onto one of the ramps they'd had built for the tractor to enter either side of the field. The man nodded with not so much as a how's-your-father and without waiting for further instruction, aimed his tractor into the middle of the orchard. Miguel mysteriously appeared to guide him with sweeping hand signals.

'Why doesn't he start at one end and work his way across?' Jean queried.'

'Jean, just let him get on with it, for God's sake. I'm sure he knows what he is doing.'

But it was clear that he didn't. The big tractor made a grand sweep of the upper and lower fields, Miguel egging him on, in and out, around and about, and uprooted twelve trees. With that, the driver turned back onto the driveway, demanded his payment in cash. Miguel stood by until the money was handed over. Ten thousand pesetas, which Miguel assured them was the going rate. The driver departed with his money, a knowing eye-wink to Miguel, and no reduction in price for the twelve felled trees at six hundred pesetas a tree. 'Seven thousand two hundred pesetas down the drain, Jean,' Jeff sighed.

Miguel kicked at one of the fallen almond trees and said his cousin had done a good job and there were too many trees anyway. Then he went home for his afternoon brandy with beer chaser. When he was gone, Jean went down into the field and sat beside a fallen tree. There were tears in her eyes for this lost soldier on a forsaken battlefield. Jeff came down carrying a bottle of wine and two glasses, and sat beside her. 'That tractor is too big,' she said.

'We'll get a smaller tractor somewhere. I promise, Jean,' he took her hand.

'Yes,' she said, the old fighting spirit returning. 'A smaller tractor.'

They sat for a while on the dry, softly upturned earth, drinking and saying nothing. Then after her third glass Jean, a trifle tipsy, looked at her husband, an angry glint in her eyes. 'You know something, Jeff? I think maybe Miguel gets a rake-off from that driver cousin of his. That would explain why he came to help this afternoon when normally he won't set foot in the field.'

'Hmm,' Jeff mused. 'You could be right, Jean. Part of his "pluck the estranjeros clean" campaign.'

⌘

Through the following year, the trees continued to flourish, so that instead of aisles of tiny sticks, they had become a veritable forest. 'Look!' They're still babies and they're so thick,' Jean exclaimed, peering at the trees hidden behind the weeds which had grown taller and thicker from being ploughed under and from the leeching of manure from the tree wells. But the small trees now had glossy flat leaves and pale shelled nuts secreted in velvety pink husks. According to their California bible they were ready to be picked.

Jeff and Jean went out with a paper carton and filled it to the brim with their first crop. They couldn't wait to crack one open and taste it, marvelling at the wonders of Mother Nature when it came to the art of packaging. Once inside the soft velvet outer jacket the wooden shell had its own brand of air conditioning with tiny perforations to let the nut breathe. The brown skin that covered the nut was more tenacious than plastic.

'You don't think about these things when you buy them in a store, do you, Jeff? Fresh nuts taste so different. So moist and sweet,' Jean observed pouring a glass of lemonade.

'Absolutely delicious,' Jeff agreed, munching away and cracking open another shell. 'The best almonds I've ever eaten. But Pepé planted them too close,'

'You told him, Jeff.' She had eaten so many she thought she would explode.

He nodded.

She sighed. 'We need a smaller tractor.'

'Mm.' he said.

A year of searching within a radius of twenty miles proved hopeless. One day they drove all the way up into the hills behind the mountain village of Ojen because a friend said he'd seen lots of small tractors up there, but no one in Ojen seemed to know the word tractor. The same in Spanish. No matter which way Jean pronounced it.

Miguel went so far as to say that no small tractors existed in Spain. But then he added that perhaps another cousin could find one and would drive it and charge them only six thousand pesetas for the day. They were less than enthusiastic because they'd seen that particular cuñado. But never sober.

One day as they were driving out of El Salto past the small dairy farm at the entrance to the main Ronda Road, when Jean at the wheel, noticed the dairy farmer's son sitting on a machine.

A tractor...! And small...!!!

She screeched the car to a staggering pit stop and was out like a flash, running up the hill towards the lad. He almost fell off the small tractor he was sitting on, Jean rattling away at him in pigeon Spanish and before Jeff could shout at her, six large Alsatians plunged in for the attack. The farmer's son stared blankly. His mother, alerted by the dogs, came hurrying out of the house in time to prevent Jean from being eaten alive.

By the time Jeff was out of the car, Jean was in the thick of explanation to the mother. The dairy farmer had a small tractor. Yes, that one. Vigorous nods. The one the son was sitting on. (Why hadn't they noticed it before???) And would the madre believe it, the Thwaites needed a small tractor? Like right now!

Yes, the farmer's wife knew who the foreigners were. Finca Santa Rita. 'Si, si. But the tractor, it is not for sale, Señora,' the woman said firmly, about to unleash the pack.

'No, not to buy, Señora. To rent! Rent, with your son driving it. To clean our field. How much would you charge?' Jean asked.

The moment the concept of commerce entered the discussion, the mother warmed to the estranjeros. She paused uncertainly. How much did they have in mind to pay?

Thinking of Miguel's scavenger nature, Jean cut in half the price he had quoted for hiring his cuñado, should he be able to get his hands on a tractor, which he said did not exist. Except for this one, barely fifty feet from Miguel's own front door, which he must have seen every single day. 'Three thousand pesetas a day?' Jean asked, expecting a Spanish barter.

The madre's eyes bulged at these crazy estranjeros! 'Si, Javier will go to your field. He will work all day. As many days as the Señora will desire.'

Through all this Jeff stood slightly apart, not wishing to interrupt the progress Jean was making. He knew she was much better at such deals, although with her fragile command of Spanish, Jeff had yet to figure out how the Andalusians understand her or indeed, how she understood their far-from-text book dialect. But she did and they did and he strongly suspected it was only by telepathy.

On the following morning, in preparation for Javier's arrival to vanquish the weeds Jean spent the rest of the afternoon picking 'wild flowers' from the field (which looked suspiciously like weeds to Jeff). 'For drying,' she said airily, and tied them up and hung them in bunches upside down on the terrace rejas, where Munchkin, who clearly knew she'd never dried a flower before, tried to pull them down on the theory that anything constructive humans might attempt should be instantly destroyed.

'Just think, Jeff. All the time we were looking we had a tractor right in our own backyard. It's just like the old song,' she said that evening sitting in the tub while he scrubbed her back.

'What song?'

She sang him the phrase: 'You'll find that happiness lies - right under your eyes - back in your own backyard!' Her voice could never carry a tune, but they were both too excited to notice. Shoving a floating rubber fish soap dish out of the way he hopped into the tub with her. 'Miguel must have known it was there all the time. Why didn't he ask them for it, do you think?'

The answer to that one came later. 'Because, my dear, 'M' is not on speaking terms with the dairy farmer,' Cynthia told them that night when the Grays came to dinner. Cynthia always referred to Miguel as 'M', in case he was lurking outside a window and overheard her and would think they were talking about him, which they were. 'Something to do with his mother, Maria. I think that the farmer was one of her unmarried husbands while he was still married to this wife. And Heavens knows which one of her children could be his. As the old saying goes, there's been more in Maria's belly than ever went in through her face.'

'If she had as many sticking out of her as stuck in, she'd look like a porcupine,' Elliot said, greedily sprinkling more cheese on his pasta.

'Really, Elliot, no need for vulgarity!' Cynthia admonished with a secret grin.

Jeff wondered what joke book they boned up on.

⌘

But mañana did not bring Javier. Nor did the next tomorrow. Miguel announced that in his opinion, the farmer's son would not come and said that they should get the big tractor back again from the Sindicado for ten thousand pesetas with his cousin driving.

Jeff said they did not care to lose any more of the trees and how was it that Miguel did not know about this small tractor? Miguel only shrugged and went out to start up the lawn mower.

Jean watched Miguel through the window. 'You know what I think, Jeff? Javier's tractor was the one 'M' was trying to hire for his other cuñado for heavens' knows how little, and then charge us six thousand pesetas a day.'

Jeff agreed, and called Miguel back in from the garden where he was guillotining the grass. He offered the executioner/cum/gardener a beer and brandy and asked him if he would go talk to the lad's mother and explain the situation. Perhaps Javier had not understood Jean's poor Spanish, which by now of course, Jeff appreciated Miguel did. Miguel was so much better at handling these important matters, Jeff said, trying diplomacy. Perhaps he could make it clear where Javier was to work, for his three thousand pesetas (Miguel winced), and that his was the exact small tractor they needed. Javier could do the job three times a year and at his convenience.

One week later and totally unannounced, just as they were about to drive down to San Pedro, Javier drove his tractor up the road and rang their just installed intercom at the gate. Miguel must have known the lad was coming because he instantly appeared in the field. He let Javier in and let him know who was boss by beginning to direct the tractor's trafficking.

Javier's first pass across the upper field was a huge success. With ease he drove his tractor between the trees. Soon the top field was cleared in neat lines of freshly turned earth. It took him half a day, and he said he would come back in the morning to clean the lower field. That left only the wells around the trees to be cleaned. Miguel announced that while he himself was not prepared to work in the field, his borracho cuñado would, for only six thousand pesetas a day, adding, 'It should take him about eight days.'

Jeff said they would have to think about it.

The second day Javier arrived on the tractor and starting down the side of the lower hill. A few minutes later the blades on Javier's tractor struck rock. He had to dismount and dislodge the sizable chunk. The whole lower field turned out to be rocky. And rockier. And rockiest. Boulders, which were supposed to have been removed by the Vivero before planting and which hadn't troubled the Sindicado's large tractor. But Javier's machine was completely disabled and he couldn't even move it to drive it home.

What could be done? The lad went away with a worried expression and Jeff was sure he was afraid his father would blame him for the damage.

For several days after Javier departed, the tractor stood forlornly at the top of the field. Then, when the Thwaites were out, Javier came and somehow got it home. They went down to the farm to see him. Said how sorry they were that his tractor had been damaged, and offered to pay for its repair. But he refused more money and asked only please, that he not be required to return ever again.

'Oh, Jeff, it's all my fault,' Jean said that night as they lay cuddled together in bed sharing that quiet moment when thoughts and worries could fly between them and they were there to comfort each other. 'Why did I think we could have an orchard, a couple of writers like us? What do we know about farms? It was a delusion of grandeur. Now all the trees will die because we can't take care of them and Greenpeace will hate us. And I was so thrilled to think I had brought them into the world. An entire hillside of them!'

He wrapped his arms around her and drew her to him again. 'My earth mother of trees,' he said, making her laugh, and taking away the pain. There was a part of Jean that would never grow up and no matter how old she got, Jeff would always see the child in her. He kissed her tenderly. They made gentle love that night and Jeff longed for an answer to the orchard dilemma for only one reason. Because he knew it meant so much to Jean.

Then a few weeks later at one of Davie's house-squatting pool parties, Jeff noticed a gardener working in the perfectly groomed garden. He had an intelligent, sensitive face. Jeff liked the look of him and went out to talk to him. It turned out that Hassan worked as a freelance gardener and took care of gardens for several of the Arab princes living on the coast. He was about thirty five, a Moroccan, spoke French and Spanish, and seemed a cut above the two younger Moroccans working with him. There was an air of authority and natural elegance about Hassan.

Driving home from the party, Jeff told Jean his secret. He had hired the Moroccan to take care of their orchard. Hassan knew where he could get a small tractor and would also take care of the trees, trim and clean them. He would charge them five thousand pesetas a day per man for everything and would start to work the following week. He even had a telephone. Jean could not believe it.

The first day that Hassan came to work, he knocked on the door and asked for a jug of water for himself and his two men and said that it would take three days twice a year to keep things in shape. He had blue-gray eyes and was thin as a reed and touched the trees with love and tenderness. Jean watched him walk across the field and wondered at his grace and agility. Hassan moved like a dancer.

Miguel was furious with them for hiring a Moroccan and said they were all untrustworthy and did not belong in Spain and one night Hassan would come and rob the house. They must take his cousin. But Jeff told Miguel that they liked and trusted Hassan, and pointed out that Miguel's cuñado had a habit of falling asleep with his brandy under a tree and they did not wish him to work in the orchard. It was one tiny victory over the El Salto Mafia.

There was a mystery about Hassan that they were not to learn for over a year. Not until he brought his small son to visit the orchard one day and they watched the child doing spectacular somersaults in the driveway. Then Hassan told them a bit more about himself. He and his family before him for three generations had been stars of the Moroccan circus. Hassan had been a trapeze artist and had travelled throughout Europe and even to Russia. But when he took one fall too many he could no longer perform. Now he was teaching his son the high wire and one day, he too, would enter the circus. As for Hassan, he oversaw the gardening for many of the Arab Princes. One of them had given him a villa and a car in Spain. His family could earn a good living and his wife worked as a cook. Hassan brought them a plate of delicious Moroccan pastries one day. And at Ramadan, Hassan worked in the field for eight hours and would not eat nor drink water until sunset. They had found the right person to look after the orchard with love.

When the Thwaites were going back to London, Hassan offered to drive them to the airport in the Prince's limousine, and would accept no money for the ride. They rode in style feeling a little guilty and very grand indeed.

When in the following spring, the villagers saw the neat rows of young almond trees, they came out on the road to admire the sight and boasted to their visitors that their village was the most beautiful in the area with a duck pond, a waterfall, a road, and now an orchard which covered the entire hillside in pink and white blossom. And they hated the estranjeros a wee bit less because they had made it all happen.

And in the following September, when little Paco took to climbing over the wall or under the fence to steal nuts and stick out his tongue at Jean, she went down and offered him a job. How would he like to earn two hundred pesetas and hour for picking the crop? And he could have some to take home to his mother. Suddenly she had three little pickers and Paco stopped sticking out his tongue.

'You know something Jeff? I think the villagers are beginning to accept us,' she said one night, and both of them felt at peace on their hill. For the moment.

It wouldn't last.

⌘

It began with a moving religious event which Jeff named 'The Cream Cake Finale'—or 'After the Stodge Was Over'. But Jean had been deeply moved by the day.

The girl was twelve and a pudding of a child whose colouring was all wrong for a Spaniard. Miguel's red haired, freckle-faced daughter Paca was clothed like a bride for her first communion. Jean wondered what foreigner had fathered Miguel. Paca came up to the finca all smiles, to show off her pretty white dress and tiny veil set on a tiara of satin band dotted with pearls. The dress was of stiff white taffeta with lace inset into the little puffed sleeves. The hem came to four inches above the new white shoes. Paca's figure had somehow not yet decided on a final shape and it remained suspended in that indefinite stage between childhood and nubile girlhood. She walked like a duck and managed to look dumpy. At least a week of Miguel's salary must have gone into paying for the dress and pride shone from his flat, round face and glowed in his wily blue eyes.

The family was already on the way to the church when the invitation was offered to the Thwaites to come along. It was a chance to watch all the children of the appropriate age in the congregation being confirmed at once. Jean hurriedly donned a skirt and grabbed a scarf to cover her head and took her camera along, not sure of the protocol of photographing such an event. But her offer to take photos of mother and daughter was eagerly accepted. And of the son. And of the other multitudinous relatives. Girls and boys, aunts, uncles, cousins, and all. It was quite a moving sight and for the occasion, and suddenly, little Paca looked almost pretty.

The church square in San Pedro was centered by a formal patch of garden inside a ring of road one block long. Down at the entrance to the town was a large park square with an ornate stone fountain and hundreds of roses, but this small square was no poor relative. It sported neat arches of shrubbery and benches and a surreal Daliesque statue of Saint Peter that hovered and loomed over all, almost as tall as the church itself. Flowers bloomed in thick profusion of reds and pinks and yellows and the El Salto villagers stood about chattering and laughing with their San Pedro betters and drinking from beer cans as the families filed into the church for the ceremony. Almost everyone had at least one child in the ceremony. The boys and girls wore deadly serious faces and the mothers wore pride pinned from ear to ear.

Inside the church, Jeff and Jean sat to one side close enough to get some good shots of the ceremony, with a central focus on Paca. It was from this church that the Saint and the Virgin and the figure of Jesus himself were carried out and marched through the town down to the sea front and back again on relevant holy days. El Salto was too tiny to have a church and when the Thwaites had given the land for the road, a deputation asked them for few extra square meters to build a chapel.

They were about to say yes when the Grays stopped them. The proposed sight would be just below the Gray's house and 'Don't you see what they're up to?' Cynthia asked querulously, 'Every time there's another death in the village, we'll have a dead body there over night and villagers moaning and crying until dawn. Can't have that, Jeff. You've got to refuse them the land.' Trying to keep everyone happy, Jeff, the diplomat, suggested that they place the chapel in the square near the duck pond but the villagers were afraid it might interfere with commerce. Commerce? This was before the Thwaites knew about the proposed kiosk and the new restaurants.

In the bright noonday sun with the heat rising to one hundred and five degrees, Jeff lined up the Tenado family on the steps of the church and Jean took pictures. Two rolls of them.

From then on, it was a custom the villagers expected of her. For some reason none of the Tenados owned a camera, and Jean decided it must be just too mechanical for Miguel to manage.

After the ceremony they returned to El Salto and repaired to an outdoor fiesta in front of Miguel's small casa. Planks set across Coca Cola cases made trestle tables on the dusty hillside. Chairs had been dragged from every house. Potato crisps, olives, chorizos, chunks of tasty bread, thick tortillas of egg, potato, and onion, Garbanzo beans in oil and garlic and Arroz a la Zamorana, which turned out to be a delicious concoction of rice and pork. And in the centre, the great communion cake with the diminutive bride doll atop (no groom).

Food was forced down their throats, awash with over-sweet, tepid Sangria and gobs of cake. The Ridgeways and the Grays, who it turned out had been invited too, made a late appearance at the feast, carefully missing the religious event. Jean had dashed back to Santa Rita and hastily found an appropriate gift for Paca and when it was dutifully presented it vanished into the house without a word. Jamming a mouthful of tortilla into her teeth, Cynthia confirmed that 'thank you' is never said for a gift, nor is it ever opened in front of the giver. The Andalucians do not consider an over display of gratitude to be in good taste.

Home at last with slight indigestion, Jeff took some anti-acid pills with a deep resolve. 'Half a melon for supper, Jean Nada mas.' Jean had barely seeded the melon when the door was shaken by thunderous knocks. A drunken Miguel and his also *borracho* brother-in-law Luciano teetered in, bearing half of a second communion cream cake frosted with white roses. Nor would they budge or even down their whiskies and Coca Colas until Jeff and Jean had been seen to have consumed a goodly portion. So much for Jeff's resolve.

⌘

Since the children had stopped playing football in the field, they had seen less of Pedro, the gentle Mongol boy. Sometimes they would find him sitting by the wall of his house just outside their new gate, a smile on his face when they came through it and often he would get up from his favourite spot and shuffle over to open the gate for them. Always as before, the small child clung to one of his hands.

As time passed, Paco's mobility seemed to decrease, as did his cheery smile or fumbled words of recognition. He would sit for long hours on the ground, leaning against the white-washed wall watched over by the growing child in his charge.

Then one very dark moonless night they were awakened by loud wailings and moans of female voices coming up from the village. The dogs picked it up with some sort of psychic sympathy and began to howl, too. The Thwaites did not learn until the next day that this chilling sound was the first mourning for Pedro's passing at the age of eighteen. He had been found sitting on the floor of his room, holding his head, unable to describe the pain that must have racked him. Their little friend Pepé, their personal town crier, came up to the house to tell them the sad news. She said that his face had turned black in the night, and they knew it was time for him to die.

Jean brought a large bouquet of red carnations into the small hot room where the coffin rested on a table. The family sat weeping in attendance. 'Did you know Jean, the word 'Mongol' comes from the word for brave. And I'd say that Pedro's whole life was brave,' Jeff said, not ashamed to allow a tear to touch the corner of his eye.

But the tragedy was not complete. The child who had been his constant companion became quite unmanageable. One day, despite all warnings, he ran in front of a motor bike and was struck down dead. This time, there had been no Pedro to deter him.

Jean and Jeff were both so depressed that they decided to accept an invitation they might otherwise not have considered. Afterwards they were glad they had. They had often seen the castle stuck in the hills above Marbella and wondered about its occupant. Now it had a 'For Sale' sign on it, and Davie was looking after it for a friend of his in the Real Estate business; the man Cynthia Gray called The Widow Walker. Naturally, Davie threw a party in it, and the Thwaites got a chance to explore this castle in Spain. When they got home that night and crawled into bed, Jean said, 'Jeff - I've got a strange idea for a story.'

'Funny,' he told her. 'So have I. Let's compare notes.' It turned out to be the Widow Walker's story about this particular castle in Spain, and they began writing it the next morning.

⌘

21: A CASTLE IN SPAIN

I'd lived in Spain for about ten years by that time. Some members of the British Colony (which includes the Americans on the Coast) call me 'The Widow Walker' because I'm a hostess's delight; always willing to escort a widowed lady to a dinner party, decked out in my still presentable blue jacket, white flannel trousers, a pale blue sport shirt or even, if it's a fairly posh do, sporting an old school tie. I didn't happen to attend Charterhouse Public School, but few people have ever queried it and Charterhouse 'old boys' don't show up much on this coast, being a more stuffy lot.

Although I was long ago a widower myself, I have never had an inclination to remarry or indeed, form a permanent relationship with a woman at my time of life. But the old hormones do play up once in a while and I content myself with collecting antique erotica, mostly Japanese, and being a silent observer of other people's foibles. I am too set in my ways to change and there is a certain routine to my days. I limit myself to a half bottle of wine a day, putter around my garden a bit and work part time in the Barata Real Estate Office in Marbella. Property on this coast changes hands faster than any place in the world, now days and although I'm British, I do sell a good deal of property to Americans. I found a good place to meet prospective buyers with money to spend at the Marbella Club bar. That is where I met Arthur.

Arthur had been a chiropractor in Connecticut, but it wasn't his dream to be a Connecticut Yankee. Castles in Spain were what Arthur dreamt about. Maybe the idea was a hangover from the illustrated fairy tale books his mother used to send him off to dreamland with as a child, or the effects of a fast game of 'Dungeons and Dragons'. Or perhaps in those formative years, the old lyrics of 'My Romance' had haunted him into action. Arthur's concept of romance presumably needed 'a castle rising in Spain'. Certainly it was a romantic idea, and Arthur saw himself as cutting a more romantic figure with a castle.

Not that he didn't have charm to the ladies. He worked and played hard at keeping himself in shape and never put on an ounce of fat, certainly in all the years I knew him. With his short-cropped dark hair, flashing brown eyes, snub-nosed youthful features and bulging biceps, it was genuinely hard to judge exactly how old he was. Some thought Arthur must be around 'thirtyish' in those early days. But others including me, believed he was a good deal older. I never actually saw his passport.

As I started to tell you, Arthur never much liked his profession, nor spoke of it. It was purely by accident that I found out what he'd done before he came to Spain. It was one day when I came upon his American high school year book tucked into his bookcase between a copy of Boccaccio's 'The Decameron' and a particularly well illustrated copy of 'The Kama Sutra', which I wouldn't have minded owning. There was a bookmark at his picture. In the year book—not the Kama Sutra.

Arthur came up just then and grabbed it from my hands before I could focus on the date, but he was certainly older than he admitted to, by a good ten years. Beneath his photo it said: 'Wants to be a Chiropractor so he can bend people to his will. Ha ha.' Americans pass that sort of thing off as humor. I asked Arthur about it and somewhat embarrassed, he admitted that he had practised that discipline. Until he retired. He'd made enough from his Chiropractic practice to live a lux lifestyle without the tactical error of getting married because he had long ago discovered that marriage was not for him. I'd discovered that, three years into my own marriage. But that's another matter.

Still, Arthur had not been rich enough to pay for a dream castle in Spain until the untimely death of his father and a bachelor uncle in the same private Lear jet crash. This double death produced two incontestable wills and provided him with an unexpected twin inheritance. Arthur shed a tear for his father, but he never much liked his uncle, and he certainly hadn't expected to inherit from the old boy. So in the end he thought a lot more of his uncle than he had in the beginning.

Arthur took the Spanish bull by the horns and retired at an age when most men were just getting their second wind. He decided to devote the rest of his days to sport and pleasure. Skiing at Aspen or Kitzbüehl in the winter, travelling the world in the Spring or Autumn—and somehow making his castellated dreams come true for all the sunny summer days ahead.

On Arthur's first trip to Spain to look for his castle he'd discovered The Marbella Club on the Costa del Sol. That year Marbella was the hangout of the International jet set. The British 'Wide Boys' and Villains kept their distance, but anyone whose name appeared in a fan mag, gossip column, or society page was heading there and that meant they too, had followers. A steady stream of newly nubile beauties pouring in on their 'hols' for ten days or so, mostly from Britain, assorted Europeans and a fistful of Americans, all hunting excitement, glamour, or possibly a rich husband. Secretaries, college girls, you name it—pouring in to catch a bit of reflected high life, if they were lucky. They could settle for a sunny beach if they weren't.

And should they be staying somewhere down the coast in a Bed and Breakfast, they'd soon learned where the Marbella Club was, and discovered that the beach in front of it was free for anyone to walk on. They could bring their own beach towel, put on their best bikini and head for it. The sand and water were the same, but the people up in the private patio above them were very different for one reason. They had money, or the use of it.

Arthur discovered he could lie out on a club deck chair and ogle the girls on the beach below to his heart's content. He could go down and chat them up, bring them up for a drink or two at the bar, and if luck was with him, end up with one or two of them in his bed that night. That first year in Spain Arthur knew for certain he had come to the right place. All he pined for was a castle.

To his regret, he also discovered that there were no castles to buy within close range of Marbella. Oh, he could have travelled inland a few hundred miles or found plenty of real castles for sale in the north of Spain, but that wasn't the reason for his wanting a castle. Arthur required it to be near the action.

He decided that the best approach was to build his own castle. Not a modern palace like King Faud had built for himself on that same burgeoning coast, but an authentic, genuine looking fake eleventh century type of castle complete with turrets and secret passages and a torture chamber where Arthur could play at his own Dungeons and Dragons. He imagined that a castle in Spain would hold an irresistible attraction for almost any young female who found her way to the coast, particularly if she was a bit kinky. I must say, his appraisal of the situation was fairly accurate.

That's when I came into the picture. I ran into him one night in the zebra-striped Club bar and we got to talking. He dropped that he was looking for a spot of land to build on, but it had to be really close to the Marbella Club. It just so happened that I had been trying to peddle a dog-end bit of land for two years which seemed to fit his requirements. I was fairly honest with him; warned him it was an extremely attenuated stretch, too narrow for a normal house, but it could actually be seen from the Marbella club below. I took him out of the patio and pointed it out to him. He had to view it immediately.

To Arthur, position was everything. He temporarily rented a villa in the Marbella Club and permanently purchased that unsalable plot perched on a perpendicular protrusion of rocky earth where you could just glimpse the Marbella Club and had a great view of the sea. I steered him to an architect and local builder (Ten percent kickback. A man must live.) who could construct the sort of fairy tale castle Arthur had in mind. Reality was not the prime requisite. It had to be built in white marble that would sparkle in the sun when seen from the Carretera de la Muerte below. His builder found a sufficient supply of the stone in a local mountain called La Concha, but known as The Magic Mountain. This did nothing for the mountain but it produced enough gargantuan boulders, some of them with streaks of crystal, to build Arthur's castle, turrets, crenulations and all.

The architect warned him that because the depth of the land was so limited, everything would have to be scaled sideways. Long, narrow rooms. Fine by Arthur. Since he intended to live in it only in the summer, his castle did not need to have any real practicality to it like electricity or central heating. It was to be a summer house with lots of candles, and hot and cold running guests for parties, parties, parties, featuring plenty of booze and a few light drugs.

His baronial main hall was no larger than eight feet deep, by about twenty feet in length. Nevertheless, he had set his heart upon a grand fireplace with an impressively carved coat of arms, so he went to one of those people in New York who trace your ancestral lineage by DNA and came up with a genealogically-suspect 16th century Hungarian Count dangling somewhere distantly from a family branch. The crest of this blue-blooded kith was duly carved by a tombstone maker in marble, to set above the stone fireplace.

Arthur drove across Spain, crossed the Alcantara Bridge over the Tagua River and in Toledo, found a repro suit of armor and a few modern reproduction swords to adorn his Hall. There was scarcely room for three bedrooms in his castle, even with a second story. His master bedroom, built flat against the side of the hill, was just deep enough for the bed, and that was slightly smaller than 'king'. No room for anything else.

Higher up the hill to the left of the main building a separate tower was reachable by a narrow stone bridge. It housed only a guest room and bathroom that owed a lot to Rumpelstiltskin and featured an ornately carved bed canopied in pale blue velvet, embroidered with gilt fleur de lys, in which to sleep a fair maiden or three. There were a few whips and chains lying about, just in case somebody forgot why they were up there and actually went to sleep.

The builder had constructed a high stone exterior wall shielding the castle. It was topped by crushed glass to deter any enemies. A winding mountain road, roughly hewn from the hillside's stony face and paved with concrete led to the great iron gate with its spearheaded perpendicular cross bars looking ominous enough to keep out any dragon. Once locked, nobody could actually enter or leave the castle.

The whole thing took about eight months to complete, to the wonder of the hillside neighbours on the streets below whose curiosity was piqued. It looked like a stage set waiting for the play to begin. Had Hamlet moved to the Costa del Sol? They didn't have long to wait. The builders were as finished as they ever would be and no Hamlet, Arthur moved in.

In the main castle, a torture chamber-cum-bar was adorned by a real skull and ceramic skull-shaped drinking cups and a few assorted instruments of torture which Arthur had handmade by one of Toledo's finest ironsmiths. There was a chastity belt which seemed hardly the point, and it was with some regret that he was unable to obtain a spike-bellied Iron Maiden from Nüremberg, but under the circumstances of what took place, it was just as well. The decor also featured a plastic skeleton chained to the wall. It usually had a rose in its teeth and wore a Spanish Flamenco hat which somewhat defeated its more sinister aspect. The black marble bar top was wide enough for the most exotic sexual encounters, particularly if one of the parties was chained up like the nearby skeleton. There were voyeurs' bar stools—but curiously enough, Arthur never invited me to any orgies that I am certain took place there. Arthur moved in with a load of luggage and three male guests he'd met in various resorts around the world, whom he'd invited to join him for one Spanish month.

This became an annual routine. On the surface, the group were an unlikely combination, held together possibly by a love of dissipation and sufficient means to support it. Sam, around forty, still worked at something in the American government, which was probably clandestine since he never spoke of it. Henri, based in Paris, had never worked a day in his thirty two years. He was extremely laid back, and I soon dubbed him 'Ennui' (but not to his face). The third man Frederick they called Freddie, who was only twenty three, had shares in the family manufacturing business in the U.K., which never seemed to require him to be in that country. One had the feeling that his family preferred he stay away as long as possible. I once made inquiries into the type of manufacture and discovered they produced enema bags and tubing equipment for high colonics.

Finally settled in, Arthur, who already had a silver Porsche, bought himself a bright red Dune Buggy that soon became an accustomed sight crawling slowly down the main street of Marbella and pausing in front of the Deporte Café. He drove young Freddie down there to show him the ropes of how to pick up girls.

'Why don't you drive the Porsche?' Freddie asked him.

'Too obvious, kid,' Arthur said cockily. 'This is a holiday car for fun. Girls figure you couldn't have a car like this unless you have several. Now learn how it's done from the King.'

Arthur would lean across the seat to any Guineveres sitting out having a coffee and politely ask: 'Excuse me, which way to the Deporte Café?'

His opening line always made them laugh and was a good conversation opener. Or if they didn't know they were sitting in the Deporte Café, he'd ask, 'Which way to the beach?' Because they were as foreign as he, and he looked fairly spectacular with his even teeth, dark haired good looks like a taller Tom Cruise, with his flashy red vehicle, they would be taken off guard and would go into helpful explanations of how he could reach the beach. He stretched these conversations further by asking even more stupid questions like, 'Is it sandy?' 'Is the water cold?' 'Do I turn left?' Since they could see the sea to the left of them, even the slowest of girls began to get wise. Then he'd let drop that just up the hill to their right—and they could see it if they turned around—he had a big white house, and that he was throwing a party.

He never used the word 'castle' because, as he once explained to me, 'The trick is, you never mention that. Then when they get up there, they figure you're so rich you've got too many other houses to mention, and the girl is yours.' It was true, they usually came quietly in pairs or in triplicate. With his amigos, he could cope with that but I'm sure Arthur could have coped alone.

He had other ambitions besides bolstering his bachelor-bonking self image; he wanted to get in with the Right Set in Marbella. His concept of who was right, were the types that hung around the Marbella Club. Arthur began inviting them to the parties and most of them came. German Countesses, English aristos, French authors, American actors and actresses, Arab Princes—those who were a bit low down on the Royal totem pole. You never knew who you'd meet. I picked up a few buyers for property at his parties.

And as a party thrower, he had an infallible system. Get a couple of girls up to the castle who could cook (All the German girls and most of the Swedish ones could. Most of the English and American ones couldn't.) and ask them how they'd like to stay a night or two and have a real big party. They felt safety in numbers. Since up to that point, Arthur and friends had acted the perfect gentlemen, the girls would say yes, enthusiastically. He would install a couple of them in the ivory tower and they would toddle down across the little, rickety stone bridge overlooking the craggy rocks below and outdo each other in the cooking department, making vast bowls of fried chicken, salad, chili, hamburgers, beans, and the like. They were not so quick on the cleaning up but they soon got the message and did it, too.

Surprisingly Arthur, also invited the un-swinging married couples of the foreign colony to these soirées, knowing they always went home early. When he got invited back to one of their parties, he came alone. Sometimes he left with one of the young unmarried women. These social types he treated quite differently and took to dinner in posh restaurants. But there were always parties and plenty of food and drink and it wasn't just the freeloaders who attended regularly.

Arthur settled into his Spanish summers, and few people knew what went on up at the castle once the gate was locked.. Then several summers on——I think it was the third one—Arthur ran into Drushka. She was tall, and solidly boned with serene, even features and a slightly upturned nose that was made for photography. She wore her long silky, black hair off her face in a hair band. Her figure was too Rubenesque to be a model, but beautiful all the same. Drushka's dark eyes were long-lashed and innocent, although that day Arthur spotted her at the Deporte Café she was celebrating her twenty fourth birthday all alone, eating a cupcake with one candle on it. It was the ideal opening gambit for a pickup. She was thrilled to be invited to his party. Arthur was the first person she had spoken to, and she could try out her school book English on him which she'd learned in Zamość, the city in Poland where she was born.

Drushka told Arthur she had come alone on this holiday and had nothing much to go back to but a dreary secretarial job which she didn't much care if she lost. She could always get another. Her mother, a widower, had just remarried and preferred Drushka not around. She wanted to improve her English and maybe leave Zamość and Poland forever, although it was a beautiful old city. Arthur told her he'd teach her a lot of things and I suppose you could say that he did.

They made love that first night and Drushka was surprised at his passion. But he didn't go too far and took proper precautions. I expect he was always careful not to become an unexpected father. The next night after the party, Drushka was washing glasses in the long open kitchen. Sam and 'Ennui' and Freddie had invited several other girls up to the castle. The guests had all left and the girls had disappeared with the three men.

Arthur came up behind Drushka, running a finger down her back. A glass nearly slipped from her hand. He caught it as it fell, setting it carefully on the counter. It had his crest hand-painted on it. He pulled Drushka around to him, and kissed her. He'd been smoking a joint and put it between her lips. She took a few drags and felt spacy. Then to her surprise, Arthur slipped a ring on her finger. She stared at it. It looked just like gold and bore his crest. Arthur had them made in Spain by the dozen and gave one to each girl he slept with. Since they were all of one size, Drushka's went on her little finger, which was still a tight fit. Arthur figured a girl could wear the ring until it turned green, but by that time she'd be back wherever she came from. Like all the others, Drushka was swept off her feet by such lavish gestures and Arthur was definitely a man for gestures. While she was trying to thank him, his mouth pressed down roughly on hers again and lingered there with unrelenting desire. 'I want you. Right now, Drushka,' he breathed. It was his usual opening line.

'What has happened to Henri and the others?' she asked, not really caring.

'They don't need us. Unless you prefer an orgy.'

She giggled and took another puff. He kissed her again forcing his tongue into her mouth. It sent a quiver of pleasure deep into her groin. Then he took her hand and led her through the hall and up the narrow staircase to his bedroom.

'I want to hold you. Possess you,' he said. 'You're mine.' That line worked on all his women. He took Drushka into the room and kissed her again, all the while expertly unfastening the row of buttons down the front of her dress, easing it from her shoulders until it dropped to the floor. Her breasts curved up tauntingly brown from the sun, dark red nipples, a generous circle. She wore no bras and full lavender flowered panties that looked like a school girl's and a glowing tan covered firm legs. Drushka helped him undress her, excited by the desire in his eyes.

'How many men have you had, Drushka?'

'I haven't asked about your past, have I?' she said, feeling very sophisticated. There had been three men, but none of them stayed for more than a year.

'Mysterious lady. But I've had hundreds of women. And now I want to have you.'

There was nothing subtle about this approach but Drushka didn't mind. It wasn't love, it was sex and that was all right, too. He drew her to the bed, pulling back the velvet bedcover with the Count's crest emblazoned on it. He took time to fold the cover back carefully, and put it on a chair. The sheets were cream satin with a large crest worked in gold thread on the center of the hem. They felt softly cool on her skin. He came down beside her, kissing her neck and then ran an inquisitive tongue along each breast. 'How many knights have fought duels over you, Drushka?'

She laughed. 'There are no knights or duels any more, even in my country.'

'That's where you're wrong, my girl. You could unleash the dragons, couldn't you? Now you've unleashed mine. And you're a prisoner in my castle.'

She laughed again. 'I can't tell when you're being serious.' Never serious, he pressed his body forcefully on top of her and she could feel the tight ripple of hard muscle She felt tingling and alive. 'Oh, Arthur, how you make me feel,' she sighed.

'I know all there is to know about sex,' he said. 'How many guys have found your 'g' spot, eh?' His finger probed delicately and drew from her a surge of feeling, an explosion of desire. Swiftly he moved to mount her and her knees came up to hold him. 'You like it, don't you Drushka? I can feel how much you want me.'

She hated to admit it but it was true. Once, she'd had a steady lover. They'd lived together for that year. But when they split up she felt relief. He had become a habit, and there was no love, no passion, no desire, only convenience. Maybe it was the joint she'd smoked, maybe she'd been celibate too many months, but whatever, now she felt insatiable. Arthur rose up resting his weight on his hands.

'I want to see your face--look at you when you come. I want to know what I can make you feel.' His hips kept their steady unbroken rhythm as he rolled onto his back drawing her up on top of him, still in control of the rhythm of their bodies. But after a few minutes he brought her back down, covering her body with his. 'That's enough domination, my princess.' Drushka was transported into the sheer rapture of gratification, floating on the joy of it. A deep moan of ecstasy escaped her lips. It was echoed by Arthur. 'You belong to me. You're mine,' he said as they climaxed.

Drushka had allowed herself to be swept off her feet with the half promise that maybe she could stay all summer as Arthur's girl friend if they continued to get along, and if she obeyed the house rules. He didn't specify exactly what those rules were, but if not, Arthur would buy her a return ticket home. They went down to the beach every day and fucked every night. She had fallen in love with Spain, maybe even with Arthur, and so she agreed.

It was some time after Drushka's arrival that I came by the castle, but I found the gate was locked and there was no answer to the bell. I thought it odd, since it was only 11:00 o'clock and the men were usually in the middle of the night's activities. No one seemed to be home. I peered through the gate, and was saw the Porsche in the shelter at the back. I didn't see the Dune Buggy but he rarely used it at night. So where were they all?

⌘

What happened that night, will never be totally known. I repeat here only what Arthur had to swear to in a court of law and told me personally much, much later.

The other girls had left and only Drushka remained at the castle. As the afternoon siesta hour ended, Drushka came down from her tower and found Henri coming out of Arthur's bedroom. From the look on his face and the state of his dress, it was clear that he'd been to bed with Arthur. She hadn't expected that. Arthur had seemed so utterly masculine, so she dismissed it thinking she must be mistaken. Arthur was smoking a joint and obviously very high. He stuck the joint in Drushka's mouth. She tried to say no, but Arthur flew into a rage. 'Dammit you have to follow the rules! Didn't I tell you?' She suddenly felt frightened and took the cigarette. Since she hadn't eaten anything all day, it went straight to her head.

At that moment, Sam and Freddie came down the staircase with their arms linked. Freddie's long hair was in a tangle. The men paused on the landing and Drushka wondered for a moment if they were all gay. Arthur went into the bar and began to mix a pitcher of drinks. 'What we need is some games,' he said. 'What say we all share Drushka?' The others laughed, and she assumed he was joking. But she was getting angry and just a little frightened. 'What is wrong with all of you?' she cried. 'Are you all gay? All of you?'

'Don't be ridiculous, Drushka. We're not gay. We swing both ways," Arthur told her. 'Ambidextrous!'

The other men laughed.

'I've had enough, Arthur. Take me down to town,' she demanded.

'You go when I say, and not before,' he told her, his voice harsh now.

'Who do you think you are?' she screamed. 'Wait until I tell all those fancy friends of yours at the Marbella Club that you're nothing but a pack of... of pillow biters!' She's learned the term from Arthur.

'Calm down, babe. Besides the gate's locked and I've lost the key,' he said and handed her a glass of the brew he was mixing. 'Here, get that down you. You'll feel more cheerful.' He kissed her on the cheek. 'I was only kidding. Let's have some fun!' He turned the stereo up full blast and started dancing around the room.

She held the drink in her hand, deciding what to do. If she tried to leave now, she was certain she would not get far. The others filled their glasses and started to drink and dance. 'Drink up, Drushka. There's plenty more,' Arthur commanded. She sipped. It tasted bitter sweet. Arthur grabbed her glass and tipped the liquid into her mouth. 'When I say drink, I mean now!' he said, eyes flashing. She gulped down the drink and felt woozy. The men were talking and laughing but she couldn't quite focus on their words any more.

'Fresh air...!' she breathed and headed out to the patio. Arthur didn't even notice. He had joined the men in a Greek style dance.

Drushka decided to go up to her tower room. She knew there was no lock on the door, but she would let things cool down a bit. Pack her few clothes and be ready for a chance to get away. Her head was spinning.

She headed up the path and started across the narrow, rickety stone bridge leading to the ivory tower, feeling quite giddy. One more step and then another; she grabbed for the railing - and then she passed out. Drushka fell over the narrow balustrade and landed in a rocky thicket some 25 feet below.

In the kitchen maybe half an hour later, Arthur turned to give an order to Drushka, but she wasn't there. "Where'd she go...?' As no one answered he shouted: 'Drushka! Come here!'

'She went out to the patio a little while ago,' Sam told him.

'I'm hungry,' Henri said. 'Let's get Drushka to cook something.'

Arthur started out, shouting her name. But there was no answer. The others followed him to the patio.

"Maybe she went for a swim," said Freddie. But they could see the pool and the water was smooth.

"Maybe she's in the tower,' Sam said.

'Yeah, the tower,' said Arthur, and started up the path to the narrow bridge, the others behind him. As he started across, Freddie cried out. 'Down there. . . ! It's Drushka!"

All eyes went to the body crumpled in the thicket below.

It was Arthur who climbed down, picked her up and carried her to the castle. He laid her out on the black marble bar in the torture room. Her dress was torn and she was very, very still.

'Jesus, Arthur!' Sam said. 'What the hell have you done?'

'You've killed her!' Henri said.

Freddie who knew a smattering of things medical from his knowledge of high colonics, felt her neck for a pulse. There was none.

'My God! This time you've really done it, Arthur,' moaned Sam, sinking to the floor, his head in his hands, half crazy with fear, thinking of his government job.

'Me..? Goddammit, it was an accident, you fucker!' Arthur said in a panic, staring at her and thinking fast. 'We were all in here!" There was a long silence while everyone thought.

'Guess we'd better call the police', Freddie said.

'Are you out of your frigging mind?' Arthur cried. The last thing we want up here is the cops. The castle's full of drugs and a lot of them are in Drushka.'

'I don't think we can pass this off as an accident,' Freddie said, looking at the girl with a clinical eye.

There was silence while each man riffled through his mind in hopes of coming up with a convenient answer. Arthur stood over her, resolution on his face. 'It's simple. We get rid of the body. So nobody traces her here.'

'How?' asked Henri. 'You don't even have an incinerator.'

'Bury her?' Sam asked.

'Not on my land!' Arthur sat on a stool, musing. 'I wonder if we could buy lime somewhere.'

'Where?' asked Henri, just coming out of his drug fog.

'We could eat her,' Freddie said thoughtfully. 'Put her on that big barbeque pit. You cooked a goat on it when that Arab was here.'

"What would we do with the bones?' asked Sam.

'Why not take her out to sea and dump her?' asked Henri.

'Arthur doesn't have a boat,' Sam pointed out.

'My bad,' Arthur said, somehow finding humor in the moment.

They sat there in silence for a few more minutes, and then Arthur said, 'Here's what we're going to do.'

They looked at him. He seemed surprisingly calm and in control. 'We wrap her up in a sheet and...' He stopped in mid sentence. 'No. No good. All mine are silk and have crests on them.'

They sat in silence again.

'There's a painter's dust sheet in the garage. I saw it,' Freddie suddenly remembered.

'Good thinking!' Arthur got to his feet and went down to the garage. He returned a few minutes later with a dust sheet covered in paint. A calm, authoritative expression lit his stubbled face. 'After all, she's just another girl on the drift,' he said. 'Right?'

The men got the body down from the bar, laid it out on the dust sheet and wrapped it up tightly. Drushka's head was bloody and her body was badly bruised from the fall. They tied the sheet in knots around her.

'Now what?' asked Freddie.

'Now we get her in the Dune Buggy,' Arthur said.

'Goddammit, Arthur! Your fucking Dune Buggy's got no top. How the hell are we supposed to hide her in that?' Sam croaked.

'The Porsche is too small,' Arthur mused. 'It's gotta be the Buggy. We'll put her on the floor in back. I'll drive. Sam next to me. Henri and Freddie can put their feet over her'. He looked at them sharply. 'It's night, for Christ's sake!'

'Okay, okay,' Sam agreed. 'But where the hell will we take her?'

'We drive up to Ronda. Drop her over the bridge,' Arthur told them confidently.

'Christ, that's an hour and a half from here!'

'So what? You have a better plan? It'll still be dark when we get there, and the bridge is at least a hundred feet above the river. We drop her over and nobody will ever find her. If they do, they couldn't trace her to us.'

'Are you sure?' Henri asked doubtfully.

Arthur's idea was the only one they had, so they took it, rather than delay.

Half way up the Ronda Road, they stopped to pick up some mammoth rocks to tie into her winding sheet. When they reached the bridge at the entrance to the town, it was past midnight and there was no one in sight. They got out the body, and although they couldn't see below too well because there was no moon that night, they managed to hoist her over the railings. There was a moment's delay and then they heard the dull splash of the body as it hit water far below. But they could tell the water was shallow. More shallow than they had counted on. They could make out that the bundle did not shift from the rocks and wash on down river. They stood there for a few more moments trying to see if it had sunk. But in the leaden night they could see nothing in the deep gorge.

'This is the bridge Hemingway wrote about in 'For Whom the Bells Toll', Sam said, staring solemnly down into the blackness.

'I always did like Ingrid Bergman,' Henri said, pensive.

'Let's get the hell out of here!' Arthur barked, turning quickly towards the Dune Buggy. He lit a cigarette and slid behind the wheel. He was as calm as ice.

When they got back to the castle, they gathered up all of Drushka's clothes and burned everything in the baronial fireplace. It stank up the room and they went out by the pool and drank two bottles of brandy without getting drunk. The next day and for two days afterwards, they bought the Spanish papers to see if there was any news. They found nothing about a body being found.

'You see? I told you,' Arthur said. 'Now let's get packed and get the hell out of Spain for a while. How about Aspen? The season starts in a few weeks anyway. We'll get ourselves a lodge and have some fun.' So Arthur and his friends prepared to leave Spain until things cooled down.

⌘

That morning the police came to me at the Barata Real Estate Office. You see, under the splattered paint on the dust sheet that the men had wrapped Drushka in, they found the builder's stamp. The police had no trouble in tracing it. When they asked the builder, he wasn't certain which of his several jobs it might have been from, so he suggested they ask me.

The Detective in charge of the case came to my office and laid a ring on my desk. It contained a crest that I was only too familiar with. 'It is terrible, Señor, what someone has done to this young woman and you are my only lead.' He showed me poor Drushka's photo and even though the body had been crushed on the rocks at the Ronda bridge, there was no mistaking her. Arthur and his friends had not been aware that at this season of the year, the river in the gorge was scarcely more than a trickle. The shroud had burst open and the body was spotted the very next day, but the police had kept the story temporarily out of the Press because it might upset tourism.

The Detective glared across my desk, retrieving the photos. 'The Court will not spare foreigners who come to our country and take the law into their hands,' he said with a scathing look, since I was a foreigner. 'Los extranjeros serán condenados a muchos años de prisión!'—meaning Foreigners will be sentenced to many years in prison.

As reluctant as I was to tell the detective what I knew about that ring, I was forced to do just that. He would have found out sooner or later from any number of girls sporting similar rings.

That all happened over a year ago now. I have visited Arthur and his amigos many times in the Cárcel, piecing together the story bit by bit. It will be at least six more months before the case comes to court. Arthur and his friends will have to convince the court that the girl had fallen on her own. But the prosecution consider that if one of them hadn't pushed her, why go to such lengths to get rid of the body?

⌘

There is only one thing to add: I have a very nice castle on the market, going extremely cheaply. It has had only one owner. I'd be delighted to hear from any of you who might be interested, and will reduce my normal 10 per cent commission to 7½ per cent because of this ridiculous story that has surfaced that the castle is haunted. Some say a woman's figure has been seen walking on the narrow stone bridge between the castle and the maiden's tower.

Well, I suppose Drushka did like the castle and she really had nowhere else to go, even dead.

You can contact me at the Barata Real Estate Office on the south side of Orange Square.

⌘

22: I HAVE THE KEY

At Santa Rita, things were not going well for Maria. Her diabetes was getting worse. It didn't stop her from eating sugary churros and she particularly loved those powdery almond cookies that got all over the floor the moment she bit into one. She would give a box of them to the Thwaites at Christmas time and brought churros with her in the pocket of her black dress when she came to clean the house, munching between floor scrapings and leaving a trail of powdered sugar in case the ants were hungry.

Jean felt it her duty to enlighten her cleaning lady about proper dietary procedures when living with diabetes. Had Maria's doctor put her on any special regimen that did not include, say *sugar*? Maria stared at Jean, then laughed and shook her head at this crazy foreigner. She was ill, Maria explained, because she'd had too many children! And since now she had only a few teeth left, she had to eat as much as she could before she didn't have any teeth at all—and could only drink soup! She offered Jean a churro before popping one into her own mouth.

Jeff told Jean that while he appreciated she was trying to help, it was impossible for Maria to understand that what she ate had anything to do with her health. Jean would have to practice her doctor skills elsewhere.

Then a few weeks later Maria announced that she was retiring and her daughter Mercedes was going to replace her. The Thwaites commiserated with her about the state of her health and held a secret celebration that night, got drunk and made exuberant love.

The next day Maria told them she would get the house really clean because she knew that Mercedes could never keep it the way she did. The Thwaites hoped that was true, but suggested that they would quite happily get somebody else instead of Mercedes, if that were the case.

'Impossible,' Maria told them. 'It is decided.'

The Maria Mafia had spoken. But before she left the house she demand a 'pahquaw'. Jean did some hasty delving through their Larousse dictionary but could find no Spanish word that sounded or looked like 'pahquaw'.

The next day Jean was enlightened by Cynthia, who explained that the word was actually 'pascua' and meant a Christmas or Easter celebration. 'But our particular Andalusians had usurped it to mean a gratuity, Jean,' Cynthia added. 'They should be asking for a 'propina'. Money in the hand, my dears. In Maria's case, she is demanding a retirement bonus of one full month's pay from you. Think of it this way; you're getting rid of her,' Cynthia said dryly, smiling to herself because another daughter, Candela worked for her regularly, and she had always been spared Maria's ministrations.

'And it *is* worth paying to get rid of her,' Jeff acquiesced philosophically.

'Let's face it, Jeff. We have no choice—and she *is* actually going!' Jean said, counting the pesetas into an envelope. Later that day Maria stuffed it into her pocket without so much as a gracias, and belched.

⌘

'Why is it none of the villagers ever say 'thank you' for presents at Christmas time? Jean asked Cynthia later.

'I told you, Spaniards don't say thanks,' Cynthia said. 'Not our Spaniards, anyway.'

The Thwaites were delighted with Mercedes. She was cheerful, didn't leave crumbs all over the floor, didn't sweep the dirt into the corners, and didn't iron holes into Jeff's shirts. So it came as something of a let-down when only a few happy months later, just when they were getting used to having no ants, one morning Maria appeared on the doorstep in place of Mercedes. A thick, wide hand swept back a greasy forelock from her brow as she pushed past Jeff saying she was bored with not working, and had decided to come out of retirement. Jeff tried to dissuade her. 'You should really be taking better care of yourself —in your condition,' he told her.

'Hmmph! I am not pregnant!' she eyed Jeff as though he might be thinking of trying it, sniffed and offered him a toffee from the bag in her pocket. Before he could refuse, she popped it into her own mouth marching into the kitchen to ride the mop. Jeff wondered how she managed to chew it with only one front tusk showing.

So there she was, back to work and no suggestion of returning her pascua. She continued to titivate the dust for two more months and the ants came trundling back. And then before they were ready for it, it was time for the Thwaites to return to London.

'I'm never ready for it,' Jean said with anticipated nostalgia, patting the new mantelpiece a friend had built over the existing fireplace from a large beam he's found in an abandoned farmhouse. Miguel had helped him and nearly destroyed the rustic beam by deciding to paint it red one day when they weren't home. He could not understand why they would want an old wood beam when they could make it all bright and shiny. The ways of the estranjeros. . . Miraculously, they had walked in just in time and managed to stop him, brush in hand.

'What can we do with Miguel, Jeff?'

'He's a handle bar short of a bicycle, Jean. Accept it.'

'But I'm not accepting Maria!' Jean cried. The next day she practised a speech in Spanish and then faced Maria in the kitchen. 'Maria we will be gone about three months and. . .' Noticing suddenly that she was scrubbing the silver off a spoon, 'No Maria!' she shouted, taking it from her hand. 'You do not use a Brillo pad on the silver!' Not that there was anything else in the house that was silver. But they'd brought down one single large serving spoon from London, which was only silver plated in any case. Maria had nosed unerringly to it, like a hound to the fox. Jean looked at it sadly. It had been a nice old spoon and now the black metal was showing through.

'It is no good, Señora. You should throw it away and get a new one.' She held up a stainless steel spoon. 'Like this! Everything new. Better to clean.'

Jean decided not to pursue this line of thinking and tucked the spoon into a drawer, wondering if she could get it re-silvered. She got back to her speech. 'Maria, it will not be necessary for you to clean the casa more than once a month while we are away. It will be locked up and will not get too dirty. But we would like you to come to the house every day to feed the cats. Naturally, we will pay you a retainer while we are gone.'

Maria shook her head with an inscrutable expression, tight lipped and ominous. She reached into her pocket and held up a shiny metal object. 'I have the key,' she said.

'Yes,' Jean, agreed. 'You do have a key. And we certainly want you to keep it so that you can get into the house to clean it— once a month and feed the cats—every day.' She hoped she was making her point.

Maria pursed her lips and folded her arms across her ample bosom. 'No, Señora. You do not understand—La llave maestra. Yo lo tengo—**I have the key**!' With that she dangled their key ring between a threatening thumb and sturdy forefinger.

Jean turned to Jeff who had entered the kitchen in time to absorb Maria's declaration. 'The key. You have the key,' Jeff nodded vaguely, sure there was some deeper meaning here.

'Yo lo tengo. I have the key.' A look of Machiavellian triumph touched the corner of Maria's thin lips. 'I will clean the house once a week, not once a month, Señora, to keep back the ants. And you will pay me in advance for the three months you are away.' A shrewd light flickered in her watery blue eyes. 'This way you can be certain that no burglars come to Santa Rita while you are gone!'

Implications of a Protection Racket loomed large.

Jeff got the message if Jean did not. Maria had the key, all right, and them under that aggressive thumb. And so when the Thwaites returned three months later, they found the house still standing, but a few less cats demanding breakfast. Maria took no blame. She had fed them regularly she informed them, but there had been an epidemic of cat flu. Fortunately Munchkin was intact and waiting for them, and Tio Rodrego still her abject slave.

But Cynthia Gray told them with a note of accusation in her voice, 'Thank God you're back, my dears! I'm sure Maria has not been feeding your cats because they have all been coming to me for breakfast. And since I now have twenty, it is a bit much, don't you think?'

'Was there cat flu in the village?' Jeff asked.

Cynthia shook her head. 'Too early in the season. Maria seems to have got you where she wants you. You must be more firm with her.'

'Firm? FIRM...? How?' Jeff wondered. Cynthia did not have an answer to that.

Then once again Maria became ill, only this time it was real. She had paused from sweeping the floor to eat an almond cookie when all of a sudden she turned quite pale and damp. Fortunately Jean was in the kitchen at the time. She called Jeff. They piled Maria into the car and drove her down the hill to her house in the square. As befitted her status of Mafia Godmother, Maria's house had the best location in the village facing the duck pond. Another of her daughters, Juana was there and they helped her up the stairs to the tiny sitting room. The Thwaites had never been invited inside before. The room was pin tidy, undoubtedly kept that way by Juana. It boasted a large television set, topped with plaster statues of the Virgin and various saints. A brightly colored print of Jesus and various photos of assorted husbands and grandchildren were hung beside a huge hand-colored photo portrait in a heavy gold painted frame of Miguel's son. The small sofa bed was covered with tiny crocheted dolls and cushions and a chair back was draped with some more of Maria's needlework. Jean suggested Maria must need her *medicina* and Juana quite expertly got out a hypodermic and injected her mother with insulin. Maria said she'd feel so much better if she could have a sweet and took a hard candy from a ready bowl.

'But why wouldn't the doctor warn her about sugar, for God's sake?' Jeff wondered later.

'Because,' Cynthia commented, reluctant to mention names, "M's mother wouldn't listen if she had one foot in the grate.'

'You mean in the grave,' Elliot said.

'Not if she's cremated, I don't,' Cynthia sniffed, which confirmed once more Jean's suspicion that Cynthia and Elliot rehearsed their punch lines.

The next morning, Mercedes was back on the job, saying that her mother was retiring and since she was too ill to come up to collect her pahquaw herself, she would collect it for her. Jeff pointed out that Maria had already had one bonus for retiring. But Mercedes only nodded and said that since her mother was retiring again, he must pay again.

Davie Davies stopped by for drinks with Cynthia and Elliot. When Jean asked him about the price of pahquahs, he said, 'Hell, Jean, you weren't supposed to pay her a retirement bonus in the first place! She'd have to work an eighteen hour week for more than a year to be entitled to that. Streuth, she's just trying it on with you two.'

'And it fit,' Cynthia put in, smugly sipping a soda water.

'It would be cheaper to send her to the French Riviera for a holiday,' Jeff grumbled.

But Jeff and Jean decided for the sake of good will, they would pay up although they drew the line at another full month's salary and offered a week's instead. Mercedes took it with no comment and said her mother was getting better. 'Not too much better?' Jeff said and Jean kicked him. They tried to be charitable and hold kind thoughts, but the news filled them with dread.

As they had feared, the second retirement did not last long either. They told Mercedes they wished her to stay, but she refused on the grounds that her mother wouldn't allow it. Once more the Tusk-Toothed One reappeared and took up her job. But soon Mercedes and Candela began appearing in her place, and still, Jean discovered, turning the wages over to Maria. The Thwaites talked it over and decided that if and when she retired again, they would definitely not under any circumstances pay a bonus or let her come back.

And as they knew it must, the day they had dreaded came. Maria announced that she was quitting for good. As her parting jab before this final retirement, she surprised them with the news that she was not retiring for reasons of health. Suddenly she was well enough to open a kiosk to sell cigarettes and candy in El Salto's small square. Right in front of the duck pond. Right in front of her door.

'Do you think she can add?' Jeff wondered.

'Add what?' Jean asked him.

'To make change. You know, to sell cigarettes to the minors,' But Jean pointed out that she'd been smart enough to get a bonus several times when she wasn't supposed to get any, and to get a concession all expenses paid, granted to her by the local ayuntamiento because she was an aging widow with no visible means of support and was a so-called pillar of the community.

'A fountain of fecundity, more accurately,' Jeff growled.

'She certainly seems to have the local authority by the balls if not some of the older males,' Cynthia remarked when she heard.

With Maria's history of amours, this might have been truer than Jean suspected. On Maria's last day she handed them back their key as though releasing them from bondage and marched down the hill like the Godmother she was. Surprisingly, this time she did not ask them for a pahquaw.

But then Mercedes told them the bad news. The local authorities had discovered that with eight strapping sons and some fairly hefty daughters, Maria had sufficient visible means of support without doling out tobacco at government expense to the locals. Maria was not going to be given a kiosk after all. Fear clutched their hearts. Would she come out of retirement yet again?

'You've got the key now, Jean,' Jeff said.

⌘

'With so many aging foreigners living on this coast, I wonder how good the medical care is if *we* should get sick', Jean asked her partner one evening sitting on the back terrace watching the fruit bats dance their usual swooping prayer to bat gods against a golden sunset. 'Remember that doctor we met at Cynthia's party? The one from Brazil or Argentina or maybe Columbia. Elliot said they have been treated by him, and he's quite knowledgeable. I took down his phone number, just in case," Jean told him.

'Hmm', Jeff said with a busy expression. 'Funny you should mention him.'

'What?' Jean asked. 'Why?'

'I was thinking about him last night. And that attractive woman he brought to Cynthia's big party at the Club. I think I've got an idea for a story about two people sort of like them.'

When Jeff told her his idea, she thought for a minute and nodded. 'Yes, Jeff. Let's write it. But the focus is wrong. It's not the doctor who should tell the story. It's the woman!'

'Hmm,' he said. 'You're right It's the woman who has just met him.'

A few days later they had worked out the story idea and the title.

⌘

24: ONE MAN'S MEDICINE

That one look. That moment divine when your eyes meet and you know you want each other. You both know—and there's no mistake about it.

That was what was missing.

Still ...

It was one of those Marbella Club Charity bean-fests after a golf Pro-Am, where a lot of people knew a lot of people but nobody knows everybody. The foreign colony is like that. Mixed types. Mixed languages. Mixed money. But it's always fairly lively. This 'do' had started around ten o'clock. In Spain people still have siestas and the evenings start later. After dinner there was dancing on the patio. I'd left my children with my mother in the English countryside and came down from London to stay with some old friends for a week. Eve, actually. We were old friends.

I've not been seeing too many people after my divorce. The whole mess has been a terrible shock to me. I've been hit by it much, much more than I'd expected. Life may be full of surprises but the law of averages says half of them should be pleasant. My Ex was not at any time, in any way at all pleasant during the whole bloody procedure.

Still, he is paying his alimony. His 'one man war debt', he called it. I call it his 'cash surrender' value.

My name is Emily Gannet and as I said, I came down to Marbella to house guest with friends. I hadn't actually wanted to go out at all that night. Not on my own. I was still, let's face it, licking my wounds. So my darling hosts had lined up the only single man they knew, a Venezuelan doctor who lived in Marbella to be their guest and my blind date. But he'd been called out on a house call at the very last moment and they'd talked me into coming along anyway.

It wasn't too bad, really. There were seven in Eve and Barry's party. I don't mind tagging along occasionally as long as I can keep other people's husbands off my bones. Some married men think if a woman is divorced for ten minutes, she's so desperate for it that anyone will do, even some balding old fool wearing his belly over his belt. Some of those guys are like leapfrogging with a unicorn; a game I don't wish to play.

I didn't really feel like getting all dressed up; but after I'd 'put on my face' and slipped into a new scoop shirt and butter beige silk Armani trousers, my favourite silk jacket and my gold choker with the diamond drop and inspected myself in the mirror, I did feel better. Funny how knowing one looks good, can make a woman feel good. Do men have that, I wonder? After all, having a husband leave you for a twenty three year old airhead just when you're turning forty can be dangerously deflating.

Not to digress, but I saw the girl once. Actually went to the place where she works and asked for her. It took a bit of brass, I'll admit but I went right up to her and told her to leave my husband alone. She called the security officer, can you imagine? Said I was threatening her. Cloud Cukoo? Still, I hadn't taken to drink or stuffing candy bars in my face, so there was still some steam left in the old self esteem.

Really good looking men are few and far between and they do stand out in a crowd as much as any beautiful woman ever does. I noticed him the moment he stepped out onto the Club patio, as though my attention had been pulled to him by a magnet. He was tall and slim, his hair was short and just going grey. He was so well groomed that I thought at first he might be an actor or even, God forbid, a male model, although his face was certainly not familiar. Why is it men think that only they appreciate beauty? I thought he was looking at me, but it was Eve, my hostess he was making for.

He greeted her, kissing her hand in that Latin way. I hadn't seen anyone do that except in old movies. 'Sorry I couldn't make it for dinner, Eve. Just got away this very moment.' His voice was deep, resonant, sexy.

'Forgivable in your profession. How's your patient, doctor?' Eve asked cheerily.

His glance slid to where couples were already beginning to dance. 'My patient. . . died,' he said. He looked back. 'Let's not talk about it, shall we? It is always so depressing. I am sworn to save lives, not to lose them.'

'Well, you got here anyway,' Barry said. 'So I guess I'd better introduce you.' He turned to me. "Emily, this is Doctor

Lopez. Emily Gannet, our friend down from London. She used to live here for a while, actually,' he added.

'Really?' he asked. 'Curious we never met.' That was the moment when he looked into my eyes. As I said, not electric. Still there was something, it cannot be denied. 'My apologies for keeping such a charming woman waiting.'

'But I wasn't waiting,' I told him, a bit too defensively. 'I never wait for anyone these days.'

'Do sit down, Eduardo,' Eve said hastily, giving me a sharp look.

The waiter brought another glass and more champagne was poured and I was beginning to relax ever so slightly. Eduardo hadn't eaten so a menu was brought and he ordered a prawn salad. I thought he must be watching his weight, and he did have a sensational figure. When he had finished, he asked me to dance.

He was surprisingly light on his feet for a tall man and he certainly had that sense of rhythm that seems the prerogative of all Latinos. That night they actually played a tango, which seems to be coming back into fashion at least in Spain and we danced it together. Dancing a tango with a South American must rate high on the accomplishment scale. I'd rate him about an eleven. For the first time in months I found myself really having fun. We drank a few brandies and seemed to laugh a lot but I can't remember what about. The spell was interrupted when his mobile 'phone rang. An emergency call. He had to leave. 'The life of a doctor,' he said apologetically and asked if he could phone me at Eve's. I said yes, I'd be there for a few more days. And then he was gone.

There's a certain empty feeling you get when you've just met someone you've really taken a fancy to and then before you're ready to be sure how much of a fancy that might be, he disappears. The image of him hung in my head for a while. Those heavy lidded large black eyes, the softly rounded vocal tones, resonant and warm. I put him out of my mind and turned my attention back to Barry and Eve. Barry was going on about the escalating cost of living on the coast and Eve was nodding agreement but not hearing a word. They'd been married a very long time.

⌘

To my surprise, Eduardo was on the telephone the next morning to ask if I'd have lunch. I tried not to sound eager and he suggested a place in the Port. I said I'd meet him to save him the trouble of coming all the way up to Eve's.

He'd chosen a popular cafe and a table on the front facing out towards the yachts. I found my total attention on him. My Ex was a nice enough looking bloke but nobody could have mistaken him for George Clooney, even that little bitch who has him now. Sorry; didn't mean to sound bitter. But I was really bowled over by the way Eduardo looked and the fact that he didn't seem to be self conscious about it. Good looking men are generally noisy as peacocks.

He told me about the Estancia his family had in South America and the horses. He talked a lot about horses and the power of their loins. Somehow, he made it sound sensual. I wondered if that was his sexual come-on to women, but he seemed genuine enough. I asked him about the patient he'd left the party for the night before. He looked away towards the tall sail-furled masts of a nearby boat and said forlornly, 'She died. I sat with her all night.' One hand rested on the table, the fingers long and sensitive, the nails carefully manicured. I touched it, affected by the sadness in his eyes. 'It must be terrible for you when that happens,' I said. 'I can see how much you care.'

His hand gripped mine suddenly with intensity. 'They are all old, you see, Emily. They come down here to a warm climate, so many from cold countries. England, Sweden. . . because they wish to retire.' He paused. 'They do not realise that their bodies have changed with the years. Then they eat a strange diet that their systems are not used to. They drink too much vino, so cheap in this country. And the first thing, they are ill. Then it gets worse and they do not have a familiar doctor here. So by the time I see them, it is too late.'

He sighed, sat thoughtfully for a moment, then went on. 'Then there are the widows and widowers who are left behind. They do not know how to cope alone, having spent half their lives with somebody they depended upon. And so they, too, become ill and die. Sometimes I think it would be better if they went with their mates. Far better. . .'

'Sort of like jumping onto the funeral pyre?' I asked, not entirely happy with his analysis.

'Oh, you may laugh, 'Emily,' he said. But the Hindus did not have it entirely wrong. What was left for the wife in those days, I ask you? Her protector gone? Nobody to look after her. Possibly better she join him.'

I laughed again. 'Come on, Eduardo. Surely you don't mean that literally?'

He looked at me and his eyes clouded over as though a curtain had been dropped. 'No. No, of course not. I do not mean it literally. Come, let us take a walk on the mole,' he said. So we walked out on the long strip of land skirting the yachts and edging the sea. Walked and did not talk.

I'd like to blame it on the wine at lunch but it wasn't that. When he asked me back to his house I wanted to go because I wanted him to take me. And he did. And it was really great. I hadn't been to bed with anyone since Jim. But like riding a bike or swimming or getting back on a horse, you don't forget, do you? I asked how we'd been so lucky as to have his phone not ring all that time and he told me he'd shut it off. I shouldn't have asked. He turned it back on and it rang immediately. It was another emergency. Eduardo looked at me with regret. 'How much longer will you be in Marbella?' he asked.

''Three more days,' I said.

'I must go.' He got up and dashed into the shower. 'Please,' he said, returning, and handed me a towel.

I can't explain what I felt like. A little liberated after the confinement of a marriage in which I had been faithful. A little my own master. Ready to do as I pleased and with whom. Certainly unsure of myself. And of him. What must he think of me jumping right into bed with him like that?

Not used to love in the afternoon, stepping out into the street in the broad sunlight from a strange man's house, I was glad I'd decided to rent a car because I never like to impose on my hosts and you can't walk anywhere on that coast.

He said he would call. He did. About nine o'clock that night. 'Can you come out?'

'How was your patient?' I asked.

'He died.' His voice was barely a whisper. 'Can you meet me? There's a disco in the port. Near where we had lunch.'

I met Eduardo about forty five minutes later. He was waiting at the bar. We took a table away from the dance floor and had a few brandies and danced. As I knew and actually hoped he would, he took me back to his house and we made love again. 'Stay the night,' he asked.

I hesitated. 'I don't know what I'll tell Eve and Barry.'

'They are grown up, Emily. Stop acting like a little girl,' he said sharply.

His phone rang. It was another emergency call. 'Will you wait for me?' he asked. 'Pour yourself a brandy. I'll be back as soon as I can.' He kissed me so tenderly I knew that this was more than just a three day fling. The impossible was happening. I was falling in love. After he left, I got up and put on one of his dressing gowns. It was silk and smelled of his skin and it got me excited all over again. So I poured myself that brandy and walked around looking at his things and finally sat down at his desk.

I'm not usually one to pry into the lives of others, but curiosity under the circumstances, is perhaps understandable if not forgivable. His diary was open to yesterday's date and I noted two names entered at the hours of eight pm and midnight, a man and a woman, certainly the two patients of the night before. And after each, the single word Muerte—dead.

I flipped back through the pages and every day or so, there were names written—and after each, the single word: Muerte. More pages more names—and every one of them dead! With a chilling sense of dread, I started to count. As I reached the number of forty five, the key turned in the door. It was Eduardo back. I slammed the diary shut.

'How was your patient?' I asked, my throat tight.

The glance dropped down again in that attitude of sadness I had begun to recognise. 'Dead,' he said.

Could a doctor be that unlucky? I did not think so. 'Do any of your patients ever live, Eduardo?' I asked, looking him squarely in the eye.

He stared back at me, startled. ' What a curious question, Emily.'

'No more curious than the entries in your diary here. I haven't got back to January yet, but so far I've counted forty five dead.'

He nodded. 'Terrible, isn't it? How they all seem to go. I administer them my very special tincture. See that they take it regularly. Even so, they never seem to recover.'

'What is it you give them, Eduardo?' I said, finishing my brandy at a gulp, feathers beginning to turn in my stomach.

'It is a tonic my father developed on the Estancia. He gave it to all the servants and even to the horses and it made them strong as bulls.'

He opened the brandy decanter and refilled my glass. 'It is really very good stuff. You have been drinking it all night - in your brandy. It prevents hangover.'

The blood drained from my head and I felt frozen to the spot. Then with the supreme effort of panic I rushed out of his house still dressed in his robe. My car was parked in his driveway. I got in behind the wheel and thanked God I had accidentally left the key in the ignition. Not a safe thing to do in Marbella. I drove straight to the police station. They were a bit startled to see a woman bolt in barefoot wearing a man's dressing gown. They thought I'd been attacked. 'Do you know Doctor Eduardo Lopez?' I began.

The Doctor. . .Eduardo Lopez. Yes, indeed they knew him. A fine man. A great addition to the community.

'No!' I screamed at them. 'A murderer. A serial killer! I have seen his list of victims! He even tried to poison me this very night! His patients, all of them are dead. You must go immediately', I told them, 'and arrest him'. My knees began to buckle. I begged them to get me to the hospital and have my stomach pumped. It had to be full of poison. 'Probably arsenic,' I guessed.

The police sent armed detectives to his house to arrest Eduardo and rushed me to the hospital by ambulance. A harrowing ride on La Carretera de la Muerte.

I do not advise you readers to request a stomach pump unless it is a matter of life or death. It is an experience best avoided. But at least I felt great relief when it was over and I was still alive. The lab report would not be ready until the following day. But the population was safe from the administrations of Eduardo Lopez. Single handed, I had put a serial killer behind bars. Probably the largest list of victims of any murderer on record. Why, I wondered, had nobody questioned him before?

The next day I was recovering from a very sore stomach on Eve and Barry's patio, having told them the entire story. They were naturally horrified. Eduardo had been their doctor for years and was a constant dinner guest, being a bachelor. So convenient when there's an extra woman and there always is. But Eve said she had never seen Eduardo attracted to someone the way he was to me. She thought it was a case of love at first sight.

And then came a call from the Detective. Would I come down to the police station? The lab report had just come back.

Barry and Eve went with me. The Detective in charge of the case read out the report. The contents of my stomach contained a goodly portion of shellfish, a large quantity of brandy and a double dose of multivitamins, particularly high in vitamin C. The tonic Dr Lopez had given me and all of his patients was a vitamin elixir. Quite efficacious, but certainly harmless.

The Inspector of Police faced me across his desk. His look was not unsympathetic. 'What Doctor Lopez told you was quite true, Señora. Most of his patients are very, very old and did not eat a proper diet. And even though he gave them his special vitamin elixir and tried to build them up, they died of natural causes. Many times there have been the Coroner's reports which confirm this fact.' He nodded, then shook his head sadly with something of the same expression I'd seen on Eduardo's handsome face. 'You know, it is a sad thing. To the foreign colony, this coast, it is like an elephant's graveyard. The old, they come here to shed their ivory and to die. He is a fine man, Doctor Lopez. He really cares about them.'

I started out of the room, but the Detective took my arm. 'I am afraid Señora that you must remain for the deposition. The doctor is preferring charges against you for defamation of character, and wrongful imprisonment.

I am almost at the end of my sentence now. After the long wait for the trial, the court sentenced me to twelve months. I got three off for good behavior and so I get out tomorrow and will go back to London on the next flight.

Unfortunately, Barry and Eve didn't want me to stay with them, which I can quite understand. And in any event the Spanish government won't let me stay, since I have had a prison sentence. The prison food is horrible, but Eduardo has been sending me some of his tincture.

⌘

25: THE FIESTA

The Thwaites felt that they now had enough stories for their short story book, and were preparing the book for submission—but to whom? While they were pondering on whether to send a copy to Jeff's old publisher, Douglas Entwhistle in New York, they got a call from their London Agent who felt the book might be better published first in the U.K.

They were discussing the question on the front terrace when Luciano came driving up the new concrete road in his old but polished car. He was wearing a clean shirt and a broad smile as he approached Jeff and Jean. Munchkin appeared out of nowhere to check out the visitor. Luciano scowled at the cat, sat down and accepted the offer of coffee which he drank reluctantly. It was not quite strong enough for a Spaniard's taste; he could still stir it with a spoon.

Luciano had come to announce that there was to be a fiesta on the following Sunday in the square in front of the duck pond and that the Thwaites were invited. One o'clock, Spanish time. It was the first time since Paca's confirmation that they had been asked to participate in any of the village festivities and they were terribly excited.

'We've been accepted, Jeff! We're really part of the village,' Jean enthused after Luciano left.

When she heard of it, Cynthia Gray lowered her darkly arched brows and said that she and Elliot would of course, be expected to make an appearance, even though Luciano must have forgotten to invite them personally.

On the day of the festival the Thwaites hadn't expected to find a table in the place of honor waiting for them right in front of Maria's house. The Tusk-Toothed One stood on her balcony eating a churro looking down on the crowd, and waved at Jean and Jeff as though it were she who had given permission for them to be there. Perhaps she had.

Small tables had been jammed solidly into the square with a clearing roped off in the center for the flamenco dancing. Everyone in the village and all their relatives from far and wide had turned out. It was the closest some of the villagers had come to seeing the crazy estranjeros and Jean, wanting to fit in, wore her concept of an ethnic skirt and shawl. The skirt had a bright splash of red flowers and the shawl had brightly embroidered flowers and a heavy black fringed border. It was the type one sees in all the pictures of señoritas in paintings and she had bought it one day in The Rostro, their Saturday morning flea market outside the bullring. Jean felt like she fit in until she saw several of the younger women dressed in smartly tailored trousers, silk shirts and gold chains.

All eyes were on the Americans as a path was cleared to their table. Plates of paella were rushed in front of them and Fantas and Sherry and wine set out on the tiny table. They could not pay for anything; they were the guests of the Barrio. All the villagers crowded around to see if they were eating enough, and smiling and advising them on which bit was rabbit, which sausage was hot, and which pepper was sweet.

At that moment Cynthia and Elliot arrived and some villagers hurriedly got up from their table to push it next to the Thwaites' for the new arrivals. It was clear they had not been included. Cynthia was dressed for a cocktail party in silver lamé trousers. She sat down next to Jean, eyed her shawl and said. 'They're embroidered in China, you know.'

'I know,' Jean said, although she didn't.

Cynthia grabbed an olive from Jean's plate and poured herself a glass of Fanta. 'Don't see how you can drink booze in the sun,' she told her husband watching him down a glass of red wine almost at a gulp.

'Thirsty,' Elliot said.

'Have you ever tried water? Besides you really must get more exercise, Elliot. You're putting on weight,' she commented archly.

'I get enough exercise, my dear, pushing sixty.' He plunged a greasy sausage into his ready lips.

'Hmmph, she said, turning to Jean. 'I suppose if he didn't annoy me sometimes, he wouldn't interest me at all.'

An area had been cleared for the exhibition dancing and a platform stage had been erected in front of the pond, the waterfall splashing a merry backdrop to the festivities. Little girls and young ladies and most of the boys under twelve were filling the dance area in flamenco costumes as colorful as dolls in the tourist shops. They formed a circle of partners, waiting for the music to begin. Guitars at the ready, the three piece band began to play the regulated dance tempos. Jean had brought her camera and began taking pictures of the children, many of whom she knew by name. Everybody wanted to pose. Her lens finder framed a splash of red polka dots, green polka dots, pink flowers, purple, orange, each girl rivaling the other in masses of ruffles, slicked back chignons brushed to the gloss of patent leather, large gold hoops or plastic flower pendants dangling at the ears.

'The villagers save up all year to splash out on fiesta costumes,' Elliot said.

'I suppose El Salto will change now.' Cynthia peered at Jean accusingly. 'Since you gave them that road, cars are regarded as a necessity in the village and children as a luxury.' She frowned. 'Personally, I've always preferred cats,' she informed anyone who didn't already know.

A Flamenco group had come from Malaga to perform an exhibition of more authentic gypsy dancing and the *cante hondo* songs played in the Marbella tourist hangouts. Luciano waved the microphone around with authority to introduce the 'acts', which consisted of groups of village youngsters dancing the traditional Flamenco and Sevilliana, their hands fluttering little humming birds above their smoothly polished hair. Mercedes, who was sitting at the next table told Jean that there was a special school in their small village to teach the children *Baile*, their traditional dance.

Then, with a fanfare of guitars Luciano stepped back up to the microphone. He spoke so rapidly in Spanish that neither Jeff nor Jean coul understand it all, until they heard their name being called. El Señor y la Señora Thwaite. Luciano gestured for them to come onto the stage.

'What on earth...?' whispered Jean. With some embarrassment, they made their way up beside him. Luciano was holding up a silver plaque mounted on a wooden board and he read from it: *A las Sres Thwaite de las vecinas del Salto del Agua en nuestra de agreddecimiento par su calabaracion en la mejara de esta barrio. S. Pedro de Alcantara 27. 8 1998 A.A.V.V. Las Flores.*

Elliot translated it for them later: *To Mr. and Mrs. Thwaite from of the neighbors of Salto del Agua Thank you for your collaboration in improving this neighborhood.. S. Pedro de Alcantara 27. 8 1998 A.A.V.V. The Flowers.*

The villagers had given them a plaque to commemorate the gift of the land for the village road.

'Thank heavens you didn't give them that plot to shelter their dead bodies,' Cynthia said.

⌘

That night as they lay in their bed cuddled together, Jean said. 'I guess now we really do belong, Jeff.'

'Yeah,' he said. 'We've finally made it, hon. From here on, it's clear sailing. Nothing can go wrong.'

'Don't tempt Murphy's law,' she whispered. But Murphy had already been tempted.

There was a letter waiting in their box at the post office from their publisher friend, Douglas Entwhistle. He said that the short stories he had read while in Spain had stuck with him and could he please see the rest of the book as soon as possible? He was preparing a new line of paperbacks for airports and he felt the short stories might just sell in this category, what with the financial climate being what it was and most publishers pulling in not only their own horns but their list of writers.

Still, with the Spanish theme, and the nature of the stories, they might just find a target. There was a big red lipstick kiss on the bottom of the letter and a P.S. from Sally: 'I've come to take the old man to lunch and am enclosing my love to you both—and to Munchkin.'

Jeff read the letter and handed it to Jean. 'Guess we'll call our agent in London. You can't say no to a publisher who asks to see your book.'

26: SPANISH DAYS AND SPANISH NIGHTS

On the far side of the irrigation canal at the bottom of their field, the tranquillity was broken by the sound of a bulldozer. Jean rushed out to the back terrace to see what was happening. What she saw was the beginning of the end. Some people call it progress.

'Jeff, come quick!' she shouted. 'Something's happening in the middle of our lovely view!'

She stared down into the hollow of the valley where a new horseshoe-shaped road was being carved out, its magnet ends facing left of their immediate view behind the Eucalyptus trees, leading onto the Ronda road. 'Whatever are they doing?' she screamed as he stepped out onto the terrace, as though it was all Jeff's fault. 'What, Jeff?'

Jeff was feeling a tad guilty because he had known about it for several days. 'It's that new development Davie was telling us about. El Asombroso, they're calling it,' Jeff said casually, unwilling to say what was really in his mind for fear of upsetting Jean even more than he knew she already was. He'd heard from the friendly Spanish chemist at the drogueria that some speculator was building another development further down the valley. Where once there were goats and chickens pecking at the fertile earth, he'd heard that a hotel and golf course would soon rise in triumph.

He only hoped it wouldn't be a high rise.

'El Asombroso, What does that mean?' she wondered, calming slightly.

⌘

'The Amazing,' Cynthia told them a few days later as they sat on the Thwaite's back terrace with Davie and watched the development of this newest of urbanisations to hit the Costa del Sol, right in their own backyard.

'The "amazing" bit will be if the speculator can finish it before he runs out of the filthy stuff.' Davie said, swilling back his second beer. 'Around here, money talks.'

'I'd say he'll need a bit more of it to keep up that conversation,' Elliot replied.

Davie Davies leaned over the terrace railing for a better look. 'The word is, his builders are three months behind in pay, and half his backers have dropped out.'

'What about the other half?' Elliot asked.

'They probably don't know yet he's lost the first half,' Cynthia said.

'Well, of course nothing ever gets built on schedule here. Or on budget. Everyone's used to that,' Davie told her flatly.

'That's because second rate people always hire third rate people,' Cynthia replied, getting up. 'Let's go have a look. What say?'

So the Thwaites and the Grays took two cars and went down to the Ronda Road and up to the site with Davie and paused at the builder's sketch posted on a small billboard, of the proposed urbanisation. No, this was not to be a hotel, or even a B and B. There were about twenty small houses to be built around the horse shoe road, and they had only begun construction on the first one, which didn't look like much.

'In fact, it looks more like it's being torn down than built up.' Cynthia said. ''

Fortunately the Thwaites were spared the sight of that first casa from their back terrace. It was hidden behind that stand of eucalyptus trees below their field.

'It will quite devalue your property though,' Cynthia assured them with a satisfied smirk a few weeks later, sitting out on the Thwaite's back terrace once again and knocking back a soda as though it were gin. 'The urbanisation utterly spoils your unbroken view.'

Elliot Gray glanced across the green expanse up to the far range of mountains. 'This whole valley will be built up one day, Jeff. And all too soon, I should expect.'

If the Grays had wanted to depress the Thwaites, they were doing a great job. Jean told Jeff later that she was sure it would never happen. It was only that the Grays were jealous of their view. 'All they have is the sea to look at.'

'That's a good enough view for anybody, Jean, even Cynthia,' he pointed out, knowing it would do no good.

'But is *good* good enough?' Jean asked querulously. 'Anyway, Jeff, you know how Cynthia and Elliot are always the life of the parties and so witty? Except it's Cynthia who generally delivers the punch lines. Well, Davie tells me it's true that they rehearse it all before they go anywhere. He says they're one gag short of a joke book.'

'Come off it, Jean. You can't believe that?' Jeff asked.

'Hhmn. Well, it could be true, couldn't it? She always leaves a bit of gossip better than she finds it. They do sound like somebody's writing their material. I mean, did you hear them the other night at the Ridgeways? Cynthia was really in top form talking about the alimony that Freddie Kravat pays his ex-wife. She said it was Freddie's cash surrender value, and "bounty on the mutiny".

Jeff nodded. 'Heard that one.'

"And when she dropped her handbag Elliot picked it up and said to her "Clumsy - always dropping things." and she just gave him a look and said: "Stupid. Always picking them up." Come on, Jeff. That had to be rehearsed. I mean, the handbag routine and all.'

He knew Jean was just upset about what was happening to their beautiful valley view.

And then quite suddenly construction on the urbanisation stopped, leaving the one house half built, and the road only laid out in gravel. Cynthia had been right about one thing. The owner had run out of money. The bad news was, in order to get out from under and recoup some of his investment, he was now selling off the plots. Just for the price of the land.

Under ordinary circumstances, few Spaniards would consider buying into an urbanisation. That was for foreigners. Too expensive. But certain locals with newly found ready cash gleaned from cashing in on the tourist market, were smart enough to pounce when developments that were going under were forced to bring their inflated prices down to something resembling reality. And so in the case of El Asombroso, it really was "amazing" because Spaniards quite amazingly began picking up the plots which after all, were situated on a gravel road with water, sewage, and electrical connections already laid on. But the Amazing building stopped for a while.

One evening a month later, Jeff and Jean sat out on the back terrace watching the birds and bats winging gracefully across yet another epic sunset and looked sadly down into the valley across their own field of newly planted almond and fruit trees, and some distance beyond their cypress fence, to the newly planted small vegetable allotments in El Asombroso.

Where houses had once been intended, weekend Spanish farmers from San Pedro had begun to erect ugly wire fences and gates around each small parcel. They were building storage sheds with nasty corrugated roofs. And slowly, slowly the Thwaites watched a lettuce patch and an orange tree or two, a few ears of corn sprouting, a pepper patch and the raw materials for building their own houses one day, burgeoning bundles of bricks and lumber, stacks of windows, piles of roof tiles, and toilet cisterns, being stored in the sheds and on the open ground. It was a mystifying sight until one night joining them on the back terrace for cocktail chat, Cynthia Gray explained it from her lofty knowledge of the territory.

'The Spanish peasants are natural born scavengers, you know. I'm certain each of those allotments is owned by a man who works on some building site somewhere, because every Spaniard is a born D.I.Y. builder, and with all the new housing, they snap up building jobs, no experience required. All they have to do is pocket a few bricks each night and soon they have enough to build a house of their own. Scavengers,' she repeated sharply.

'If you ask me, I think they're pretty smart,' Jeff said trying to look on the bright side. 'I wish we could have rebuilt Santa Rita like that.'

⌘

A few weeks later, they were working in their study, Jean at her computer, typing away when Jeff paused to sniff the air. 'I smell smoke!' he told Jean, who was on her feet immediately and looking out across the top of the eucalyptus trees that grew down the hillside along the edge of their land down to the irrigation channel. Smoke was definitely rising from the trees and blowing in at them. They rushed out to see what was burning.

On the hillside under the eucalyptus trees just beyond their new fence were a group of village children, some of them no older than five, fanning and beating the underbrush into flame with long eucalyptus branches. The Thwaites rushed down the field to their fence bordering the grove.

'Stop! Stop!' Jean yelled, all her Spanish eluding her in the moment of panic. But the children merely smiled and waved and continued to set fire to the underbrush sensibly standing behind the wind blowing away from them in the direction of Santa Rita, The flames seemed to be getting dangerously high and licking up the trunks of the eucalyptus trees.

'Stop! What are you doing?' Jean shouted at the small pyromaniacs. Then the Goat Man appeared from behind a tree. He seemed it was he, leading the children's attack.

'They're trying to burn down our house. Get the hose, quick, Jeff.' She waved her arms frantically at the Goat Man but he didn't seem to notice, busily directing the little fire makers' activities.

Jeff scrambled back up the field and connected the hose. The flames were fast approaching the latest addition to the cypress hedge they had only just been planted along that side of the field. Jeff turned on the water, bringing the hose to play across the cypresses. It dribbled out in a weak stream.

'What's wrong with it?' Jean called.

'Dunno,' he called back.

'Jeff...! We have four thousand litres of water stored! We also share a well with the other houses. We also have mains water, and plenty of hoses. So why can't we get any water when we need it?'

Jeff did not attempt to answer this, and called out to the Goat Man in Spanish to ask him to stop setting fire to the land. The Goat Man only waved and smiled and continued to direct the children in burning off the field showing no concern for the safety of their trees.

As the fire passed over each stretch of earth, the children seemed to be following it up and beating it out with their branches, to some extent keeping it in control. But it was doing the eucalyptus trees no good and it had almost reached their tree fence. Jeff fed the water across the branches of the tender new cypresses moving up and down the row as fast as he could, to get them all soaked.

Jean, who had been stamping the ground like a frightened mare, squealed at him. 'What on earth are they doing that for, Jeff?'

'Damned if I know, Jean. Maybe he's teaching them the art of arsonry.'

'Well, I've had enough!' Jean ran back up to their car and drove down to Miguel's house to get him to call fire department. Miguel came up to the field with her, and leaned over the fence to talk to the Goat Man. His manner was measured and casual, not at all perturbed at what he saw. When he came back to the Thwaites, he told them,' No need for the fire department, Señora. The children, they have the fire under control as you can see.'

'In control? They're setting it! Why? Why are they doing this?' Jean screeched at him.

'The children are trained to clean the field in this way and the insectos who bite the goats, they will not be so plentiful in the next summer.' He lit a cigarette from the butt of the one he was smoking and flicked it at a cypress tree, which responded with a sizzle.

⌘

Jeff and Jean had a lot to learn about rural life in Spain. They were absorbing more every time they came to stay in their ramshackle finca and loving it more every visit. But now once again, they were returning to London, and then going to New York to close the deal on their new book, Spanish Days and Spanish Nights with Douglas Entwhistle.

Later that afternoon Jeff and Jean stopped by the Farmacia in San Pedro de Alcantara to tell the pharmacist, Jose and his assistant Josefina that they were going to be away for three months. Their new Spanish friends were quite used to the Thwaites, and had been invited a few times up to Santa Rita for drinks and tapas. They wished them a pleasant trip and while

Jeff was chatting with Jose, there was some whispering going on between Josefina and Jean.

'What was all that whispering about?' Jeff asked as the drove back up the hill.

'Girl talk,' Jean said and he knew he was going to get nothing more out of her.

When they got back to Santa Rita, Maria was waiting on the terrace sitting in a wicker armchair and eating a churro. A certain fear gripped Jeff when he saw her because she never came up the hill now that she was officially no longer employed. Maybe she was hoping to return to work with the thought of more 'pahquaws'.

Maria rose as they came up the steps and greeted them. For a change, she was actually smiling which, while it revealed her few remaining tusks, it did give her face a more cheerful aspect. She was holding a small wrapped package.

'You are leaving tomorrow,' she said in Spanish.

'Yes,' Jeff replied. For three months.'

We will be back in September,' Jean added.

'Mercedes will look after the house once a week,' Maria said firmly.

Jeff breathed a sigh. Maria wasn't planning another 'comeback' tour.

Jean nodded. 'I'm sure everything will be fine, Maria. But in case of any problem, Miguel should always have the Grays phone us in London.'

Maria jammed the rest of her churro in her mouth and handed Jean the package. 'I have made this for you,' Maria said.

Knowing that the Spanish villagers never opened a gift in front of the giver, or never thanked them, Jean was not sure how to react.

'OPEN IT,' Jeff hissed.

Jean untied the string. Inside was a needlework cushion cover, stitched with brightly colored flowers on a white cotton background. They know that Maria had made such needlework cushions for her own home and it must have take many hours to make.

'It will brighten up Santa Rita,' Maria said.

'Yes it will, Maria, and it will have a place of honor when we return,' Jean added and she said, 'Thank you.'

'The village will welcome you in September,' Maria said and turned to leave.

Jeff offered to drive her down the hill in the car. She thought for a moment, and then accepted with a sly smile. Jean could read her mind. The villagers would see her getting a ride in the estranjeros' car.

Jean watched them drive down to the gate and turned back to the house. They would be leaving in the morning.

They had been accepted.

⌘

All packed and ready to go, Jean climbed in beside Jeff, their light luggage carefully stowed in the boot of the taxi. She hadn't told Jeff what she knew she must tell him, although she had known for two months. But it never seemed the right time. Was there ever a right time, she wondered, because she wasn't exactly certain how he would take it.

"Jeff. . .?"

He was looking out the window at Santa Rita as the taxi turned down the driveway.

'Jeff,' she said, 'We're going to have a baby'. She let the words hang in the rising heat of a late June morning.

'I know, hon,' he replied patting her hand and smiled his crooked smile at her.'

'You know?' she asked, astonished. 'But how? How could you know?'

The way you've been eating. Sucking lemons all day and pigging out on almonds. Not at all like you. Besides, your blue dress is a bit pinched through the middle.'

'Hmm,' she said thinking that sometimes he seemed like he was inside her head. 'So. . .why didn't you say?'

'I was waiting for you to tell me. When you were ready.

She was silent for a minute. 'How do you feel about it, Jeff?'

'How did you think I feel? It's fantastic!'

'It'll change our lives, you know.'

'I certainly hope so,' he replied with a grin.

'Jeff. . . oh Jeff, you're really happy?'

'It could be the greatest thing that ever happened to us.'

'In a world of great things. Like finding each other.' She kissed him on the lips, prodigious emotion behind the light touch.

They looked back at Santa Rita, seeing it diminishing from the taxi taking them to Malaga airport.

'The blue bedroom would make a nice room for the baby,' she said.

Jeff nodded. 'He'll love 'Santa Rita.'

'Or she. . .' The taxi spun out into the Ronda road, heading down to La Carretera de la Muerte.

Santa Rita pray for us. . .' she sighed under her breath.

'What?' Jeff asked

'Santa Rita,' Jean repeated. 'Pray for us.'

Oh,' he said. 'For all three of us then, please.'

⌘⌘⌘

PAT SILVER-LASKY

Born in Seattle, Washington in 1925, Pat Silver-Lasky's new book *Under The Magic Mountain* marks an incredible 75 years as a professional writer. She studied at the University of Washington, Stanford University and Reed College, where she produced and directed their first play.

As Barbara Hayden, she produced, wrote, directed and acted in the first live TV drama series from Hollywood, Emmy nominated *Mabel's Fables* for KTLA in 1949 and appeared in feature roles in films and played leading and co-starring roles on television throughout the 1950s.

As an A.S.C.A.P. writer, she wrote lyrics for 14 published and recorded songs with her first husband Tony Romano, including *While You're Young* for Johnny Mathis. They also wrote songs for two films at Columbia Studios.

As Pat Silver, she wrote as a team with her late husband, Hollywood screenwriter and author, Jesse L. Lasky Jr. Together they wrote their verse play, *Ghost Town* which won several awards. Then eight films, 119 TV scripts, four books including *Love Scene* (1978) the acclaimed biography of Laurence Olivier and Vivien Leigh. Pat directed their play *Vivien,* in Los Angeles and later in London; the American best selling historical novel, *The Offer,* 1981 (republished with additional material in 2015). Their TV series, *Philip Marlowe, Private Eye* (as writers and show runners) won awards in America and Holland.

Since Lasky Jr.'s death in 1988, Pat has written 4 books. *Screenwriting For The 21st Century* (2004), *Ride the Tiger* (2010), *Scam Schemes Scumbags* (2012) with Peter Betts and *A Star Called Wormwood* (2015). Her latest book, *Hollywood Royalty, A Family in Films* was published by BearManor Media (2017).

Pat lectured on script writing at several American Universities and was Script Consultant and Guest Lecturer at the London Film School (1991-1999). She now lives in Orange County with her husband, cartoonist and painter Peter Betts.

⌘⌘⌘

Website: patsilver-lasky.net

Printed in Great Britain
by Amazon